Winds of Betrayal

Monica Koldyke Miller

To Becky,

From Mom,

Monica Koldyke Miller

1/5/00

Photography by: Rebeccah Liechty

ISBN: 1514103273
ISBN 13: 9781514103272

Acknowledgements

First and foremost, I thank God, from whom all blessings flow.

To my loving husband and children, whose unfailing support allowed me to realize my lifelong dream.

Thanks to Sergeant Leonard Corral in ensuring Sheriff Hadley interrogated like a lawman.

Many thanks to Bobbi Ray Madry, Laurel Steill and Les Edgerton for keeping me humble in my writing skills.

Special thanks go to Louisa May Alcott, author of "Hospital Sketches." Her first-hand experiences inspired many of my scenes between healer and patient.

Finally, to everyone else too numerous to mention; there's no greater compliment a writer can receive than to be told to "write faster!"

chapter I

Reagan Burnsfield sat in his study, glancing over mail as he sipped coffee. Hands roughened from years of lumbering sifted through letters of varying importance. A slim white envelope caught his eye. The postmark revealed it came from Indiana, yet he didn't recall having done business with anyone there. Tearing it open, Reagan skimmed the contents, and as he did, his hands started to tremble. He flipped to the last page to reveal the writer's identity and with that knowledge began again.

> *Dear Reagan,*
> *Though this news may be shocking, it's with great trepidation I'm asking for your help. Months ago, I'd left home to visit my Aunt Emmaline in Lars, Indiana. It was my intent to make this my*

home, but my plans have been spoiled, for I've taken ill and my doctor fears the worst. If so, I'll soon be unable to take care of my responsibilities.

I must confess I'd fallen in love with someone. I foolishly believed he returned my love, twisting his attention into something it was not. To my shame, I even forced myself upon him while he was besotted. You can imagine why I had to leave. I've a child, and unless someone steps forward, he'll be committed to the Lars Orphanage. Aunt Emmaline's beyond the age to care for him and I can't ask his father, for he has no memory of that night.

I'm begging you to take pity of my circumstance and find a place in your home to adopt my son. He's christened Gaeran Samuel Hampton. I've informed the mistress of the orphanage to wait thirty days before considering other parents. I further ask you tell no one of this, except Amanda. I pray you'll give Gaeran the love and devotion I feel and not speak unkindly of me when he's older. Please believe I cannot reveal the father's identity for it would destroy his chances of growing up in a happy home. You are my only hope.

Elizabeth

Reagan stared at the letter, his gut twisting. Visions of a phantom lover once again played in his mind; visions he had told himself were nothing more than the result of too much drinking while separated from his wife. Though it had occurred over a year ago, he'd never been able to banish the notion something untoward had happened in that hotel room. And then, there were the scratches. He couldn't remember how he'd received them and the telltale marks nearly ruined his reconciliation with Amanda.

Reagan recalled Elizabeth revealing her feelings for him at Camilla's birthday party and her dismay when he'd rebuffed her. He hadn't dwelled on the incident because his attentions were focused on regaining Amanda's affections. He realized suddenly, that her admission had come on the heels of his last night at the hotel. *Could Elizabeth be the phantom lover that eluded his memory?*

Reagan rubbed his brow, forcing himself to recall any shred of memory that would prove him wrong. That night, he had visited Sam Hampton, Elizabeth's father, about a business deal Sam helped broker. When he arrived at the Hampton's, Elizabeth was on her way out but tarried long enough to accompany Reagan to the study. There, she informed her father she'd be dining with Camilla and in the course of conversation decided she would also spend the night. Reagan had consumed a fair amount of alcohol both during his meeting and afterward, in his hotel room. He had fallen asleep and arose alone, though his dreams had been filled with erotic images. It seemed inconceivable Elizabeth could've been the one in his dreams for he neither invited her to Rochester Hotel, nor let it be known he had a suite.

Yet, there were the scratches. Amanda had discovered uniform markings on his back and immediately surmised the worst. He had no idea how he'd received them and couldn't give a satisfactory answer. It remained a mystery to this day.

Reagan read the letter again.

If Elizabeth had known his whereabouts that night, could she have entered his room? But how could she slip in through a locked door? Reagan dismissed the idea when he suddenly recalled his father had entered the hotel room the next morning with no key. *The door had been unlocked!* Sometime during the night, someone had used a key. It all made sense now. The images of lovemaking, the rose scent that lingered on his sheets. He had supposed he had gotten the sachet from Elizabeth as she escorted him to the study and he had somehow transferred them to the sheets. But, if she had been in his bed, so would her scent.

Reagan groaned as a scenario played itself in his mind. Elizabeth, in her eagerness to reveal her feelings had somehow obtained a key and entered his room. In his drunken state he didn't know the lover of his dreams had been real, and in that condition, he had done the unthinkable. The results were devastating. It now appeared Elizabeth was attempting to unite father and son with this final act.

Reagan sat motionless, his mind racing over his options. He could do nothing, burn the letter and tell no one. The child might be adopted and never learn of his ignoble beginnings. Or, as is often the case with children in orphanages, he would languish without proper food or love. Reagan's sense of duty immediately rebelled. His child shouldn't have to suffer. He had to think of something else.

He could discreetly give the letter to Sam, Elizabeth's father, who'd surely raise his grandson despite the stain of illegitimacy. But, what if Sam refused? Would the shame be too great for a respected mayor? If he lost his position, how would he raise the boy? With no wife to ease his burden, Sam might feel overwhelmed and unable to care for the babe. No, the child needed both a mother and a father. Gaeran needed to be adopted.

Perhaps, he could find loving parents here in Cantonsville who would raise him without anyone knowing the circumstances of his birth. Several possibilities ran through Reagan's mind of couples who could afford a child in need. Yet, what reason could he give them to travel to Indiana when so many local children needed adopting? And, could he watch from afar, knowing the boy might be his flesh, unable to hold that which was his? Thinking of his own son, Reagan knew he'd never want anyone but himself to raise his child.

Yet, what could he tell Amanda? He nearly lost her when she discovered the scratches and if he confirmed her worst fears, how would she respond? Would she take Jesse and flee? He couldn't bear being separated from his loved ones and yet, could his fears justify abandoning his other son? Reagan's insides heaved, his heart congesting with anguish as one thought pushed forward beyond all others. Gaeran needed him. He must find a way to bring him home.

Reagan folded the letter and placed it inside his vest pocket. He would speak with Amanda but needed time to settle upon what he would say. One thing was certain. He would telegraph the Lars Orphanage of his impending visit. He didn't know how Amanda would view his actions, but he must convince her they were the right thing to do, and quickly.

chapter 2

AMANDA LAY JESSE down for a nap after his morning feeding. She then sat down with needle and thread to mend one of her husband's shirts. She hummed to herself while stitching, but lay down her mending when the door opened. Reagan entered, kissing her brow before standing beside the crib.

"How's the little fellow doing?"

"He's become a tyrant when he eats," Amanda said. "I don't know where he puts it."

Reagan chuckled. "He's a Burnsfield. If there's something we want, we go full bore until we're satisfied."

"Still, I'll be relieved when he's weaned. He's not fed more than a few hours before he fusses for more."

"That won't be for some time yet," he said, stroking Jesse's clenched fist. "In the mean time, you could use some help. I've hired a nanny, starting next week. It's time to let another take over for awhile so you can get some rest."

"I know I'm often tired, but a nanny? I love taking care of Jesse. I can't think of a time where I'd want another to tend him."

"I can," Reagan said, grinning. "I miss you at night. You scarcely lay down before you're up again, spending all your time in the nursery. I miss touching you and—"

"Reagan, really!"

"What? I'd think you'd be grateful for a full night's sleep."

"I suspicion your motives," Amanda said, lifting a brow. "It sounds more like I'd be trading one sort of sleepless night for another."

"Well, that too," he said, shrugging. "But eventually, both our needs will be met. Besides, it's better for Jesse. Once he begins toddling, you'll need your energy to keep him out of mischief."

"By then, I'll think a nanny's a good idea. Perhaps, I'll even allow a playmate or two. You won't think me remiss if I go back to helping Aunt Ella with her sewing circle, would you?" she said, fingering her needle. "It'd only be a few hours a week. That wouldn't be neglecting our babe, would it?"

Reagan's demeanor seemed to turn sober though Amanda couldn't say why. His voice softened even as his back stiffened. "No. As I said, there's nothing wrong with having help. As long as we do what's right.

Raise him properly. Shield him from harm. Isn't that what parents do?"

Amanda furrowed her brow. "Of course it is. You seem upset. Is something wrong?"

Reagan's shoulders slumped. Turning from the crib, he sat on the footstool near Amanda's feet. "Yes, there is." He pulled papers from his pocket and held them out. "I received a letter from Elizabeth. She's in trouble and asking for our help."

Amanda took the letter and unfolded it, reading swiftly. "Oh, no!" she gasped, a hand covering her mouth. "I can't believe it."

Reagan stared at his hands. "I too—was shocked—when I read it. It seems too bizarre to believe. And yet, I feel we must do something. Elizabeth wouldn't have contacted us unless she had nowhere else to turn."

Amanda stared at Reagan, her voice strained. "You don't think—I mean—is it possible *she* could've been the one who scratched you? She said the father of her child was besotted—and—you'd been drinking at the hotel. You couldn't recall what happened. Did your memory ever return?"

Reagan's face clouded. He shook his head. "No. I've still no real recollection of that night. I'm sorry," he said. "I wish I could give you an answer."

"What about *before* you drank yourself insensible?"

"What do you mean?"

"Did you see her when you went to the Hampton's that night?"

"Briefly. She'd escorted me to the study. While there, she told Sam she was going to Camilla's to help plan her birthday party. She left long before I did. I've no memory of seeing Elizabeth after that."

"I see," Amanda said, sighing. "If you haven't remembered by now, you probably won't. I suppose it's preposterous to think she could've done such a thing. After all, you were married at the time."

Reagan opened his mouth, but then shut it, rubbing his hands as if quelling the urge to say something. "I guess we'll need to decide whether or not to take the boy," he said. "I mean—she told the orphanage someone would be coming."

"Surely, there's other kin besides her father who could take the child."

"No, there's only Sam and his sister, Emmaline. We were contacted because there is no one else."

"Are you serious? Won't it seem strange so soon after Jesse's birth?"

"I'm not concerned what others might think," Reagan said. "Elizabeth wasn't a close friend, but she's asking for our help. What else can we do?"

"I'm not sure adopting her son's the answer. Besides, what if she recovers and wants him back?"

"I'll tell you what. I'll go to Lars. If her doctor thinks she'll recover, I'll ensure she has enough money for herself and the babe. If however, the worst happens; would you be opposed to me bringing him back?"

Amanda searched Reagan's eyes, moved by his concern. "I understand why she'd want her child in a good home. I suppose we should do what we can. All right, you may go and if necessary, bring him back. We'll see about finding a family for him. Ever since the War, mother's been involved with Children's Aid Society. She'll know what to do."

"What if she can't place him?" Reagan persisted.

"If that happens, we'll discuss other options. I don't think we can decide until then."

"I see," he said. "I'll leave immediately. I should be back in a few days."

"What'll you tell your father?"

"Nothing more than I have to," Reagan said, rising. He took the letter from Amanda's hands. "We can't tell anyone about this. Not even our parents. After all, we don't even know if I'll be bringing him back."

"Of course," Amanda said. "I promise."

After Reagan left, Jesse began to stir, interrupting her thoughts. It wasn't until later Amanda would wonder about the relief she saw in her husband's face. Or, was it gratitude? She couldn't decide.

chapter 3

IN LARS, REAGAN left the train depot with directions to the orphanage. He hired a buggy and within the hour found himself knocking on a well-worn door. A young girl answered and after listening to his request, escorted him to the open doorway of a small office. Inside, sat a middle-aged woman, primly dressed and her hair in a tight bun.

"Mrs. Seymour, Mr. Burnsfield is here to see you about baby Gaeran."

Mrs. Seymour looked over her spectacles as if sizing Reagan up before gesturing him in. "Sally, please see that tea is brought at once. Mr. Burnsfield has come a distance and needs refreshment."

"Yes, ma'am," the girl said before leaving.

"Please have a seat, Mr. Burnsfield." She indicated one of two chairs in front of her desk. "I'm sure you're tired."

"Thank you." He settled into the nearest seat. "I came as soon as I could."

Mrs. Seymour rose and opened a drawer cabinet behind her desk. Retrieving a file, she resumed her seat and once again perused Reagan's form. "Let's not waste any time, Mr. Burnsfield. Miss Hampton informed me a family friend would come for her child. Frankly, I didn't believe anyone would until I received your telegram. Now that you're here, shall we proceed?"

"Mrs. Seymour," he said. "Before we start, can you tell me how Elizabeth's doing? I know she wasn't well."

She folded her hands, looking at him intently. "I'm sorry to say, Elizabeth succumbed to pneumonia less than two days ago. We've had little Gaeran for just over a week, long enough to know he's perfectly healthy."

Stunned, he continued. "Did she change her mind about who's to have her child?"

"She didn't, Mr. Burnsfield. Women like her have no resources and they don't make demands. Elizabeth was different. She appeared on our doorstep when she first became ill, asking a lot of questions. When summoned to her bedside, she felt adamant whomever she'd written would come. She made me promise to wait thirty days before adopting out her child. She needn't have worried. It's unfortunate, but we lose most babies to sickness before we can place them."

"I didn't realize—"

"As distressing as those facts are, Mr. Burnsfield, it doesn't dampen my resolve. My goal is to save as many children as I can and in that light, I'd like to settle the matter of Gaeran." She picked up her pen. "You *are* here to adopt the child, aren't you?"

"Yes. If Elizabeth hadn't improved, I planned on adopting him."

"Very good." She began writing. "We've a few legal procedures, namely petitioning the court. After establishing a few facts, we'll begin immediately. Can I have your full name, Mr. Burnsfield?"

"I'll do everything necessary. However, I'd like this to be done quickly as well as quietly. Elizabeth's father will soon arrive and may find out about her baby. It's possible he'd come here, demanding the boys' whereabouts. Who knows if he'd want the child, but I don't want him creating havoc because I adopted his grandson." Reagan withdrew Elizabeth's letter and handed it to Mrs. Seymour. "Please read this. Afterward, I'm sure you'll agree the adoption shouldn't be made public."

Mrs. Seymour took the letter and read it before setting it aside. "I understand how difficult it'd be if that happened. But, I don't believe Mr. Hampton would do such a thing. After all, spreading the news would needlessly tarnish his daughter's reputation. Most people in this situation want the problem to go away, not bring attention to it."

Reagan leaned forward. "Perhaps, but I can't take that chance. Did her aunt know about the letter Elizabeth wrote?"

"Elizabeth said she told no one. However, I believe Emmaline overheard our conversation. So, it's possible she knows one had been sent."

"If she did, she'd pass that on to Sam. He wouldn't know the father was unaware of her situation. If he discovers I was the one who came, he'd believe me responsible. You can see the position I'd be in."

"According to Elizabeth, the father was out of his mind with drink. All you'd need to do is show him this letter. Once he realizes you had nothing to do with it, you'd be absolved."

Reagan took a deep breath, releasing it slowly. "About the time this happened, I'd been separated from my wife. I stayed at a hotel and oftentimes, eased my loneliness with liquor—"

Mrs. Seymour stared at Reagan over her spectacles. "Am I to understand *you're* the besotted fellow of whom Elizabeth spoke?"

"I'm almost certain, but memory can't confirm it. If Elizabeth's father discovers I've adopted Gaeran, he'd question me ceaselessly. I don't have to tell you what this would do to my wife or the scandal it would cause."

"This is highly unusual," Mrs. Seymour said. "Although from Elizabeth's letter, she seemed adamant you take her child. So, if we can manage a private adoption, I've no objections." Just then, Sally brought a tray. Mrs. Seymour waited until two cups had been filled before continuing. "I'll contact Judge Pritchard this afternoon. His wife, Anna, is a supporter of our orphanage, and a friend of mine. Due to the situation, I'll request no notices be placed in the paper."

"Thank you, Mrs. Seymour," he said. "I trust that if Sam comes to inquire of the child, you'll keep this confidential?"

"My loyalties are to the children. If silence guarantees a placement, so be it."

"You've my gratitude," he said. "And to show it, I'll arrange a years' payment for doctor visits. I'd also like to give a donation for any other needs."

"That's not necessary, Mr. Burnsfield. It'll seem like bribery. However, these are hard times and *after* it's final, I'll gratefully accept charity. Our children suffer enough from being orphaned. Keeping them fed and clothed shouldn't be one of them."

Later, Mrs. Seymour led Reagan through the baby ward. Infants and toddlers were placed two to a bed, many crying with arms outstretched. She stopped at the furthest crib, lifting one out. "He's not taken well to his surroundings and hasn't eaten much. I'm afraid he's a bit thin. Mr. Burnsfield," she said, placing the child in his arms, "this is Gaeran."

Reagan cradled the babe, fighting sudden tears. "He has Elizabeth's eyes," he said, brushing a strand from the babe's face. "He's beautiful."

"Though Elizabeth called the child by his middle name, my recommendation would be to always call him Gaeran. He'll need a clean break from his past. However, by whatever name you choose, you'll soon get to know each other."

"You're right," he said. "Gaeran seems to suit him."

"I'd recommend hiring a wet nurse for your trip home. We've precious few volunteers, but it wouldn't be difficult finding a woman if she's well compensated."

"Can you give a recommendation?" Reagan said. "I only ask that she's healthy and able to stay until he's weaned."

"I'll interview our wet nurses today. Any that show interest will be given a doctor's bill of health before being offered the position."

"Thank you. Now if I may, I'd like to find a place to stay until the adoption's arranged."

Mrs. Seymour lifted Gaeran from Reagan's arms. "You'll find many rooms for let along Chauncey Avenue. Or, there's a hotel near the train station."

"I'll opt for a boardinghouse," Reagan said. "Hotels get me in trouble."

"I understand," Mrs. Seymour said, placing Gaeran back inside the crib. "You've enough entanglements as it is."

chapter 4

SAM HAMPTON FELT a recurring ache as he traveled by rail to retrieve his daughter's body. His suffering had started early in life with the death of his parents and lingered while being raised by his older sister, Emmaline. He later married and had one child before his wife passed away suddenly. Anguish, coupled with feelings of abandonment rode him mercilessly with every calamity. He had found happiness while Elizabeth lived. But with this latest blow, he suffered grievously. He belonged to no one. His life held no profit save an aging sister and a lifetime of losses.

Yet, nothing prepared him for what he saw when he entered Elizabeth's bedroom once he reached Emmaline's home. A tiny cradle occupied a corner, filled with knitted blankets and a solitary rattle.

Sam turned to his sister, who hadn't stopped weeping since he knocked on her door. "What's the meaning of this?" he said, pointing.

"I-I didn't expect you this soon," she said, daubing her cheeks. "I should've had them removed. I'm sorry—"

"Do you mean to tell me Elizabeth was *pregnant?*" Sam thundered. "How could you let this happen? Why wasn't I told?"

"Sam, please calm down. Elizabeth was expecting when she arrived. She begged me not to tell you. It must've happened before she left Cantonsville."

"*Before*— ?" Sam's fingers curled into fists. "Who'd she say was responsible?"

"She never told me," Emmaline said. "All I know is she planned to stay and raise little Sammy. She said she couldn't go home."

"She had a boy?" he said. "She named him after me?"

"I didn't attend the christening, but she always called him Sammy," Emmaline said. "I assumed that was his given name."

Of a sudden, his lip quivered and his voice became strained. "Where is he?"

"Elizabeth had the orphanage take him. She said everything had been arranged."

Sam gazed around the room, stopping at the cradle. Though still outraged, a budding joy took root. *Part of Elizabeth lived!* Walking over, he took a blanket and held it against his face. "My Elizabeth had a son," he whispered, weeping fresh tears.

"Please don't cry." Emmaline touched his shoulder. "She wanted to protect you. She said if anyone learned of Sammy, you'd be disgraced."

"Why should I care about that?" he said bitterly. "Everyone I love has been taken from me! What evil have I done for God to treat me so?"

"You can't mean that," she said. "Only God chooses which burdens we must bear."

Sam turned to his sister with scorching eyes. "Are you saying he meant for my Elizabeth to die? Why would he take my parents, my wife and after that, my daughter, and finally my grandchild? What kind of God asks that of anyone?"

"No—I mean—I don't know," she said, stepping back. "It's just, these are hard times, and many are suffering. It's our lot to endure."

"I'm sick of enduring! Look what it's got me. Nothing! Except for Elizabeth, my life's been worthless." He shook his fist. "I can't bear it anymore! I'm going to find my grandson." He stormed toward the door. "And anybody that doesn't like it can *kiss my ass!*"

Two hours later, Sam stepped outside the orphanage door. He felt drained of emotion as he left the porch to walk the boarded sidewalk. No amount of pleading, arguing or threatening had opened the mistress's lips on where Elizabeth's child had been taken. She insisted the babe had been locally placed and that the adoption was private. The only paper she produced was a statement from Judge Pritchard declaring the laws of Indiana had been complied with satisfactorily.

His prayers seemed to have fallen on deaf ears as his chances of finding his grandson evaporated like a wisp of smoke. With a start, he realized the cadence of his feet tramped in unison with words that sprang from a hatred he didn't know existed. *I'm going to kill whoever got Elizabeth pregnant! I'm going to find him and kill him!*

chapter 5

REAGAN OPENED THE front door, allowing the nurse with Gaeran in her arms, to enter. He followed, setting down two traveling cases before taking the sleeping child. "Maisy, I'll show you the nursery and then take you to your room. Afterward, I'll introduce you to the rest of the household."

"Thank you," she said, picking up her traveling case.

Reagan led the way upstairs, walking the length of the hall before opening a door and entering. "Here's the nursery," he said, placing Gaeran in a day crib. "Your room will be across the hall. I'll have a crib brought tomorrow so Gaeran can stay with you at night." He reentered the hall and opened a bedroom door, revealing a spacious room. "Please take a couple hours to refresh yourself. Afterward, I'll have cook bring some tea."

"Thank you, sir," Maisy said, then closed her door behind her.

Reagan had taken no more than a step when his own chamber door opened and Amanda hurried out. "Reagan," she breathed, kissing his cheek. "You're home!" She looked around the hallway. "I heard voices."

Reagan thought he had prepared himself, but words fled and he simply opened the nursery door. "You did. I'll explain in a moment, but first I'd like to introduce you to Gaeran," he said.

Amanda entered and stood by the bassinette. "He looks frail," she whispered. "Does he need a doctor?"

"The doctor in Lars said he's healthy, but exhausted. I'm sure being taken from Elizabeth has frightened him. Providing stability is the best we can do."

"I take it this means Elizabeth—worsened?"

Reagan nodded. "She died before I arrived. That's why I brought him home."

"Poor child!" Amanda said, her face softening. "I'll contact mother about placing him. It seems cruel putting him back in an orphanage, but maybe he can be put at the top of the list."

"Amanda, there's more." Reagan took a deep breath, laying a hand on the child's back. "My earlier introduction was incomplete. This little one is Gaeran Samuel Burnsfield, the newest member of our family."

Stunned, Amanda's jaw dropped. "W-what are you saying?" she said. "You've adopted him? He's—he's now our son?"

"Yes. But, I can explain—"

"How could you?" she said, choking. "Didn't we agree Children's Aid should try adoption first?"

"After what he's endured, I didn't think he'd survive. I was afraid—" Reagan stopped, realizing she wasn't ready for truth. "—I know what we agreed to, Amanda, but it seemed the right thing to do. We've more than enough to provide for him. He'll be like a brother to Jesse."

"I don't understand. Why us?"

"Why not us," Reagan countered. "What's wrong with us adopting?"

Amanda shook her head. "Don't you realize how strange it'll look? We've never mentioned adopting and suddenly we've another son. Didn't we create enough gossip when we got married? What if someone found out we adopted Elizabeth's child? I couldn't live through another scandal!"

Reagan's lips formed an angry line. Taking her arm, he led her from the room, releasing her once inside their bedroom and behind closed doors. "Listen! I don't care what anyone else says. We were asked to take Gaeran in by Elizabeth, who was in trouble. She felt it best he be adopted by someone she knew. She believed you the best choice."

"But, she didn't ask me," Amanda said, arms akimbo. "She asked you. I can't help but wonder why."

"I'm assuming it's because of my relationship with her father. He and I worked closely on a business deal. She may've thought Sam approved of me. Other than that, I've no idea." Reagan hated himself for his partial lie. He had a pretty good idea why, but no way to confirm it. For Gaeran's sake, he prayed the truth would never be known. "I'm sorry it ended this way. I'd hoped Elizabeth would recover. She didn't, so I did what I thought best."

Amanda's eye's filled with tears. "Tis obvious, you didn't care what I thought! Just like that," she snapped her fingers, "you broke your word. I can't believe you did this without consulting me!"

"That's not true!" Reagan took a step as Amanda retreated. "I do care! You'd have done the same thing." He struggled to maintain an even voice. "Gaeran wasn't thriving. I feared he'd perish. I—I adopted him to keep him alive."

"And how'll you do that, now? Surely, you don't expect me to—I won't—nurse that child." She threw up her hands. "That's asking too much!"

Reagan shook his head. "Of course not. I hired a wet nurse to accompany me home. Her name's Maisy and she's agreed to stay until he's weaned. She's in the guest room opposite the nursery."

Amanda folded her arms, turning away. "It seems you've thought of everything. I hope you've also thought what we're going to tell everyone. I won't know what to say when we show up places with two children instead of one."

Reagan's face darkened. "You make it sound as if I committed a crime! With orphans filling streets, I'd say we're to be praised for doing our civic duty." He came and stood behind Amanda, his voice softening. "I know I acted in haste. I'm sorry. I should've consulted you first. Please don't be angry."

Amanda sniffed, looking over her shoulder. "Won't Mother be upset when she finds out we didn't adopt through her? She's especially proud of her placements."

"She'll be thrilled for any child snatched from harms way. How could she be otherwise?" Reagan touched Amanda's shoulder, relieved she didn't pull away. "We'll have both our parents over for dinner and introduce them to Gaeran. It'll be alright. I promise."

A knock on the door caused both to jump. Reagan went to open the portal while Amanda wiped at her tears. "Mr. Barrington has stopped by. He's waiting in the front parlor," said a servant.

"Thank you Aida. Please tell Beau I'll be down shortly. Mrs. Burnsfield's a bit tired and may not join us."

"Very good, sir."

Reagan shut the door. "Do you feel up to company? I know how much you enjoy his visits."

"I couldn't possibly," she said, turning away. "Please, give my regrets. Beau can always tell when I'm upset."

With a sigh, Reagan left the room, feeling he'd bungled the one introduction that meant the most, that of his wife to his son.

chapter 6

"MON AMI, HOW are you?" Beauregard said, grasping Reagan's hand. "I visited a few days ago, but Madame said you were on an unexpected trip. So, I come today."

Reagan smiled at his longtime friend. "I'm glad. But, I've a feeling you weren't too upset to have had Amanda all to yourself."

"Oui! Madame Burnsfield is très beau! Moi never tires of her charms," he said, winking. "Mayhap, next time you'll be gone longer? You've been stingy with le fleur."

"The *flower* is taken. And, I don't share," Reagan said, chuckling. "I thought the matter settled at our wedding. You were there, remember?"

"Tis true! You've said the better man won the prize." Beau bowed with a wave of his hand. "But, who knows? Madame may yet tire of such a brute as you."

Reagan punched his shoulder. "What are you saying? You'd switch places with me?"

"Absolument," he said impishly. "What are friends for?"

Though spoken in jest, Reagan felt pricked. He didn't want a reminder of how upset his wife was at this moment. He took Beau's arm, steering him toward the settee. "So, how've you been? I've heard you became partner at Barrington Hotel. Am I correct you're no longer satisfied being your papa's desk clerk?"

"Oui!" Beauregard laughed, displaying white teeth. Though shorter, he had little trouble gripping Reagan's shoulder. "I've decided I need real enterprise. My investment will allow even more ventures."

Reagan grinned as they reached the settee. "To my recollection, the only ventures you chase are feminine."

"Non! This is different. This summer, I stayed in a beautiful lodge in Catskills. It suddenly came to me; a resort would be a perfect vocation! Who better to bring our city culture and romance, than a Frenchman?"

"We have hotels already. How will you compare?"

"It'll be a grand structure. Nothing will be like it!" Beau punctuated the air with wide gestures. "We'll build large porches for families and—and even their dogs! In one yard will be croquet for ladies and for gentlemen, tennis and bowling greens. There'll be walking paths, carriage rides and picnics by the river. Gardens with exotic flowers, benches and private grottos for newlyweds—"

"Or lovers?" Reagan grinned as they both sat near the hearth. "It sounds too ambitious for a man who's made leisure his only occupation."

"L'ambition ne vieillit pas," Beau quipped. "Ambition has no rest. I am become like you, mon ami. I'll now be a businessman."

"I'm happy for you. But, won't your father view a retreat as competition to Barrington Hotel?"

"Non! Mon père's hotel accommodates travelers. My resort will be a destination! People will feel they're in New York, not Cantonsville, Ohio." Beau's eyes were like lit coals. "I found an ideal spot, twenty beautiful acres along the river. It's quiet and it's secluded. Not only will people come from far away, but those nearby who want to vacation without traveling long distances."

"I agree, it's ambitious. Will you finance it through Bruester Bank and Trust?" Reagan asked as a maid entered with a tray. She deftly filled two teacups.

Beau accepted a cup, grinning. "Ah, that's where *you* come in. As Monsieur Bruester's son-in-law, you could help present my idea, but in more festive settings than a bank."

"What'd you have in mind?" Reagan asked, taking tea the maid offered, but ignoring the scones.

"But, where is Madame?" Beau asked, looking around. "I wanted to hear what she thinks of my plan."

"Amanda isn't feeling well. She said to give her regrets."

"Tsk!" Beau shook his head. "As bonne mère, I'm sure she's doing everything herself."

Reagan waited until the maid left. "That'll soon change. I've hired a nanny for Jesse. And, since we're on the subject, you'll be the first to know we've adopted another child, a boy about Jesse's age."

Beau's face lit. He clapped together his hands. "How wonderful! I've heard Emily uses her influence in placing orphans. It's hard to say 'no' to your mother-in-law, eh?"

Reagan fumbled with his tea, clearing his throat. "Uh, the adoption wasn't through Emily. As a matter of fact, I'd received a letter from an old college friend who'd been crippled in—in the battle of Port Republic. After losing his wife, he couldn't care for his child."

"I read about that awful battle in the papers," Beau said. "Many died. Does your friend live nearby?"

"Ah—*no*," Reagan took a sip before continuing. "His wife moved to Indiana while he was gone, and he followed later. I just returned from there today with the child."

Beau set down his cup. "My apologies. Surely, you're tired. I should return another time."

"Absolutely not," Reagan said, relieved to change the subject. "Please tell me how we fit into your plans."

Beau's face brightened. "My hope is Amanda will invite a few friends for dinner and of course, George. Then, I'll explain my idea and perhaps discuss financing over wine. Your parlor will be more comfortable than an office. Once he's reminded I'm your good friend, he'll be inclined to listen, no?"

"Don't pin your hopes on that," Reagan said, chuckling. "It might be to your detriment you remind him."

"Posh! Everyone knows ever since you saved Amanda from that knave, Derrick Banning, you've been the twinkle of Monsieur's eye."

"You were there too, my friend."

"Until I got shot," Beau said, shrugging. "After that, I wasn't any help."

"Still, you haven't any worries George won't remember you."

"But, I wasn't the one who bloodied my knuckles on that murderer's face. And now you're once again a hero, rescuing a friend's baby." He picked up a scone, spreading it with jam. "But, you didn't mention your friend's name. Do I know him?"

Reagan's mind raced over his college friends and people he hadn't thought of in years. Only one arose that he knew couldn't be traced. "Eisen. His name is Eisen Paine."

chapter 7

Doctor Artemus Turner had just hung his coat when a knock rattled his office door. He swept the portal wide, viewing a man with an obviously scarred hand. "Come in," he said, indicating a chair. "Please, have a seat. I've just arrived myself." He then took his own chair behind his desk. "I see your hand's been injured. What can I do for you?"

"I'm Miles Alexander," the man said, removing his hat. "I'm from the 34th Volunteer Infantry. I was shot a year ago. I need you to say my hand is healed enough to return to my company."

Turner's brows rose. "Who's requiring the evaluation?"

"Because of the damage, Surgeon Brashear issued a certificate of disability. He insists on a doctor's consent before rescinding it."

"You're the first soldier to request going back," he said. "Let me see your hand."

Miles stretched out his hand, palm upward. Turner gently flexed each finger before turning over the hand to palpitate the scar tissue. "Your tendon's torn and there's bone loss," he said matter-of-factly. He then bent it forward and back, observing range of motion. "Grip my hand as hard as you can."

Miles squeezed his fingers, yet strain showed in his eyes. "What do you think? Am I sufficiently healed?"

Turner released Miles' hand. "Hold on, soldier. Open your fingers as far as you can. Then move each one independently and then make a fist." He watched as Miles opened his hand until it looked like a shallow bowl. He then barely touched each finger to his thumb before making a loose fist.

"Well?"

Turner shook his head. "You're hand isn't useless, but I'm not convinced you could handle a gun."

"But, I'm needed."

"Why the hurry? You need more time to strengthen your hand."

Miles blue eyes remained unwavering. "I don't think that matters, sir."

Artemus noted the man's squared shoulders and quiet determination. With wavy hair neatly combed, he carried an air of authority. "You're an officer," he said, finally.

"I'm Warrant Officer Miles Alexander. I'm ready to return to my regiment."

"*Warrant* Officer Alexander—that mean's you're a doctor."

"Whatever I am," he said, "I'm ready to go back."

Artemus sighed. "But, you're right hand dominate."

"How'd you know?"

"You wouldn't be here if you weren't. Look, I understand your desire to return. But, I know what's required of a battlefield doctor. You must be able to handle a suturing needle and enough strength to amputate limbs. Gruesome as that is, those poor soldiers would suffer more if you're incapable of swiftly executing your duties."

"Brashear swore I'd never regain its use, but I've kept my hand limber. I've been suturing cloth—"

"It's not the same and you know it," Artemus said, standing. "The only way to prove you're strong enough is to cut a branch the size of a man's thigh bone. If you can do that, then I'll consider it. The blacksmith has a tool shed out back. Let's borrow a saw and see what you can do."

Soon, both men stood near a woodpile. Miles wiped sweat from his brow before gripping a handsaw. Turner held open his timepiece as Miles began sawing a branch with short, faltering strokes. He had cut halfway when Artemus snapped shut his watch.

"Stop. I'm afraid it's not good enough. You lack strength."

"I'll work harder," Miles said, handing the tool to Artemus. "Perhaps I'm not manipulating the scars enough. If you assist with both your hands verses one of mine, I'm sure I'll improve."

"Listen, I'm amazed with what you've done. I know how painful scar tissue is. With bone fragments, I'm sure it feels like it's been crucified."

"The whiskey helps," Miles said, putting on his coat.

Artemus rubbed his jaw. "I'm not opposed to working your hand, but I've a better suggestion. I could use your talents to help soldiers, just not the way you're thinking."

"What do you mean?"

"I've been commissioned to create a hospital for wounded soldiers. Your passion indicates a high degree of dedication and I need someone to hire and train staff. Your hand wouldn't be an issue since we'd be caring for men who've already survived battle wounds but aren't healthy enough to go home. Besides, I'll be there to assist."

"So, you're saying you won't certify I'm fit for duty?"

"Not if you want me telling the truth. Think about what I'm offering. If you accept, I'll pay fifty dollars a month. Not quite what the Army pays, but then again," he said grinning, "you shouldn't get shot while working." Before he walked away, Artemus patted Miles' shoulder.

"Traitor!" Miles muttered, scowling at his scarred hand.

chapter 8

AMANDA SAT IN her chambers by the fire, nursing Jesse. In the privacy of their room, she didn't cover her exposed breast and it gleamed in the firelight. Reagan sat nearby, glancing at the mantle clock. It had taken time for Amanda to accept Gaeran's adoption, reluctantly declaring she would forgive him so long as he never abused her trust again. Reagan had eagerly agreed, silently thanking God for Amanda's natural kindness.

"Dinner went well," he said, loosening his collar. "Both our parents seemed overjoyed we'd adopted Gaeran and each took turns holding him."

Amanda smiled. "Yes, they did. Although, I held my breath when you explained how it came to be. Everyone accepted your story Gaeran came from a widower who'd become disabled."

"I told you it'd be all right," Reagan said. "These are trying times. Many families have taken in orphans. Sheriff Hadley adopted a boy headed for the work house. He said a twelve year old needed school more than an apprenticeship."

"I'm sure he'll fit in with Jim's other kids," she said. Suddenly, her smile faded, replaced with concern. "Once this gets around, what if someone would try contacting Mr. Paine? I know it's a remote possibility, but if anyone did, our alibi would be undone."

"Don't worry. Even if anyone snooped, they wouldn't find him."

Amanda lifted Jesse to her shoulder and patted his back. "How do you know? It's hard keeping secrets with so many busybodies around."

Reagan chuckled. "If it weren't for those busybodies, we wouldn't be married."

"This is different," she scolded. "How do you know the truth won't come out?"

"Because," he said, rising to kiss her brow, "Mr. Paine is a fiction of my imagination."

A soft burp from Jesse punctuated the silence as Amanda stared at Reagan. "What do you mean? I thought you said Eisen was a college friend."

Reagan lifted Jesse from Amanda's shoulder, cradling the sleeping child. "Eisen was someone I created to use as an excuse when I wanted to leave school for—entertainment—purposes."

"Entertainment?" Amanda's eyes widened. "You don't mean—"

Reagan grinned. "I'm taking Jesse to the nursery where he's staying tonight. And, you're going to let Mrs. Stuttart take care of him until morning."

"Just because you hired a nanny, doesn't mean I won't hear him cry."

Reagan's eyes lowered to where her dress parted. "Tonight you'll be either too busy or too tired," he said. "You'll need your rest."

Amanda's skin came alive in the wake of Reagan's perusal, tingling as though he had touched her. Her cheeks instantly stained, remembering her own thoughts had traveled that same path lately. Since Jesse's birth, she'd had little time nor inclination to attend to wifely duties. But now, as the child neared five months, she felt fully recuperated and even anxious to resume those moments of bliss.

As Reagan left with Jesse, Amanda rose to rummage through drawers, pulling out a silken shift. Cobalt blue with copper threads, the garment had been created by Ives Du Monde. She had blushed at its short hem and daring slits. Yet, Reagan had delighted in it, purchasing it on the spot while shopping at Bostwick's. She retreated behind the changing screen, doffing her clothes and pulling the shift over her head. The cloth had barely settled over her hips when she heard Reagan reenter the room.

She then sat at her vanity, removing hairpins while he leaned against a bedpost, watching. Amanda loosened locks that cascaded to her waist, then taking a brush, stroked her hair into a shimmering mass. Reagan became fascinated with firelight reflecting off the copper shift and how provocatively the material clung as she moved. When her fingers hovered over one of several perfume bottles, he stepped forward, brushing away her hand.

"Nay, not that one," he said, reaching for a different decanter. "This is my favorite."

Amanda smiled as she accepted the bottle. "It's always the rose water." She touched the stopper behind each ear and across her throat. She then turned on the bench, facing him and lifted her lips invitingly.

Reagan had longed for this time of reacquainting and determined to savor each moment. He reveled in her beauty from her porcelain skin and ebony locks to her full breasts curving sharply above a narrow waist. He knelt, parting her thighs to encompass him as his fingers smoothed her hair in a sensuous caress from nape to hips. The Attar of Roses mingled with the scent of her hair creating a tantalizing perfume that ignited desire in the pit of his stomach. He could scarce control his excitement as Amanda leaned forward to press her lips against his while unbuttoning his shirt and pushing it off his shoulders. His heart nearly stopped when her breasts played a teasing game of cat and mouse against his chest.

With hands still on her hips, Reagan drew her close until they were intimately pressed together.

One hand slid up her back while the other began a slow ascent along her waist. His lips found her throat where perfume filled his head with memories of past lovemaking. Amanda gasped when one hand found a breast, peaking against his palm. A warm tingling pulsed throughout her being, becoming a white heat that threatened to consume her. She brought his face back to hers, their lips and tongues melded in a sensuous exploration of warm cavities of their mouths. Reagan's hands never ceased moving as he delighted in every curve. Finding the edge of her shift, he pushed it upwards, slowly caressing her thighs until gripping her hips. Then in one fluid motion, he lifted her and stood, enjoying sensations of her nestled against his groin.

"Reagan!" Amanda said, laughing. "You'll drop me."

"You weigh but a feather," he said, teasing her ear with his tongue and turning toward bed. "But if you insist, here you go." He gently tossed Amanda among pillows before shedding his clothes and joining her beneath the covers. Reagan looked into her eyes of liquid indigo, marveling at her beauty. Though he had been smitten the first time he saw her, she now exuded a more womanly beauty that made her exceedingly desirable. "You're so beautiful," he said, lifting her hand to his lips. Kissing her palm, he then placed it against his manhood so she could feel his need. "I've been waiting to show how much I love you," he said, kissing her forehead, "to hold you—touch you," then her nose and then her lips.

Though his body demanded fulfillment, Reagan whetted his appetite by caressing Amanda in ways he knew would heighten her pleasure. He touched, tasted and explored every part of her until she writhed in anticipation and not until she begged him to love her did he lower himself between her trembling thighs. Amanda accepted him fully, rising to meet him, her belly rubbing against the hardness of his. She felt the strength of his body as her fingers traced over his biceps, shoulders and ribs. They were two beings coming together as one. A merging, blending of bodies. Awe turned to rapture as their union, begun with restraint, gave way to eager, uncaring haste. Reagan sensed Amanda's imminent bliss and his control crumbled. His possession became complete and groaning, he shuddered as waves of pure physical pleasure washed over him the same time Amanda cried out. Straining together, each sought to satisfy the full measure of their passions and not until the last shred was spent did they lay in exhausted stillness.

Pulling rumpled sheets up around them, Reagan turned his face into her hair as it spilled over pillows. The scent reminded him of long nights waiting for their pleasurable interludes to resume. He marveled that since meeting Amanda at her debutante's ball, it was only she who could stir his blood until his passions seethed.

chapter 9

THE FUNERAL FOR Elizabeth Hampton took place the day Sam brought her body home. Before leaving Lars, he had wired his servants to post a death notice, make arrangements with the cemetery and then drape the house with crepe. And due to the length of time since her death, he omitted the usual practice of parlor viewing. Instead, he took her pine box directly to the funeral parlor where he had her body placed inside a cherry wood coffin. That afternoon, the hearse arrived and once the coffin was loaded, headed directly to the cemetery. Six black horses adorned with ostrich plumes pulled the wagon, followed by Sam's carriage and lastly, the pastor who would perform a private ceremony. Workers unloaded the casket inside an iron fence bordering the graveyard. Fire-red maple leaves crunched beneath feet, giving notice to the otherwise silent passage.

Despite sympathetic callers, the mayor forbade anyone to join him. Not knowing who had impregnated Elizabeth, it might have turned into an inquisition of any man who would've attended. Instead, he mourned alone.

Sam stayed long after the pastor left, utterly forsaken and unable to relinquish his last act as parent. Not until the sun dropped behind trees did a caretaker gently lead him away so the grave could be closed.

In a stupor, he went home and locked himself in his study where servants heard nothing but weeping and periodic slamming of the liquor cabinet door.

chapter IO

CAMILLA MUELDER HAD married Leroy Spelding for the sole reason he had been the wealthiest man available. Since then, her gay existence had become as lackluster as her husband's dull blond hair. The exhilaration of her engagement and wedding had ebbed, leaving her evenings filled with tedious recitations of his day at the bank. She had thought riches would make up for having a less than appealing husband. But, after one year of marriage, Camilla felt near suffocating. She missed the attention she had garnered at balls. Where she once graced the arms of many young swains, she now rarely danced with anyone save Leroy. Even that distraction had been curtailed with the palling effects the War had on Cantonsville society.

So it was with eager expectation, she invited Leroy's friend, Braegar Calderon, for an extended visit. Though he had moved away after purchasing coal mines in southern Ohio, he often returned, keeping ties with childhood friends. His business prospered from steamboats operating on Lake Erie and when rail lines expanded west and south, he became the largest coal supplier in Ohio. He was handsome, charming and rich, with a wicked sense of humor. And, it hadn't escaped Camilla's notice he had become far richer than Leroy ever hoped to be.

In celebration of his return, Camilla planned a dinner including Beauregard Barrington and Lorelda Hargrove. She invited Beau for his attentive bent and Lorelda because her plain visage gave stark contrast to Camilla's beauty. Being the only beautiful woman among three men, Camilla would be assured constant male attention.

"I hope you're not wearing that suit to dinner," Camilla said. She stepped aside as her husband entered their bedroom. "It's become shabby. We don't want Braegar thinking we can't afford decent clothes."

He sighed while removing his jacket, recognizing her ill disposition. "I wouldn't think of it," he said.

She watched him loosen his tie, her foot tapping in tempo with her simmering impatience. "You really must go to the clothier, Ives Du Monde. He's brilliant with men's attire. I'm sure he'd suggest more becoming styles."

"Why?" Leroy said, snorting. "What's wrong with my tailor?" He stepped over a pile of soiled stockings, placing his tie in a drawer. "Really Camilla, this room's a disgrace. I'm ever stepping over your gowns and-and under things!"

"You only allow help twice a week. What do you expect without full time staff?"

Leroy hung his jacket in the wardrobe before unbuttoning his vest. "I'd expect you to pick up after yourself. You don't see *my* clothes littering the floor. And not only that, look at the dresser Mother gifted you." He flung his arm toward the bureau heaped with broken fans and rumpled kerchiefs. Perfume bottles, some with missing stoppers occupied a corner of the scratched and badly stained surface. "She'd be appalled. I don't know how you find anything in that mess."

"How dare you!" Camilla said, her voice rising. "Do you think I'm living like a banker's wife? You're richer than most yet stingier than a pauper!" She pointed her finger. "You keep our purse strings so tight I can barely clothe myself. Look at my ring!" She mockingly held it toward him. "It isn't near the size that damnable Burnsfield bought for his tramp of a wife! Being caught like they were, she's lucky she got anything, let alone that huge diamond."

"Amanda isn't a tramp," Leroy said. "It's unfortunate they were captured by bounty hunters. It's my understanding George gave permission for Reagan to escort her without chaperone."

"Unfortunate for *you*, you mean," Camilla said, her eyes slitting. "You were set to ask her hand in marriage until that happened."

"Everyone knew I considered Amanda a good match. After they'd been apprehended, Mother convinced me to look elsewhere."

"She was right. I can't believe Amanda's invited anywhere, save her own parlor."

Leroy stared down his bony nose at her. "You know as well as I do, Amanda's father co-owns the bank with my father, Ezra. So, I doubt she would've been shunned forever. Besides, her marriage fixed everything. As to my misfortune," he said, shrugging, "I hardly think she's the cause."

Camilla missed the barb as she stomped her foot. "It's not fair! She has a bigger house and full staff while we've only a cook and part-time help. Why can't we be like them?"

"As his banker, I know Reagan's income far outweighs mine. They deserve to live any way they choose. And, he can certainly purchase whatever baubles he wants for his wife." Leroy turned, pulling pressed trousers and a clean shirt from the wardrobe.

Unable to sway him, Camilla's lip curled. She closed space between them, rifling through his clothes. "Look at these. Gray! Black! Brown! Not a gay color among them. You dress like a stick in the mire. It's no wonder your disposition's sour."

"Being frugal is a virtue," Leroy said patiently. "In these times, one doesn't know what the War will bring."

"Oh! I'll never understand why I married you!" Camilla grabbed a perfume vial and smashed it on the floor. "Just wear your best. I've invited Beau and Lorelda so Braegar will have something to discuss besides your stodgy old job!" Turning, she flounced from the room, missing Leroy's sigh as he laid his clothes on the unmade bed.

chapter II

"WE'RE SO PLEASED you came," Camilla said when Mr. Calderon descended the stairs. "I hope your room felt comfortable after the train ride."

"Exceedingly," he said. "I slept very well." He nodded to Leroy, who joined them in the foyer. "Your brandy had everything to do with that, I'm sure."

"It's one of few indulgences I allow myself," Leroy said. "Besides, I know you've become accustomed to finer things in life."

Camilla silently thrilled at that tidbit. She lowered her lashes demurely. "I hope it wasn't difficult taking time for us," she said. "My husband tells me you're quite an important businessman."

"It's never difficult when a winsome woman waits," Braegar said, bringing her hand to his lips. "Besides, I've wanted to get to know the lady who fetched my friend to the altar."

"I pray you're not disappointed," she said. "You've always known Leroy and mayn't be pleased with his choices."

Braegar shook his head. "On the contrary; he's surpassed all expectations. I find it a mystery how he managed to capture such a lovely dove."

"I think I've just been insulted," Leroy said, laughing. "But, the simple truth is, I discovered the woman of my dreams. You could too, if you'd ever settle down."

Braegar chuckled. "Let's leave that subject for another day." He then gripped Leroy's shoulder. "Yet, marriage seems to agree with you, my friend. You're looking more a banker everyday. You've meat on your bones and acquired a distinguished look."

Camilla's eyes were drawn to where Braegar's gaze rested on Leroy's silvered temples. "Let's hope that has more to do with banking worries than me," she said, smiling. "Dinner's about to be served, but first we've guests in the parlor. Shall we?" She accepted Braegar's arm, noting the material of his suit felt softer than anything her husband owned. And though he wasn't quite Leroy's height, his torso appeared powerfully built. She reluctantly left his side when they entered the parlor, stepping toward her seated guests.

"Braegar, I'd like you to meet Lorelda Hargrove." Camilla indicated a plain, thirty-something woman, dressed fashionably but without jewelry.

Braegar's eyes showed kindness when Lorelda fidgeted, then reddened at his approach. He took her hand. "How do you do?"

"Very well," she said. "Pleased to meet you, I'm sure."

Camilla touched her honey gold hair before continuing. "And this is Beauregard Barrington, an old and dear friend whom I've known for years. Beau, this is Braegar Calderon, a friend of Leroy's who now lives in Chester."

Beau stood before shaking Braegar's hand. "Bonjour, Monsieur Calderon. It's a pleasure to make your acquaintance."

"The pleasure's mine."

"What a beautiful ring!" Beauregard noted the signet sheathing Braegar's finger. "Is it a family crest?"

Braegar smiled with pleasure. "It is," he said, holding it out. Red and silver filigree filled the space otherwise emblazoned with a sword between facing lions and a falcon above an armored helmet. "These symbols represent Calderon bravery during William of Normandy's Conquest in 1066. I, of course, make no such claims of glory. My courage lies in business, not the battlefield."

Beauregard chuckled. "Business can be just as dangerous when one risks everything."

Braegar canted his head. "Yet, success often follows daring decisions. You could even find pleasure sitting on a barrel of gunpowder. The trick," he said, smiling, "is learning when to jump off."

"I bow to your greater experience," Beau said, dipping his head. "My skills cannot compare."

"What then, can you brag about? I'm sure your talents are many."

"Only a few. Most of which I don't get paid for," he said. "Although, I admit, being hotel concierge allows me to enjoy the company of beauteous madams and demoiselles."

"You've the more pleasurable occupation, Braegar said, grinning. "And, how lucky am I, to have dinner with two such ladies?"

Lorelda's eyes rounded and her cheeks darkened when Braegar's gaze once again fell on her. A smile lit her face which she promptly hid with a discreet cough.

Camilla saw it too. "Why, thank you, gentlemen," she said, stepping between them. "But, beauty shouldn't be a woman's only adornment. Having grace and refinement is just as attractive." She made a show of turning toward Lorelda, who saw the hint of malice in Camilla's eyes. "Oh, and respectability can't be overlooked," she said, turning back. "Don't you agree Mr. Barrington?"

Beau clicked his heels, nodding curtly. "Oui, Madame! As ma mère says, 'beauty without virtue is a flower without perfume.'"

Braegar suddenly struck his forehead. "Barrington! I knew that name sounded familiar. Are you, by chance, related to the owners of Barrington Hotel?"

"Oui. Mon père built it almost ten years ago."

"I should've realized when you mentioned being concierge. It's a beautiful hotel. Perhaps, I'll stay there next time I visit."

"Nonsense," Camilla said quickly. "We wouldn't hear of it, would we, Leroy."

"Of course not, my dear." When Camilla's frown lingered, he added, "You'd honor us by staying with us whenever you come to Cantonsville."

"I'll keep that in mind," Braegar said, eyes resting on Lorelda, "especially when you invite such charming guests."

Camilla silently seethed. It was *she* who should be fawned over, not Lorelda. Thick set with sparse brows, Lorelda had been used as foil against Camilla's beauty since the first time they met. Quiet and unassuming, Lorelda rarely ventured into conversation unless invited. Camilla had no doubt Braegar was being solicitous out of pity, but decided to take no chances. "Beau, would you be so kind to escort Lorelda? I've placed her beside you at the table."

"My pleasure," Beau said as he held out his arm. "Mademoiselle?"

As Beau led Lorelda into the hall, Camilla smiled at Braegar. "Would you do me the honor?" Glancing at Leroy, she spoke over her shoulder.

"Dear, could you please shut the blinds? The afternoon sun fades the carpet."

Once everyone had been seated in the dining room, the first course was served. Camilla opened her napkin before grasping her wineglass. "Beau, you must tell us about your plans. Leroy says you've a splendid idea for a resort."

"The bank's considering a business loan," Beau said, looking at Leroy. "And, I hope I haven't offended you by petitioning George. After all, he's Reagan's father-in-law, who's like a brother to me."

"Not at all," Leroy said. "My position doesn't involve lending. You were wise to go directly to one of the owners."

"A resort?" Braegar's brows rose. "What a novel idea! I've never considered Cantonsville large enough for vacationers. What makes you think so?"

"Because, it won't be inside the city," Beau said. "I've obtained property along the river. There's raw beauty, yet it's peaceful and serene. Nature, at it's finest. It'll be *irrésistible*."

"Is that wise?" said Camilla. "I think I'd prefer theaters and restaurants to consorting in the woods."

"There'll be many amusements to keep one satisfied," he said. "You could spend afternoons having tea or strolling gardens. And, I'm sure Madame wouldn't tire of books from the library or our chefs' creations."

She sipped wine. "Maybe not, but 'twould bore Leroy to death."

Beau's chest rose proudly. "Au Contraire! Do I not know men are vigorous creatures? My resort will offer many robust activities. Fishing! Hunting! Riding! Anything a man desires. Afterwards, they'll return home rested and refreshed."

"Anything?" Braegar winked. "At White Sulphur Springs, I found companionship of the lovely kind. Dare I hope this resort will have—similar—refinements?"

Leroy coughed. "That's Tennessee's notion of entertainment. I'd remind you our company's too tender for such trifles and better left until amongst ourselves."

Braegar chuckled. "Of course. I wouldn't want your guests thinking I'm a rake." He affected contrition. "My pardon, ladies and you too, Beau. And yet, I'm intrigued. What sort of retreat do you have in mind?"

"Though everyone's welcome, it'll be family oriented with activities for all."

Leroy nodded. "That'll bring a wider clientele. The bank will surely find that favorable when considering your loan."

Braegar rubbed his jaw. "Sea resorts have unique attractions. Even though there's a river, we've no sand beaches or hot springs. Why would anyone choose to come here?"

"Good question, Monsieur Calderon. You're not the first to ask. First, my rates will be lower. That'll be attractive to those on a budget. Secondly; there'll be less travel getting here. Lastly, northerners usually holiday in the south. That's now impossible with the War. So, it's the perfect destination for those unable to go east or to the ocean."

"Have you thought of a market strategy?" said Leroy.

"Monsieur Bruester asked that, too. He suggested advertisements in several newspapers in Ohio and Pennsylvania." Beau raised his shoulders. "Who am I to disagree? I proclaimed his suggestion brilliant."

"A wise choice to tell your lender," Leroy said, laughing.

"That's what I thought," Beau said. "But, that's not all. I'll also provide transport to and from the train station. And, as an incentive, anyone booking the first season will get two days of free meals. Eventually, word of mouth from satisfied customers will bring others."

"Good and good." Braegar nodded. "And, what'll you call your little piece of heaven?"

Beauregard smiled widely. "You've nearly said it! I've named it *Paradis Pavillon*."

"Splendid name! Will you be open year round?" he asked in sudden enthusiasm. "Because if you are, I know someone interested in providing you with tons of coal."

Everyone laughed as Beau chuckled along. "Perhaps, once my loan's approved. For now, I'm planning summer occupancy."

To everyone's delight, he then spent the better part of an hour describing the interior features of the resort and how the grounds were being readied.

"Sounds like you've thought of everything," Leroy said. "Since I'm no expert, Braegar's your man. He's frequented much of the Eastern Seaboard. He'd know what clientele would look for in a resort."

"Ahh, I could pluck your mind!" Beau said. "Why don't we dine soon at our hotel? My complements, of course."

Braegar seemed pleased. "I'd love to, as long as Mrs. Spelding doesn't mind my absence from her table."

"Of course not," she said, daubing her mouth. "And, please, call me Camilla." Her eyes flitted toward Lorelda. "And speaking of absences; much has happened since you've been away, Braegar. Did you hear about the mayor's daughter, Elizabeth? She died while visiting her aunt in Indiana. Her father refused to allow anyone at her burial. Very mysterious, if you ask me."

"No, I hadn't heard," Braegar said. "Wasn't she an only child?"

"Yes. But why she'd been gone so long no one seems to know," Camilla said, leaning forward. "Lorelda thinks she ran away."

Everyone looked at Lorelda who had been quiet until now.

"I-I overheard my parents talking," she said, looking from one to the other. "They supposed darker reasons why she left."

Camilla's eyes brightened. "Your parents are friends of the mayor, are they not?"

Lorelda nodded. "He'd been over for dinner several times. I suppose he didn't like being alone."

"Come now," Camilla said. "There's no need to be coy. What did he say about Elizabeth?"

Lorelda sat straighter at everyone's attention. "Well, it wasn't until he and Father retired to the study that Mr. Hampton said how much he missed his daughter. He told Father, who told Mother, who then told me that he'd written Elizabeth several times asking her to come home, yet she refused. Mother believed she used her aunt as a ruse to run off. But since it now appears she never left her aunt's home, we must've been wrong."

"Oh, I wouldn't be so sure," Camilla said, licking her lips. "Although she never said so, I had the impression Elizabeth was smitten. It wouldn't be so hard to believe she'd left for a lover."

"But that doesn't explain why she died," Leroy said. "Let's not spoil dinner with gossip, dear. We wouldn't want our guests thinking we made a habit of discussing other's misfortunes."

"Rest assured, your reputation's safe," Braegar said. "If there's juicy news to be told, it can wait until after dinner. I'm rather enjoying the company of your charming guest," he said, smiling at Lorelda who blushed again. "But for now, I'm happy to continue discussing Beau's idea." He turned toward the Frenchman. "So tell me, do you need additional funds? I've been looking for a place to invest since Ohio keeps raising my taxes."

"I'm humbled," Beau said. "But, since I'm now Papa's partner, I've enough income. Coupled with the loan I hope to receive, my proposal should be funded."

"I see," he said, shaking his head. "I'm always late to the dance. I'd buy more war bonds, but that's so boring. I'd rather find something entertaining to spend money on."

"My! My! All this talk of finance," Camilla said. "Since it's time for dessert, shall we discuss lighter topics?"

Leroy held up a hand. "Forgive me for interrupting, but I need to mention something. Doctor Turner's been commissioned by Governor Dennison to turn the Winslow house into a soldier's hospital. It's not a business proposition, so the bank can't lend funds. My father Ezra, and George Bruester, as the bank's founders, have decided to solicit donations instead. Since businessmen have greater resources, I'd appreciate you thinking on this during your visit, Braegar. And Beau, once your resort's up and running, perhaps you'd consider a small donation."

"Say nothing!" Beau said. "It'd be a privilege. I'll speak to Father. I'm sure Barrington Hotel will have much to offer."

"You can count on me, as well," Braegar said. "Anyone tending the wounded has my support."

"I'd like to make a contribution, too." Lorelda looked as surprised as anyone she had spoken out loud. "I-I mean, I'm sure my father would consider a gift."

"Hear! Hear!" Braegar raised his glass. "I salute those who employ feminine persuasion for a purpose." He smiled, seeing her happy expression. "Madam, your kindness is admirable."

"Why, thank you." Lorelda fairly beamed. Thus transformed, she seemed less awkward. "If father's agreeable, I'll have his donation sent to the bank. It mightn't be much, but every little bit helps."

Camilla lowered her eyes to hide her seething. *How dare Lorelda seek attention!* "Why, as part of Ladies' Aid, I'll raise money for the hospital," she said suddenly, looking up. "I'll also organize a fair for people to donate bandages and such. It'll be just like the packages we sent soldiers last year."

Leroy blinked, his eyes widening. "Why, my dear, that's a fine suggestion! Doc Turner will be encouraged at the news."

Camilla felt her importance rise in Braegar's admiring glance. "I'll speak with Mrs. Farrington at our next meeting. And if you're so inclined Braegar, maybe you'd stay long enough to oversee fundraising. Amongst friends, I'm sure we could raise a tidy sum."

"Agreed!" He said, slapping a palm on the table. "I'll let my secretary know to wire me if a need arises. Otherwise, I'll stay through the holidays and do some good before returning home."

Only Camilla noticed Lorelda's deflated posture. She smiled, her nostrils flaring in triumph. "I'm sure shopkeepers would gladly donate scrap cloth, especially with people buying material for winter clothes. Since I'll be busy, Lorelda, would you be a dear and inquire of them the next time you're about? It's all for a good cause."

Lorelda took a large gulp of wine before answering. "Of course." Her eyes rose to meet Braegar's. "As Camilla pointed out, it's for a good cause."

It wasn't until Lorelda and Beau's departure and the others retired to the parlor that Camilla returned to her earlier conversation. She lowered the magazine she had been reading while the men set up a chessboard. "Now that we're alone, I can finally tell you about Elizabeth," she began.

"If you must, my dear." Leroy sighed, looking at Braegar. "I apologize. There's no stopping the woman once she sets her mind."

Braegar chuckled. "It's all right, really. Otherwise I'll never hear the scuttlebutt." He sat back, giving Camilla his full attention. "Please, go on."

Puckering her lip, she affected a moue of distaste. "A shocking scandal occurred last year. And, I believe there's a connection between *that* and Elizabeth Hampton, the girl who just died."

Amused, he raised a brow. "What scandal?"

Leroy looked pained, but remained silent as Camilla leaned forward. "Why, Amanda Bruester got caught in the woods with Reagan Burnsfield by bounty hunters!"

"Bounty hunters? In Cantonsville?"

"The rumors say both were involved with runaway slaves," she said, becoming animated. "Elizabeth discovered the news, quite accidentally of course. Naturally, she told me what she knew and who'd keep that information to themselves? They were accused of breaking fugitive slave laws! The judge held an inquiry, but Amanda's parents were there and used their influence to keep either of them from being charged."

"Perhaps, lack of evidence was the reason no charges were brought," Leroy said. "Sheriff Hadley sent deputies to look for evidence. I heard all they found was a rock with a scarf tied around it. Not exactly proof of guilt, if you ask me."

Camilla smiled tightly. "But very mysterious, don't you think? And, if what you're saying is true, that left only one explanation why they'd be alone in the woods. They were having a *tryst*! Everyone thought so and she practically admitted it when questioned at my own dinner table. It wasn't long before the rumors forced them to marry. How strange that after Elizabeth tells what she learned, she leaves town and ends up dead? Too coincidental, if you ask me."

"With Camilla, nothing's coincidental," Leroy said. "There's intrigue everywhere."

"Things are not always as they appear," Camilla said. "If not for Elizabeth, Reagan wouldn't have had to marry Amanda."

"Are you saying Reagan Burnsfield had something to do with Elizabeth's death?" Braegar asked.

"Not directly. Leroy claims Reagan never left town."

Leroy moved a pawn. "He'd been at the bank every day for a week before Sam got the news. He'd have had to have been two places at once to accomplish the deed."

"And who's to say he didn't hire someone?" Camilla retorted. "No one knows what happened. Sam isn't saying, so we're left with conjecture."

Braegar studied the chessboard. "No doubt we'll never know. I never really knew Reagan or Amanda. From what you're saying, I'm wishing I had." Camilla missed the wink he gave Leroy. "But, I have to admit, it sounds very mysterious indeed!"

chapter 12

WOMEN OF VARIOUS ages and a few boys crowded the porch of Winslow house. The Cantonsville Daily had posted notices that volunteers and hired help were needed. Listed duties included cleaning, laundry and cooking as well as providing basic needs for wounded soldiers. No less than twenty gathered that morning.

Amy Burnsfield stood near her friends, Olivia Hollis and Mallory Dagget. Having turned eighteen and with no pressing duties, Amy had declared her resolve to volunteer. Her parents gladly gave their blessing. Unsure how one dressed for volunteering, Amy chose a subdued day dress with velvet trim. She pinned her blond hair beneath a bonnet, allowing a few tendrils to escape.

"Do you suppose there'll be prisoners of war coming with the injured?" Mallory asked in a hushed voice. "Poppa says I can't volunteer if they're sent here!"

"No, silly!" Olivia said. "Only men from our area will likely come so they're near their families." She then touched Amy's arm. "Mallory's only here to find a husband!"

"I am not!" Mallory said, shaking her dark curls. "I'm here to help the War cause." She then smoothed the front of her expensive gown. "However, if I become friendly with one or two, what's the harm in that?"

"You do realize most will be lying down," Olivia said. "They may not notice your décolletage."

"Oh posh!" Mallory's hand flew upward, covering her open collar. "I felt near choking and removed my pin. Besides, everyone knows there're no soldiers here today."

Amy said nothing for just then a man opened the front door and stepped outside. "Good morning everyone," he said. "I'm Doctor Turner. As you know, the Winslow house will soon become a soldier's hospital. We'll receive our first patients next week. In that light, we're anxious to sign up volunteers but will supplement any shortfall with those seeking employment. If everyone would please come inside, we'll place your name on a roster, doing our best to match a job with your talents. After going over your duties, we'll make a schedule. Some of you may be selected to assist doctors in their rounds but the rest will be assigned domestic duties."

Entering the reception hall, Doctor Turner indicated a man with wavy hair sitting behind a table next to several empty chairs. "Doctor Alexander will be in charge of appointing staff. Please sign your name, what position you'd like and whether you're applying as a volunteer or paid help. Afterward, please take a seat in one of these chairs. Once we've reviewed the list, we'll assign your duties then show you around."

As soon as Mallory spied the young doctor, she hurried to be first in line. "How do you do? My name's Mallory Dagget. *Miss* Mallory Dagget. I'm here to volunteer."

Miles handed her a pen. "Please sign the roster, Miss Dagget."

Leaning low, she scribbled her name, giving him a glimpse of her bare neckline. "Will I be working with you?" she asked breathlessly.

"That depends," he said. "We'll need to make sure all posts are filled. Some are more urgent than others. Tell me, what position are you looking for?"

"I can do anything except change bandages. The sight of blood makes me retch."

"There'll be plenty of jobs not directly involved with the injured. Do you have a preference between kitchen and laundry?"

Mallory looked taken aback. "I didn't mean I couldn't be around soldiers. I just wouldn't be able to tend their wounds. But, I could be your assistant. I'm used to giving orders."

Miles suppressed a smile. "What else can you do?"

"I'm good at talking," Mallory said, becoming excited. "If any soldier's lonely and needs someone to talk to, I can sit for *hours*. I'm good at storytelling too." Her eyes widened suddenly. "Why, I could keep a roomful of soldiers entertained all day!"

"I see. I'm sure we'll find you a job somewhere." He looked past her. "But for now, we need to sign up others."

With reluctance, Mallory set down the pen. She took a seat, eyeing those in line.

At her turn, Amy signed her name and wrote "volunteer" behind her signature.

Miles noted her poise as well as her neat handwriting. "We sometimes need letter writers for those too injured to write. You may be a candidate. But before you decide, I must warn you, it's not for the squeamish. You'll be exposed to foul smells and bloody wounds. Would you be willing to do that?"

"I'll do whatever's necessary. I understand most jobs will be unpleasant."

"I like your attitude," Miles said, tapping his chin. "I've one more question Miss Burnsfield. Are you accustomed with medicines or chemical substances?"

"I'm familiar with maladies and home remedies, if that's what you mean."

"Have you studied botany?"

"Of course," Amy said. "I passed all my science studies."

"Good. I think I've a position for you. That is, if you can spell as well as you write." Before she could respond, he pointed behind her. "Next!"

Thus dismissed, Amy went and sat beside Mallory as that one leaned toward her.

"I think Doctor Alexander likes me," she whispered, inspecting her perfectly manicured nails. "He asked me all kinds of questions and wanted to know what I'm good at. What did he ask you?"

"He wanted to know if I could spell," Amy said, perplexed. "Do I look stupid?"

Mallory patted Amy's hand. "Don't worry. I'll put in a good word for you."

chapter 13

AMANDA SEARCHED HER desk, looking for her shopping list. She then began rummaging Reagan's desk nearby, pulling open each drawer until she found it mixed among some mail. As she closed the drawer, an envelope tucked in back caught her eye. Looking closer, she realized it to be the letter Elizabeth had sent.

Since Gaeran's adoption, Amanda tried forgetting the letter's contents and its implications from her mind. She'd accepted Reagan's explanation that Elizabeth believed them the best couple to raise her baby. Not having seen the letter since Reagan first showed her, Amanda opened it and read it again.

For some reason, the ending struck her as odd, her mind emphasizing certain words.

> ...I pray *you* will give Gaeran the love and devotion *I* feel and not speak unkindly of me when he's older. Please believe I cannot reveal

the father's identity for it would destroy his chances of growing up in a happy home. **_You_** are my only hope.

Amanda's fingers shook, realizing Elizabeth's plea had been written to Reagan alone. She seemingly expected Reagan to love the child just as *she* would. And why would revealing the father destroy Gaeran's chances of growing up in a happy home?

Amanda groaned as all her doubts came flooding back. She replaced the letter in the drawer, sighing. With Elizabeth gone, there wasn't any way to verify what happened that night. But as she left the study, it occurred to her there was one person who could validate Elizabeth's story. In fact, there was a Ladies' Aid meeting that very afternoon being held at Clara Farrington's. She could still find out. She hoped with several women in attendance, she'd arouse no suspicion with whatever small talk she would make.

~·~

Clara Farrington, a diminutive, middle-aged woman, cleared her throat as she stood in her parlor. "Ladies, I want to thank you for coming. I see many new faces and appreciate your interest in our newest cause. It's been brought to my attention that Doctor Turner's leading the effort in turning Winslow house into a soldier's hospital. Once again, the Ladies' Aid Society has been called upon to gather necessities. Previously, we sewed clothing and uniforms which were sent to our enlisted men. We're widening our efforts to include donations so this hospital will lack nothing in food or medical care."

"You may contribute any number of ways. One of our members, Camilla Spelding, has generously offered to hold a soldiers' fair which will be held right before Thanksgiving. Items gathered and money collected will go toward sending supplies to our soldiers. If you want to assist in planning this bazaar, please let her know. Otherwise, our efforts will be focused on canvassing businessmen for donations as well as placing donation boxes in every merchant's door. We'll need others to visit friends and neighbors, appealing for useful items. We've made lists to take with you," she said as Matilda Harper began passing out hand-written papers. "My secretary, Mrs. Reckewig will record your chosen project in the minutes of today's meeting. We'll present our collections to Winslow Hospital this Saturday before the soldiers arrive. After that, we'll focus our efforts on the soldiers' fair. Are there any questions?"

Henrietta Livingston raised her hand. "If there's no stigma to donating clothes of the dearly departed, I'll be happy to clean out my late husband's closet. I've been loathe to get rid of his things, but

I believe Frederic would've wanted them to be of some use."

"Nothing useful will be turned away," Clara said. "Ladies, this is a perfect example of giving within your means. Mrs. Livingston lives frugally due to being widowed these many years, yet she's found a way to be generous! If everyone looks to her example, I'm sure we'll provide Doctor Turner with abundant supplies."

"My sewing circle can donate quilts we've been working on," Gabriella Bruester said, setting down her teacup. "We'll also spin yarn for anyone who knits."

As several women began offering ideas, Amanda turned toward Camilla, whom she deliberately sat beside when the meeting began. "A fair is a wonderful plan! Did you get the idea from reading about sanitary fairs in the papers?"

Camilla took a sip of tea before responding. "The notion came to me at a dinner party. Leroy spoke of raising funds to our guests, both of whom are important businessmen. You know Beauregard of course, but I don't believe you've ever met Braegar Calderon. He owns coal mines in southern Ohio and lives in Chester. Being such a good friend, he's agreed to stay long enough to help raise money for the hospital."

"That's quite generous of him," Amanda said, stirring her tea. "Has he been here long?"

"A few days."

"It's a shame he wasn't here for your birthday." Amanda put a smile on her face. "I-I mean, Reagan and I could've met him. Speaking of which," she hurriedly added, "I've been wondering for some time now, about *last* years' birthday party."

"What about last year's party?" Fast losing interest, Camilla reached for a scone.

Amanda braced herself, speaking quickly. "I know I should've asked sooner, but I so enjoyed the confections you made last year. I wondered if you still had the recipes. I seem to recall Elizabeth saying she helped you with the refreshments. I didn't know if they were your recipes or hers."

Camilla's head snapped up. She looked at Amanda closely. "Elizabeth told you that? When? Hasn't she been gone these many months?"

Amanda struggled to keep her voice light. "She'd mentioned it after last years' party. I-I thought that's what she said, but perhaps, I misunderstood."

Of a sudden, Camilla smiled sweetly. "Oh? What exactly did she say?"

Amanda hoped no one overheard her next words. "Well, I thought she mentioned spending an evening at your house to plan your party and it got so late she ended up staying the night." Unable to decipher Camilla's change in expression, she continued. "And so, I hoped you might still have those recipes."

"How very interesting," Camilla purred, nibbling her scone. "I must look up those recipes. However, I mayn't be able to locate them. Since marrying Leroy, I've still several boxes to unpack."

Amanda felt Camilla had side-stepped her question and pressed on. "So I remembered correctly? Elizabeth did help with—the confections—and such?"

Camilla leaned forward, green eyes bright. She spoke low enough her voice wouldn't carry. "I don't know why Elizabeth would spread such tales. She never helped plan my party nor did she ever spend the night. Perhaps she was protecting someone and secretly went elsewhere. Can you think of a reason she might do such a thing?"

Amanda felt a stab of apprehension. She recalled another time Camilla had drawn her into a conversation only to ambush her with cruel accusations. Although they were sitting in Clara's parlor, Amanda didn't know the limits of Camilla's malevolence. She raised her brows innocently. "I must've been mistaken, then. If she didn't do either of those things, I'm sure I'm recalling a different situation. Please don't give it another thought."

Hiding her dismay, Amanda directed her attention back to the meeting. She later left Clara Farrington's with a list of suggested donations and a fear Reagan had lied about his encounter with Elizabeth as well as his time at the hotel. She had to discover whether Reagan could've fathered Gaeran. She hoped the adoption records would show whether or not he had been conceived while Reagan stayed at the Rochester.

chapter 14

A CRISP BREEZE stirred dry leaves beneath the buggy as it traveled toward Cantonsville. Braegar rounded a bend and immediately pulled up when he spied a rather rotund man walking the same direction he was headed. Hatless and covered in dust, it appeared he'd been thrown from his horse.

"May I be of assistance?" Braegar asked. As the man turned toward his buggy, Braegar grew alarmed. "Mayor Hampton? Are you all right?"

Sam Hampton squinted against the sun as he stood unsteadily. "Do I know you?" he asked.

Braegar hurriedly climbed down and took Sam's arm. Though the air was cool, the mayor's face shone with perspiration. His clothes were stained and the smell of whiskey clouded the air. "I'm Braegar Calderon. You knew my parents, Emma and Gregory." Gently, he led Sam toward the buggy. "Here, let me take you home. Did your horse bolt?"

"S-stupid animal! Got spooked or somethin'."
He looked around. "Where's my hat?"

Braegar looked up and down the road, spying
the missing article several yards away. "I'll help you
into the buggy and then get your hat," he said. After
several attempts, Sam got his foot on the step and
grabbing a brace, hoisted himself up while Braegar
lifted from behind. As the mayor dropped heavily
onto the seat, Braegar trotted back and retrieved the
bowler hat. Once inside the buggy, he placed it in
Sam's hands. "I'm afraid it's been stepped on."

"Stupid horse!" Sam said.

Braegar slapped the reins. "Were you going
somewhere?"

Sam rubbed his brow. "Already did. Went to
Eliz'beth's grave."

"Oh," Braegar said. "I heard about your loss.
Such a tragedy."

Tears fell from Sam's eyes as he leaned against
the cushion. "My Eliz'beth's gone! Taken! Taken, I
say!" He dug a hanky from his pocket and daubed
watery eyes. "Everything's been taken from me!"

"Is there anything I can do?" Braegar asked,
placing a hand on Sam's shoulder. "My parents, God
rest their souls, would've wanted me to help any way
I could."

"Only if you find my Sammy," he muttered,
punching his ruined hat. "Sammy's gone. They won't
tell me where he is!"

Braegar looked at the mayor. "Who's Sammy? And, who won't tell you where he is?"

"Sammy's all that's left of my Eliz'beth. I went to get him and they'd already taken him away." Sam crushed the hat in his hands. "That bitch wouldn't even tell me who adopted him!"

Braegar said nothing for several minutes. As he neared town, he turned down a side street. "I'm taking you home the back way, so no one sees you've had an accident. It wouldn't look good for the mayor to look—unkempt."

"Thank you, my boy," Sam said, mopping his brow. "You're right. I'm feeling a bit unwell."

Braegar guided the buggy to the back entrance of the Hampton home. He jumped down and hurried around as Sam stumbled out. Braegar gripped his shoulders while the mayor sagged against him as they walked. The back door suddenly opened and a man rushed to assist.

"Dudley," Sam said, holding up the remnants of his bowler. "My hat got kilt. Damn horse!"

Dudley looked apologetic as he braced the mayor's other side. "I'm sorry, sir. Sometimes, Mr. Hampton gets like this when he visits the cemetery." They managed to get Sam through the door and up the rear stairs to his room, laying him on a bed.

"I'll take it from here," Dudley said as Sam began to snore. "Thanks for your kindness." Leaving the room, Dudley closed the door. "This has been a trying time for the mayor. I pray you won't judge him too harshly. He recently lost his daughter."

Braegar shook his head. "Rest assured, he has my sympathies. No one knows how they'll react to a tragedy." He then touched Dudley's arm, looking worried. "Yet, on the way here, the mayor sounded angry. I fear he intends to do someone harm."

"Don't worry. Mr. Hampton won't remember a thing when he wakes up. I'll doubt he'll even recall who brought him home."

"What a blessing," Braegar said, relieved. "That way, he won't be embarrassed if we meet again."

Dudley nodded. "One last thing, can I count on your discretion? If anyone hears how you found him—"

"I won't tell a soul. After all, I know how it feels to lose loved ones," Braegar said, extending his hand. "I must be on my way. I'm having dinner at the Barrington Hotel."

❧⟡

"Monsieur Calderon, how good of you to come!" Beau emerged from the Barrington Hotel office and shook Braegar's hand. "Please, come this way. I've reserved a private table." Leading him to the dining hall, Beau's enthusiasm continued. "I'm eager to share my ideas before my plans are finalized."

Braegar laughed as they entered the dining room. "I'm happy to be of assistance. In fact, I just came from viewing your property. I wanted to see the lay of the land. I must admit, you've purchased the best tract for Paradis Pavillon. Even if I bought land on either side, it wouldn't be as favorable."

"Oui. I've spent much time considering what's needed. Your words give me confidence."

"I'm humbled." Braegar gave a short bow. "I'm also honored. It seems my return to Cantonsville has been worthy on many fronts. First, I'm asked to help raise funds for Winslow Hospital and now to advise a fellow entrepreneur."

"I wish I could repay you with more than dinner," Beau said as they stepped inside a small alcove where a waiter stood in attendance. "This is our most private table."

"That could be remedied," Braegar said with a grin, "if you'd reconsider my offer. My coal operations don't allow much time to mingle with gentlefolk. Becoming affiliated with Paradis Pavillon would allow me to indulge my flamboyant side."

Both men sat and were immediately handed menus. "I'll reconsider if the bank declines my loan. Fortunately for me," Beau said good-naturedly, "I'm best friends with the banker's son-in-law. Gives me an advantage, I'll admit."

Braegar gave an exaggerated sigh. "I've heard about the Burnsfield marriage. If only I'd met you sooner perhaps we could've been partners! But, I'll not belabor the point. I'm sure Mr. Bruester will recognize a good business plan." He turned his attention to the menu. "Now, what do you recommend?"

"There are many excellent dishes. The chicken pie French style is *merveilleux*," he said, kissing his fingertips before popping them open, "as is the venison with currant jelly. However, one of my favorites is Ficandeau of veal. All of which will be on Paradis Pavillon's menu."

"I'm impressed." Braegar said. "I'd no idea Cantonsville had such talented chefs. Will your resort cooks copy this menu?"

"I've commissioned a master chef who'll arrive a month before we open Paradis Pavillon. He'll spend that time with Chef Édouard, perfecting my menu and arranging food deliveries. He'll also bring pastry chefs!" Beau's eyes lit with pleasure. "There's nothing so unforgettable as a sweet confection at the end of a memorable meal."

"It seems you've thought of everything. My compliments."

After ordering, Beau began sketching on paper he pulled from his pocket. "I've employed Monsieur Walsh who built the Lyndel in St. Louis. He's joining my ideas with Italian and French models, yet on a smaller scale. Here," he said, tapping his pencil, "at the main entrance you'll see a grand staircase that splits half-way up and curves to either side. The vestibule will be marbled with a frescoed ceiling. The baggage area, coat rooms and offices are on the first floor. In the rear will be laundry, kitchen and service rooms."

"I like it so far," Braegar said. "Go on."

"On the second floor there'll be private parlors for ladies and a gentlemen's club room. Here's where the dining room will be, and over here, the ball room," he said, indicating spots on paper. "Of course there'll be single rooms and suites upstairs and stables around back."

Braegar pulled his chin. "And, what's the layout for outside activities?"

"The woods have riding trails, but on the grounds I'd like courts for tennis and croquet. And over here, I think gardens." Beau paused, his voice slowing. "What say you, Monsieur?"

Braegar looked intently at the sketch. "I find nothing amiss. One question, though. Will your front entrance have something unique?"

"We envisioned a piazza with sitting areas."

"Nothing more grand? Have you considered a fountain, say in the middle of a circular drive?"

"Non! It hadn't occurred to me," Beau said. "What an excellent idea!"

"I know there's no mineral spring here, but a bath house would draw additional patrons. It's quite popular in New York."

"True. But, I don't think I'd want restricted areas where children might wander."

"There are ways to accommodate." Braegar said. "Simply build cottages next to a bath house where guests have privacy. I guarantee you'll find those willing to pay for that particular pleasure. I'd also recommend a gentlemen's saloon. Music and refreshment make good investments if pretty ladies provide them."

Beau laughed. "You're persuasive, my friend. I appreciate your ideas. However, changes must be approved by Monsieur Walsh. I'll mention them at our next meeting. Ah! Here comes our meal. Please, let's enjoy!" Setting aside his paper, Beauregard took up his glass of wine. "To Monsieur Calderon! May our friendship last for all time."

"Hear! Hear!" Braegar said, clinking together their glasses. He looked at the sumptuous dish before him. "If this tastes as good as it looks, I must meet Chef Édouard and see where he creates such masterpieces."

chapter 15

"I can't believe I've been assigned kitchen and laundry duty!" Mallory said, leaving Winslow House Hospital. "I wanted to entertain soldiers. How can I do that if I'm washing clothes?"

"Entertainment isn't the most pressing need right now," Olivia said, pulling her shawl tighter. "Besides, Doctor Alexander said things may change if we get more volunteers. Most of us were assigned multiple duties."

"Easy for you to say! You get to keep records. Your hands won't get chapped, like mine." Mallory held out her hands. "Look at them! How could he expect these hands to sit in water all day?"

"We came to volunteer," Amy said as they neared a waiting carriage. "We're helping the War cause, remember?" The driver set the step then opened the door, assisting the girls inside. "I certainly wasn't expecting anything fun. And what better job would there be for Olivia? She's kept records in her father's shop for years. Surely her experience proves her the best choice for the job."

Mallory flounced on the seat, looking dejected. "That's another thing! You get to follow Doctor Alexander around, writing notes. When you're not doing that, you'll write letters for the soldiers. It's not fair!"

"I didn't ask for it," Amy said as the carriage began to move. "Doctor Alexander chose my duties. He mentioned the job could make me nauseous. If I remember correctly, you told him you'd become ill at sight of blood. I'm sure he was only thinking of your delicate nature."

"Perhaps others will volunteer, allowing you to change jobs," Olivia offered.

Mallory's eyes lit. "You're right! I'm sure that'll be the case. I think Doctor Alexander likes me. After all, he did consider my tender stomach."

"Regardless, we're to report for duty tomorrow," Olivia said, smiling. "I'd advise you not to wear your finest, Mallory. If you splash water on a dress like your wearing, you'd ruin it for sure."

"But I haven't any plain dresses! Whatever shall I do?"

"If I were you, I'd ask one of your servant's for one of theirs. Oh, and don't forget an apron. You're bound to get wet." Olivia did her best to look sincere. "Find one that covers your bosom. On windy days, wet clothes can flap about and soak you in no time."

chapter 16

AMANDA OPENED THE home safe, removing Gaeran's adoption papers. She then sat, holding the folio with shaky fingers. She had waited until Reagan departed, knowing he'd spend the day at the mill. She felt torn. If Elizabeth had conceived around the time Reagan stayed at the Rochester, her worst fears would be realized.

Was that enough proof to condemn the man she loved? Reagan openly admitted not knowing how he'd gotten scratched. Yet, nagging doubts persisted. Could a man be so drunk he couldn't recall bedding a woman? Amanda had often played the scenario in her mind, never finding a satisfactory solution. It seemed impossible for Elizabeth to discover which suite Reagan occupied, obtain a key, make love and then exit without his knowledge or consent. The most she could hope for was that Gaeran's birth pointed to a time outside Reagan's stay at the hotel.

Taking a deep breath, Amanda unfolded the document and quickly found Gaeran's birth date.

She then counted backward to his approximate conception. When she saw it overlapped Reagan's stay at the Rochester, her heart sank. She stared at the page, not knowing what to do. She looked at the date again, counting forward this time. With a start, she realized Gaeran was born only two weeks before Jesse. Elizabeth's pregnancy would've occurred right before Camilla's birthday party.

Amanda recounted the events as if it were yesterday. She had withheld her affections after stumbling upon papers that seemed to indicate Reagan had wed for financial gain. Their alienation became complete when he later moved into Rochester Hotel. It wasn't until Reagan's father forced him to return home that they attended a party together under the guise of a truce. On the ride home from Camilla's, Reagan had seduced her. The next morning and after they had made love, Amanda discovered strange scratches on his back. Because they were uniformly scored and she didn't cause them, she could surmise only one thing. Reagan had slept with another woman. Yet, her accusations remained unanswered because Reagan's heavy drinking had erased his memory. The arrival of Elizabeth's letter resurrected those lingering doubts.

And, that hadn't been all.

On the heels of that calamity, another had arrived. Reagan had been jailed when the body of a very pregnant Molly Carnes, had been found in his office. Though accused of killing the strumpet, after being seen with her, he had been exonerated. Derrick Banning, who'd been blackmailing Reagan, had planted her body at the mill. Not only that, but he was the likely father of her babe. Amanda knew this because the cad admitted it when he had kidnapped her during his failed escape.

Tears blurred her vision. Once before, she had acted impulsively when she happened upon damning information. This time, she'd seek more specifics until she knew whether or not she had indeed, been betrayed after all.

chapter 17

CAMILLA SAT AT her desk, looking over her roster for the soldier's fair. Had anyone viewed it, they'd have seen she had delegated all work to others. With no one knowing the extent to which each duty had been allocated, it would leave praise to fall solely on Camilla.

She turned her head at the sound of the door opening. "Ah, there you are, my dear," Leroy said, entering the study. "I came home on time, as requested."

Camilla stood, tolerating Leroy's kiss. "Good! Lorelda will be our dinner guest tonight."

"Again?"

"I wouldn't think you'd mind. Of late, she's taken pains to refine herself. I don't know what's causing it but I suspect she's jealous."

"I hadn't noticed. Perhaps she's finally overcoming her shyness."

"You don't notice anything!" Camilla said. "I've seen the change. The poor girl wore hideous earrings her last visit. She looked positively painted with rouge."

Leroy poured a drink from the sideboard. "She's a late bloom. It's only natural she would enhance herself if she's settled on finding a husband."

Camilla stared at Leroy's back, a sneer forming. "Mayhap, she's settled on someone *else's* husband. She's never before spoken so much. I hadn't realized how grating her voice can be."

"Then why keep inviting her?" Leroy said, taking a seat and unbuttoning his suit. "Surely, there are others who'd grace our table."

Camilla adjusted a candle on a nearby table. "There are scant single women among our friends and we need to give Braegar a dining partner." She looked up, her eyes narrowing. "Yet Lorelda talks more to you. Before, she spoke only when necessary. Now, she offers all kinds of prattle."

"Maybe it's because I treat her like a guest and not a table ornament," Leroy said, setting down his drink. "Frankly, I don't know why she's tolerated your friendship all these years. You treat her badly. I choose not to and she's responding to that kindness."

"Lorelda's been useful."

"Somehow, my dear, that doesn't surprise me," he said. "I hope Lorelda's past loyalty will keep your tongue tightly reined. I don't want her insulted at my table. Besides, I find her newfound charm agreeable compared to your incessant gossiping."

Camilla stepped closer, placing hands on her hips. "Well, I don't want her unleashing her newfound charms on Braegar. He's too kind to rebuff her and she'll likely get ideas."

"Of course, we can't have *that*," Leroy said. "You'd rather Lorelda remain a spinster than find happiness. I, on the other hand, hope she finds someone. I don't expect it'll be Braegar, but at least she's trying."

Leroy couldn't know Camilla seethed at any who dared challenge what she considered hers. Whether it was a husband she despised or the attentions of a man she secretly admired, mattered not. What she coveted was hers alone until she cast it away. "It's embarrassing to see her act like a school girl. And if I can't redirect Lorelda then you'll need to warn Braegar."

Leroy snorted. "I'd only embarrass him. With Braegar's experience, he doesn't need me to point out the obvious. Besides, he's enjoyed the company of several ladies since coming home. I'm sure Lorelda's aware of that."

"Nevertheless, if you don't say something, I'll be forced to remedy the situation myself." Camilla opened the sideboard and removed a decanter, setting it on a nearby tray. "I've made all the preparations. Braegar will spend time before dinner with you. You'll have drinks. Then, you casually mention he shouldn't encourage Lorelda or be too attentive. If he has any pity, he'll realize he's doing her a favor."

"This is ridiculous!" Leroy said. "What do you expect me to say?"

"I've already thought of that," Camilla said sweetly. "You can say 'Lorelda becomes infatuated with the slightest interest shown her. Be careful, or you'll find yourself engaged before you know it.'"

Leroy lifted his drink and downed it. "Camilla, you're an evil woman."

Instead of becoming enraged, Camilla drew close and lowered herself onto his lap. Having denied him for weeks, she knew her nearness would provoke a response. Touching his face, she brushed her lips over his before kissing him. His reaction was immediate. Soon Leroy had the pleasure of touching his wife in ways he hadn't for awhile. "Tonight," she purred against his neck. She pressed herself against him and nipped his ear. "Take care of this for me and you'll not be sorry."

It wasn't until Camilla left the room that Leroy poured himself another drink, muttering, "Methinks, I married a devil!"

chapter 18

WHEN REAGAN ARRIVED home that night, he went directly upstairs and into the nursery. Olga Stuttgart, the hired nanny, sat in a rocker, knitting. Jesse clutched a rattle as he lay on a blanket near the hearth.

"Hello, Olga. How's the little fellow doing?" he asked, squatting down before picking Jesse up. Giving him a kiss, Reagan then laid him on his tummy, placing wooden blocks within his reach. "Let's spell your name," he said, placing lettered blocks in a row.

"He's *goot*," Olga said, her hands never ceasing. A slight accent confirmed her German heritage as did her sturdy frame. Her gray hair had been meticulously braided and pinned in a knot. A crisp apron covered her dress and she appeared stern as a schoolmarm until she smiled. "Mrs. Burnsfield just finished his afternoon feeding and is now dressing for dinner. She said to tell you she'd like a word with you."

Just then, the door opened and Maisy came in, carrying Gaeran. "Good afternoon, sir." She swept past him to place the baby near Jesse. "The babes seem to enjoy each other. So, I bring Gaeran in most days, to spend time with his brother." Gaeran and Jesse both began smiling and babbling when they spied each other, causing Reagan to laugh.

"That's good! Hopefully, they'll learn to get along and be best friends."

"Ja," Olga said, nodding. "Already, they begin to look more alike."

Reagan felt a moment of alarm as he looked at the boys. Despite being the same age, there were distinct differences. Gaeran was thinner, though catching up to his adopted brother. His hair wasn't as dark as Jesse's and his eyes were brown to Jesse's blue. Not seeing a physical resemblance, Reagan considered their personalities. Of the two, Gaeran seemed more withdrawn. He expected time and stability would resolve his apparent shyness. But, were there similarities? Reagan couldn't decide because he hadn't spent as much time with them as their caretakers. But, if they noticed a likeness, how long before Amanda would?

Although, the pieces fit together, he still wasn't certain Gaeran was his. He had never told Amanda of Elizabeth's bold offer the night of Camilla's party. That he had rebuffed her meant nothing if he'd already bedded her! His claims of innocence would ring hollow against the presence of a living, breathing baby living under his own roof. Whether or not to divulge that theory was a battle he waged daily.

Standing, Reagan turned toward the door. "Good day, ladies," he said. "It seems my wife calls." Moments later, he stood in front of the fireplace where Amanda sat, hands folded in her lap.

"Please sit," she said, indicating an empty chair. "We need to talk." She looked at him fixedly once he settled against the cushions. "I must know everything. Once and for all, you must tell me everything about Elizabeth."

Reagan's heart skipped a beat. "But, I have told you," he said, leaning over outspread knees, "all that I can remember."

"This time, I'll ask the questions." Though Amanda's face remained impassive, her back was stiff. "Let's start at the beginning. How did you come to be invited to the Hampton's in the first place?"

Reagan sighed before running a hand through his hair. "I'd received a letter requesting my presence for dinner. Sam's other guest was his cousin, Mr. Hayes, who worked under the Secretary of War."

"I don't understand. Why were you invited?"

"Sam was interested in making connections between our city and the war cause. If there were contracts to be had, he wanted Cantonsville to be among them."

"Why would he do that? Did you or your father ask him?"

Reagan's composure slipped, realizing the direction of Amanda's queries. Not knowing the consequences, he decided only to reveal that which he knew for certain. "Well, not exactly," he said. "As a matter of fact, it was Elizabeth who first mentioned it to me. Quite unexpectedly, I might add."

"Elizabeth?" Amanda looked taken aback. "Why would she have done that?"

He smiled half-heartedly. "This is going to sound worse than it is," he began. "But, the first time Elizabeth spoke of the mayor's involvement was at our wedding. I'd mentioned something about reminding her father I'm in the lumber business. That's all. I never expected anything to come of it and was quite surprised when we received an invitation to dinner with Sam's cousin."

"We?"

"Father and I, I mean."

"Then, why didn't Thomas go with you?"

"Reagan tugged absently at his collar. "We had an argument, and I forgot to tell him." It sounded lame, even to his ears. "I meant to," he added," but even after I realized I'd forgotten, I was so angry I decided to go alone."

"What were you arguing about that made you so angry?"

Reagan rubbed his brow. "Is that important now?"

"By the looks of you, it is. Why don't you tell me? Or, did you forget that too?"

"No," he said, gazing at his hands. "If you recall, you and I weren't on good terms when we returned from camp. Father was upset we were sleeping in separate bedrooms. He told me I needed to regain your good graces. Or, should I say, *lectured* me."

"You-you argued about that?" she said, gasping. "What'd you say?"

"To mind his own business."

Amanda's fingers tightened in her lap. "Is that when you began staying at the Rochester?"

Reagan nodded. "But, I never brought a woman there, I swear!"

Amanda seemingly kept a tight hold on her emotions. "Is that also the time Elizabeth told you she helped Camilla plan her birthday party?"

"Uh, no," he said. "She told me that on my second visit to find out whether his cousin had arranged any contracts."

"Did your father go with you that time?"

"No." Reagan could see hope dwindling from Amanda's face with every detail. "That was my last night at the Rochester. After that, I came home."

"You said you got drunk that night. So, you should be able to recall what happened *before* you drank yourself into a stupor. As best you can, I want to know what interactions you had with Elizabeth."

If not for the time Reagan had spent thinking about that night, he never would've remembered as much as he now knew. With dread, he recited nearly word for word what Elizabeth had said as she escorted him to the study and then poured drinks for him and her father. Reagan insisted that's when she told Sam she was staying at Camilla's for the night to help plan the party.

Amanda's face paled as he spoke. She stared at him for several seconds. "So, you're saying she told you the lumber contracts were her idea? Why would she do that?"

Reagan had hoped to somehow avoid that question, for the answer was the most damning of all. And yet, telling the truth was more honorable than lying to his wife. He had promised himself he'd never do that again. "I didn't find out why until afterward, the night of Camilla's party."

Despite knowing he had done nothing to invite Elizabeth's affections, he also knew what his next words might do to Amanda. "Please understand," he said, rising to kneel before her, "I've never mentioned this before because I feared how you'd take it." He spoke softly, willing her to hear his sincerity. "That night, I danced with Elizabeth while you were dancing with Anson. During our conversation I questioned why she interceded on my behalf with Mr. Hayes. Her answer shocked me as much as it's going to shock you." He then took a deep breath before continuing. "At first, she said she knew how business operated, and 'twas always better if friends profited before others."

"I'm confused," Amanda said. "What does that have to do with anything?"

"I'm assuming with her father being mayor, it wasn't uncommon to have businessmen frequent their table. Merchants often make agreements over dinner. She would've been privy to a lot of trade dealings. That's how I took it, anyway."

"And, because of that, she offered to help you?"

"Yes."

"Though odd, it's not shocking. There must be more."

"There is," he said. "She first let me know it was she who caused the meeting with Mr. Hayes. She then told me there were even more things she'd do if I'd let her. She implied I was being neglected since — since she'd heard I was staying at the Rochester — and she'd heard you and I were estranged."

"Good Lord! So, she knew which hotel you were in!"

At her accusing look, Reagan spoke in a rush. "I told her I wasn't interested! I said you were the perfect wife and that I didn't do business that way."

She tried to rise, but Reagan gripped her tightly. "I didn't encourage her! I never invited her to the hotel and I've no memory of her being there!"

Amanda pushed away his hands. "Tis obvious she wanted you! Why wouldn't she go to your hotel?"

"She went to Camilla's," Reagan said in sudden relief. "She told Sam she'd spend the night if it got too late. Don't you see? She couldn't be two places at once."

"You're lying!" Amanda stood, glaring into his eyes. "I spoke to Camilla at the Ladies' Aid meeting. She denied everything you said about Elizabeth staying that night or even helping plan her party!"

"What?" Dumbfounded, he stood also. "But, that's what she said! You can ask Sam! He'd have no reason to lie."

"I'm *not* going to ask a grieving father what his dead daughter said more than a year ago!" she said angrily. "How could I?"

Reagan drew near. "You're right. I'm sorry. I wish otherwise, but I don't remember much of anything at the hotel."

Amanda heard the catch in his voice. She stepped back, staring. "Then, tell me what you *do* remember."

Reagan's mind raced over his past encounters with Elizabeth. He knew how damning they seemed despite how innocent it had been at the time. If he disclosed his visions of a phantom lover, it could very well end his marriage. Yet, after nearly losing her once to deception, Reagan felt he had no choice. He'd have to bare it all, even his own suspicions.

Taking her hand, he led Amanda back to her seat. He then pulled his chair close. "I've told you all my lucid memories," he said. "But, I've never mentioned a nagging feeling there might've been more." He looked into her eyes. "I remember cursing myself for drinking too much. I left Sam's—*alone*, and went to the Rochester. No one was in my room when I got there, and no one was there when my father came bursting into the room the next day." Reagan rubbed his forehead as he formed his next words. "However, the only thing I'm not sure of, what hasn't made sense to me, is a vague memory or-or a dream. I've only had flashes of something or someone, I don't know. It's plagued me ever since, but I've never been able to discern if it was a dream or—worse." His face etched with chagrin. "The only thing I can't account for was a slight scent of perfume on the sheets. I assumed I'd transferred it from my clothes when I escorted Elizabeth to the study. I didn't want to consider any other possibility."

Amanda looked stricken as her worst fears were verbalized. "But how—?"

"I don't know how!" he growled, jumping up to pace the floor. "But, it wasn't until later; I realized my father had entered without a key." Reagan stopped pacing and rubbed his neck abstractly. "I suppose I could've forgotten to lock the door, but I can't be certain."

Amanda dissolved into tears, covering her face. "It must be true! It must! It can't be anything else!"

"Please, Amanda," he pleaded, touching her shoulder. "Please believe I've never wanted anyone but you. Not then. Not now. I just don't know what happened that night."

Amanda struck away his hand, her voice hard. "If you suspicioned it, how could you bring that—that—bastard—into our home?"

Reagan couldn't have looked more shocked if she had slapped his face. It was so unlike Amanda to speak cruelly. "But, I don't know for sure. I can't claim anything from a wisp of a memory! How could I?"

"You owed me that!" she said, sobbing. "You neither told the truth nor gave me a say in the matter! You denied my right to protect our son—!"

"Gaeran is innocent—"

"That won't mean a tinker's damn when it gets out that Reagan Burnsfield flaunted his indiscretions under his wife's nose!" She flung her arm outward. "How long before I'm a laughingstock?" Ignoring her anger, Reagan knelt down, gathering her in his arms. "I can't endure another scandal. I just can't," she muffled against his shoulder.

"You won't," he said softly. "How could anyone know when even I don't know?"

"If she told someone—anyone—all will be for naught."

"I don't think she did. From her letter, she didn't want anyone to know. And besides," he said, holding her face so she couldn't look away, "I don't know if I'm the father. All I know is I could be."

Amanda searched his face, wanting desperately to believe him. After the trying events that led to her being wed in the first place, she felt her life had become idyllic. She loved her husband, her child and her life. But now, everything seemed as shattered as a broken mirror and just as impossible to mend. Amanda didn't know whether her trust could stand another bout of betrayal. She suddenly shivered, thinking she could again be swept up in a tempest that wouldn't abate until everything she held dear, lay in ruins.

chapter 19

ON THE NIGHT of September 16th, the 28th Ohio Infantry had taken position opposite a stone bridge crossing the Antietam Creek, near Sharpsburg, Maryland. As dawn broke, soldiers could hear sounds of battle on their right and left, but no orders were given to advance. By afternoon, as fighting ebbed and flowed on other parts of the battlefield, General Burnside finally gave the order for his troops to attack Confederates positioned across the creek. After twelve hours of savage combat, both sides suffered crippling casualties...

Ohio quickly petitioned for and received from Washington an order to remove the sick and wounded sons of Ohio from Tennessee and Cumberland valleys and bring them home. After enduring weeks of convalescence, permanently disabled soldiers as well as those requiring prolonged treatment could once again breathe native air and look upon familiar objects and faces.

The first wave of wounded and sick arrived by rail, having survived the field hospital and steamboat journey. With no time to build, hospitals were formed from existing buildings. The Winslow House Hospital was one such transformation as Cantonsville joined the ranks of cities eager to take in Ohio's brave soldiers.

Doctor Turner hadn't time to dwell on the enormity of his undertaking as cots on the first and second floor filled. Some were carried on stretchers, too weak to walk while others limped on crutches, bloody bandages binding stumps of amputated limbs. The first order of business was to ensure exhausted and thirsty soldiers were made comfortable. They were given water, or if they preferred tea with bread and butter. Once soldiers were evaluated and their treatment and diet prescribed, the job of healing began.

As Miles' attendant, Amy took notes on soldiers' conditions while Olivia did the same with Artemus. Between records that arrived with the wounded and observations of both doctors, treatments were formulated, to be amended as patients responded.

Doctor Turner had earlier laid out staff regulations that would be strictly observed. And though, this wasn't a military-run hospital, it would be run in similar manner, excepting certain military protocols. Doctor Turner, with Doctor Miles' input, decided to forgo requiring those injured and who are able, to stand at attention during inspection. Additionally, both doctors relaxed age and gender restrictions of volunteers as long as they performed their tasks. However, they scrupulously adhered to Surgeon-General Hammond's official orders in running a hospital, especially cleanliness and care of sick and injured soldiers. With this in mind, they selected both men and women, young and old to jobs operating a well-run hospital. The duties for nursing positions varied slightly from those cooking and cleaning, as in a pinch, one could be called upon to aid another. However, it soon became obvious both acts of service had unfavorable points. The sights and smells of washing soiled bedding were nearly as pungent as caring for the wounded themselves. Since many illnesses that beset soldiers involved internal diseases, diarrhea accompanied most of them to Winslow House. It didn't take long for those who lacked a strong stomach to decide that volunteering or even earning a wage wasn't worth the blood and stench assailing their senses. Within a fortnight, nearly half the original staff had resigned their positions.

It took far less time for Amy to overcome the horror and realities of war. Initially shocked at the injuries and suffering, she soon realized her acts of service could never compare to those she served. She determined she would summon courage to alleviate whatever suffering she could.

Whenever she wasn't making rounds, Amy did simple chores of sweeping around and under beds, offering small talk and banter along the way. Questions of home and family were asked and answered, sometimes with sadness, always with longing. She ran errands, purchasing combs, shaving mugs or bottles of rose water for a soldier's loved one. On her way home, she delivered packets to the post office, returning the next day with books and newspapers for those wanting to pass time in that manner. What began as a service, blossomed into a calling as she increasingly showed up on off-duty days.

It didn't escape Doc Turner's notice, who decided to elevate Amy's position to ward-master. She now inspected each room or "ward" every morning, ensuring they had been properly cleaned and beds freshened with linens. She oversaw supplying each patient with clean clothes and attended those doing laundry. Yet, with all her responsibilities, Amy still found time to mingle for a time in each ward. To those who were dismayed at their wounds and disheartened with pain and effort of life, she gave a challenge, a dare to live. Friendly and cheerful, Amy soon coaxed a smile from all but the worst cases. As their spirits lightened, they began cracking jokes and more than a few humorously solicited her with marriage proposals.

Miles, on the other hand, felt her absence from his side in a completely unexpected way. Not having her quiet, efficient, note-taking presence by his side caused a surprising surliness that lasted most mornings. Without realizing it, he trailed her route as she inspected wards and he made rounds. His eyes were continually drawn to her slender form as she bent to smooth a soldier's cover or check sheets for stains.

Tearing his eyes away, he returned to the task at hand, reaching for the color coded card attached to the end of one of the beds. "Why is this marked 'low diet' when I specifically requested 'half diet?'" he asked, holding up the yellow card.

His stern look turned to exasperation when Polly, the newly-assigned assistant only gave a blank stare before flipping through her notes. "I'm-I'm not sure, Doctor. I'm sure I wrote down your orders." She stopped on a page and reread her notes before looking up, wide-eyed. "I-I guess my mark of a downward arrow, meant 'low' but when I updated your orders, I forgot and mistook it for 'one-half.' I'm so sorry, sir! It'll never happen again."

Before he could upbraid the girl, Amy walked over and handed him a blue card from her apron pocket. He almost smiled before resuming his stern look. "From now on, you will take precise and neatly written notes, or we'll find someone who can."

"Yes, sir!" Polly said, her lip on the verge of trembling.

Miles continued to the next bed where Amy had stopped to wipe the brow of a young lad. Stepping near, he noticed the boys' eyes were open. "Well, there you are," he said gently, leaning down to feel his forehead. "When you arrived, your fever had worsened. We weren't sure you'd recover."

The boys' eyes turned reluctantly from Amy, who'd been tenderly ministering him. "Yes, suh!" he spoke, finally.

Miles recalled the brief notes on the boy. Being so young, the battlefield doctors hadn't wasted time discovering which side he had fought on. They simply bound his wound, which consisted of a single stab from a bayonet. While sharing space with the injured, a fever had taken over, causing delirium. The boy, diagnosed with Typhus, was sent along when Ohioan's disabled were ordered home.

"How old are you, son?"

"Fourteen, my last birthday."

Miles' brow lifted. "Why, that's very young to be in the army, isn't it?"

"Yes, suh, but I thought it my duty."

Miles cut away his bandage. "It's a good thing your size didn't warrant a bullet," he said. "Or, you mayn't be here now."

"If you say so, suh."

"Where are you from?" he said, cleaning the wound gently.

"Mississippi, suh!"

"Mississippi? Well son, you're a long way from home." He discarded the soiled cloth before rewrapping his injury. "You're in Cantonsville, Ohio at a hospital called Winslow House." Miles suddenly noticed the boy staring at his hand.

"What happened to you, suh?"

He held up his hand so the lad could see it clearly. "I was hit with a rebel bullet."

The boy's lips upturned. "Should'a hit higher," he said, raising his chin.

"'Twas a stray shot. The battle was over and I'd been tending the wounded."

"Lucky shot, you mean."

Miles grinned. "If you say so. What's your name?"

"Dwight Sherwood."

"Why, that's a Northern name. We'd scant information on you. All we knew was that you'd been picked up after the battle. By your clothes, the doctors weren't sure which side you belonged to."

"Yes, suh; my father's from up north, but he's lived in Virginia many years, and is now a good Southern man."

"I see. And, your mother, where's she?"

His little thin lip quivered. With effort, he controlled his voice. "She's dead."

Empathy etched Miles face. "Your mother must've been a wonderful woman," he said softly. "I'm sure she taught you to be a good boy, avoiding what's wrong and to keep yourself from falling into bad habits."

His eyes, half concealed beneath long, soft lashes, welled up. "That, she did. My mother taught me to pray. I've kept out of scrapes, and had no troubles 'cept once, and I didn't even ask for that one."

"Well, son, you're very young and very sick. You're unable to endure hardships of war. If you get better, you'd best return home, don't you think?"

A slight flush passed over his face. "Not til the War is over, *suh!*"

Miles felt a rush of emotion that a mere child could be so brave. His eyes rose to meet Amy's, which shone with equal compassion. "Well, Dwight, let's first get you well. We'll worry about that later. Is that all right with you?"

His hand swiped at his tears. "Yes, suh! I'm a marker, and I hope to be up and in the field again. It's my duty."

Miles gave the boys' shoulder a gentle squeeze. "We'll do our best. And, all I can say is, if every Confederate were like you, we'd be in trouble for sure."

Dwight's lip twisted into a lopsided grin. "They *are*, suh! They are!"

chapter 20

CONSTRUCTION OF PARADIS Pavillon began the first week of November. Reagan had insisted Burnsfield crews clear the woods to ensure Beauregard wouldn't be overcharged by others. Unbeknownst to Beau, Reagan supplemented the fee with his own funds while providing premium timber at below market prices. It was his way of repaying Beauregard for his years of friendship. And, though the Frenchman had been like a brother, it wasn't a bond he feared losing.

What beset his mind was how to rebuild his crumbling relationship with Amanda. After divulging the extent of his fears—for he couldn't confirm nor deny them—Reagan lived in a world of uncertainty. Despite his intentions, he found himself once again, estranged from his wife. She first bore Gaeran's presence with reluctant, than later, agreeable acceptance. But now, she invariably took Jesse with her for any excuse to keep him from the nursery. Whenever Amanda visited others, she brought along Olga, indicating they wouldn't return until late evening. If things remained as they were, it would soon be obvious trouble had come between them.

Worse, were the nights. Having waited patiently after Jesse's birth, their one glorious interlude had whetted his appetite no small amount. Just knowing her own desires had bloomed, but now held in abeyance, caused a torturous suffering in both body and mind. He lay in bed, sleepless, reliving their moments of bliss until his body screamed for release. Yet, Amanda's rigid back indicated a lack of forgiveness for her feelings of betrayal. He could no more broach her cold shoulder than he could scale the frozen peaks of the Rockies.

Worst of all, he had no escape. Once before, he found himself in a similar situation. Then, he had fled his bedchambers, taking residence at Rochester Hotel. From that situation, this new, even thornier one arose. This time, there'd be no safe haven, no avoiding the object of his desire and no liberation from his roiling need. If he'd taken pity on himself, he should've avoided observing Amanda in various states of undress, when she bathed or when she nursed Jesse. But, like a man parched with thirst, he slaked his cravings with prurient espying until he found himself on the balcony, cooling his fevered brow. Unlike the last time, he found no way to regain Amanda's trust who, with fierce determination, declared she would protect the most precious thing in her life. Her child.

⊱⊰

The week before Thanksgiving became a blur of activity for women of Cantonsville. Along with newspaper notices, congregations in the city had been inundated with announcements of the Soldier's Fair being held at the fairgrounds the following Tuesday. Clara Farrington's formidable reputation preceded her as she canvassed businesses daily, collecting donations.

Booths were erected inside several large tents bursting with items for sale. Tables became crowded with patriotic souvenirs, trinkets, porcelain, books, personal and household items, toys and saddlery. From an anonymous source, a collection of Revolutionary War relics, guns, swords and artifacts from former battlefields as well as flags, tomahawks, and arrows were loaned for viewing to create excitement and patriotism. Though it remained unspoken, everyone suspected old-man Galloway most likely emptied his attic, for the veteran of the War of 1812 sat nearby, smiling, as items were carried in.

Spices and dry goods filled a table near fresh pastries supplied by Chef Édouard from Barrington Hotel. Donated produce and hand-crafted tools from area farmers sat in baskets. Barrels had been installed at every tent opening where clothing, linens and yarn could be dropped upon entering as well as guarded money boxes for those preferring monetary donations. Games of chance were set near a local artist who sketched patrons for a two-dollar donation.

Amanda stood behind the table designated for infant clothing. Having donated Jesse's too-small gowns and unused cloth diapers, she decided to volunteer her services rather than walk the fairgrounds with her husband. It'd be easier than pretending they were still a happy couple. After Reagan had revealed the full extent of his memory, Amanda felt her heart had been dealt a deadly blow. In times past, hurt or anger followed one of their quarrels. Now, she felt devoid of emotion. It was as if she'd taken refuge in a hidden sanctuary and so long as she remained, nothing penetrated. Not even love.

Behind this buffer, she felt safe. Strangely however, this condition also prevented her feeling anything else. Coldness had settled over her. Where before, she had taken delight in everyday duties, she now performed them without joy or happiness. She didn't understand it, but it served her needs. Did her love for Reagan survive? She didn't know.

Amanda smiled as two women approached.

"Why, there you are, dear." Emily smiled as she turned to her companion. "Didn't I say she'd be tending one of the tables? Since having Jesse, she's become preoccupied with anything to do with babies."

"Oh, Mother," Amanda said, making her voice light. "I'm simply doing my part. Besides, you're no different. Once you got involved with Children's Aid, you've done little else."

Emily laughed, shaking her head. "Yes, it's true! I've found my calling after all these years. First, I lose half my weight worrying over my daughter's future, and then I put my new-found energy into finding homes for orphans. Poor George didn't know what to think. It's as if he'd married two different women."

"That was over a year ago, Mother. I'm sure he's grown accustomed to the new you. Besides, I've never seen Papa happier."

"Perhaps you're right," she said. "If this war wasn't so awful, I'd say it was more of a blessing to me than anyone I've helped."

"Emily! Don't belittle your services!" chided Katherine, Amanda's mother-in-law. "Everyone's grateful for the children who've been placed, thanks to you."

"And yet, my own daughter sought to adopt a child elsewhere," Emily said, feigning disbelief with hand over her heart. "If I didn't know better, I'd think something amiss."

Amanda laughed nervously. "Of course not! Reagan made that clear the night we introduced you to Gaeran."

"Yes, my dear. I'm only jesting. I think it's wonderful what Reagan did for his friend." She turned toward Katherine. "Although, I don't remember hearing about Mr. Paine before. Have you met him?"

Neither woman noticed Amanda bite her lip as Katherine shook her head. "Not that I recall. Although, that doesn't mean Reagan didn't mention him. It's been many years since he attended college."

"Is-is there something you needed?" Amanda said, desperate to change the subject.

"We wanted to luncheon with you, if your replacement comes before noon. We decided we'll take our break around that time and visit the dining tent," said Emily. "What do you say, dear?"

Amanda nodded. "I'll ask Mrs. Livingston. She's due to drop off more clothes."

Katherine laid a hand on Emily's arm. "I suppose we should return to the jeweler's table. We promised to finish the morning shift. Although, if I stand there much longer, I'm afraid I'll purchase the remaining stock."

"Not unless I do, first," Emily said, touching the pin on her dress. "I saw this the minute I arrived and snatched it so fast; I thought I'd be accused of thievery." Both women turned the way they had come, chatting and laughing as they disappeared into the crowd.

With a sigh, Amanda began straightening stacked clothing. Despite obsessing on what she should do, she was no closer to having an answer. She feared she would choose wrongly. The last thing she wanted was for love to cloud her judgment.

Yet, try as she might, cracks in her self-imposed armor had already begun to form. Having to share *with him* her table, her home as well as her bed was a constant reminder of her predicament. How long before someone realized the timing of Elizabeth's death and Gaeran's adoption? How long before the whispers began? Fear widened those cracks until every scenario she envisioned ended in disaster. Slinking feelings of hurt and anger crept inside, until finally, her heart rebelled. Over and over it gave voice to what she dreaded most. *Betrayal! Betrayal!*

Tears stung her lids as Amanda realized how easily she had fallen in the same pit her mother had once occupied. In her youth, Emily had been secretly engaged to Thomas Burnsfield, but their betrothal had been cut short by her blue-blooded sire. Emily's anguish turned to anger when young Thomas refused to fight for her hand. Long afterward, her hostility found vengeance on her poor husband, George. It wasn't until Amanda's kidnapping and rescue nearly two years ago that a lifetime of bitterness had been erased when her mother and Reagan's father reconciled their past. How ironic that Emily felt free while Amanda now choked on similar venom.

She pushed aside her thoughts as a prospective buyer approached. For now, she wouldn't dwell on her problems. She needed more time to think. A small, persistent notion however, had taken root in Amanda's mind. Once before, she had considered leaving her marriage. That had been swept away when Reagan had been cleared of the strumpet, Molly Carnes's, murder. But now, a different wind blew; a tempest that threatened the foundations of her existence. Once chosen, there'd be no turning back. Would she crumble or hold fast beneath its ravaging aftermath?

chapter 21

LORELDA HARGROVE IMPROVED her complexion with a concoction of egg whites boiled in rose water, alum and oil of sweet almonds. Beaten to the consistency of paste then spread on a muslin mask, she wore it every night. For her hands, she mixed soft soap, oil and mutton tallow. After boiling, she added spirits of wine and musk. She slathered her hands then wore gloves while sleeping. After two weeks, her face glowed and her hands felt soft.

Sitting before her vanity, she powdered her face. After curling her hair, she used combs to secure an upswept appearance while allowing ringlets to fall to her shoulders. Then, she applied small circles of rouge beneath the outer corners of each eye, and a touch on the center of her lips.

She appraised her image in the mirror. Though not a small woman, Lorelda had, with the help of two maids, cinched her thick-set waist into a heavily-boned corset. She then donned a new gown, daring for her, in color and design. Never before had Lorelda drawn attention to herself with such particular care. Usually, her attire consisted of drab colors designed to blend into her surroundings. This gown, spotted in Peterson's Ladies National Magazine, became her coveted next gown. The silk fabric in colors of beige, ecru, taupe and cream were woven into a large plaid pattern, trimmed with velvet. The bodice was trimmed with brown velvet tabs of diminishing width to promote a slimming effect. Metal shank buttons, attached just inside the border of each tab, boasted a thin gold chain draped alluringly over her ample bosom. White lace peeked from beneath three-quarter Pagoda sleeves while the jewel neckline was adorned with a Venice collar.

Lorelda finished the ensemble by attaching a brooch near her throat. Pleased with her appearance, she then misted herself with gardenia-scented perfume before gathering up her heavy cape. She decided she'd no longer stand in the shadows like faded wall paper. Tonight she *would* be noticed. And, as far as she was concerned, Camilla could go to hell.

きゃ くら

Camilla planned an extravagant party the first week of December celebrating the success of the fair and hospital collections. She knew she needed her husband's consent, yet chaffed at the notion she had to ask. Since Leroy held his purse strings so tight, she used the only method she knew would work. She slept with him. Afterward, she felt blameless to the many receipts she incurred for food, hired help and ballroom orchestra.

Camilla smiled as she counted RSVP's. She had purposely invited one less man than women. It galled her that Lorelda continued to parade herself before Leroy and Braegar in ever more alluring fashion. At first she'd been amused at her clothing combinations and too-rouged cheeks. However, the clashing fashions began to calm the same time her "face paint" became less obvious. Not only that, Lorelda began appearing at other peoples' dinner parties as her timidity diminished. It shouldn't have bothered her, as Lorelda was considered by most, to be an unmarriageable woman. Having passed the age of thirty, she was invited out of respect for her parents, Joseph and Alma Hargrove. Her father, having founded Hargrove and Sons, Attorneys at Law, was the most feared lawyer in Cantonsville. Lorelda was their only daughter.

Camilla, however, neither feared nor respected Hargrove. As long as she appeared friendly to his daughter, she felt safe from censure. And lately, it'd been too long since she had basked in the accolades of her peers. Tonight, there was only one person she thought of as she dressed. And, it wasn't Lorelda Hargrove.

chapter 22

AMANDA ALREADY RUED her decision to attend the Spelding celebration. The belief she could pretend happiness for one night fled the moment the RSVP had been sent. She knew too well what happened the last time she and her husband had called a truce in order to attend Camilla's birthday party. Reagan had seduced her on the carriage ride home and the result was her son, Jesse. At that time, her anger toward Reagan had already begun to falter, and it didn't take much to quell it completely. This time, Amanda's wrath seemed to be gaining momentum. Her numbness had worn off, and in its wake came a simmering outrage. She didn't know if she could act normal around those who knew her best. Not only would ever-observant Beau be near, but her parents as well as Reagan's. It seemed impossible. And yet, Amanda felt an obligation to not dampen everyone else's joy. She had to find a way to celebrate the suc-cess of the Soldiers' Fair and Winslow House contributions without giving credence to her troubled marriage.

⤜⤛

The Spelding dining table had been expanded, with three leafs inserted for all their guests. Camilla and Leroy graced each end, surrounded by some of the largest donators. Invitees included the parents of Reagan, Amanda and Beau. Of course, Braegar was the guest of honor and to pay homage to the Winslow Hospital, Doctor Miles accepted the invitation, which included Amy, Olivia and Mallory. Camilla secretly decided the three hospital volunteer's youth and beauty would be the perfect foil against Lorelda's attempts of attractiveness. No one but Lorelda suspected her placement between Olivia and Mallory was anything but a kindness.

At Camilla's nod, Leroy tapped a fork against his wineglass. When conversation paused, he held up his glass. "As you know, we've gathered to celebrate the success of the Soldiers' Fair. Everyone here deserves credit. It was a grand occasion."

"Hear! Hear!" The men chimed, lifting glasses.

Everyone took a sip before Leroy continued. "The full tabulations will be revealed in a moment," he said, smiling at Camilla, "however, I'd like Doctor Alexander to explain what Winslow House received due to everyone's efforts."

All eyes turned to Miles. He looked strikingly handsome in a worsted black suit he had purchased for the occasion. "Thank you, Mr. Spelding. Mrs. Spelding," he said, pulling paper from a pocket. He then cleared his throat. "Winslow House received six barrels of assorted clothing, including blankets and bandages. We also received two hundred pounds of canned food, meal, flour, spices, onions, potatoes, jellies and foodstuffs too numerous to mention." He paused and nodded to Beau and his parents. "And from Barrington Hotel, we received a barrel's worth of sheets, linens, towels and napkins. Our soldiers will be the best dressed, best bedded men in town." Everyone laughed politely. "Lastly, we received $13,995 in donations to be held in a special account at the Bruester Bank and Trust." Miles folded the paper and tucked it back in his pocket. "We, at Winslow House can't thank you enough for your generosity."

"'Twas a pleasure," Braegar said, smiling. "And I hope I'm speaking for everyone when I say it's the least we can do to repay these men. The real heroes are the soldiers themselves. And in that vein, I've been told Mr. Burnsfield, the elder, has even more news."

All eyes turned to Thomas who, with his thick hair and hazel eyes, gave sharp testimony to being an older version of his son, Reagan. He stood, patting his wife's hand before speaking. "I must confess, if it hadn't been for Amy's work at the hospital,

I wouldn't have known the extent of its needs. Her stories made me realize we should do more. Being in the lumber business gives me that opportunity. And so, Burnsfield and Burnsfield Lumber Company will pledge fifty thousand dollars worth of lumber for renovations or extensions to Winslow House."

As spontaneous murmurs erupted, he held up a hand. "Wait. There's more. George and Emily Bruester purchased property next to the hospital in anticipation of said expansions. And finally," he said, grinning, "Charles and Yvette Barrington have contracted Mr. Walsh, architect for the soon-to-be Paradis Pavillon, to be at your disposal. Mr. Walsh will meet with you to get specifications. He'll draw plans so when you're ready to build, so are we."

A round of applause punctuated the surprise on Miles' face as Thomas sat down. "I'm humbled," he said, looking at each in turn. "I can't wait to tell Doctor Turner. I wish he were here. He's the true founder of Winslow House and he'll be the one to decide its needs."

"Have the good doctor come to my office at the bank," George said. "I'll deed the property over and we'll set up the paperwork with Miss Hargrove's father, who's an attorney. I'm sure he'll donate his services as well."

"The contract for your lumber is tucked inside the deed," Reagan said. "Please inform Doctor Turner to contact me when he's ready to build."

"I'll be sure to," Miles said. He then looked at Amy, sitting next to her parents. "You knew about this, didn't you?"

"Of course!" she said with an impish smile. "But, I was sworn to secrecy."

"Now, I understand why you claimed we needed more beds even when I said there wasn't room."

Leroy felt, more than saw his wife's meaningful look across the table. He cleared his throat. "I'd now like Camilla to give the fairs' tabulations. My dear?"

Camilla gave her best imitation of demureness, lowering her gaze briefly. "Some of you know my cousin, Marietta Stowe. In one of her letters, she'd mentioned how bazaars were a good way to collect donations. I brought the idea to a Ladies' Aid meeting, and we came up with a plan. Those who'd already canvassed merchants for Winslow House made another round to collect for the Soldiers' Fair. Between that and the fair itself, we were able to send sixty boxes of food and clothing to the 7th Ohio Volunteers."

"Much of our success was due to our guest, Braegar Calderon. Although he no longer lives in Cantonsville, his loyalty's been our good fortune. Mr. Calderon, with the help of Leroy, spoke to merchants, asking them to close their businesses either entirely, or for a half-day so workers and townspeople alike would venture to the fairgrounds." She smiled at the Burnsfield men. "I understand you closed your mills that day."

"It wasn't a hard decision," Thomas said. "When Katherine returned from her Ladies' Aid meeting, she informed me the mills would be closed whether I liked it or not." Laughter again punctuated the air. "However, I believe it was the *women* of Cantonsville who made the fair successful. They did most of the planning, preparing, prodding men—"

"Hear, hear," Beau said, holding up his glass. When he realized no one had joined him, he shrugged. "I thought it time for another toast."

Leroy chimed in. "You're quite right, Beau. Though everyone contributed, our women carried the load. I want to thank you all, but especially my wife, for coming up with the idea. We owe her a debt of gratitude." He then held up his glass. "To Camilla."

"To Camilla!" everyone said.

No one noticed that Lorelda didn't join the homage. She kept her gaze downcast as Leroy continued. "Lastly, we can't forget our contributors. Braegar made sure every man of means had been contacted. Knowing what was collected, I'm sure he twisted more than a few arms."

"You speak truth," said Beau's mother, Yvette. Though small in stature, she often won notice with her vivacious, sharp wit. By the gleam in her eye, today would be no different. "I've had the pleasure of meeting Monsieur Calderon when he came to Barrington Hotel. I vouch; he's capable of charming the money from anyone's purse, even my stick-in-the-mire husband!"

"Yvette!" Charles said, sputtering. "Your jests are more suitable among those who know you best." Having acquired wealth late in life, he worried at offending those he still considered his betters. He looked around contritely. "My apologies. My wife has a Parisian's sense of humor."

"I'd rather say, a wicked sense of humor," Braegar said, grinning. "It's been a real pleasure to have made your acquaintance, Madam Barrington."

Yvette bowed her dark head in acknowledgement. "Oui! 'Tis a pleasure indeed. You must have some hidden French blood, Monsieur Calderon. Until now, only my son, Beauregard has understood what it is to have true *charmant*."

"Ahh, yes!" said Braegar. "His charm has garnered ample support for Paradis Pavillon. Congratulations are in order. I've heard construction has begun."

"It wasn't easy winning over creditors," Beau acknowledged. "Mr. Bruester may be a good friend, but he's a formidable businessman."

"Extending credit's the quickest way to lose a friendship," George said. "I can't risk bad investments, even among friends. As you can imagine, I went over Beau's finances with a fine tooth comb. Luckily, everything's in order, including assurances from Charles, owner of Barrington Hotel."

"Co-owner," Beau corrected. "I've joined mon père in partnership. It allows me to fund Paradis Pavillon."

"That's all well and good," George said, grinning. "Just, don't miss a payment!"

Beauregard nodded his agreement among the ensuing laugher. Though he noticed Amanda's quiet demeanor, it wasn't until asking her to dance later that evening, he discovered the reason.

"What's the matter, ma petite?" he said, escorting her to the ballroom. "You look much sad."

"'Tis nothing," she said. "I was up late with Jesse. I'm just tired."

"Il ne faut pas laisser croître l'herbe sur le chemin de l'amitiè."

"Oh Beau," Amanda said, giggling. "You know I can't speak French!"

"I said, 'Let not the grass grow on the path of friendship.' It's obvious, there's ought amiss, ma chéri. I'd be pleased if you'd tell me what's troubling you."

Amanda looked away. "I'm sorry. It's nothing I can discuss."

Beau pondered her words while guiding her in a waltz. "Is your son unwell? You could speak with Doctor Alexander. I'm sure he wouldn't mind."

"Ah—no. Everyone is well, thank you."

Beauregard spoke so only Amanda could hear. "Has Reagan been neglectful? He's surely an oaf when it comes to understanding ladies."

"No, of course not," she said, near choking. "He's been the p-perfect husband."

"Ah, mademoiselle! Reagan is many things, but even I know, perfect is not one of them. He's done something, no?"

"I suppose you could say he's neglected keeping me informed of certain things," she said. "Call me silly, but I think it's best kept to myself."

"I understand. It's no secret that is known to three. At least, let's enjoy the music, ma chéri," Beau said, smiling. "Just remember, when it comes to men, there's no joy without *annoy*." They swept past other couples on the dance floor, among them Camilla and Braegar, deep in conversation.

"So you see, I need a sleeping potion," Camilla said. "Chamomile tea hasn't helped my insomnia."

"I'd be happy to prepare a mixture for you," Braegar said. "I'll leave it in the kitchen. You'd only need a few drops in your tea. I'd recommend adding sugar due to its bitterness."

"I'm sure it'll help," she said as the dance ended. Then taking his arm, they began walking off the floor. "Now that everything's over, how long will we have the pleasure of your company?"

"Not long enough, I'm afraid. Business calls me home."

"Surely, you could stay until the New Year," she said. "It's been terribly dull since the War began."

"I'll consider it, I promise," he said, patting her hand. "I can't recall a time when I've been so loath to leave."

"I must admit," Camilla said, putting her hand over his, "it's been an immense pleasure having you." She allowed her fingers to caress his skin. "I pray you'll soon return."

Braegar stopped a moment, facing her. "The pleasure's been mutual. I must extend my compliments to Leroy for having obtained such a beautiful wife. I should be so lucky someday."

Camilla smiled. "Why, Braegar! You make me blush. Had you stayed here, you could've had any woman. You wouldn't have looked twice at me."

As a new dance began, he continued escorting her off the floor. "My dear, had I stayed, you wouldn't be gracing the arm of a banker." He grinned at his own jocularity. "At least, I'd have given him a run for the money."

Camilla thrilled at the implication. "Mayhap, you would've won," she said, giving his arm a squeeze. "We've so much in common; we'd have made a good match."

"It's too bad, my dear," Braegar said, sighing. "Alas, we'll never know. Leroy's friendship forbids me from sampling that which isn't mine. Perhaps, in the next world, we'll have an opportunity. As it is, I must content myself with the leavings."

As they neared where others stood, Braegar's eyes traversed Lorelda's dress in apparent appraisal. "Why, my dear, you look positively stunning," he said, stopping to take her hand. If I've Camilla's permission, may I have the pleasure of the next dance?"

Camilla tried catching Lorelda's eyes with a look of disapproval even as she uttered, "Of course." She was denied satisfaction, however, because Lorelda never looked her way. She had to step aside when Braegar led his new partner onto the floor.

chapter 23

REAGAN HAD DUTIFULLY danced this night, with every female except Amanda. As he approached his wife, he could feel more than see her bristle. Ever since he confessed all, she had spurned his attempts to assuage her feelings. He had been patient; thinking time would heal her heart. As of yet, her only concession had been allowing him to accompany her to social events. Even now, it appeared her dance with Beauregard hadn't improved her temperament. Wary of provoking her displeasure, he stood beside her, watching couples dance. "It's been a wonderful party so far," he ventured.

"If you say so," Amanda said, all the while smiling to anyone glancing her way.

"Aren't you enjoying yourself?"

"As much as I can, under the circumstances."

Reagan fought a sudden urge to shake her. "I'm trying my damnedest to rectify those circumstances," he said, whispering. "Why can't you understand that?"

"Understand? How can you not understand the position you've put me in? This isn't something that can be swept under a rug. One must get rid of the dirt!"

Reagan tamped down his ire, knowing full well the veracity of her words. A scandal like this could take years to die. "There's nothing we can do about it at the moment," he said, feeling the need to comfort her. "Would you at least, allow me the pleasure of this dance?"

If not for the close proximity of Beau, who seemed intent on watching their behavior, Reagan believed she would've declined. She accepted, however, placing her hand on his arm. Once on the dance floor, he forced her stiff form a little closer. "Careful my dear or you'll have tongues wagging."

"I don't know what you mean," Amanda said tartly. "I've been careful to look as if nothing's amiss."

"You do realize we're in the lion's den. If you appear unhappy, Camilla will have gone no further than her own lair to observe and spread her tales."

"Her attention seems elsewhere," she said, glancing toward Camilla. "She's barely spoken to me."

"You've apparently caught Beau's regard. I've seen him watching us ever since you two danced together."

"I've told you before; Beauregard knows when I'm troubled." She looked into Reagan's eyes. "More so than my own husband, I might add."

"Amanda, I want nothing more than to fix this *thing* between us. Tell me what I must do and I'll do it."

"I want this to have never happened! I want proof you've not played me false. Until then, I can't stand for Jesse to be near *him*."

Reagan's voice thickened and she found herself gazing into stormy eyes. "So, I'm to cast Gaeran away like a leper? Elizabeth paid dearly for her sins. And I may be worthy of the same, but not Gaeran. He's innocent."

"And what about Jesse?" said Amanda, equally fervid. "Should he suffer for your sins or the taunts that'll surely come? This stain not only falls on us, but our families. Or, have you forgotten that I, as well as my parents, know what it's like to be shunned?"

"No, madam, I haven't," he said. "Neither have I forgotten how my name was abused when we were captured by bounty hunters. I let them believe we'd been caught in a tryst rather than betray your Aunt Gabriella for transporting runaway slaves. You didn't protest my disadvantage when I became your alibi, though the rumors branded me a rake!" Reagan's voice softened at her stricken expression. "Amanda, our love got us through that, and more. We'll get through this too. I promise."

Amanda didn't respond, for the music had ended as they neared where Miles and Amy stood talking. When Miles gallantly offered his arm, she wasted no time allowing him to escort her back onto the floor and away from Reagan.

⮞⮜

Sam Hampton lived in a world split between hatred and despair. Unable to accept Elizabeth's death, he often drank himself into oblivion. Once sober, he veered again into rage and the cycle repeated itself. Finally, in the recesses of his being, he realized this behavior wouldn't solve his problem. But, what could he do?

He could avenge his loss.

Yet, in order to know what to do, he needed to know where it began. Being mayor had earned a measure of status, which in turn, had opened doors to influential families. That access had somehow exposed Elizabeth to the cad who had ruined her, then caused her to flee from home. Denied the comforts of a daughter and the grandchildren she would've borne, Sam settled on the only course of action left. He would discover who the scoundrel was and make him pay. And, if that ruined his own life, he deemed it worthy.

With shaking hands, Sam opened the door to Elizabeth's room. Until he learned of her death, the maid had dutifully kept her room dusted and tidy. Afterward, he had forbidden anyone to enter her chambers. Now, as he stood just inside the door, the dust layers claimed finality to her absence. Elizabeth would never come home. Tears formed as he opened her jewelry box and fingered the contents. He found a tiny ring she had worn as a child, but soon outgrew. He next picked up the necklace he had purchased for her eighteenth birthday. A string of pearls she had spied in the jeweler's window. He wound it around his hand, recalling her joyful tears after opening her present to discover the coveted gift. He had given her anything she wanted, and yet it hadn't been enough to keep her from seeking love elsewhere. His hand formed a fist so tight, the string burst, scattering pearls onto the floor. He dropped the remnants into the jewelry box and then began rifling bureau drawers.

Sam didn't know what he was looking for. But, once he found it, he would decide his actions. If there were clues, they'd surely be found in this room.

chapter 24

CAMILLA HAD ENJOYED her party immensely. She had been thanked personally and publicly and it fed her ego no small amount that she seemingly caught the eye of someone other than Leroy. Initially, she had planned on putting a few drops of Braegar's sleeping potion in both her and Leroy's bedtime tea. Having recently fulfilled her wifely duty, she had no desire to extend her benevolence further. However, Camilla determined she wouldn't let her charms go to waste. She secretly dumped the vial's contents into one of the cups before handing it to Leroy as he sat in bed.

She then undressed while he sipped, uncharacteristically hanging her clothes in the wardrobe. After folding each of her underclothes and placing them in drawers, she donned a clingy shift.

"Will you be done soon?" he asked, eyeing her silk-clad form.

"Patience, my dear," she said, smiling. She sat at her vanity, removing pins from her hair. Then, taking a brush, she ran it over her golden locks until they shimmered in the lamplight.

Camilla kept glancing at him in the mirror, noting his drooping lids and unsteady hand. Rising, she took his cup and set it aside. She returned to her vanity, selecting a scent before applying it over her bosom. She then stood watching him until she heard a faint sound of snoring. After lowering the wick until all she saw was the outline of his body, she silently crossed the floor, closing the door behind her.

Camilla stood outside Braegar's bedchamber, knocking lightly. Soon, the door opened. Braegar must've hastily donned a robe for his bare chest could be seen between partially wrapped folds.

Of their own volition, Braegar's eyes swept Camilla's body, clearly seeing the outline of her breasts beneath the thin material. Surprise etched his face. "Is something amiss?"

"I must speak to you, privately," Camilla said. "Could I have a moment of your time?"

Braegar looked up and down the hall. Seeing no one, he stepped aside. Camilla brushed past him, her scent wafting beneath his nose. Closing the door, he turned and stepped near. After another long appraisal, he spoke low. "To what do I owe this—pleasure?"

Now that she had entered his room, Camilla was lost for words. Her lips parted and her breath grew rapid, but she could only stare as he closed the gap between them. She recognized desire in his eyes, yet he resisted touching her. "This puts me in a difficult situation," he said. "If you don't leave, I won't be responsible for what happens."

"Don't worry. Leroy's asleep," she said, speaking low. "I doubt he'll wake until morning."

A smile spread across Braegar's face. "I thought you were the one who needed the sleeping potion."

Without speaking, Camilla placed her hand inside his robe, feeling quickening pulse beneath her fingers. Braegar suddenly reached out, pulling her near with one hand while cupping a breast with the other. Camilla gasped as she felt her nipple peak beneath his palm. She lifted her mouth as his descended hungrily. For several moments she felt sensations she hadn't enjoyed in awhile as her hands roamed beneath his robe. Just when her knees began buckling, Braegar lifted her and carried her to his bed. Tossing her among pillows, he disrobed, displaying his full desire. Ripping back the covers, he joined her, seizing her hips and rolling until she lay atop him.

"Is this what you wanted?" he said, running his hands over her derrière. He then grasped the silken material, gathering it in his hands. Slowly, he pulled it upward until her bottom half lay exposed.

Camilla felt his powerful legs beneath hers. Having become accustomed to Leroy's gangling thinness, it excited her to feel wanted by what she considered a real man. She wriggled to a sitting position and pulled off her shift, exposing herself to his gaze. Then, bending low, she slanted her mouth over his, feeling more powerful than when she had snared her marriage proposal from Leroy.

chapter 25

IN DESPAIR, MAYOR Hampton sank to the floor next to the bed. He had looked through the wardrobe, nightstand and every drawer in Elizabeth's bureau. He even leafed through books on her shelf, imagining a hidden letter with an incriminating signature. Yet, he found nothing. Elizabeth had left no evidence who her lover had been or that she'd even had one. Still, pregnant she had been and no one got that way by themselves.

Feeling the need for a drink, he gripped between mattress and bedsprings, pushing himself off the floor. As he rose, his fingers brushed something hard. Sam lifted the edge of the mattress, his heart racing. With shaking fingers he pulled out a book, recognizing it to be a diary. He opened it, his eyes racing past entries she had obviously made as a child. Flipping forward, he found a key tucked between two pages. Holding it up, he stared, noting a stamped number. He looked at the entry dated July 17, 1861.

'Today's the day. I'll tell Papa I'm going to Camilla's to help plan her birthday party. I'll convince him I'm to spend the night. He has a meeting, so it shouldn't be difficult. That's when I'll let my love know I should be his wife, not her!'

Sam nearly dropped the book. The bastard was married! He turned the page, reading swiftly. *'He wants me! He said he's always wanted me and can't live without me! Sadly, he fell asleep before we could make plans. I can't wait to see him at Camilla's party.'*

The next dated entry was July 24, 1861. The rage in Sam became palpable and his hands shook. *'All is for naught! The drunken bastard didn't even remember me coming to him. He won't leave his wife. I could just die! What will I do? How can I ever show my face around him again?'*

Sam read further, but no entries revealed a name. When he got to the pages describing how she planned on visiting her Aunt Emmaline, the notations stopped altogether.

Sam squeezed the key as if it could somehow divulge its' secrets. He now knew two things. One, Elizabeth had a rendezvous with a married man and two; the bastard had attended Camilla's birthday party. It wasn't much to go on. He would start with this key. The number at the top indicated it came from a hotel or boarding house. With any luck, he just might discover which. With that accomplished, he might possibly learn which of Camilla's guests used such a facility during that time. Of course, no one boasted about such things openly. But, it would narrow possibilities to which scoundrel caused Elizabeth's pregnancy and ultimately, her death.

ॐॐ

A dark-clad figure peered over a woodpile outside the kitchen entrance, watching a maid through the window. Setting two cups, teapot, cream and sugar on a tray, she carried her burden through swinging doors, unaware a stranger stood outside in the cold night air. With the kitchen now empty, the door opened silently and the stranger entered. A kerosene lantern lamp, left burning to light the room was soon unscrewed and its' contents dumped on stacked wood near the stove. Striking a match before tossing it, the woodpile became engulfed with flames. Then, the figure put the lamp back together, setting it on the edge of the stove where it was sure to fall near the woodpile, implying the maids' negligence. The miscreant left quickly, hurrying through the dark to an awaiting horse, where once mounted, fled with the alacrity of a soul being chased by the devil himself.

chapter 26

THE DISCOVERY THAT Barrington Hotel had caught on fire spread faster than the newspaper reports claiming the mishap had destroyed kitchen, storage and laundry rooms. After a frantic headcount ensuring all guests were accounted for, Charles Barrington issued vouchers for a complimentary visit at a later date. He also made arrangements with Angelo's Ristorante down the street to cover all meals until his patrons checked out. And then he closed his doors until further notice.

Reagan found Beauregard in what used to be the hotel kitchen, directing clean up efforts. "Ah, my friend," Beau said, wiping soot from his hands. "You come to see the désastre?"

Reagan tried not to appear shocked. Viewing the charred ceiling, he calculated the floor above was also ruined. "I'm so sorry, Beau. Do you know what happened? The papers said the fire began in the cooking area."

"Oui. The fire warden believes a lamp fell near the wood box. Although. the maid swears she didn't leave it there." He sighed as he looked around. "It matter's not. Whatever the cause, we must *reconstruire* if our hotel is to survive."

"If it's lumber you need, don't hesitate to ask," Reagan said, laying a hand on his shoulder. "I'm sure Father would reallocate a contract or two to get you on your feet."

Beau nodded. "Merci. Mon père fears if we delay, we'll lose much clientele."

"Tell your father we'll deliver lumber the moment we get a list of your needs. And don't worry about payment. We'll wait until you have funds."

"Non!" Beau said firmly. "I've already halted construction on Paradis Pavillon. All resources have been diverted, including our architect, Monsieur Walsh. Without Barrington Hotel, there won't be enough money to fund the resort. You'll be paid the moment we receive shipment."

"It's really not an issue—" Reagan began.

Beauregard's hand shot up. "I insist!" He then gentled his tone. "Your friendship means too much. I'll pay immediately and fully. Even if Paradis Pavillon cannot be, we must have Barrington Hotel. It's all we have."

"What's the harm in extending time?" he persisted. "Tis obvious you're in a pinch."

"Qui paie ses dettes s'enrichit," Beau quipped, clicking his heels and a quick bow. "Out of debt, is riches enough!"

"I see," Reagan said, sighing. "Let's do it your way."

Beau smiled, kicking a burnt chunk of wood. "Too bad you don't also make bricks. We'll need plenty in the rebuilding so this never happens again."

"That's a wise choice," he said, "especially if you've not fired the maid."

Beauregard laughed, pointing to what appeared to be a lad working a broom. "So insistent was she, she's donned britches to help clean up."

He then turned as a man with a handle-bar mustache entered through what used to be the back door. "Sheriff Hadley! When did you get here?"

"I've been here awhile," Jim said, nodding to Reagan before turning all business. "I wanted to look around and now I've a question." He held out two cigar stubs. "I found these on the far side of the woodpile. Do you allow your employees to smoke outside?"

"Non!" Beau said, looking at the cigar remains. "Besides, we employ boys to fill and clean our stoves. They're not old enough to smoke."

"Neither could they afford these," Sheriff Hadley said, pulling a band off one of the stubs. "These are Montecristo's and they're expensive. I don't know if any of our shops carry them, but I'll find out."

"What does this mean?" Beau asked.

"Perhaps nothing, but it seems rather odd that the remains of expensive cigars were found outside your door. It almost appears as if someone were waiting behind the woodpile, where they wouldn't be seen."

"May I?" Reagan held out his hand.

"Sure," Jim said. "Take a look."

Reagan lifted one and looked at it. "I can tell you they are, indeed, sold in Cantonsville." He handed it back to the sheriff. "I received a box of these for Christmas from father. I'm sure they're the same brand he smokes."

Beauregard's jaw dropped at Jim's sudden, inquisitive look. "Surely not! Mon ami would never do such a thing. Why would he?"

"Oh, I don't know," drawled Sheriff Hadley. "Mayhap, in order to sell more timber?"

Reagan's brows shot up. "Jim! You know me better than that! I'd gladly donate timber to Beau before I'd do such a thing."

"I know, I know," he said, grinning. "I couldn't help myself. However, until I know if this means anything, I'd like to keep this bit of information out of the papers."

"I'll say nothing," Beau vowed. "In fact, I never saw those vile things." He held up both hands and looked away. "Tell me nothing, sheriff. If there's a Monsieur Bad Man afoot, you catch him."

"This may turn out to be unimportant," Jim said, pocketing the stubs. "If they're sold here, it could be anyone. Even a poor man sometimes craves a good smoke."

chapter 27

"SO, TELL ME dear, how are you adjusting having two babies around?" asked Gabriella Bruester as she sat in her parlor, opposite Amanda. "I hope they're getting along with each other."

Amanda set down her teacup, idly stirring its contents. "Very fine, thank you." She looked at Jesse playing on the floor, nearby. "And yes, they seem to get along. Once Gaeran's weaned, I'm sure he'll be well enough for visits. But, for now, he needs to stay with his nursemaid." She smiled brightly. "Which reminds me, I've been meaning to ask you something. You've never said what happened to Nell's baby the night Reagan and I were caught by bounty hunters. I'm wondering if you can now tell me."

Gabriella set down her own teacup. "I suppose I could. Its difficult letting go of old habits, you know."

Amanda nodded, waiting for Gabriella to gather her thoughts.

"That night, Ben took us to our original destination. As you know, Nell died from her injuries. We had to bury her without a marker in order to protect the safe house." Gabriella stared at her tea, remembering. After a moment, she seemingly shook herself. "We then left the child there and returned home. Later on, I received a carefully worded letter indicating a certain 'orphan' had been adopted by a family, traveling north."

"How frightening it must've been. Were they ever caught?"

"As far as we know, they made it to wherever they were headed, thank God."

Amanda shook her head. "I still can't believe you were a conductor for all these years. We never knew!"

"Of course you didn't. How else could I've done it?" She picked up her cup, taking a sip. "It's against the law, you know."

Amanda burst out laughing, causing Gabriella to smile as well. "That's just it. Who'd have believed a woman of your—maturity—would've been so bold? I mean, you walk with a cane; you're no bigger than a mite, and yet you did such dangerous things."

Gabriella patted her white hair, pinned in a bun. "Why, my dear, that's the only way to fool those who should've been minding their own business."

"You wouldn't be...still...would you?" Amanda let the question hang.

"Fortunately or not, it's impossible for my friends to pass undetected around all that fighting. However, I'm praying Lincoln will settle the matter once and for all."

"That's good," Amanda said. "But, in the meantime, it looks as if you've traded one good cause for another."

"Oh posh! I don't know what you mean."

"Well, besides your sewing circle, you've also joined Ladies' Aid. You continue supplying provisions to the Negro settlement, and how many times have you paid Doctor Turner for a sick child's care?"

"You don't expect me to do nothing when I could help, do you? Isn't that what you did when you adopted Gaeran? You saw a need and acted. I'd say you're just as worthy as I am, my dear."

Amanda's countenance lost some of its glow. "I don't compare, Aunt Ella. I'm not brave, like you." Though visiting Gabriella always lifted her spirits, Amanda felt a familiar weight upon her shoulders. She had thought she'd be able to confide in her dear aunt, but couldn't bring herself to admit Reagan may have been wantonly indecent with another woman.

❧❦

"You've been neglecting your hand," Doctor Turner said, looking up from his desk.

Miles frowned as he handed over the monthly statement of hospital funds. "I haven't had time," he said. "Besides, I don't think further manipulation will improve it."

"It's not just progress I'm talking about. If you don't work your injury, you'll lose what strength you've achieved."

Just then, Amy entered the open door. "Excuse me, Doctor Turner. I've listed the food donations. Olivia's also written weekly menus so nothing spoils." She held out several papers. "That is, if you approve."

Artemus took the sheaths, looking from Miles to Amy. "I've another duty to assign you, Miss Burnsfield." He ignored Miles' sudden look of chagrin. "I need you to manipulate Doctor Alexander's injured hand twice a day. It needs to be done every morning and evening before you leave."

"That won't be necessary," said Miles, reddening. "I'll manage myself."

"Obviously not," Artemus said before redirecting his attention to Amy. "I require at least fifteen minutes each session. However, the more strenuous of the two will be the evening, where I'll allow Doctor Alexander a small libation for the pain he'll suffer."

"I'd be happy to," she said. "But, I'm not sure what to do."

"Don't worry, I'll show you exactly what's needed," he said. "And, you'll report directly to me. If he misses one session or gives you any difficulty, you're to let me know immediately." He then turned to Miles. "This is non-negotiable. I can't have soldiers see you neglecting your injury while expecting them to improve theirs. Is that clear, Doctor Alexander?"

"Surely, Miss Burnsfield has enough to do without burdening her with another duty," said Miles. "I'll find a willing soldier to do it."

"And have you intimidate them into not following my orders?" said Doctor Turner. "I trust you won't threaten Miss Burnsfield, or I misjudge your character. Both of you be in my office at six-thirty. And, Doctor Alexander, I recommend a pint of whiskey. You're not going to like what Amy's going to do." Artemus ignored her startled look. "That'll be all, Miss Burnsfield. I'll look over these diet tables today."

chapter 28

BRAEGAR LEANED FORWARD, sputtering coffee onto the morning newspaper before holding it aloft. "Did you know that Barrington Hotel caught fire?"

Looking alarmed, Leroy set down his own cup. "Good heavens! What happened?"

Braegar's finger ran down the front page article, stopping halfway. "It says it started in the back of the hotel." He paused and quickly read. "Ah, good! No one was hurt, but how sad for the Barrington's."

"Let me see," Leroy said, taking the paper. "Heavens! This says kitchen, and laundry rooms as well as part of the second story were destroyed. The whole of it must be rebuilt before Barrington Hotel can operate. Heavens!" he repeated. "This can't be good, for them or the bank."

"I'm sure the bank insisted on insurance," Camilla said, taking a dainty sip of tea. She looked beautiful in a golden toffee dress and jacket with an overlapping pointed closure. A large brooch, clasped at the collar, contrasted against her white blouse. "I wouldn't be overly worried," she said, giving Leroy the briefest glance.

"My dear, the bank insisted Beau insures Paradis Pavillon, for which we hold the note, not Barrington Hotel. I've no idea how the Barrington's are positioned for a loss there. If not, I fear they'll be in dire straights."

"This is dreadful!" Braegar said, slapping the table. "If you'll allow me, I can be of service. It's a pittance to extend monies to bridge the gap between rebuilding the hotel and loan payments. Just tell me what to do."

Camilla laid a hand on Braegar's arm. "What a wonderful friend you've turned out to be." She let it linger there as she looked toward Leroy. "What do you think, dear? Should he go to the bank and present his offer?"

Leroy shook his head. "You should discuss this with Beauregard. After all, he hasn't missed any payments. However, I'm sure he'd be happy to consider your offer. I know the Bruester Bank and Trust would be grateful for this assurance."

"It'll be my pleasure," said Braegar, patting Camilla's hand. "I've grown very fond of everyone during my visit. If I can help, I'm most happy to oblige."

Camilla's cheeks darkened as she reluctantly removed her hand. "We've been doubly blessed to have you. I-, I mean—*we*—will loathe seeing you go."

"Then we'll simply have to make the most of the time we have," he said, smiling. "These next weeks will undoubtedly, be the most pleasurable I'll have in a long time." Braegar then stood. "I'll consult an old lawyer friend of mine. He'll be able to instruct me on how to offer my assistance until Mr. Barrington recovers from this unfortunate accident. Then, if he's willing, I'll bring papers to the bank to officiate a transfer of funds. Would that be agreeable?"

"I'll let father know the moment I get to the bank," Leroy said, looking relieved. "If this works out, we can't thank you enough." He held out his hand, accepting the strong handshake. "Thank you, Braegar! Thank you!"

chapter 29

REAGAN KISSED JESSE and Gaeran before their respective nannies took them to bed. He inwardly cringed when Amanda avoided this ritual, which she did by leaving the parlor before the children were taken upstairs. He followed her into the library, slamming the door behind him.

Amanda whirled, apparently startled.

"I've just about had my fill of you shunning Gaeran," Reagan said, advancing into the room. You don't even treat him like a guest, let alone one of our children. When will you quit punishing him?"

"When I know whether or not he's truly yours," she said, her own anger rising. "You expect too much! You think I can create love like *that*?" She snapped her fingers. "Well, I can't! I'm not sure I even want to. Every time I see him, I see you in Elizabeth's arms."

He drew near, his words falling like stones. "I see a little boy who lost his mother. A mere child, whose only need is to be loved." His voice filled with emotion as they stood two paces apart. "I see a baby, for God's sake!"

He desired taking Amanda in his arms. At the same time he wanted to shake her. "This has to stop," he said thickly. "Everything you fear will come true if you continue acting this way. I'm sure the nannies have noticed, if not the whole staff. I insist you act as if Gaeran's a gift, not a burden. It doesn't matter to me whether or not I fathered him."

"It matters to me," she said, moisture filling her eyes. "I've tried getting past this, but I can't. All I know is Elizabeth gave you every clue to her desires and you somehow didn't notice. Even after she likely bedded you, you still have doubts. It's seems too incredulous to believe." Amanda's lip trembled while her shoulders lifted then dropped. "I fear it is hopeless. I have nothing to give this child."

Reagan's heart ripped as twin spikes of pain and despair pierced his soul. His hands clenched at his sides. "What am I supposed to do?" he said in a near whisper. "I want do what's right."

"I don't know," she said, dissolving into tears. "I feel like everything's ruined!" She wiped her eyes with the backs of her hands. "I fear something bad will happen and I'll lose everything."

"Come here, you little fool," he said, drawing her against him. "Don't you see? It's fear that's causing your unhappiness. Don't let it ruin *us*."

They stood thus entwined until her sobs turned into sniffles. Though he tried not to, images of Amanda yielding to him played havoc in his mind. "Here," he said, giving her a hankie, "you've watered my shirt." He waited until she'd daubed her cheeks and blew her nose before upturning her chin with a knuckle. "You've lost nothing. Why can't you see that?" He suddenly wanted to kiss her lips, so close to his. Her perfume reminded him of long nights spent without easing his passions.

Amanda's eyes were pools of liquid indigo, studying his face. "I don't know how to explain it. I'm afraid the truth will out. If it does, there'll be no quick fix like last time. We've a living, breathing child who'll be a daily reminder of your indiscretions. Maybe you don't care if we become a laughingstock, but be assured, I do!"

"So, we're back to that," he said, irritation suffusing his amorous thoughts. "We're going in circles, don't you see? We have to resolve this. Gaeran's health is still fragile. What choice do we have but to make him part of our family?"

Amanda misread the conflict in Reagan's face. "Would a warmer clime help?" she asked. "Mayhap, the cold weather is ailing him."

"I hope you're not suggesting we send Gaeran away, because I won't do that." His fingers bit into her arms, yanking her against his chest. "I'll have no more talk of this, do you hear?"

As he stared into her eyes, desire finally won out. Of their own volition, his arms encircled her, preventing retreat. He pressed his lips against her rapidly pulsing throat, finding the delicate place behind her ear. Her warmth played havoc with his senses, plucking at memories of unrestrained ardor. When she didn't pull away, he captured her lips, savoring their soft trembling. He had been too long without the comforting softness only a woman could give and Reagan determined he wouldn't be deprived another night. Slowly, he tested her resolve by dropping a hand to her lower back and then beyond.

He felt Amanda stiffen before she pressed a hand against his chest. "You can't fix this problem with that," she said raggedly. Her eyes glittered, searching his face. "I don't know how. But, for all our sakes, I need you to fix this."

A hopeless frustration took a hold of him. "Fix what?" he snapped, releasing her. "There's nothing left to fix! I was presented with a problem. I did what I thought right." His hands flew up, fingers splayed. "You've put me in an impossible position, *woman*! I won't choose between those I love and those to whom I'm obligated. What kind of man would I be to abandon a child, possibly my own?"

Amanda pointed an accusing finger. "All I know is our son's future may be in jeopardy. And, I won't allow that, either."

"It seems we're deadlocked," he said, ignoring the pain in his chest. Whether his heart pounded with passion, conviction or both, he didn't know.

A knock at the door prevented further words. "Begging your pardon, ma'am," a maid said, when bid come in. "But, Jesse needs a feeding before being laid down."

Reagan remained long after Amanda departed. His eyes wandered the room his wife had tastefully decorated. What had once been a home of warmth and comfort had become a place of enmity. He wondered what future hell awaited him. He doubted it would be worse than the one he just created.

chapter 30

SAM HAMPTON KNEW he would be too well known to do the job himself. So he sent Dudley to traipse between hotels and boarding rooms, giving well-rehearsed dialogue to those in attendance. He stated he found this key, quite by accident of course, and wondered if it belonged to their establishment. When they said no, Dudley thanked them, pocketed the key and moved on. It was late afternoon by the time he reached the Rochester Hotel. Approaching the desk, he gained the notice of the attendant.

"How may I help you, sir?"

Dudley fished the key from his pocket. "I happened to find this near the entrance to the Theatre Royal. I'm wondering if it might be one of yours."

"Let's take a look," he said. As soon as Dudley placed it in his hand, the clerk smiled. "Yes, it looks to be one of ours." He turned to the board behind him and searched through numbers, stopping where identical keys hung. "It seems we've already replaced it," he said. "Both keys belonging to that suite are already here." He hung it with the others before facing Dudley. "Our patrons often lose keys, so we're constantly replacing them. But, thank you kindly for returning it."

Dudley cleared his throat. "You're welcome. I'm curious, however. Is there any way to tell how long that key's been missing? Or, how often that suite is let?"

"It's one of our finest suites, so it's engaged less often than our regular rooms," the clerk said. "Yet, I don't recall those particular keys turning up missing, so it must've been awhile ago."

Dudley's eyes fell to the register lying open. "I don't suppose it'd be permissible to look through the registry and see who may've occupied those rooms, would it?"

The clerk clamped a hand over the register. "Certainly not! If a patron wanted that information known, I'm sure they'd have to be the ones to do so."

Dudley surreptitiously removed a wad of bills and pushed it across the counter.

"My query concerns the summer of last year. Those patrons being long gone wouldn't be available to ask. Let's just say I'm a curious fellow, willing to pay."

After several moments, the clerk pulled the money toward him. His eyes grew wide. "Good

Lord!" he whispered, opening the wad. "What did they do?"

"I'm paying to get information, not give it."

The clerk swallowed as he looked around the lobby, then back to Dudley. "All you want is a list of anyone who occupied that suite last summer?"

"Yes. The months of June, July and August will do nicely."

The clerk crushed the wad into his fist, stuffing it into a pocket. "It'll take time. I need to go back through old registers. If I'm caught, I'll lose my job."

"When can I expect a list?"

"I'm working until midnight. I think I can do it by then. But, I can't promise I'll be able to go through all the books."

"That's when I'll return," Dudley said. "Good day, sir." He turned and left, anxious to give the mayor this bit of news. He didn't know exactly why Sam wanted the information, but felt whatever it was; it would forever alter the course of the person Sam was looking for.

❧❦

"What do you mean he couldn't find it?" Sam slammed a fist on the parlor table, a game of solitaire laid before him. "All he had to do was look through some old registers!"

Snow still covered Dudley's shoulders, giving his overcoat a dappled appearance. "Yes sir. I know sir. He—he said that particular ledger was still with Sheriff Hadley. I presume it's because it was entered as evidence during Mr. Banning's trial."

"Hell and damnation!" he roared. "Must I do everything myself?"

"I'm sorry, sir. He checked the other registers and none covered the months you wanted. It appears the key is a dead end."

Sam's mind had already begun to turn. Out of two possibilities, there was now only one avenue left. He would have to find out who attended Camilla's party.

chapter 31

"SO WHAT ARE your plans for the day?" Camilla asked Braegar while sipping breakfast tea.

"Very busy, I'm afraid. I'm meeting with a lawyer to draw up those papers we discussed, in order to assist Beau, if he so chooses."

"I'm sure he'll be more than delighted," Leroy said, daubing his mouth with a napkin. "I can't imagine the stress of having to delay Paradis Pavillon while repairing Barrington Hotel. Father mentioned how concerned the bank had become with these developments. He calmed considerably after I told him of your offer."

"I'm pleased to be of assistance," he said, smiling, "although, I've no idea whether Beau will accept."

"He would, if he realizes how far it'll go to ease the banks' peace of mind," Leroy said. "I know father's expressed misgivings of a quick recovery."

"Mayhap, Ezra could give him gentle encouragement. As a businessman, I understand the perils of new enterprise. Misfortune can cause even the most fervent financier to withdraw support."

"I'll mention it today," Leroy said. He then turned to Camilla. "And what's on your agenda today, my dear?"

"Shopping for Christmas," she said. "I've several things on my list."

"Ah yes!" he said, nodding. "Just don't forget about our budget. Gold can't grow on trees, you know."

"I appreciate the reminder, but I'm well aware of our limitations."

Leroy nodded, missing her warning look. "Unfortunately, I've had to take into consideration our recent donations. It sounds paltry, but they add up." He raised his brows. "Should I assume Ladies' Aid will continue asking for contributions?"

"Of course!" she said, nostrils flaring. "I can't be the only one not contributing. I haven't old clothes to give and I don't do needlework. Money's all I have to offer."

Leroy looked pained. "That's regrettable, my dear. Wouldn't selling baked items at a bazaar work? We've had tasty confections—"

"Confections!" She looked aghast. "What *is* it about confections? Amanda recently asked about those recipes."

"Well, maybe that's what she had in mind. It's a good wife who can stretch a dollar, even for a good cause."

"I doubt it," Camilla said. "It felt like a ruse. She claimed Elizabeth told her she'd spent the night at my house to help plan my birthday party last year. What ridiculousness! Why would Elizabeth lie about that?"

Leroy shrugged. "If she did, she must've had a reason. What did you say?"

"I put Amanda in her place. I told her I wouldn't know why Elizabeth would spread such tales. If she had, it was most likely to sneak away to meet a man. By the look on her face, she must've thought it was Reagan."

Now it was Leroy who looked aghast. "Heavens! I pray you didn't say *that*?"

"Of course not," Camilla took another sip of tea. "I only implied it. You know I think Elizabeth's disappearance is somehow linked to that lumberman. She'd spread the tale of Amanda's arrest. Why wouldn't he want revenge? I mean, the man had to marry the wench after that!"

Leroy looked contritely toward Braegar. "My apologies. This subject is most unseemly. I know of no connection linking Mr. Burnsfield to Elizabeth's death, let alone an affair!" He glanced sternly at Camilla. "And, I'll hear no more tales. Is that clear?"

"I only implied that to ruffle her feathers," Camilla said, shrugging. "Besides, no one else heard me. It just slipped off my tongue."

Leroy stared at his wife, incredulous. "That kind of rudeness is beyond ugly, my dear. From now on, I ask that no gossip, unfounded or otherwise, crosses your lips."

Camilla lowered her eyes, enraged at being rebuked in front of Braegar. "Of course. 'Twas thoughtless of me. I'll do better, beginning today."

"About today," Braegar said in the ensuing silence. "I won't be here for dinner. I've friends I promised to visit before returning to Chester. I'll likely stay the night as I'm sure we'll be up late reminiscing old times."

Camilla looked accusingly at her husband. "I hope our little spat hasn't dampened your spirits. I apologize if we've made you uncomfortable."

"That's not the case, I assure you," Braegar said. "My plans were decided yesterday. You've been more than gracious hosts." He leaned back, folding hands against his middle. "In fact, I find it refreshing you consider me part of your family inasmuch as you speak freely in my presence."

"We certainly don't want you feeling unwelcome," Leroy said. "Your coming's been good for so many reasons."

"And yet, even I know what happens," he said. "Fish and company stink after awhile. It's about time I give you time to yourselves."

Leroy smiled. "Agreed. Let's give Camilla's duties a rest. Shall we expect you back tomorrow?"

"Mayhap, or even the next day," Braegar said. "I've left a few things unattended and time grows short." He gave a meaningful look to Camilla. "Besides, I've shopping of my own to do and I need a secret place to hide my treasures."

༺ ༻

Camilla wasted no time knocking on Braegar's door once Leroy left for work. She held out a clothes basket when the portal opened. "I've brought your wash," she said breathlessly.

"You could've had the maid do that," he said, taking the basket and setting it aside. "I've everything I need for my travel bag."

"I sent the maid home," Camilla said. "I told her I had a headache and needed rest."

He looked amused. "I thought you were shopping today."

"Later," she said, entering and then closing the door. Knowing her perfume wafted beneath his nose, she began fingering his lapel. "Must you leave right away?"

Braegar lifted her hand, kissing her palm. "What do you prefer?" he asked. "Because I can leave whenever you wish."

"You could wait an hour," she whispered.

When he seized her, she coiled her arms around his neck, crushing her mouth to his in sudden intensity. He pulled apart the hooks at her bodice before yanking down the material covering her bosom. He then dipped his head, using his mouth to tease her peaking areolas, already familiar with what pleased her. She gasped, her fingers flying over the buttons of his shirt, pulling it open.

Camilla experienced a heady thrill as Braegar lifted her with one arm while sweeping a nearby dresser with the other, sending items crashing to the floor. Setting her down, he lifted her skirts while she tugged open the placket of his pants. Within moments, they were joined in a heated embrace as Braegar's hands firmly gripped her hips, thrusting powerfully inside her.

Camilla's heart beat wildly at being the object of his desire. His eagerness fed her lust, taking her to new heights as she clung to him. Her fervor only increased his passion as Braegar claimed her mouth in a brutal kiss that soon ended in a frenzy of motion and mutual cries of carnal release.

"I'm going to miss this when I go," he said, greedily savoring a few more strokes. "You've been an experience I'll not soon forget."

"Then, why go? Let others run your company. Move back here. We'd never have to be apart again," Camilla said repairing her bodice.

"I'd extend my holiday if Beau accepts my offer. That'd give us a few extra weeks. Excepting that, a business like mine can't be run by others. Besides, sooner or later, we'd be found out," he said, withdrawing. "Why not enjoy this while we can?"

"I wished you'd never moved away!" Camilla said with vehemence. "I loathe being married to that man!" She leaned against the wall, palming his cheek. "Take me with you. I'm not too proud to get a divorce."

"Now, Camilla, you know I can't do that." He handed her a towel from the forgotten basket before repairing his clothes. "Leroy's a friend. I can't very well take his wife. He won you fair and square."

"He wouldn't have if you'd have been here," she said, easing off the dresser. "I wish to God I'd never married him!" She daubed herself before tossing the cloth. "How dare he upbraid me at breakfast?"

Braegar laughed. "There's been centuries of women who've ruled their husbands with remedies from nature. One could tame them or maim them."

Camilla shook out her skirt before glaring at him. "I'm sure I don't know what you mean. You could just take me away and be done with it."

"Too many encumbrances, my dear," he said kissing her nose. "One never knows what a cuckolded man might do. Leroy might shoot me, and he'd be justified."

"But, what am I to do?" she said, wailing. "I want to be with you."

"Then I suggest you keep giving Leroy your sleeping potion so we can enjoy the time we've left. I'm happy to keep scratching your itch."

"And, what'll I do once you're gone? I can't divorce Leroy. I've no means of supporting myself."

"You'll eventually outlive him, my dear. Perhaps, your final years will be pleasant enough once you've inherited his money."

"I wouldn't need it were I with you," she countered.

"I'm a cad when it comes to beautiful women," he said, stroking her cheek. "But, I see no reason to ruin Leroy's life. Let's just savor this time, shall we?"

Camilla grew surly with her inability to sway him. "Perhaps, he'll choke on his tea and save me the trouble," she said, opening the door and stomping out. "He could die for all I care!"

She missed Braegar's quizzical look as he wondered if she meant what she had just said.

chapter 32

MILES AND AMY sat facing each other in the cramped space of the hospital pantry. An oil lamp sat on the floor. "Have you had adequate liquor?" she asked, taking his hand into hers.

Miles snorted. "I can't believe Doctor Turner's making you do this. I've done this myself a hundred times. I don't need you to perform the task."

She leaned over, dipping two fingers into a tin. "This liniment is a mixture of mutton tallow, oil, spirits of wine and musk," she said, applying a soft glob to his skin.

"In other words, I'm going to smell like a woman."

"Are you going to complain the whole time?" she said, using her thumbs to massage his scar. "Even though you're my superior out there, in here, I'm in charge."

Miles said nothing as Amy began applying pressure before turning over his hand and gently stretching each finger. Then, turning his hand again, she used her thumb to massage perpendicular to the scar in a cross-friction technique.

Beads of sweat appeared on his brow as she palpitated each finger. "Ahh, careful," he burst out, jerking his hand. "That hurts!"

"I'm sorry," Amy said. "Perhaps, you need a drink."

"I'll know when I need alcohol," Miles said, muttering. But after another few minutes, he leaned down and snatched up the whiskey flask near his feet. Taking several gulps, he coughed, breathed deeply, and then croaked, "Go on."

When she'd completed the torturous task, Amy then instructed Miles to perform movements with individual fingers. "I'll keep a record of your strength and flexibility," she said, giving his hand a final pat. "Doctor Turner made it clear I'm not to cheat in any way, if I'm to help you."

Miles held out his hand and shook it. "It's useless," he said. "You've rubbed my nerves to oblivion."

"He said the first sessions may seem to make it worse. But once we begin breaking down scar tissue, everything will improve."

"There's no *we* in this," he said, frowning. "I get to enjoy this all by myself."

"Just think what a good example you'll be setting," Amy said. "Most of these men have serious injuries. They'll be encouraged, seeing your efforts."

"I doubt it! They've enough troubles of their own to worry about."

Amy sighed, deciding she had said enough. If he wanted to wallow in the muck of self-pity, she wouldn't listen. She lidded the tin, and then shelved it before retrieving the lamp, waiting for Miles to rise. He scooped up his whiskey bottle and pocketed it before following her out the door. "I'll be here fifteen minutes early tomorrow to work your hand," she said, setting the lamp on a sideboard and pulling her coat from the closet.

As she slipped it on Miles retrieved his coat and shrugged into it. But handling buttons with only one good hand proved too much and in frustration, he gave up.

"Here," she said, reaching out. "Allow me." Never having been this close, his nearness had an unnerving affect on her. She avoided his eyes as she worked the buttons. When she reached his collar, she had the distinct impression he'd drawn even closer. Glancing up, she noted his dilated eyes and his breath had a distinct odor. "I think you've had enough to drink, Doctor Alexander."

He grinned suddenly. "Maybe you should accompany me to my apartment and help me undress."

"Now I *know* you've had too much," she said. If not for the fact Doctor Alexander had never before displayed churlish behavior, she might've been insulted. However, she had been around injured men long enough to realize that pain and the substances used to dull it, often loosened tongues. "I'll have one of the steward's assist you to your quarters, if you wish."

Miles donned his hat before assuming a stiff stance. "If the lady refuses my company, I'll suffer the distance alone." He then held his hand toward the door. "After you."

Amy wound a scarf around her neck then proceeded down the passage, pulling gloves from her pockets. "Are you sure you haven't had too much whiskey? I'd feel responsible if some evil befell you."

Miles opened the door, a cold blast nearly unseating his hat. With pursed lips, he tolerated a shiver before speaking. "I believe the weather's sufficiently cold to keep me from dawdling along the way. I'll escort you as far as your buggy, Miss Amy."

Taking her arm, Miles walked firmly though a bit unsteadily, to the outbuildings behind the hospital. After the stable boy brought out her covered buggy, Miles insisted on helping her inside.

"I'll see you in the morning," she said, taking the reins. "It won't be as painful tomorrow, I promise."

"I wouldn't be so sure," he said, almost forlornly. "My wound never heals."

"With Doctor Turner's treatment, your injury should improve. Time, as you know, mends most anything." Then, slapping the reins, she left Miles standing, alone and very much bereft of her company.

chapter 33

LORELDA SAT AT her vanity, tweezing her brows into a more pleasing appearance. She then began brushing her hair, recalling conversation at the dinner table. Sam Hampton had been an unexpected guest, mostly because the mayor came minutes before dinner was announced. The Hargrove's gladly accepted his company, the first since Elizabeth's untimely death. They were solicitous and compassionate; knowing Sam's devastation from rumors of his drunken rides to the cemetery.

Sam, however, seemed sober, if not purposeful as he directed conversation toward, not away from his daughter. In fact, Alma Hargrove later wondered if the mayor had taken leave of his senses. He seemed determined to discover all who fell within Elizabeth's circle of friends.

To Lorelda, Sam's cheerful demeanor felt forced when he asked who had attended Camilla's birthday party two years past. She named a few, mystified to his intense questioning. Soon after, she excused herself, claiming a need to ready for a trip to visit cousins in a nearby town.

She smiled as she dipped her finger in colored paste and smoothed it over her cheeks. She would indeed, visit her cousins, but not before stopping along the way for a planned rendezvous with the man of her dreams. Lorelda envisioned Camilla's fury if she had only known how Lorelda had worked Leroy's sympathies to do her bidding. Indeed, there was no greater satisfaction than plucking a morsel from the lips of another. Especially, she thought, if that person was none other than Camilla Spelding.

❧

"Monsieur Calderon! How good of you to come." Beauregard indicated a chair at his table at Angelo's Ristorante. "I just received a note from Ezra Spelding you had news which would be beneficial. Of late, I could use some good news."

"If I may be so bold, I've a proposition that greatly pleases me." He took a seat opposite Beau, waving away the proffered menu. "Let's say it'll be the last good deed I do before returning to Chester once New Year arrives."

"At least, have a beef tea. It's refreshing on a cold day," Beau said. At Braegar's assent, Beauregard sent the waiter to do his bidding. "Now, what can I do for you?"

"I read of your misfortune in the papers. Although you didn't lack resources before, I'm hoping to lend assistance, with your permission, of course. I took the liberty of mentioning it to Leroy and he agreed that extending funds would go a long way in keeping the bank from becoming; shall we say—nervous—about meeting your obligations. My only wish is your dreams aren't dashed because of an unfortunate fire." He then pushed a paper across the table with a large figure written upon it.

Beau dropped his fork. Only this morning, the elder Barrington had informed him of their evolving financial situation. Since travel dropped considerably during cold weather, the Barrington Hotel survived on summer income to carry them through winter. After studying their books, it became obvious that without the ability to generate income, expenses would exceed savings by the first of the year. Most of the purchased building materials for Paradis Pavillon were unsuitable for hotel renovations. And, even if he found a buyer to liquidate his inventory, he'd sustain considerable loss.

"Mon Dieu!" Beau exclaimed. "Incrédule! As a fact, I was considering asking my lumber supplier, who happens to be a friend of mine to delay payment. I hesitated as our friendship is most dear."

"Wisely said," Braegar said, nodding. "Those who mix friendship with finances, tend to lose one or the other. My proposal allows you to keep your fellowship intact. I, on the other hand, will return to Chester with only a business deal between us."

"I—I don't know what to say." Beau laid a hand over his heart. "I'm at a loss for words."

"Please let your answer be *yes*," Braegar said. "I've a contract written up. It only requires your signature and funds will be immediately transferred. He withdrew folded papers from an inner pocket and passed them to Beauregard. "Since I have the bank's blessing, I hope you'll accept."

"What is your rate of return?" Beau asked as he skimmed the contract.

"I ask for nothing as long as you're able to repay the sums within five years. You'll have ample opportunity to recoup your losses by then. I'll receive no return except having done a good deed."

"No return? That's not a smart business decision," Beau said, pushing his plate aside. "What if I chose not to repay you?"

"That's what my lawyer asked," Braegar said, chuckling. "Out of an abundance of caution, he put in a stipulation to guarantee my interests. If, by some imprudence you neglect to repay me, I'd obtain twenty percent ownership of Paradis Pavillon. However, I don't believe you or the bank will let that happen. Please, let this be my gift to you. I will, of course, require the bank's signature to approve and verify the legality of my paying your note. The additional monies can be used however you wish. Mayhap now, you could put in that fountain to the entrance of Paradis Pavillon?"

"You're generosity exceeds comprehension," Beau said. "Why would you do such a thing?"

"As I've said before, I've been looking for ways to defray taxes. This investment will show no return, so in actuality; you're doing me a favor. Besides, my hosts have asked me to stay longer. This venture gives me an excuse. I'd delay my departure until I'm assured Dame Fortune is restored to you."

"This is indeed, a fortunate turn of events," Beau said, beaming. "I'll show this to mon père immédiatement! Ah, here comes your beef tea!"

chapter 34

A COLD WIND scattered snowflakes across the paths of those disembarking from the train. No one noticed the plain-faced woman carrying a traveling bag into the depot. Once there, she inquired about renting a livery for her and the small trunk the conductor lifted from the train. She arrived at a nearby hotel where she signed her name on the registry. Lorelda then took the key and climbed to the third floor, entering a suite which had been previously paid for. She immediately unpacked, laying out her best clothes. She spent the next part of an hour dressing her hair and applying her newly gained skills of enhancing her looks. With luck, she'd soon meet the man who had quietly and delicately sought her notice. Being courted by a gentleman of means was the most exciting thing she had ever experienced. No wonder Camilla sought the attention of others, even under her husband's nose. It felt intoxicating!

Lorelda recalled the thrill of being asked to dance by Braegar at Leroy and Camilla's party. He had complimented her appearance, indicating she had grown more attractive at each encounter. A blush stained her cheeks while exhilaration lit her eyes. With surprising glibness, Lorelda found herself telling Braegar about her upcoming trip to Waynesburg, where she planned visiting cousins and shopping for Christmas gifts.

Braegar listened, claiming it a splendid idea. He declared that he too, should adopt her plan. Before their dance ended, he had asked her to think about combining forces, making their holiday shopping more pleasant. He would even provide a suite at a hotel to freshen herself from her travels and have a quiet meal until he joined her.

Too astonished to agree outright, Lorelda only stuttered a promise to consider his offer. For days, it consumed her thoughts. She savored the idea of a tryst, even if it only meant an afternoon stroll on his arm. There'd be no harm, she reasoned. Braegar had always been a gentleman, his conduct faultless and his conversations polite. He had never acted improperly, even with Camilla who obviously fawned over the rich bachelor. How Leroy failed to recognize his wife's behavior was beyond comprehension. It was obvious to her how Camilla fed her ego seeking notice of every available male.

Lorelda couldn't point to a time Braegar had expressed any desire outside expected decorum. And yet, it went beyond conventional manners to invite an unmarried woman to a secret rendezvous. When she finally realized it was her company he sought instead of Camilla's, her yearnings won out. Yet, it took days to gather courage to undertake such a wanton thing.

She had written a sealed note, passing it to Leroy to give to Braegar, claiming it her holiday gift suggestions. And, Leroy mustn't read it lest it spoil her surprise. It was, in reality, her travel dates and times.

She received a missive two days later with the name of the hotel in which a suite had been rented. He agreed to meet her that afternoon where they would wander numerous shops before dining together.

It wasn't until Lorelda heard a key in the lock that she realized she hadn't been sure he'd actually come. She looked down and gasped, realizing she was only clothed in her chemise. With more aplomb than she felt, she hurriedly donned a robe before the door swung open.

☙❧

Reagan sat at his desk, turning over the thorny issue of Elizabeth's child. He knew he must consider Amanda's fears if he were to regain her good graces.

Yet, he struggled with any solution that included forsaking Gaeran's adoption.

Once again, he relived the day he had gone to Lars. Upon learning of Elizabeth's death, he'd felt an overwhelming desire to protect that which was—or could be—his. Now, that core impulse threatened the existence of everything he loved.

A crushing helplessness overcame him until from the depths of his despair, a tiny thought emerged. Once taken hold, his mind bandied it about until it blossomed into a full course of action. He opened a desk drawer and withdrew pen and paper. He wrote swiftly then folded and stuffed the missive in an envelope before heading out.

On the way home, he decided he would use the excuse of the holidays to carry out his plan. He wasn't certain it would solve his problems, but his marriage couldn't continue as it was. Once in place, he prayed Amanda wouldn't perceive it as a final act of betrayal.

chapter 35

"TELL ME," AMY said, massaging Miles' hand. "Where is it you call home?" The cramped pantry allowed little room for them or the stools on which they sat. With knees touching, Amy concentrated on her duties to keep from relishing her proximity to the handsome doctor.

"I grew up in Orwell, in Ashtabula County."

"Orwell? Is that a city?"

"It's barely a village, so I'm not surprised you haven't heard of it."

"What was it like growing up there?" she said.

"Unremarkable. Chores included chopping wood, feeding chickens, weeding the garden and other unpleasant tasks. Father insisted I work at neighboring farms to learn their trade and to keep out of trouble. Oh, and did I mention chopping wood?" he said. "I hated that."

Amy laughed. "Yes, you did. I think I'd have loved it. I wasn't allowed to roam outside or get dirty.

If I wasn't taking school or music lessons I was learning how to walk, how to talk, how to cook and sew. Do *this*, don't do *that*," she said, drawing her mouth into a pinched moue. "If I had to take care of myself, I'd probably perish from ignorance."

"Don't lament your upbringing. I've known many who would've traded places at the crook of a finger."

"Mayhap," she said. "I suppose one always wants what another has." After a few moments silence, she spoke again. "What made you decide to become a doctor?" When he didn't answer, Amy glanced up, catching him staring at her mouth. She dropped her gaze, rubbing with renewed vigor.

"Easy!" he said, flinching.

"I'm sorry, but this is how Doctor Turner showed me."

"Field doctors have more tenderness," he said darkly. "I think you're secretly enjoying this."

"And, you're nothing but a bellyacher." A grin curved her lips, though she remained on her task. "So please, tell me how you came to be a doctor."

Miles sighed. "If you must know, my father's a country doctor. As a child, I often went with him on his travels. Since many of his patients had four legs, not two, I became well-versed in diagnosing and treating animals. Afterward, we'd discuss various cases, human or otherwise. I found I enjoyed it.

When I got older, I started volunteering my own observations and remedies." He shook his head. "Then, I got too big for my britches. I thought myself smarter than my father and told him so. It wasn't until he insisted I defend the rationale of my theories that I realized how little I knew. So, I applied to medical college, graduating just as the War broke."

"Was it difficult? The War, I mean."

"More than I imagined. My training didn't prepare me for the reality of battle. It felt overwhelming. In order to save some, we had to ignore the rest."

"What do you mean?"

"With hundreds brought in, we assessed each soldier, determining those who had a chance over those who didn't. The most likely to survive were those whose injuries we could amputate and then sew up. We had no cure for anyone shot in the vitals."

"Could nothing be done for them?"

"We gave morphine to the dying and sedatives to those who could wait. I tried not to think about it. But, I've often wondered if I misjudged their injuries."

"You're only human," Amy said softly. "I'm sure you did the best you could under the circumstances."

"Maybe," he said, grimacing. "But, not likely. I've dreams that say otherwise."

Forgetting her task, she cradled his hand. "I'm so sorry! It must've been horrible."

When his expression remained somber, she abruptly changed the subject. "You told Dwight you'd been hit by a rebel bullet. Is that true?"

"Very deft," he said with a chuckle. "But, you're right. Another topic is in order."

He then cleared his throat, sitting as upright as the short-legged stool allowed. "What exactly would you like to know?"

"If what you said to Dwight was true. You'd been shot by a rebel?"

"The rebel part was. I just didn't tell him it was by the very one I'd been tending."

Amy's eyes widened. "How's that possible?"

"Our infantry stumbled upon a band of rebels trenched between two mountain ridges. We exchanged fire until most fled, leaving their dead and injured. I'd been tending the wounded when one shot me for my trouble. He'd hidden a pistol beneath his body."

"But, you were only trying to help him!"

"I believe his last words were, 'Damn Yankee, go home!'"

"*Last* words?"

"As soon as his gun discharged, my assistant shot him dead."

"How fortunate 'twas only your hand!" she said. "You could've been killed!"

"You're right," Miles said. "I had just knelt down and was reaching for a bandage when his gun went off. The bullet pierced where my...uh, lap had been."

Unbidden, Amy's eyes dropped to that area and she blurted, "That would've been awful!"

"More than you know," he said, grinning.

"Oh! I'm so sorry! I didn't mean—*that!*" Flustered, she bent to her task. "Let's continue, shall we?"

He sighed. "If we must. But, I think you've done enough for one day, don't you?"

"Doctor Turner said—"

"What Turner doesn't know won't hurt him. My hand's much improved." He wiggled his fingers. "See?"

"That's because we've been working it," she said. "We've no choice but to continue." She turned his hand, palm up. "If you need a distraction, tell me what Doctor Turner's decided for the new building."

Miles braced himself as she applied pressure to his index finger. "He's designing a floor plan which includes bathrooms and latrines on every floor. I also gave him your suggestion of a dumb waiter for the kitchen and a separate one for the dispensary."

Amy nodded as she worked. "It's more efficient. We're constantly running up and down stairs with food, medicines, and supplies. I've heard he's considering a laundry room. Is that true?"

"Complete with boiling caldrons, washboards and ironing tables."

Amy paused. "Will there be a linen room?"

"What would you prefer?" he asked.

"Well, if there's shelving or cabinets, it'd be more convenient if it's all in the same room."

"I'll be sure to mention it."

If Amy meant to thank him, the moment was lost when the door suddenly opened and Polly stood immobile, mouth agape. "Oh, excuse m-me," she said, stammering. "I came to fetch more salt for Cook."

Miles appeared equally flustered to be caught in the pantry. He leaned back, while waving his free hand. "Please, get what you came for!"

Polly reached in, scooping up the jar. "I'm sorry to interrupt—"

"This isn't what it seems," he said. "Doctor Turner ordered rehabilitation on my hand. This is the only spot of privacy to be had. I pray you won't spread any gossip?"

"Of course not, sir!" she said, clutching the jar. "I won't tell a soul." She abruptly turned then shut the door.

"I think you've scared that poor girl out of her wits," Amy said. "Ever since her mistake with the diet card, she's acted like a frightened butterfly."

"I hadn't noticed," he said, wincing. "Aren't you about done?"

"Not yet," she said. "As a matter of fact, you've half the female population of this hospital mesmerized."

"W-what?" he said. "That's preposterous."

"Haven't you noticed how Mallory moons over you? She follows you around like a puppy."

"Her assignments are in the laundry room," he said. "I don't know what you're talking about."

Amy laughed, her eyes a molten chocolate. "Well, I've noticed how often she visits the linen closet when you make your rounds. And, most of the kitchen staff whispers about—"

"That's quite enough, Miss Burnsfield. I've enough on my mind without having to worry about such trifles. And, as a matter of fact, I think we've done enough for today." Rising, he attempted withdrawing his hand while Amy refused letting go. In the close confines they bumped roughly and she became unbalanced. Reflexively, Miles grabbed her arms, pulling her upright and against his chest.

For several seconds Amy found herself staring at lips so close, she only had to lean forward to touch them. Startled at where her thoughts led, she looked up, catching his amused regard. "Oh!" From the recesses of her mind, she heard a voice telling her to pull away. Yet, she stood immobile as Miles' amusement turned to something else. His eyes dilated and his breath deepened as he slowly closed the gap. The shock of contact was nothing compared to the sudden warmth flooding her insides. As his lips moved over hers, she thrilled at his nearness. His hands burned a path up her back until he compassed her with his arms. The realization that she was kissing her supervisor finally sank in and Amy leaned back, eyes wide. "Doctor Alexander!" she said breathlessly, "We mustn't!"

"Mayhap, it's time to call me Miles," he said, chuckling as he released her, "as we've just had a *thorough* introduction."

Amy's cheeks burned bright red and she felt near suffocating. "This—this, oh!" She reached for the door, but stopped, keeping her back to him. "I trust that we'll never speak of this and in fact, shall forget it ever happened." She then opened the door, exiting with a swish of skirts.

Miles bent over, placing the lid on the forgotten liniment. "Well, Miss Amy" he said to himself, "we mayn't speak of it, but I guarantee I'll never forget!"

chapter 36

REAGAN'S RESOLVE TO implement his plan grew with each passing hour. By evening, he determined that not only would Amanda accept his decision, she would agree. Well, not right away, he reasoned, but eventually. Their marriage remained in peril until they resolved this, and he'd be damned if he'd lose his family without a fight.

He had cleared Amanda's calendar, writing hasty notes of cancellation to be sent, and then informed Maisy and Olga of his plans. After swearing them to secrecy, he instructed a chamber maid to pack a small trunk for her mistress. And then, taking a deep breath, Reagan sent a servant to tell Amanda he wanted to speak to her in the library.

The mantel clock had chimed the nine o'clock hour before the door opened and Amanda swept in. "Aida said you needed to see me," she said, frowning. "Couldn't it wait until we'd retired? I was bathing Jesse."

"Olga's just as capable. Besides, I needed to speak with you before then." In reality, he feared their voices would carry into the nursery. And if there were disagreeable words, it would be better to have them away from prying ears. "Would you please sit?" He then took a chair beside her. "I've been thinking about what you said about Gaeran. I'm sure you remember since we discussed it in this very room."

Amanda nodded, clasping her hands. He saw interest spark in her eyes. "I do."

"And do you remember asking me to *fix* this problem?"

"Of course," she said. "What've you decided?"

"First of all, I want you to know how much I love you and Jesse. I also realize this adoption has caused a breach between us." Amanda's eyes were riveted on Reagan, and she looked as if she held her breath. Still, she remained silent, waiting. He had prayed she'd somehow relent, saying how sorry she was for putting him in this position. He had hoped she'd realized it his duty to do what was best for Gaeran. But her jaw stayed shut.

"I'm going to do whatever it takes to preserve our family," he began. His heart increased tempo as he threw down his gauntlet. "So, I've decided we're going to Lars. To the orphanage—"

Amanda's breath caught. "Lars? Are you mad? Didn't the mayor find out about the baby?"

"Yes. Mrs. Seymour wrote that Sam came, demanding to know his grandson's whereabouts. However, she refused to reveal the adoptive parents."

"Everyone knows Elizabeth died in Lars! We might as well announce we adopted her child! Besides, we've plans for the holidays. We can't possibly leave."

Reagan had braced for resistance and kept his tone level. "Madam, I'll ask you to remember these walls are not so thick and we're not alone in this house. Kindly keep your voice down." He stood, his temple pulsing erratically. "We're going. I've already cleared our calendar and wrote apologies to be sent, tomorrow. Your bags are packed. Olga's coming also, since there'll be times it won't be convenient to have Jesse with us."

Amanda's visage battled between anger and curiosity, with the latter winning out. Her voice calmed, though her tone remained tense. "I know I asked you to fix this. But, going to Lars is too obvious. Someone will put two and two together."

"I thought of that too. I've told the staff we're taking a holiday in Pittsburg and Olga won't say otherwise."

"But, Reagan, why are we going?"

Reagan turned to stare at the fireplace, thrusting hands into pockets. "I've decided to let you choose what's to become of Gaeran. The only stipulation is that you must see what I saw. If you can show me where I erred in my decision, then—then I'll consider other arrangements for the child."

Had Amanda seen the sorrow on his face, she may've understood Reagan's pain in placing this power into her hands. She couldn't know the battle he had waged before coming to realize that without her support their marriage would fail.

He sensed her nearness moments before she placed a hand on his back. "I understand. Thank you," she said.

He hoped she would speak words of comfort. That she consider all options, even keeping Gaeran. But, she didn't. She left, shutting the door on her way out.

Long after the household settled in their beds, Reagan stood before the fire until it crumbled into embers. Though his decision seemed the only logical choice, the heaviness in his heart indicated there'd be no good outcome for the child named Gaeran.

chapter 37

"SO TELL ME, my dear, when did you meet Leroy and Camilla?" Braegar patted Lorelda's gloved hand, tucked beneath his arm.

"I've known Camilla most of my life," Lorelda said, her gaze sweeping the sidewalk on which they trod. "My father represented her parents in a land dispute when we were children. Although it wasn't until Camilla's coming out ball that we began socializing."

"Ah yes! Your father is Joseph Hargrove. I'd nearly forgotten he handled my parents' estate after they died."

"Were you very young?" Lorelda asked. "That must've been a difficult time."

Braegar's cheerful expression turned thoughtful. "I was in my teens. And, yes, it was hard losing them both."

"I'm so sorry," she said with obvious sympathy. "How'd you cope?" She knew what it meant to be lonely.

"I'd been on summer break from college when my father's heart failed. Within weeks my mother died also. Everyone said it was from a broken heart."

"Such a tragedy! I'd have been devastated."

"That was long ago," Braegar said. "But, it taught me how to bear grief. Not only that, to always seek happiness. It's become my consolation, if you will." His chest expanded and he smiled handsomely. "As my actions attest, I've replaced those sorrows by seeking out beauteous companions and creating fond memories wherever I go."

Lorelda blushed at the tacit implication. She barely noticed wares displayed in storefront windows. "And you, Mr. Calderon, how long have you been friends with the Speldings?"

"I've known Leroy since primary school. Camilla and I were introduced years ago at a Christmas ball. But, she had so many suitors, I'm sure she barely remembers."

"Camilla seems to have that knack," she said. "That's my first memory of her, as well. But, I don't recall seeing you at any of her balls."

"That's because I'd moved to Chester by then and only became reacquainted with her at their wedding. However, this visit has allowed our friendship to fully bloom."

"How happy I am for you," she said. "I'm sure Camilla's the richer, let alone the soldiers who've benefited from your generosity."

"Bah! Nothing is labor if it's enjoyed." Braegar's brow suddenly furrowed. "It's just occurred to me, you and I should've met at their wedding. Weren't you there?"

"'Twas happenstance I didn't get an invitation," Lorelda said, barely glancing his way. "Camilla assured me I'd been on her guest list. She said she later found the missive had somehow fallen beneath her desk."

"Oh, how regrettable," Braegar said. "I'm sure it was an unfortunate oversight. I consider it my loss, as had you been there, we'd have become acquainted sooner."

She warmed at his consoling words. "You're most kind. It would've been a pleasure. And, I'm happy we're now able to enjoy each others company."

"Yes," he agreed. "I find it refreshing to converse without—" he paused, looking apologetic, "—interference." At Lorelda's questioning look, he continued. "My dear, it hasn't escaped my attention that Camilla often controls our conversations. It would be ungentlemanly not to abide by her wishes." He chuckled at her widening eyes. "I am, however, a man of my own mind. If I wish to know someone better, that's my decision."

Lorelda's heart fluttered, her eyes misting. "It's my wish, too."

"And look at our opportunity," he said, smiling. "There's none to hinder us or anyone to mistreat you."

"Camilla wasn't always this way. There were times she treated me well."

"My dear, you needn't defend her. I've seen how she uses you. And yet, I'm a guest in her home. It's not my place to rein her in. That's up to her husband."

"Leroy's too soft hearted, and she can be quite determined."

"It matters not. As I said, I'm here to enjoy life's pleasures. If an opportunity arises I don't deny myself. Besides, my acquaintance with Camilla has its benefits. Because of her, we've become friends—ally's—of sorts." He looked amused at her expression. "Have I shocked you, my dear? I'm being frightfully blunt. But since we only have today, I'm dismissing formalities in order to make the most of our time together."

Lorelda looked into his handsome face, realizing she fell short of the beauty he'd surely been accustomed to. "Why me?" she asked, lowering her gaze. "I'm no one of importance."

Braegar's expression softened as he lifted her chin. "Everyone has something to offer," he said. "I see value when others don't. So no more talk of you not being important. Camilla has no idea what an asset you are." He slowed as they came to an intersection, guiding her across the street and onto the next boardwalk. "Let's not talk of disagreeable things. We're here to shop and enjoy ourselves."

Braegar stopped in front of a hat shop window, perusing the colorful display. "Speaking of shopping, which do you prefer? I think the derby with feathers, don't you?"

Lorelda caught her breath. Indeed, among all the hats, he had chosen the most beautiful. She leaned in, noting the abundance of lace accentuating the curled feathers. "I agree," she said. "That one's the most beautiful."

"Let's go in, shall we?" Braegar had already turned toward the door. "I'd like a closer look."

"Oh, that's not necessary," Lorelda said. "I've only money for Christmas gifts."

"This is my treat," Braegar insisted, opening the door wide. "Come. Let's see how it looks on you."

As soon as they entered the store, a smiling, middle aged woman stepped forward. "Welcome. How may I be of assistance?"

"We'd like to see the ladies derby with purple feathers."

"You've exquisite taste," the proprietress said, lifting it from the display. "As you can see, it's made from the finest wool, dyed deep purple. It's designed for both strolling and coach attire." She turned the hat, describing each adornment. "The brim has two rows of ruffled, netted lace framed with gimp braid. See the crown's black floral lace? It's designed to form a trailer. On you, madam," she said, eyeing Lorelda's height, "it'll gently sweep your shoulders." With a knowing smile, she continued. "The braid banding the crown is French Passementerie. And as you see, these feathers curve sideways and toward the front, accenting the purple flower from which they're attached." She pivoted the hat with a flourish. "Completing its beauty is a floral bow attached where the trailer begins."

She then proffered the hat. "It'd greatly please me so see how madam looks with it on."

"So would I," Braegar said. He removed the stick pin and hat she wore while the owner placed the new hat on a suddenly blushing Lorelda.

"It's so ornate. It mayn't match my dress—"

"Nonsense!" the woman said. "It's a beautiful contrast against your gray cloak."

As Lorelda viewed herself in a mirror, the proprietress deftly inserted a black pin. She then stood back. "I must say, you do justice to the hat, madam."

"Indeed, she does," Braegar said, withdrawing his wallet. "We'll take it." Within moments the purchase had been completed. Lorelda felt conspicuous in the stylish hat as they once again gained the boardwalk.

She carried a hatbox in which the hat she had previously worn had been wrapped. They visited many shops, making purchases and conversing about those whom each knew. By the end of the day, Lorelda was thoroughly smitten. Conversation ebbed and flowed around events and mutual friends. She felt her importance rise at her ability to provide Braegar understanding of all that had transpired since he moved to Chester.

With reluctance, Lorelda realized they were returning to the hotel where their purchases had been sent throughout the day. Braegar had been a perfect gentleman, even insisting they share a final meal before parting. As they entered the hotel's dining area, Lorelda felt a twinge of sadness her glorious experience would soon be over. It entered her mind that she had a room until tomorrow. She was a woman who had never experienced a man's attention or touch. And she wondered what it was like. As they looked over the menu, Lorelda contemplated whether or not she too, should create fond memories which could last a lifetime.

chapter 38

EARLY THAT MORNING, Reagan and Amanda boarded the train with Olga and Jesse. They traveled south to Warren where they then boarded a train heading west. Reagan paid for a sleeping car for Amanda's comfort and a place to retire when Jesse became hungry. It wasn't until the train approached Tiffin that he announced they would spend the night in a hotel rather than travel all night.

After making inquiries in the depot, Reagan had their baggage taken to the nearest hotel and arranged for two suites. Once the nanny was settled across the hall and with a crib, he returned to his room.

Closing the door, he observed Amanda struggling with the laces at the top of her ankle boot. "Here," he said, hunkering down in front of her chair, "allow me." He brushed away her fingers and worked the knot apart before loosening the laces and removing her boot.

Amanda closed her eyes and wriggled her toes. "Oh, that feels so much better. I've worn these before, but they seem unusually tight."

"We haven't traveled since you've had Jesse," Reagan said, unlacing the other boot. "I hate to be the bearer of bad news, but Mother swore her feet grew larger after having me and more so with Amy."

Amanda's eyes popped open. "Are you saying they'll grow bigger with each child?"

Reagan chuckled. "I'm not saying that. It's just what Mother said happened to her." After removing the other boot, Reagan pulled a chair close and sat down, lifting a stocking covered foot into his lap.

"I'm just going to massage away the soreness," he said when she eyed him warily. Although spoken in truth, Reagan knew he wouldn't reject any opportunity to undo their estrangement. That she even tolerated his touch was a victory.

Whatever Amanda intended to say was lost as his fingers began working in a circular motion, causing instant relief. Sighing, she again closed her eyes. For several minutes she basked in pleasure, grateful for his ministrations.

Almost without realizing it, Amanda's other foot found its way into his lap. His fingers seemed to find every sore spot, knowing when to apply pressure and when to gently knead the area. Amanda leaned back, her attention waning until she felt a hand above her ankle. She opened her eyes, surprised to see him looking intently at her.

"Is something amiss?" she asked. She attempted to pull her foot from his grasp, growing confused when he resisted. She halted at the glint in his eye, recognizing that look. "That's enough," she said, pushing herself upright. "I feel much better now."

Amanda stood to rummage through her small trunk. "I promised Olga I'd return to feed Jesse before retiring. Please excuse me." She stepped behind the dressing screen, soon emerging in her nightclothes.

"Olga will let you know if Jesse's hungry," Reagan offered half-heartedly as she removed her hairpins. "Why don't you wait until then? It might be several hours, yet."

Amanda ignored the obvious reason for Reagan's protests. If a scandal broke, she couldn't allow a lapse of judgment to impede her decision. She needed to be clearheaded and certainly *not* pregnant. "I'd rather take care of it and not be awakened in the middle of the night," she said, knotting her robe. "You needn't wait up."

Without further words, Amanda exited the suite. Reagan could hear her soft tap on Olga's door and then voices before everything fell silent. With a curse, he rose, jerking loose his necktie. Desire roiled in his gut, having been whetted from thinking he had gained a measure of acquiescence from his wife.

He removed his shirt before pouring water into the washbasin to splash his face. He knew he couldn't force the issue if she were determined to resist, especially in a hotel with strangers nearby. But as he dried his face, it occurred to him he could make it damned uncomfortable.

Reagan strode to the fireplace, grabbing a poker. With precise movements, he spread apart logs and shifted ash around. As a precaution, he hid the small wood rack under the bed. He next stepped to the window, opening it just enough to allow a draft. It wasn't long before the air began to cool. He then blew out the lamps, leaving the dying fire the only illumination.

He smirked as he undressed and slid between sheets, being sure to take the side closest the fireplace. Amanda would have to choose between cuddling up to her very willing husband or freezing on her side of the bed. Pulling the covers toward him, he then waited until he perceived she had returned.

With his back to the fireplace, Reagan heard Amanda poke the fire then pace the room, obviously looking for the hidden wood. After hearing an audible sigh, he opened his eyes just enough to see her round the bed and remove her robe. Carefully, as to not wake him, Amanda gingerly lifted the sheet and climbed in. True to his speculation, she lay as far away as the mattress permitted. Yet, it wasn't long before he felt her groping for the covers. If the quilt hadn't been snugly tucked beneath his arm, she would've gained its warmth. Yet it resisted her tugging. Again, she lay still as if attempting to sleep. After several interminable minutes, he felt Amanda shift closer.

Reagan knew his body radiated the heat she wanted as she'd often claimed in happier times. So he waited patiently, feeling the room grow colder by the moment. Slowly, as to not disturb him, Amanda scooted backward until her rump just touched Reagan's thigh and her back grazed his chest.

Sighing in pretend sleep, Reagan's arm casually draped over Amanda's waist, bringing the warm cover with it. He felt her stiffen, but when he didn't move otherwise, Amanda slowly relaxed. She then burrowed beneath the warmth of his arm, wriggling contentedly.

Feeling her so close, Reagan's heart thumped in his chest. He fought the urge to seize her, instead bringing his knees forward until his thighs lay against hers in an intimate embrace. With only the thin shift between them, Amanda could certainly feel his arousal. But, thinking him asleep, she nestled into her pillow and softly sighed. Within moments, he heard her even breath as the warmth of his body lulled her to sleep.

Almost of its own volition, his hand sought a warm breast, cupping it loosely. Yet when nothing happened, his fingers ever so gently began exploring its contours. The idea of forced ravishment abhorred Reagan, but his lustful cravings drove him to edges of husbandly persuasion. Like a man long starved, he couldn't resist sampling the banquet set before him. Yet, it wasn't enough to fondle his wife. He wanted the gratification only a woman soft and willing could give. Applying gentle pressure, Amanda's body turned toward him, her lavender scent assailing his nostrils with heady sweetness. It wouldn't be ravishment, he reasoned, if the feast could be mutually shared. All the better, if he could awaken the appetite of the main course.

With infinite slowness, Reagan plucked the buttons of her gown until her bodice parted. Reaching inside, his fingertips traced a circular pattern over an areola, causing a sudden puckering. When no shrieks of protest burst out, Reagan raised himself just enough for Amanda to roll onto her back, exposing her mouth. In the dim light, he could just see her parted lips and leaning over, tested their softness against his.

Amanda resisted rising from the tentacles of sleep as she basked in a sea of sensations. Caught in a dream, she envisioned herself holding Jesse as he nursed contentedly. But something kept grazing her mouth and Amanda roused herself just enough to brush it away.

Beneath her fingertips, she felt manly stubble covering a face directly over hers. Confused, Amanda turned toward the form in an effort to make sense of what was happening. She came suddenly awake when she realized her shift, now near her hips, was moving even higher and something warm and wet came into intimate contact with a bare breast.

Gasping, she was suddenly consumed with a wave of ardor that left her temporarily helpless. Before she knew it, Reagan managed to wrest the gown from her, leaving no protective barrier. "What—wait," she said, struggling to sit up. Yet her efforts were useless as she remained pinned to the bed, parrying against hands that knew her vulnerabilities and took full advantage.

Amanda was shocked that Reagan dared such an overture while she slept unawares. Yet, she resisted screeching her objections; fearful someone might burst into the room. Instead, she tried commanding her treasonous self to ignore his seduction by sheer dint of will. However, with his weight nearly upon her and nowhere to retreat she couldn't regain control of the situation, let alone her traitorous impulses.

In an effort to thwart his obvious intent, Amanda pressed both hands against his chest. But she found them suddenly trapped above her head with one sweep of his hand as he continued his assault with his mouth. Her body rebelled against her resistance, causing white hot desire to flood her loins as Reagan's tongue became a firebrand against her skin.

If Amanda thought drawing her legs up would impede him, she soon discovered her error. Her movements allowed him closer access as he expertly positioned himself between her thighs. The sudden pressure *there* made her writhe in near ecstasy and she involuntarily arched against him. "Reagan," she rasped, "wh-what are you doing?"

Reagan's mouth caught hers in a possessive kiss before whispering back, "I'm making love to *my wife*." He moved against her sending fervent shock waves throughout her body. "And," he muttered thickly, "she's loving me back."

Amanda shook her head in denial even as Reagan lifted her unresisting hips to accommodate his position. This treachery by her own body vexed her. She'd foolishly thought she could resist his charms by keeping her distance and spurning his advances. She now realized the folly of her reason.

Her breath became ragged when she felt his probing shaft moments before it thrust fully inside her. As his hard belly pressed against the softness of hers, Amanda knew there was no turning back. With intentional slowness, he moved, causing unbearable shards of pleasure to pulsate in quickening waves until soft whimpering escaped her lips.

Once before, she'd been at odds with Reagan, denying his husbandly rights. She had first refused then freely gave herself because she had been the only one to consider. But that was before Jesse. Before Gaeran.

She willed herself to ignore this raging hunger, this assault on her senses. It became a battle she was destined to lose as her body's demands overwhelmed her ebbing will. Suddenly, Amanda couldn't stop herself from joining him thrust for thrust as urgent need overpowered her judgment.

They sought mutual fulfillment as Reagan's mouth slanted over hers, his tongue parrying in equal tempo to their bodies. It became a joining. A blending. They were husband and wife. Man and woman. Lovers, straining and cleaving as one. Against all logic, Amanda felt a burgeoning, primal urge to be completely possessed, her hands traversing the length of his powerful back until claiming his rounded backside.

The impact of her hands urging him deeper sent Reagan's senses into blinding ecstasy. His lips broke from hers and his breath became a torch against her neck, increasing his frenetic rhythm. When he convulsed with blessed release, Amanda's body tensed rapturously then exploded into a thousand bits of unbearable pleasure.

At last, they lay spent; she felt lips brush hers in a languid caress. "That, my love is exactly what we needed," he said, enjoying the subsiding sensations of love play. With infinite tenderness, Reagan shifted Amanda until she lay against his hard chest, wrapping her in an intimate embrace.

The room had become lit with a thin shaft of moonlight, affording Amanda the sight of moving curtains against the window. Long after he'd fallen asleep, she laid awake, wondering which destiny lay in store. Neither staying nor leaving would deter a scandal. How could she choose rightly? It was obvious she couldn't sustain bitterness or even indifference when it came to her husband. Without that protective barrier, leaving her marriage would take a terrible toll. Yet, staying would certainly cause irreparable damage for Jesse's future. Cradling his hand with hers, she quietly wept.

chapter 39

AFTER LEROY RECEIVED the signed contract between Braegar and Beauregard, he promptly turned it over to his father, Ezra. The elder had fully intended on completing the contract with his signature. However, an unexpected interruption had left it on his desk, unsigned. His secretary couldn't leave it unattended and upon spying the folder, decided Ezra's partner could just as easily finish the process. And so he gathered the papers and entered George Bruester's office.

"Excuse me, sir," he said. "But, Mr. Spelding's left for the day and I overheard him say these papers needed signed then filed at the courthouse. Would you be available to look them over?"

"Of course, Mr. Rawlins. Do come in," George said. "Ezra left after receiving a message his wife had fallen. She may've broken an ankle."

"Oh dear, I hope she'll be all right," Rawlins said, laying the contract down. "It'd be a shame to be abed this time of year."

"I agree. Now, what do we have?" he asked, picking up the papers.

"I'm not sure. Leroy brought them in." He looked a little sheepish. "I never intend eavesdropping, but since my desk is outside the office, I overheard him say something about Paradis Pavillon. I'm assuming it has to do with our recent loan to Mr. Barrington."

"I see." George looked through his bifocals, scanning the contract. "I think I know what this is. It looks as if Mr. Barrington is receiving a bit of additional assistance from our friend Braegar Calderon." He flipped to the last page where there were already two signatures and one empty line marked *banker*. He smiled as he lowered the contract. "Thank you Mr. Rawlins. I'll be sure to have this ready before I leave today."

"You're welcome. I'll be sure to file it first thing in the morning."

After Rawlins left, George began with the first page, reading swiftly. Flipping the page, he nodded to himself, mentally checking each requirement. As he neared the last page, however, a frown began to form and he reread one sentence three times. He furrowed his brow as he flipped back a page to reread its contents as well. He tapped his fingers, ruminating on the meaning of the default clause as well as the obscure way it stated the due date.

Shaking his head, he decided it wasn't his place to question a contract already signed by both parties. He picked up his pen and held it over the page. Still, he couldn't bring himself to sign. George then read the contract once again.

"This can't be right," he muttered. "I must be misunderstanding something." He set down his pen, and then looked at his watch. *It won't hurt to wait one more day, he thought. I'll run this by our bank lawyer tomorrow.*

రిం∞

Camilla spent the morning in the drawing room decorating the table-top Christmas tree with silver foil, pine cones and spun glass. She spent an equal amount of time looking out the window for Braegar's arrival. When she spied the livery conveyance coming up the drive she hurried to prepare tea. She had just set down a tray of scones, jam and cucumber sandwiches when Braegar was ushered into the drawing room.

"Good afternoon, my dear," he said, approaching. "You look exquisite."

Indeed, Camilla had taken particular care to look her best. Her hair, loosely gathered in a hair net, curved gently against her nape. She wore an ecru gown with double ruffles across her bosom and spaced, twin ruffles undulating near the hem. Wide, pagoda sleeves overlaying a white flounce enhanced her slender wrists, which rested against a tightly cinched waist. Camilla appeared like a golden angel, standing in front of the mantel where firelight encircled her with a tawny aura. She knew how beautiful she looked for she had practiced this pose many times in front of her mirror. She needed to be irresistible. With Braegar's recent absence, she had made up her mind. She couldn't bear life without him.

Camilla extended her hand. "I'm so pleased you've returned," she said. "I've prepared refreshments." She then sat on the sofa, patting the cushion beside her. "Please, won't you join me?" She poured two cups of tea, handing one to Braegar. She waited until he took a sip before dropping all formalities.

After glancing toward the door, she leaned forward, speaking low. "I'm going to leave Leroy. I want out of this marriage."

Braegar smiled, looking bemused. "My dear, I'm certainly the last person to give you marital advice. But, do you think it wise? I mean, wouldn't it arouse suspicion to do so now? Mayhap, you could wait until spring, long after I've left. You wouldn't want to cause a scandal."

"I cannot!" Camilla said, urgency creeping into her voice. "I loathe my husband. I can't bear his touch." She boldly laid a hand on his knee. "You can't leave me here. I'm begging you to take me with you."

"What if you later regret your decision and wish back your secure life?"

"I have no life," she said. "Anything's better than being chained to that—that *bore* the rest of my days."

Braegar sighed as he shook his head. "I must warn you, some have branded me a cad. I admit to being a feckless fool around women. You may want to reconsider knowing I make no promises of a future."

"I'm not asking for a betrothal," Camilla said. "Those are things one decides later on." She dared touch his cheek, running a thumb over his lips. "We'd take plenty of time to decide our future."

"As usual, you've a wanton means of persuasion," he said. "I fear a dangerous combination, you and I."

Camilla smiled in triumph, her hand dropping. "Not dangerous. Powerful. We can do anything, together."

Braegar looked at her intently. "If you do this, there'll be consequences. Once a reputation is ruined, especially for a lady, it's near impossible to recover. I hope you understand what you're choosing; what'll likely happen."

"If I'm gone from here, it won't matter. I now realize what I've been missing. Besides, you may yet decide I'm worth keeping." Camilla had earlier decided if she couldn't claim him outright, she'd thwart all interlopers. Men were to be manipulated. Rivals crushed.

"I hope you realize I'd no intention of destroying your marriage. If I'd have known, I would've resisted your charms. I don't want to be responsible for ruining anyone's life, not even Leroy's."

"You didn't ruin my marriage. You just made me aware how awful it is."

Braegar sighed. "Still, I couldn't bear to see his face when he learns you're leaving and right after Christmas! Perhaps, to avoid ugliness, you could stay for a time with your parents. I'll return to Chester and you choose when and how to break the news. That way, we aren't accused of playing Leroy false. At least, we should spare him that."

Camilla's eyes flared. "I don't *want* to wait. Why should I?"

"I'm not saying you must. I'm only thinking of what's best. The bank has yet to finalize my loan. It'd be a blow to the Barrington's if our actions caused the bank to decline my offer."

"I don't care! I'm suffocating here," she said, mewling. ""If you feel anything for me, you'll do this."

Braegar lifted her fingers, bringing them to his lips. "Allow me to think about it. Let's wait until the loan's secure, and then find a way to do this without undo pain. Leroy's still my friend and I wish him no harm. Perhaps, by then I'll have thought of a solution that'll satisfy everyone."

"In the mean time," Camilla said regaining her teacup, "I need another vial of sleeping potion. I hope you'll have it ready tonight." Her eyes warmed as she took a sip. "I've missed you."

Braegar shook his head. "My dear, you've a voracious appetite. I'll have it sitting just inside my door on top of the curio cabinet by the time dinner's served. In its proper dose, it should last until I leave for Chester."

Camilla nodded. "Thank goodness for remedies from nature."

Braegar reached for a scone, slathering it with jam. "My dear, goodness has nothing to do with it."

chapter 40

REAGAN'S CALM COUNTENANCE belied the turmoil roiling his gut. Both he and Amanda had been ushered into Mrs. Seymour's office. Having been there once, and now sitting next to his wife, he thought the room especially cramped.

Mrs. Seymour entered with a tray, setting it on her desk. "Good morning, Mr. and Mrs. Burnsfield," she said as Reagan rose to his feet. "Please, do sit. There's no formality here."

She poured a cup of tea, handing it to Amanda. "It's a pleasure to make your acquaintance, Mrs. Burnsfield. Your husband's a man to be admired, coming to our rescue as well as Gaeran's. We're grateful. With the War, it's difficult finding resources."

Amanda nodded. "Reagan told me about your situation. We're glad to help."

Mrs. Seymour poured a cup for Reagan before sitting. "I understand this isn't a social visit," she said. "I'm happy to answer your questions and then

I'll give you a tour. I hope you're not easily distressed, Mrs. Burnsfield. We do our best, but I must warn you, you'll witness various forms of suffering."

"Suffering?" Amanda looked taken aback.

"Unfortunately, yes," said Mrs. Seymour. "I won't beat around the bush. We're ever battling maladies common to needy children. Yet, even if we're fortunate enough to ensure a sound body, their poor hearts are often mangled."

Amanda's hand rose to her throat. She looked at Reagan.

"I believe you had some questions for Mrs. Seymour," he said gently.

"Yes," she said, fingering the locket around her neck. It held a lock of Jesse's hair. "I—I wasn't expecting Reagan to adopt Gaeran. I mean, we hadn't agreed upon that option. I thought Elizabeth's family should've been contacted first. I need to ask why they weren't."

"I see," Mrs. Seymour said. She opened a desk drawer and pulled out a file. "I kept this nearby after learning of your intended visit." After adjusting her spectacles, she opened the folio, perusing its contents. "Ah yes, I remember now." She looked at Amanda. "Mrs. Burnsfield, I don't know what you've discussed with your husband, but since you're here to learn the truth, I'm going to tell you all I know." She turned piercing eyes toward Reagan. "Is that permissible?"

Though dreading this moment, Reagan felt resolute. "Please. Feel free to explain everything. I want nothing kept from my wife."

"Let's start with Elizabeth," Mrs. Seymour said. "Miss Hampton came to the orphanage inquiring how one placed a child. At the time she was quite ill. Soon after, she summoned me to her deathbed. She let me know she'd written to a person she believed would come at her request. I understand your husband received that letter." At Amanda's nod, she continued. "Elizabeth made me promise I wouldn't place her child for a period of time unless it was to whom she'd written. I felt duty bound to honor her wishes. But frankly, I was surprised anyone responded."

Amanda took a sip of tea. "I understand Elizabeth had been staying with her aunt. Why didn't she raise the child?"

"That would be Emmaline. The woman is elderly. Even if she had the energy, she didn't have the funds. The child would've ended at our door eventually. Elizabeth must've realized this because she insisted I take Gaeran."

"Did Elizabeth say why she contacted my husband and no one else?"

Empathy etched Mrs. Seymour's face. "No, Mrs. Burnsfield, she did not. In fact, I didn't know the letter's contents until your husband showed me.

I can only surmise Miss Hampton did what she thought best for her child."

"What would've happened if Reagan hadn't come? Wouldn't Gaeran have been adopted by now?"

"That's a good question, Mrs. Burnsfield. I can only give you the facts as I know them." She again opened a drawer, pulling out a large binder. Unwinding the lacings, she withdrew a thick stack of paper.

There was silence as Mrs. Seymour scanned the top page before setting it in front of Amanda. "This particular child had been rescued from the poorhouse. His parents could no longer feed him. Unfortunately, by the time we took him in, he'd developed tuberculosis. Thankfully, we kept him isolated and from infecting others, but he soon succumbed to the disease." Amanda had barely skimmed the notes when a second sheet covered the first. "This young girl had been placed a few months ago. Afterward, I found out the woman of the house beat her. We took her back and thought we'd found another home where she could work as a domestic. All she'd wanted was the opportunity to attend Sunday school. My supervisor discovered the new family refused to take her to church with them because of her pockmarked face. Even worse, they tried to pawn her off on another household because she was, in their view, too ugly."

The shock on Amanda's face didn't stop Mrs. Seymour. She placed another page in front of her.

"This is a list of young boys who had to be separated from bigger boys." At Amanda's questioning look she said, "When existence seems unbearable, it's not uncommon for those angry at life to prey mercilessly on younger ones. As hard as it is to leave children at the mercy of some adults, it can be worse to leave them subject to older kids angry at their fate."

The headmistress placed a hand on the remaining pile. "Illness is a constant problem. Scarlet fever, tuberculosis, measles, we've had them all. I count blessed every child who finds a home, even though most end up indentured on farms or working as domestics."

"What of the babies?" Reagan asked, although he looked at Amanda.

"Unfortunately, we lose more than we place, Mrs. Burnsfield. The longer they're here, the more likely they'll get sick. I'm comfortable saying Mr. Burnsfield likely saved Gaeran's life. He was thin and not responding well when we received him. May I ask how he's fairing now?"

"He's thriving," Amanda said, pulling a hanky from her sleeve, daubing her eyes. "I had no idea. My mother volunteers at Children's Aid Society in Cantonsville. She's never mentioned such circumstances."

"If I were a betting woman, I'd wager it's not good business to herald challenges of the human condition. Our goal is to place children in homes, not raise them in institutions. I'm sorry if I've upset you, Mrs. Burnsfield. I understood that you needed truth, unvarnished."

"Those poor babies," Amanda said. "How can it be?"

"I don't know how it is in Cantonsville, but here in Lars, infants are last to be placed. Most who adopt do so because they need apprentices or farm hands. Only families with means can afford children that can't give in return. Unfortunately, these poor little ones are the hidden casualties of war." She then stood. "If you're ready, Mrs. Burnsfield, I'd like to show you our humble establishment."

chapter 41

SAM PACED THE length of his study, frequently stopping to gaze at his watch. After what seemed hours, he heard a soft rap on the door. "Come in!" he said, pocketing his watch.

"What did you find out?" he said to the one who entered.

Rosa, Sam's cook for many years, studied his face fearfully. "Not much, sir. I visited cousin Lucia, just like you asked. But she didn't recall Miss Elizabeth ever spending the night or even visiting last summer."

"Did you tell her it was right before Camilla's birthday party?"

"Yes sir, just like you said. I told her Elizabeth mentioned she intended helping Camilla plan her party. But, Lucia said she would've known if Camilla had an overnight guest."

"What of the party? Were you able to get the guest list?"

"No sir. Like me, Lucia's a cook. She could tell me approximately how many people attended and what she served. But, she never had access to any list. Even if she had, it would've since been thrown away."

Her gloved hands worried the edges of her cloak. "Will that be all, sir?"

The mayor turned away, gripping the back of a chair. "You may go." Long after the door closed, Sam's mind roiled. He knew from Elizabeth's diary her lover had been married. She knew he planned attending Camilla's party, which meant he was likely among her circle of friends. Knowing she hadn't spent the night at Camilla's, he now knew which night she apparently had her tryst. However, without that guest list, he couldn't determine the culprit. He'd simply have to ask Camilla herself.

He didn't care how odd it seemed, or how curious. He knew he risked that others would infer why he was prying into Elizabeth's past. The only thing that mattered now was inflicting the same pain he felt. If he didn't throttle the bastard to death, he'd leave him in shambles. A married man, once exposed, would find his marriage over and his reputation ruined. That, he could do. *Would* do, he swore, slamming his fist against the chair.

❧❧

"I vow, that's too bad!" he said, peering into the looking glass. "I weren't a bad looking feller, but now I'm done in." He touched his swollen, gun-shot cheek. "By gosh, there'll be a thunderin' scar! What'll my intended say when she sees me?"

Miles took the mirror, handing it to Amy before applying a salve. "We'll not fret about that now," he said. "Let's work on healing you first." He placed gauze over the wound, finishing by rolling a strip of cloth around his head, pinning it in place. Of necessity, it covered one eye. "Once a scab forms, we won't have to wrap you so and you'll have use of both your eyes."

Wilber looked at Amy with his one eye appealingly. It was apparent he wanted a woman's point of view. "If your intended's sensible, I'm sure she'll honor your wound as proof of your bravery," she assured him. "I think a scar's the finest badge a soldier could wear."

He nodded, though still uncertain as Amy picked up her tray and followed Miles into the hall.

"I want to thank you for taking Polly's place," Miles said, pausing beyond the door. "She sent word of her absence only minutes before she was to report for duty."

"It's no trouble. I enjoy seeing the men's progress." Suddenly, Amy felt her throat constrict as she realized how close together they stood. Ever since *that kiss* she felt guarded around Miles. It wasn't that she found him unattractive. In fact, just the opposite was true. But, not knowing his intentions, she chose to avoid all but the most seemly behavior. "Am I finished?" she asked.

"No, we've one more. He's a recent arrival. He's been placed with the seriously wounded."

"Isn't that Doctor Turners ward?"

"It is," he said. "But, since I tended Caleb when he first arrived, he's asked for me ever since."

"Under your care, I'm sure he'll be fit as a fiddle."

"I'm afraid not," he said. "Despite his small wound, I've no hope he'll survive."

Amy looked perplexed. "You don't mean he must die? If he's survived so far, he surely has a chance, doesn't he?

"He got shot in the back. A man less strong would've succumbed by now. It's to his detriment that youth and vitality has kept him alive thus far."

"But, why send him here if it's hopeless?"

Miles lowered his voice. "He wasn't expected to live. He was being sent home for burial. When the wounded arrived and he was still alive, they brought him with the others. He'll be sent the rest of the way home when it's—it's—over."

"Isn't there anything we can do?" she said. "Can't we at least make him comfortable?"

Miles shook his head. "He has broken ribs and his lung's been pierced. To breathe is torment. I can't ease his pain since he must lie on his back or suffocate. I'm afraid it's going to be hard 'til the end."

Amy swallowed the lump that threatened. "Does he know? I mean, that he won't—"

"I haven't told him," Miles said, sighing. "He's been so brave. I haven't the heart to take his hope of going home to his family." He then touched her shoulder. "If it's too difficult, you don't have to do this. I can tend him myself."

Amy would've broken down if not for having learned to bottle tears for solitary moments. Instead, she stiffened her back "Of course, I'll come. It'll be a privilege to meet Caleb."

"Then smile when we go in. Who's to say what'll happen? It's not only medicine that cures." At her questioning look, he said, "These boys pine for mothers and sweethearts. They pine for home. You become their substitute when you give tender care."

Before she could respond, Miles opened the door to the next room. Though the room was brightly lit, it felt somber as the wounded lay silent, occupied in suffering. Amy realized it lacked the jocularity of other wards with men in various states of healing.

A moan could be heard as Doctor Turner peeled off a bandage from a soldier's festering leg. So intent on his job, he didn't turn to greet the two entering the room.

Miles approached a bed, laying a hand on a young man's shoulder. "Caleb, I'm here to change your bandage."

Turning his head, Caleb smiled weakly. "Good morning, Doctor," he said, his eyes rising to meet Amy's. He seemed to study her as she took in his pensive eyes and hair flung wildly over his brow.

Miles squatted down and slowly lifted him to a sitting position. "Caleb, I'd like you to meet Miss Burnsfield. She's going to assist me today."

"Hello, Caleb," she said, smiling. "I understand you've just arrived."

"Yes'm," he said as Miles unwound the bandage from his torso, dropping the cloth into a bucket. Miles next peeled bloody gauze covering a jagged hole inside a purple-black bruise. It revealed ribs too thinly fleshed for a full grown man.

"I'd been told I was going home when they first got me on the train," Caleb said conversationally, "but they must've decided to keep me here a spell. I think being knocked around in those confounded ambulances worsted my injury."

"Are you ready?" asked Miles, opening the bottle containing liquid bromine.

Caleb drew up his legs and leaned forward, placing forehead against knees. "Yes, sir." He braced himself as Miles cleaned the area before applying bromine directly onto the wound.

Amy watched as Caleb gave no outward sign of suffering until she noticed tears rolling down his cheeks. He looked lonely and forsaken, and her heart heaved in her chest. Setting down her tray, she knelt, gathering him in her arms and whispered, "Let me help you bear it, Caleb." Only then could she feel how rigid he held his body to keep from crying out.

Once Miles covered the wound with gauze and plaster, Amy handed him a fresh roller, helping re-wrap Caleb's torso. Then together they assisted their patient onto his back. "I hope that's better," she said.

Gratitude laced with pain, filled his eyes. "Thank you, ma'am, it's just what I needed! I'm sure I'll be fit as a fiddle in no time."

Suddenly, Amy felt near choking. Excusing herself, she fled to the laundry room where she released hot, pent up tears.

chapter 42

AMANDA'S THOUGHTS HAD spun in circles since leaving Lars. They had boarded the train and traveled east where she knew they would stop for the night in Tiffin. Any outrage she may've felt at being reminded of her husbands' transgression had been forgotten amid her memories of the orphanage. She could scarcely erase the vision of babies crying or lying listless in tiny beds. Having imagined large airy rooms where toys abounded, she instead walked through cramped wards where dirty diapers and illness odors lingered despite abundant use of vinegar scrub and placement of lavender packets. That conditions were worse than her husband described made her nauseous.

At the time, she had said little, avoiding Reagan's eyes as he anxiously watched her reaction to every revelation. They toured the home while Mrs. Seymour described their daily routine, pointing out areas where Reagan's benevolence improved living conditions. The children's hopeful looks of being rescued tore at her heart. Disappointment showed clearly in their eyes as the couple continued past. More than anything, Amanda felt ashamed. Ashamed that she had been so wrong, that she'd acted so outraged at Gaeran's adoption. She now knew it was the only thing Reagan could've done. In fact, had he not, it would've proven him heartless.

Amanda rode for hours, insisting on holding Jesse even when he became restless and Olga offered to take him. She held him fiercely, kissing his brow with tear stained lips. It wasn't until reaching the hotel in Tiffin that Reagan took the babe. "Amanda, you're exhausted," he said, placing the sleeping child the nanny's arms. "You need rest."

"But, what if he wakes and needs me?" she said, watching Olga enter her room.

"Olga will come for you," he said, unlocking their door. "She's across the hall. I've ordered dinner to be sent to our rooms so you can relax until then." After the porter deposited their luggage, Reagan shut the door. "If you'd like, I'll have a bath drawn. It'll help you sleep."

Amanda stood, her head lowered. "Oh Reagan," she said, bursting into sobs. "I can't believe how stupid I've been!" She felt strong arms cradling her as she buried her face in his chest. "I'm so sorry!"

"Hush," Reagan whispered, rubbing her back consolingly. "You didn't know. How could you?"

"I'm evil! All I thought about was how it would affect me—Jesse—I never once realized Gaeran would've perished there!"

She heard him chuckle. "Milady, I've considered you many things, but evil isn't one of them." He lifted her chin, wiping her tears with his thumb. "I'd rather think you're an intractable mule, perhaps."

"That's not much better," Amanda said, sniffing. "You're implying I'm a stubborn ass!"

"Well, I'll admit you got the stubborn part right." He then kissed her nose. "And, if you don't cease your weeping, the staff will think me a cad. Now, cool yourself while I hang our clothes in the wardrobe."

Obediently, Amanda entered a side room where a porcelain tub stood next to a commode furnished with basin, pitcher, washcloths, soap and towels. On a shelf rested shaving mug, razor and strop. Pouring a quantity of water, Amanda wetted a cloth before pressing it to her cheeks. She dipped the rag twice more before daring a look in the mirror. "I look horrid," she said, observing her red, swollen eyes. "What must you think of me?"

"I think you're a tender hearted woman who's had her sensibilities stretched," Reagan said, finishing his task. He then stood in the doorway, leaning against the jamb. "I'd thought to shield you from the raw conditions I'd found. Maybe, if I hadn't, you wouldn't have had to see them for yourself."

Amanda looked at her husband with new eyes and a rush of emotion. "I should've been grateful you saved Gaeran. I should've trusted you. I can't imagine anyone surviving those conditions, let alone a baby. Can you ever forgive me?"

"I thought you'd never ask," he said, reaching for her. They embraced just as someone knocked on the door. "There's our supper. Should I ask for a bath?"

"Yes, but please make sure there's plenty of firewood. I about froze last time we slept here." She didn't understand the mirth in his eyes or his sudden burst of laughter as he went to open the door.

chapter 43

"HOW NICE TO see you, Mr. Hampton," Camilla said, extending a cup of tea toward her guest. "Had I known you'd intended to visit, I would've asked Leroy to delay going to the bank. With Christmas only a week away, I'm sure he could've gone in late."

She sipped from her cup, glancing at him over its rim. Though a smile curved her lips, her eyes were lit with curiosity. She couldn't wait to discover why he came to see her when he had never done so before. She desperately hoped it had something to do with Elizabeth.

Sam sat ramrod straight, his cup forgotten in his hands. "I—as you know, I lost my dear Elizabeth recently."

Camilla forced sympathy to knit her brow. "I'm so sorry for your loss," she said, setting down her cup. "Leroy and I were great friends of Elizabeth. We were devastated to learn of her death." Well practiced tears formed beneath her lashes. "If there's anything we can do, we'd consider it our duty."

"Why, yes—yes, there is," he said, looking relieved. "I do have a favor to ask."

"Anything. Anything, at all," she said. "What can we do?"

"Well, this may sound odd," Sam's eyes flicked about the room, "but, I—I want to t-thank Elizabeth's acquaintances. I mean, she always spoke so highly of her friends, and—and now that she's gone, I want them to know how much they meant to her."

Camilla hid her disappointment, smiling brightly. "I'll be sure to pass that on to Leroy. It goes without saying, we miss Elizabeth very much." She studied his face while taking another sip. "Unless, of course, there's anything else?"

Sam's cup rattled against its saucer and he promptly set it down. "As a matter of fact, there is," he said. "You see, I wouldn't want to omit anyone who I mayn't know about. And, as she'd mentioned all her friends were invited to your birthday party, I'd hoped you could give me your guest list. So, I can thank them individually, that is."

Camilla's eyes narrowed. She'd heard of his recent drinking bouts and so wasn't surprised his appearance bore the marks. His eyes had become mere slits above pale, sunken cheeks. The fleshy jowls, recently shaved, boasted nicks from hands that obviously shook. The puzzle piece that didn't fit was his agitation. A grieving man who spoke of thankfulness wouldn't appear so *angry*. Something was wrong. Suddenly, Camilla was very, very interested.

"Which list do you mean? Surely, you don't mean the one from last year?"

Sam gripped his knees tightly. "That's the one. I'm sure you've since invited different friends and it'd be awkward if I approached someone who didn't really know my Elizabeth."

"That was before I married," Camilla said thoughtfully. "Mother did most of the planning, including invitations. I wouldn't suppose she'd still have that list after all this time. However, I could probably write down who I remember being there. Would that be sufficient?"

"Very much so," he said. "It's important I thank everyone; even if they didn't seem overly friendly or who may've been married. My daughter wasn't in the habit of discussing her friends and who she may've grown close to."

Camilla heard a nearly imperceptible sneer in his words. Her mind flew to the swirling rumors of Elizabeth running away because of a lover. All at once, it made sense. Sam seemed to be searching for reasons his daughter left. Or, was he looking for reasons of her death? She simply had to know.

Camilla rested a hand against her throat. "Please, tell me," she said, her voice quivering, "was

Elizabeth upset with me? Is that why she left? If I did something wrong, I'd never forgive myself."

He shook his head. "I'm sure you weren't the reason. She hadn't felt well and thought a visit away would do her good."

Camilla scrutinized this tidbit. She dare not question if Elizabeth's had actually been ill, knowing what that might imply. She chose a circuitous route. "Still, I can't help but wonder if she felt poorly due to some hidden sorrow. My Aunt Edith, God rest her soul, died of melancholy after Uncle John died. The doctor said she just pined herself away."

"Sorrow?" Sam looked at her sharply. "Tell me! Did Elizabeth ever mention being upset about anything?"

Her eyes rounded in innocence. *He'd just eliminated a nervous ailment.* "Oh no! She seemed quite happy. I'm sure I supposed wrong. Please forgive my imprudence."

The mayor nodded. "In that case, I'm back to my original question. Did Elizabeth mention someone she had grown close to? An exceptional friend, perhaps? Someone I can thank for being so—so *good* to her."

Camilla felt a prickling along her neck when Sam's eyes grew malevolent. Triumphant she knew what the mayor sought; she dared one more probing question. She leaned forward, almost holding her breath. "Should I be recalling anyone in particular?"

chapter 44

"THANKS FOR COMING on short notice," George said as he ushered Reagan into his office. "I understand you and Amanda just returned from Pittsburg. I trust it was a nice vacation?"

"Yes, it was," Reagan said as he took a seat in front of George's desk. "I came as soon as I opened your letter. Though it stated you wanted an immediate audience, it didn't give a reason why."

George closed the door before sitting. "Ah, yes. I'm afraid that was purposeful." He folded his hands on the desk. "I'm in a difficult situation," he said. "A situation no banker wants to find himself in."

Reagan's curiosity piqued. He couldn't imagine a circumstance his upright father-in-law wouldn't know what to do. "What can I do to help?"

George opened a folder, taking out what appeared to be a contract. "There are strict rules of conduct when it comes to privacy between banker and lender," he said, laying the contract on his desk.

"Even in situations when we're not the ones loaning the money but facilitating between parties." He cleared his throat, looking uncomfortable. "As long as the terms are agreed to, it's not our place to object. However," he said, again clearing his throat, "until the contract's been signed by all parties, it's not binding."

He then stood. "Reagan, I'm going to step out of my office. I'll be gone for several minutes. As I've advised you, I'm not at liberty to divulge what amounts to a private act between two parties. As you sit here, *unattended,* I trust you'll remember my words." Mopping his brow, George walked to the door and then spoke without turning. "When I return, I'm going to ask you if there's anything you'd like to invest in. If so, as co-owner of the Bruester Bank and Trust, I'll arrange an expedited transfer of funds."

After George left, he couldn't see the astonished look on Reagan's face. Nor could he see that within moments Reagan snatched up the contract and began reading.

ॐ

Camilla could hardly contain herself throughout dinner. It felt an eternity until she could give Leroy his evening tea with sleeping potion. Once he dozed in his bed, she hurried down the hall, knocking softly. Without waiting for a response, she entered, rushing into Braegar's arms for an ardent kiss.

"You'll not believe who visited today!" she said as Braegar lifted her in his arms.

"Does it matter?" he asked, allowing their combined weight to fall into bed. "I doubt we've much time."

Camilla propped herself on one elbow, staying his parrying hands. "Yes, and don't worry. I gave Leroy a heavy dose. He won't wake 'til morning."

"In that case," he said with a laugh, "I'll bite. Who was it?"

"Mayor Sam Hampton, that's who, and you'll never guess what he wanted!"

Braegar sighed heavily. "It seems we must play your game." He too, propped himself on an elbow. "You may tell your story, but be warned," he said, running a hand over her hip. "I'll not listen for long."

"The mayor requested I reconstruct the guest list for my birthday party. Not this year, but *last* year's party. He's coming for it tomorrow."

"Why is that important?'

"It's the last party Elizabeth attended."

"It doesn't signify," he said, his gaze dropping to her bosom. He plucked at the ties, exposing bare skin. "I've more important things to think on. Namely, how I'm going to please you."

"It's significant," Camilla said, "because he gave me a way out of my marriage."

Braegar stared, temporarily forgetting the lacings. "How?"

"Of course, he didn't come right out and say so, but I believe he's searching for the reason, or more accurately, the person who forced Elizabeth to leave."

"I don't understand. How does that free you?"

"With my artful questioning, it became obvious Elizabeth had to leave. At least, the mayor believes she became involved with someone. A male someone, if you know what I mean."

"Are you saying it was Leroy?"

"I don't know, but I'd certainly implicate him if it helped my cause. All I'd have to do is say he'd been giving Elizabeth undo attention. The mayor will likely do the rest. Once it gets around Leroy was the reason for Elizabeth's departure, no one will condemn me for leaving him. In fact, it'd likely be expected."

Braegar looked at Camilla thoughtfully. "Was the mayor drunk?"

"Well, he looked a little unkempt, but he was sober. Why?"

"I never told you I'd once found Mr. Hampton, very inebriated and thrown from his horse. He'd been to the cemetery. While taking him home he said someone had taken Sammy from him. When I asked him who that was, he said Sammy was all that was left of Elizabeth. I surmised Elizabeth must've had a child because he also said they wouldn't tell him who adopted him. Who *they* were, I can only guess."

Camilla gasped. "Elizabeth had a child? Why didn't you mention this before?"

"Spreading tales is hardly good form, my dear. I didn't see the need for ruining a dead woman's reputation. Had I told you, it would've been all over town by now."

"But, wasn't the mayor afraid you'd tell someone?"

"According to his driver, he wouldn't remember our meeting. He doesn't realize anyone knows his secret."

"This is even better than I'd hoped," Camilla said, laughing. "Don't you see? If Leroy's accused of fathering Elizabeth's child, I'll get my divorce!"

"Do you actually think Leroy guilty?"

"Of course not," she said, rolling her eyes. "He could barely touch me on our wedding night. I had to *teach* him what to do."

"Then why brand him so?"

"Adultery is grounds for divorce. A child is proof of adultery. It's as simple as that."

Braegar lifted Camilla's chin. "That still doesn't make it acceptable for you to leave town with another man. This must be handled delicately. Do you understand?"

"Of course," she said. "But, it doesn't take away the pleasure of getting rid of that ghastly man."

"I don't understand why you married him, Camilla."

"I was bored," she said, shrugging. "And, to be honest, I was jealous of that wench, Amanda."

"Amanda Burnsfield?"

"Yes. I'd almost ruined her reputation when Reagan squelched my fun by marrying her. I needed a diversion, and Leroy provided it."

Braegar shook his head. "My dear, you are an evil woman. I'm not sure if even I should trust you."

Camilla's eyes gleamed as she took his hand, placing it on her breast. "You're not the first person to tell me that," she said, drawing near his lips. "But, you should stop talking now."

chapter 45

EARLY THE NEXT morning, Camilla penned a list of all who attended her birthday party. Since Sam wouldn't come for it until that afternoon, she planned to later go through her clothes, deciding which items she'd take. Afterward, when Braegar provided her an extravagant wardrobe, she'd destroy everything Leroy had ever purchased.

However, her plans were forgotten when Braegar entered the library just as she finished sealing the envelope. His usual good humor appeared absent. "What's the matter?" she asked, rising.

"It seems your Mr. Burnsfield has thwarted your pleasure once again," he said, handing her a missive. "I just received this from the bank. For reasons unknown, Reagan managed to advance funds to Beau before my loan was finalized!"

"What do you mean? How does this thwart anything?" she asked, opening the letter and scanning its contents. "Maybe it's for the best. You mayn't want to do business with the bank once I leave Leroy."

Braegar picked up the envelope containing the guest list. He tapped it against the desk. "Did Reagan attend your birthday party last year?"

"Well, yes," she said, splaying her hands. "Beauregard is everyone's favorite. He livens any gathering. In order to assure his presence, I invited Reagan, who happens to be his best friend. Why do you ask?"

"I don't like being outmaneuvered, my dear. Beau's concept won't bring Paradis Pavillon to its full potential. However, once we became partners, I intended to persuade him to alter his plans."

"I thought you only did this to keep him from default?"

"Opportunities come in all forms. And, I'm not one to waste an opportunity. I only needed time to convince him."

"I don't understand how lending money gets you that," Camilla said.

"Money buys influence, my dear. Once I held his debt, he'd either come around to my way of thinking or find himself the poorer for it."

"Poorer?" Camilla repeated. "You just said you'd both make a lot of money!"

"Either with him or without him, Paradis Pavillon is a potential gold mine. You see," he said at her confused look, "my loan has certain advantages.

Once in place and if not repaid by agreed terms, I'd become controlling owner."

"You mean you'd steal it?"

"It's business, my dear. Not unlike how you plan ending your marriage. By any means necessary," he said, throwing himself into a chair. "I'm not sure how that lumberman got involved, but I won't have it taken from me!"

Any loyalty Camilla felt for Beau crumbled beneath her desire to help Braegar. She rounded the desk, kneeling before him. "What'll we do? This letter says Reagan already made the loan."

"This is where you come in," he said, lifting her chin. "You've raised treachery to an art form. I need your skills."

Camilla smiled wickedly. "What do you want me to do?"

"Delay giving this list to the mayor. Tell him you need more time or that you're indisposed. I don't care what you do; just give me a few days."

"How will that help?"

"I'm going to show Reagan the prudence of selling me his note. And, here's my form of persuasion," he said, holding up the envelope.

"My guest list?"

"I'll tell him if he doesn't cooperate he'll be branded the father of Elizabeth's child. Reagan's history with unsavory women will no doubt provide fodder. Didn't Lorelda say he recently adopted a baby? How convenient! Even he will understand how devastating the accusations will be once that information is given to Sam Hampton."

"Now, wait," she said, frowning. "That's my ticket out. How else will I obtain a divorce?"

"Let's make a bargain," he said, drawing her closer. "There's no reason we both can't benefit. Once Reagan gives me what I want, you can still give this list to Sam." He brushed his lips against hers. "Either way, you won't have to deal with your problems again."

In response, Camilla coiled her arms around his neck, kissing him deeply. In the recesses of her soul, her sense of power grew darker, thicker. Serpentine. It rose like a spring, forming fangs that dripped with venom, looking for a place to strike.

chapter 46

REAGAN NEVER FELT happier. Not only had he gained the good graces of his wife while avoiding tragedy for Gaeran, he had averted what he considered a bad business deal for his friend. After George Bruester had returned to his office, he had taken his seat and as promised, asked if there was anything Reagan would like to invest in.

Answering in the affirmative, George had, with the swiftest of actions, transferred several thousand dollars from Burnsfield and Burnsfield to Beauregard Barrington's business account. He then recommended they wait until after the holidays to mail Beau the paperwork so he had time to inform Braegar his contract had been declined.

With only four days until Christmas, Reagan felt he had already received his gifts. He began opening mail, whistling a tune cavorting in his mind. However, it stumbled to silence when he spied an envelope with a coat of arms. Tearing it open, he read swiftly.

> *Dear Mr. Burnsfield,*
>
> *As you know, I've been a guest of the Speldings while also enjoying frequent visits with our mutual friend, Beauregard Barrington. Due to the fire, I offered an interest-free loan to rebuild the destroyed portion of his hotel, which he accepted. I've just been informed by the Bruester Bank and Trust that while my loan offer was greatly appreciated, you'd already begun paperwork, which superceded mine. I'm puzzled how this came about because he recently signed an agreement with me. Despite this, I've hope we can work out an arrangement that's mutually beneficial.*
>
> *Let me tell you about the day I found Mayor Hampton returning from the cemetery. Sorely grieved, he mentioned something valuable had been taken that belonged to his daughter, Elizabeth. He tried retrieving this item only to find it had been signed over to a new owner. This item is very precious and I believe he'd do anything to recover it. Furthermore, Mayor Hampton asked for my help in its recovery. I'm happy to oblige. My search will begin with anyone who's recently obtained a similar item. Regardless of intent, I'm sure it'll prove ruinous to whoever has it. Once you realize the se-*

*riousness of my endeavor, I'm sure we'll find a way
to settle this matter.*

*I understand you've recently adopted a child.
Congratulations.*

*Yours,
Braegar Calderon*

For several seconds Reagan stared at the signature in disbelief. Amanda's fears had without warning, come to pass. Worse, he'd no strategy to correct it. "Damn! Damn! *Damn!*" he swore, folding and placing the letter in his pocket. He stood, and then abruptly sat down. He had to think!

Reagan frantically searched his mind for any other solution than what the letter implied. However, without knowing the extent of Braegar's knowledge, he couldn't decide. His frustration grew as there seemed no way to avoid capitulating to the blackguard. If he refused, he risked everything.

Reagan's personal ethics of finding the right path had been until now, an easy one. However, this time it seemed he would have to choose between two unsavory evils. Who could more easily survive the brunt of betrayal, his own family or Beauregard?

If he ever doubted Braegar had knowingly constructed an ambiguous, deceptive contract, he no longer did. The bastard had nearly stolen Paradis Pavillon and was now resorting to blackmail to get it back.

Reagan rubbed his jaw. If he refused, he held no doubt Braegar would follow through with his threats. But, why would a successful businessman do such a thing? Reagan recalled vague memories of Braegar being orphaned as a teen and later becoming a successful businessman before moving to Chester. He knew nothing more until they met at Camilla and Leroy's celebration dinner.

Reagan weighed if his family could withstand the revelation it was he who had adopted Elizabeth's child. For months, the scandal surrounding his marriage had set tongues wagging. This would be worse. Social invitations would cease, possibly forever. That wouldn't overly upset him, but it would devastate Amanda. To whom would she visit or invite to tea? Never to be invited where friends and acquaintances gathered would be social death.

Would it also cause cancellations of lumber contracts? Being in business with Thomas meant his parents could suffer too. And, Amy? Just eighteen, what chances would she have of a fitting marriage? Not just his sister, but his children! In sick realization, he knew the worst was yet to come. Gaeran would be branded a bastard. Reagan imagined the taunts, whether from schoolyard or street would be devastating. This wasn't something he could visit upon innocents. He couldn't—wouldn't do it.

The alternative meant he would imperil the future of his lifelong friend. As a lad of fifteen, Reagan had happened upon Beau being thrashed by a pair of tormentors. He had halted the scuffle, but not before blackening their eyes for brutally attacking the smaller boy. Henceforth, Beauregard had considered Reagan his brother, shielding the hard-knuckled lumberjack from slights of others with his razor sharp wit. As their friendship grew, so did their bond; whether hunting or playing cards, both appeared well suited to the other.

If he allowed Beau to be defrauded, he'd be giving Braegar success in whatever evil he planned. Seeing the contract, he realized the man coveted Paradis Pavillon. After reading this letter, Reagan knew the bastard would do anything to get it.

With a heavy heart, he pulled out a sheath of paper and penned a response, requesting an immediate meeting. If he cooperated, he'd insist on drawing up the transfer papers himself. He wouldn't be ambushed again by the shifty coal baron.

chapter 47

"MISS BURNSFIELD?" CALEB touched her gown as she laid a knot of heath and heliotrope on his pillow. His pale face, tinged with gray, shone with moisture. "Would you mind writing a letter?"

"Of course not," Amy said. "Just give me a moment to get pen and paper." Moments later, she had settled in a chair, a tray upon her lap. Having earlier noticed a thin band on his finger she asked, "Shall it be addressed to wife or mother?"

"I'm not so young; ma'am, twenty-five in June, and I've been what you might call settled these ten years, for mother's a widow. As the oldest, it wouldn't do for me to marry until Annabelle had her own home and Johnny a trade. We're not rich and so I had to be father to the children and helpmate to my dear mother." He looked at her wistfully. "But now, I'm thinking God's got other plans for me. And, so I should give my best council as would be expected of me."

Amy stared at the paper, knowing if she glanced at him, she'd burst into tears. "Shall I write to your mother, then?"

"No, ma'am, to Johnny just the same. He'll break it to her best, and I'll add a line to her myself when you get done. I'm hoping to get a response, so I know they'll be okay."

Despite her best efforts, Amy's vision blurred. Only through sheer dint of will did she finish dictating his instructions to his family. After he penned his final words, she folded and addressed the letter, promising to post it that very afternoon.

જ⊷⊰

A light snow began to fall as Reagan entered the darkened interior of River Saloon. He knew of the establishment, for many lumbermen frequented it both before and after a long winter of timbering. With Christmas only days away and many factories closed, the bar had become crowded despite the early hour. He walked between tightly packed tables, spying Braegar sitting at a corner table and smoking a cigar. A liquor bottle and two glasses occupied the center space.

"Greetings!" Braegar said, motioning toward a chair. "Please, join me."

Reagan ignored the salutation, taking a seat across from him. "Your letter got my attention," he said. "Although, I'm not sure what the hell you're implying."

Braegar took the cigar from his mouth. "Getting your attention was my primary goal. And now that I have it, I'm prepared to do business with you."

"I don't make it a habit of doing business with snakes," Reagan said. "But, I'm curious what you have to say, and so I'm here."

"A wise choice," he said. "Did you bring the contract?"

"Tell me, what were you hinting about Elizabeth? That I stole something from her? I can assure you I'm no thief. Besides, I can't imagine the mayor confiding in you, let alone having you search for anything of value. It doesn't make sense."

"Ah, I see we're fishing," Braegar said. "That's understandable. Let me put it this way. You have something I want. I know something you wouldn't want exposed. Something that'll adversely affect those you love. It's in both our interest to make an exchange. Now do you see?"

"I've been exonerated from any scandal you may've heard about. There's nothing about my life that hasn't been exposed," Reagan countered. "I think you're bluffing."

"Everyone has skeletons in their cupboard," he said, smiling. "It just so happens, I stumbled upon one you won't be able to prove isn't yours."

The hackles on Reagan's neck rose. He changed the subject, trying to regain the upper hand. "I know what you tried doing with your loan. You made it appear Beau had five years to pay it off, when in reality, the due date was sooner. If he didn't catch it, he could've defaulted. I also noticed it wasn't clear who then would've had controlling ownership."

"He read the contract. I can't help it if he mightn't have noticed what I said wasn't exactly what was written."

"It was sleazy and underhanded. You took advantage of Beau's trust. I could've convinced the bank to bring charges. However, they wanted to avoid embarrassment, especially since Leroy, whose father co-owns the bank, happens to be your host. You're the one who should walk away, thankful you're not sitting in jail right now."

"I'm protected by caveat emptor," Braegar said, shrugging. "That contract would've been binding; will be binding, once you and I finish our business. Now, do I need to spell out exactly why this transaction is to your advantage? Or, can we simply agree that you've a past that cannot afford to be dredged up."

"I've no idea what you're talking about," Reagan lied. "You'll have to enlighten me."

Braegar drained his glass before speaking. "I've learned quite a bit during my stay. It's enough to turn a saint's hair white. You've been busy, my friend. Your history includes a dead, pregnant strumpet and being forced to marry after a compromising situation. I've even heard you may've had something to do with Elizabeth's disappearance. Revenge perhaps, for her spilling about your arrest by bounty hunters?" He puffed on his cigar, grinning. "In other circumstances, we could've been best of friends."

"The only thing busy has been Camilla's malicious mouth," Reagan said, snorting. "But, of the three you mentioned, two are no longer living and the third is my wife. I'd say you've no witness to testify."

Braegar tapped his cigar against an ash receiver. "Sometimes, a person reaches out from the grave, especially if that someone carried a bastard child."

Reagan felt his composure slipping, yet managed an even voice. "What are you trying to say?"

"Let's just say, I know Elizabeth left town because she was pregnant. I know because Mayor Hampton told me as much. I also know that you've recently adopted a child. Coincidentally, that child's about the same age as Elizabeth's brat."

"And, how would you know that?"

"I don't," he stated flatly. "But, that won't matter once I tell the mayor who was giving his daughter undo attention before she left town."

"You weren't here to witness that fabrication. He wouldn't believe you."

"But, he will believe Camilla," Braegar said. "She's prepared a list of everyone who attended her birthday party last year. You see, he's very anxious to learn who his daughter associated with. In fact, he's actively pursuing the matter."

"There were a lot of men there. How could he know who the culprit was?"

"Camilla will tell him so."

"That bitch!" Reagan spat. "Why would she lie about that? I was a gentleman around Elizabeth as well as every other woman at that party."

"She'll do it because I asked her to. But, more importantly, Sam will believe her."

"You've no proof," Reagan said. "I'll deny anything she says."

"You could," Braegar said, nodding. "But, can you survive the repercussions? Could your family? I don't have to tell you what it'll do to your wife, let alone your children. It won't matter whether or not you're culpable. With your past, everyone will believe it. So, there's really no difference." He leaned back, taking another draw before blowing smoke. "I don't even care that you mayn't be guilty. So you see nothing you can say or do will prevent me from ruining you. That is, if you refuse to cooperate." He allowed his words to sink in. But after several interminable minutes and when he got no response, his pleasant visage turned icy. He pointed to Reagan's jacket, where he noticed a slight protrusion. "Now, is that our contract?"

chapter 48

REAGAN ALMOST DIDN'T hear the question. He suddenly couldn't take his eyes from the cigar pointed at him. Reaching into his pocket, he withdrew folded papers. "I didn't trust you to write the language," he said, tossing it onto the table. "I've already seen how you play with numbers."

Braegar snatched it up, reading quickly. "What's this?" he said, laughing. "You've stipulated the contract isn't binding until my cheque clears the bank?"

"I've every right to protect my investment. Surely, you can understand. You're a liar and a thief. If I'm going to do business with you, I must ensure your money's good. And, since today's Saturday, I can't deposit a cheque until next week."

"I'll grant you that," he said, slapping his hand on the table. "Barkeep! Bring me a pen!"

After the bartender brought a pen and inkwell, both men signed the contract. "Well, my friend, it's been a pleasure doing business with you," Braegar said, pushing a cheque toward Reagan. He then folded the contract and placed it in an inner pocket. "Have you thought of what you're going to say to the bank about this turn around?"

"I'm going to tell them I had a change of heart," Reagan said. "I'm sure they'll think I've lost my mind."

"Just be sure they finalize my original contract. Once that's done and my cheque clears, you and I'll never have to cross paths again."

"Somehow that doesn't ease my mind. What assurance do I have you won't implicate me anyway?"

"As long as I get what I want, you've nothing to fear," he said. "Besides, there's another who can be linked to Elizabeth in your place."

"Why ruin anyone? You have what you want!"

"I do," he conceded. "But, why should you care? It won't be you."

"What's to keep me from warning Beau about the original contract?" Reagan said, unable to tamp his ire. "Once told, I'm sure he'll refuse your assistance."

Braegar's eyes narrowed. "If that happens, I'll do everything I said I would. I'll take great pleasure in destroying you, your wife and your children. Do you doubt me?"

"Not in the least. You're a proven scoundrel," Reagan said, studying his face.

"Yet, I'm feeling provoked to tell Beau he's about to be swindled."

"But, you won't do that, will you?"

Reagan sighed, scooping up the cheque and folding it. "No. If Beau learns anything, it won't be from me."

Braegar nodded while tamping his cigar. "You've made a wise choice. Shall we shake on our accord?"

"I'd rather not, but I'll gladly accept one of those fine cigars," he said. "I don't believe I've tried that brand."

Braegar grinned, pulling one from his inner pocket. "I always keep a spare. Should I light it for you?"

"No thanks, I'll save it for later," he said, tucking it into his pocket. "I don't feel like celebrating right now."

Reagan left immediately. He couldn't wait to visit Sheriff Hadley. Until this moment, all hope of salvaging the situation seemed lost. Now, he desperately hoped what he held in his pocket would answer his prayers. If not, Reagan had just committed a heinous act of betrayal. He'd knowingly abetted a criminal against his lifelong friend.

❧❦

"You say he's blackmailing you?" Sheriff Hadley asked, staring at the cigar Reagan had handed him. "And, this is your proof?"

"No," Reagan said, "that's what I'm hoping you can use to prove Braegar set fire to Barrington Hotel. It looks exactly like the one you found behind the woodpile."

Jim looked at the band closely before opening his desk drawer, pulling out a metal box. "Let's take a look," he said, opening it. He picked up the stub and held it next to the cigar. "Well, I'll be damned! It's the same brand." He looked up. "But, it doesn't prove he's the one who started the fire. Clancy gave me a list of those who regularly purchase these from his shop." He leaned back in his chair. "I even asked for anyone he recalled buying them only once. Braegar Calderon's name wasn't one of them."

Reagan rubbed the back of his neck. "What about Leroy?" he asked. "Braegar could've gotten those cigars from him."

"You know, Leroy's name *was* on that list," Hadley said, opening another drawer. He removed a sheath with the sheriff's neat handwriting. "I put him last on my list to speak to since I couldn't imagine a banker setting fire to a business. However, due to this information, I'll go to the bank first thing Monday morning." He looked up again. "Would you please sit down? I'm getting a crick in my neck talking to you."

Reagan finally took a chair in front of the sheriff's desk. "Forgive my ill manners, but the last time I sat in your office you accused me of murder."

Hadley laughed, running a hand over his mustache. "That I did! And, if I recall correctly you were being blackmailed then, too." He shook his head. "You do have a penchant for getting into trouble."

"This time, I came directly to you," Reagan said. "I expect you to do your job and find me a way out of this mess."

Jim shook his head. "I'm no magician. I won't make promises I can't keep. Besides, just because Braegar smokes the same brand as our pyromaniac doesn't make him the culprit."

"Who else benefited from that fire? It's mighty suspicious, if you ask me."

"Suspicion alone won't hold up in court. You know that, as well as I do. This," he said, holding up the cigar, "is no smoking pistol."

"Well, what are you going to do?" Reagan asked. "I can't let this happen to Beau."

Jim sighed as he pulled a pencil stub from behind his ear. "Tell me everything you know. Let's start with what information Braegar's using to blackmail you. Maybe there's a way to stop him."

Reagan took off his hat, worrying the brim with his hands. "I could find no chink in his armor. I'm afraid we'll need to look elsewhere."

Hadley sat back, looking askance. "What are you saying? Is what he's accusing you of, true?"

"It's possible," Reagan said, shrugging. "I'm not sure. But, for propriety's sake, I'd rather not talk about that until I must."

"Alright," Hadley said, his pencil poised over clean paper. "What can you tell me?"

chapter 49

"DON'T YOU THINK we should call off our dinner party?" Leroy asked, looking out the window. "It's been snowing all day and it doesn't look to abate anytime soon."

"Of course not," Camilla said. "If the storm worsens, Lorelda can certainly spend the night. This is our last gathering before Christmas. Besides, we're celebrating Beauregard and Braegar's agreement. It's fitting we thank Braegar for what he's done."

"My dear, you're acting as if he's saved Beau from certain doom. 'Tis nothing more than a loan to ensure the hotel gets repaired and begins producing income again."

Camilla bit back the retort on her tongue. She despised when Leroy corrected her. Instead, she smiled sweetly as she focused on her embroidery. "You're right, of course. How foolish of me to think otherwise."

Leroy returned to his chair. "I'll be glad once the holidays are over," he said, picking up his newspaper and shaking it open. "Though I've enjoyed Braegar's company, it's wearying being constant host."

Camilla gritted her teeth. *He* wasn't the one who planned their dinner parties. *He* didn't ensure their servants did extra cleaning and laundry. Thankfully, the cook worked full time. Otherwise, she believed Leroy would've expected her to prepare meals as well. With effort, she maintained a pleasant expression, reminding herself she'd soon be rid of the buffoon she had married.

Yet, Braegar's looming departure still unnerved her. He had returned from his meeting with Reagan claiming success. So why were shards of fear piercing her heart? Camilla pushed away the notion; reminding herself her future was assured. Once Braegar got his contract, she wasted no time visiting Sam and handing over the list. As he tore open the envelope, she recounted fictitious examples of Leroy giving attention to Elizabeth. Whenever Sam asked about her married guests, she kept redirecting the dialogue, insisting Leroy spent the most time with her. All at once the mayor blanched, and thinking she had succeeded, wished him well and went home.

"The new year is sure to bring unexpected pleasantries," she said, plying her needle with sudden enthusiasm. "I wouldn't be surprised if our lives improved for the better."

"Perhaps," Leroy said while turning the page. After a few minutes silence, he continued. "It looks like General Burnside embarrassed himself at Fredericksburg. He reported victory before being forced back across the Rappahannock. By all counts, we lost thousands more soldiers than the enemy."

"Please," Camilla said, rubbing her forehead. "It sickens my stomach to hear such things. Must you recount every battle you read about?"

Leroy looked up. "Have you tried tea with bitters? It calms most sour ailments."

Camilla rose. "What I need is to *not* hear about war and death!" She flung her tapestry hoop before heading toward the door. "I'm going to see our guest rooms readied in case we need them." She stopped and held up a warning finger. "It's Braegar's last dinner with our friends. So you best find something pleasant in that paper to discuss."

Long after she had left, Leroy stared at the doorway, struck by her increasingly volatile temper. Before, she'd only grow testy if he pursued his husbandly rights too often. And, that hadn't happened for weeks. *If I didn't know better*, he thought, shaking his head. *I'd say she was expecting.*

❧❧

"We're so pleased everyone could make it," Camilla said, unfolding her napkin. "As you know, Braegar will be returning to Chester after the holidays." She smiled at him and then her guests. "Tonight, we're celebrating his many acts of generosity."

"Hear, Hear," Leroy said, raising his glass. "A toast! Not only for his works of charity, but for ensuring Barrington Hotel will remain sound after he's gone."

Everyone clapped as Braegar waved his hand. "Please, we've already covered this ground. As to the loan, it's temporary. Yet, I'll admit, this devil is looking forward to being a part of paradise. He winked and then laughed with everyone, raising his glass. "Tonight, I want to express my appreciation to Leroy and Camilla for hosting me these many weeks. And," he raised his glass toward Lorelda, "to the friendships I've gained. May they be strong and life long." Lastly, he lifted his glass toward Beauregard. "Finally, I want to salute a man who had a vision I'm proud to be a part of, even if only for a short time."

"A beau jeu, beau retour." Beau quipped.

"Hear, hear," everyone chorused before sipping.

"What did you say?" Camilla asked, setting down her glass.

"One good turn deserves another," Beau said. "I hope to someday return the favor to Monsieur Calderon. Besides repaying him, that is."

"It'll be repayment enough seeing Paradis Pa-villon becomes everything it should. However, if you allow me a suggestion or two, I'd consider it an honor."

"I'm sure Beauregard would be happy to hear you out." Camilla looked at Beau expectantly.

"Of course, mademoiselle." Beau turned to Braegar. "I insist you join me for breakfast at Ange-lo's. Say, eight o'clock? I'll bring the blueprints and an open mind. Would that be agreeable?"

"That'd be splendid!" he said. "I'm humbled by your kindliness. But enough about me." He then looked toward Lorelda sitting next to Beauregard. "My dear, you must tell us about the book I saw you reading in the library. Wasn't it *The Suspicions of Mr. Whicher?*"

chapter 50

"What do you prefer?" Camilla asked, standing at the sideboard where liquors were stored.

"I'll have whatever Leroy's drinking," Braegar said. "He has excellent taste."

Leroy sat near the parlor fire, knees crossed. "I'll have the bourbon, my dear."

"Beau?"

"Bourbon, of course!" he said. "It's a cold night, and the wind's positively foul."

Camilla poured three drinks then offered them on a tray. "You know you're welcome to stay, Beau. I've already readied a room for Lorelda. I'd feel dreadful if you had trouble getting home."

Beau lifted the proffered glass. "It's no problem, mademoiselle. I'll get there long before I turn *se glacer.*"

Camilla next poured two sherries, giving one to Lorelda who sat on the sofa. With reluctance, she joined her since all other seats were taken.

"Now that everything's set, how soon will you reopen Barrington Hotel?" Leroy asked, smoothing an errant lock of hair. "I understand the fire destroyed a large area."

"Oui," Beau said, nodding. "We've cleared debris and have begun reconstruction. However, I'm awaiting confirmation from the bank that my account's been credited before ordering new tables and stoves."

"That's odd," Leroy said. "I would've thought you'd have received the paperwork by now. I'll see about it when I go to work tomorrow."

"Perhaps, it's been delayed due to the holiday," Braegar said, glancing toward Camilla. "I'm sure there's nothing to worry about."

Camilla took his cue. "Let's not spoil the evening with any more talk of business. Why don't you tell how it came to be I got my portrait?" She indicated a painting on the wall. "Everyone will agree it's a more entertaining story."

Braegar rose and stood by the fireplace, gazing at the large, heavy-framed portrait of Camilla standing with one arm casually resting on a banister while the other held a fan low against her skirt. A dress of light blue silk, white bodice and short sleeves accentuated her honey-gold hair as did the colorful, heavily chorded draperies behind her. "It's magnificent," he said, setting his drink near Leroy. "I don't recall seeing it before."

"Camilla's always wanted a portrait," Leroy said, glancing over his shoulder. "I decided to have one made as a gift for Christmas. Unbeknownst to her, I'd taken one of her photographs to a local painter. It wasn't until later; I discovered she hated the dress in the photograph. I knew the painting had already been started so I spirited her favorite dress out of the house and took it to his studio." He chuckled at the memory. "It was no small task. Camilla never leaves home before I depart for work."

"Oh dear," Beauregard said, sipping his drink. "I'll bet that was a quandary."

"It was chaos when she looked for the gown, but couldn't find it. I tried telling her the washerwoman had it, but I finally had to admit I'd taken it myself."

"I thought to wear it for Thanksgiving dinner," Camilla said, her voice strangely sweet. "So, of course, I wanted to inspect it for rips or stains. You can imagine my distress when I couldn't find it."

"Unfortunately, in explaining its absence, I had to spoil the surprise," Leroy said. "So, to make amends, I promised to hang the portrait the moment it was finished and not wait until Christmas."

Everyone turned at Lorelda's sudden laughter. "I beg your pardon," she said, removing her hand from her mouth. "But, that's not quite how it happened." She looked at Camilla with venomous eyes, blurting, "She accused the maid of stealing it."

Camilla's jaw dropped at her exposure. Clamping her mouth, she immediately placed a smile on her lips. "It wasn't as dramatic as all that," she said. "I merely asked if it might've been misplaced." She reached over to pat Lorelda's arm. "It wasn't an accusation, I promise." Withdrawing her hand, she raked her nails over Lorelda's skin. Satisfaction coursed through her when she saw from the corner of her eye, her friend wince. She didn't understand where Lorelda's sudden enmity came from, but she wouldn't tolerate it.

If not for her ability to mask emotions, Camilla couldn't have maintained her pleasant visage or smooth, modulated voice. However, Lorelda knew her too well. She recognized the tamped fury and barely pursed lips. It was worth suffering the hidden assault to finally throw down the gauntlet. Lorelda had finally had enough. She could no longer tolerate the hidden barbs, the veiled slights. Once Braegar departed, she would never again darken Camilla's threshold.

She sensed something was about to happen and Camilla, its agent. She couldn't discern what it was, but it felt hidden. Foreboding. Didn't Braegar once admit his willingness to dismiss formalities if time was of the utmost? Well, so could she.

If possible, she would find a way to warn Braegar. Something was amiss. Lorelda knew the signs. The calculating eyes, the shift of inflection and too wide smile all pointed to a scheme in the making. Rubbing her injured wrist, Lorelda decided she'd use time and tide to speak privately with Braegar. Spending the night, she hoped, would provide the perfect opportunity.

chapter 51

CLAIMING A HEADACHE, Lorelda soon excused herself and retired to her bedroom. Finding stationary in a drawer of her writing table, she scribbled a message and hastily slid it under Braegar's door before returning to her room. She then sat down to read. After another hour, she could hear voices and the sound of a closing door. She peeked down the hall. Despite seeing a light beneath Leroy and Camilla's door, it remained dark under Braegar's. Thinking he tarried downstairs, Lorelda decided she would venture out on the pretext of returning her book to the library. With luck, she'd find Braegar alone.

Lighting a candle, Lorelda made her way downstairs. She walked the hall between parlor and study, glancing into both rooms. Disappointed in finding them empty, she decided to return her book to the library then wait in her room. He would surely come once he found her note. With footfalls muted by carpet, she entered the library. She made her way to the bookcase and finding an empty space, slid the book in its place.

Suddenly, Lorelda heard muffled voices. Fear struck, for she recognized Camilla's soft lilt the same time the doorknob turned. In a panic and without thinking, Lorelda blew out her candle and set it down moments before flattening herself against the wall. She groped backwards until feeling a cold draft, her fingers touching frosty window panes. Just as she slipped behind heavy drapes, she saw two people enter. Camilla and Braegar! Lorelda shrank further back, praying darkness would shroud her. Yet, despite speaking barely above a whisper, their voices could be clearly heard.

"I must know tonight," Camilla said, setting down her candle. "Are you taking me with you or not? I did everything you said. I gave the list to the mayor. I made him think Leroy had been the one fawning over Elizabeth. He'd have to be a dolt not to fathom my words."

"I told you, this must be handled delicately. You can't leave before Sam accuses Leroy of fathering her child. Otherwise, you'll be disgraced. That's no way to start a new life."

"What difference does it make?" she said, clutching him. "I won't be around to suffer their scorn. Besides, after the story gets out, I'll not be blamed for leaving him."

Braegar gripped her shoulders. "Patience, my dear. A reputation is easier kept than recovered. We've already laid the groundwork. Now that Sam has the list and with what you told him, he'll put two and two together. Once he accuses Leroy, you'll be free. That way, both our reputations will remain intact."

"You're playing me false!" Camilla cried fearfully. "Why else would you leave me here? You know I can't stand when he touches me!"

"No, I'm not," he said, at once soothing. "Don't you see? If we're found out, it would jeopardize your divorce as well as my relationship with the bank. We play this right; nothing ends but your marriage. I—we've worked too hard for this. We mustn't ruin it now." He then drew her close, his eyes two lit coals. "Just keep doing what you're doing and it'll soon be over. I promise."

Trembling, Camilla touched his face. "Do you swear?"

"I swear," he said, his mouth hovering over hers. "By the time I leave, you'll know exactly where your future lies."

Between narrowly parted drape panels, Lorelda spied their heated kiss. She felt bile in her throat, realizing how blind she'd been. *How could she have imagined a man would prefer her over Camilla?* Her mind raced over every compliment, every occasion which culminated in that one, glorious day. She had often relived those moments; convinced he had found her worthy of attention. She had been a fool! Not only had Braegar misled her, he and Camilla were plotting a fraud on Leroy.

Suddenly, Camilla broke their embrace and looked around. "Do you smell something?"

Lorelda's heart thumped rapidly as Camilla gazed about the room before spying the snuffed out candle. She held her breath until Camilla laughed lightly. "It's only a candle. Lorelda must've forgotten hers when she borrowed a book," she said, giving him one last hug. "I must hurry. I'm to prepare Leroy's tea."

"Then go. We mustn't take any more chances until he's been implicated with Elizabeth's condition."

The room grew dark after they left. With shaking fingers, Lorelda parted the drapes and stepped into the room. She dared not take her candle now that it had been spotted. And so, with halting steps and outstretched arms, Lorelda found her way to the hall and silently crept upstairs. Once in her room, she wrung her hands, deriding herself for having tucked a note beneath Braegar's door. What excuse could she devise to deflect her rashly penned words? After what she witnessed, she knew the enormity of her miscalculation. She opened her balcony door, allowing frigid air to cool her brow.

Her thoughts were interrupted when the bedroom door swung open. Fearfully, Lorelda turned to face her visitor.

chapter 52

THE DOOR CLOSED with a click. "Where were you just now, Lorelda?"

Lorelda's eyes grew wide. "What do you mean? I've been here. I had a headache, remember?" She took a step back, recognizing fury.

Camilla moved toward her, raking Lorelda with a contemptible gaze. Raising her hand, she struck her hard across the face. "*Liar*! You were in the library. I smelled your candle then saw your fat self hiding behind the curtains."

Lorelda held a hand over her cheek, stunned. "I—I..."

"What's the matter, cat got your tongue?" Camilla stuck a finger in her face. "I caught you spying, you pathetic thing!"

"You'll never get away with it. I won't let you."

"Won't let me what?"

"You—you're doing something bad to Leroy. I heard you!"

"Did you now?" Camilla said, sneering. "All you heard was what Leroy has coming to him. I discovered Elizabeth was his *convenient*. Poor girl, she fled when she learned she was having a child. No one will expect me to stay once it gets around."

"I don't believe you. That's just an excuse to divorce him." Lorelda felt her indignation rise. "It's dishonorable to sully your marriage that way. How you got Braegar involved is beyond me."

"I went to him for advice."

"Advice? Is that what he was giving you in the library?"

"It's none of your business," Camilla said, her hands forming fists.

"It's too late," Lorelda said. "I won't stand by and let you destroy Leroy. I owe him that much. He's always been kind to me."

"You'll say *nothing!* Do you understand?"

Lorelda no longer felt her stinging cheek. She stood a little taller, allowing her disillusions to puddle at her feet. She'd lost once again to beautiful Camilla. Braegar wasn't hers and never would be. So be it. She decided to unleash the one weapon she had left, aiming at Camilla's soul.

"Whatever you granted Braegar, know this," Lorelda said, wiping trickles of blood from her lip. "It wasn't enough to keep him from coming to me. We met less than a fortnight ago. Not only did he proclaim how poorly you've treated me, he bought me a gift—"

"So what!" Camilla said, interrupting. "You're nothing but a pathetic, ugly spinster. I'm sure he felt sorry for you!"

Lorelda's bitterness receded as she recognized who was more pitiful. "Perhaps. But, that's not the impression I got when he spent the night in my hotel room." Lorelda smiled at Camilla's shocked expression. "I'd say you're no less a plaything than I. Once divorced, don't be surprised if you find your lover chasing the next pretty face."

Murderous rage spilled from Camilla's eyes as her worst fears were spoken out loud. "How *dare* you! I could kill you for uttering such lies!"

❧ ❦

Deep into the night, the winds' sharp teeth forged albescent drifts that crested and troughed like a rigid sea. Mournful echoes whistled around corners, rattling doors and windows, causing both man and beast to burrow more deeply into their beds. Outside, widely spaced lamp posts, like sentinels guarding barren streets, bore witness to the swirling whiteness and within their glow, exposed the storms ferocity. At length the squall finally abated, leaving drifts around buildings and across roads. Silence descended as frigid temperatures hardened snow, making travel difficult, even by foot.

In the wee hours of the morning, the town snow warden harnessed horses to home-made snow rollers weighed down with rocks. He began the laborious task of driving through city streets, beginning in the retail district and working his way through residential avenues. As the wooden rollers rotated, they flattened drifts to a uniform height. Later, when the townspeople awoke, their horse-drawn sleighs would easily slide atop compressed snow.

By the time the eastern sky began to lighten, the snow rollers had already driven past the Spelding residence on its way to the edges of town.

Camilla awakened to a low, hoarse sound. *"W-water..."* Rising up, she looked to where Leroy lay beside her. However, it wasn't until she lit a lamp she could see her husband appeared flushed and soaked in sweat.

Alarmed, she hurried to pour water from a pitcher. "Leroy," she said, yanking back covers before holding a glass to his lips, "drink this."

Despite spilling much of it on him, she managed to get some in his mouth. He lay back, staring at the ceiling. "...h—head hurts..."

She next wet a cloth, wiping his face. "What's wrong?" she asked. "Are you ill?" When she got no response, Camilla hurried out the door and down the hall. She knocked on Braegar's door and after no response, went inside. In the early morning light, she could see the room was empty. Instantly, she remembered he'd agreed to meet Beau that morning for breakfast.

She went swiftly to the maid's room and pounded on the door. "Tillie! Wake up!" Camilla kept knocking until she heard movement inside.

The lock clicked before the door swung open. "Yes, ma'am?" the maid said, rubbing sleep from her eyes. "Is something amiss?"

"Go and fetch Doctor Turner. Leroy's ill." Without waiting for a response, she hastened back to her room to get dressed. As she pulled off her nightgown, she glanced at the teacup sitting on the bedside table. *I wonder*, she mused inwardly. *Perhaps, I needn't worry about a divorce, after all.*

chapter 53

SAM HADN'T SLEPT since receiving Camilla's guest list. He had barely listened to her prattle about Leroy, knowing he searched for a married man. He had read the list twice before realizing there was only one male listed who had already been wed at the time of the party. *Reagan Burnsfield.*

Shaken to his very core, Sam had wracked his memory for any hint of behavior that would've validated his supposition. He could recall no untoward conduct while either of them had been in his presence. Besides the gathering he had thrown before elections and their encounter before Elizabeth visited Camilla, there was only one other time Reagan had been in his home. And, that was the dinner where he'd introduced his cousin Bertram to Reagan. Had Elizabeth's suggestion of joining local business with the War cause been more than happenstance? He recalled his own enthusiasm and insistence on bringing the two together. That by itself wouldn't be enough. He needed proof of unsavory behavior.

Could it have been an unknown swain to him and her friends? And yet, he had Elizabeth's diary. There was no doubt the culprit had been married and had attended Camilla's party.

No, it had to be someone he knew.

And then it came to him.

He hadn't really believed the oft-repeated story of Reagan and the murdered harlot, Molly Carnes. Rumors swirled Reagan had been wantonly indecent with the girl, fueled by Clara Farrington's insistence she saw Molly and Reagan depart the same carriage outside the dressmaker's shop. When Molly's body had been discovered inside Reagan's office, Sheriff Hadley had no other recourse but to arrest the lumberman. That the strumpet had been pregnant only added to the salaciousness of the act. However, Reagan had been exonerated once evidence proved Derek Banning was both murderer and father of the child. And, that's what Sam had always believed.

Until now.

He questioned whether anything he had been certain of was the truth. If a man were capable of heinous deeds, how difficult would it be to hide a second affair? Moreover, the results had been the same, Sam thought bitterly. Both women had ended up pregnant and dead.

After Camilla left, he had locked himself in the study. Trays of food went ignored as well as concerned requests he open the door. After two days, Dudley hadn't been able to convince the mayor to leave his study. Had he been able to, he would've been shocked at the blood-shot eyes and unkempt appearance. He would've been further astounded to know the mayor hadn't consumed a drop of liquor.

Sitting at his desk, Sam read the list for the thousandth time. Though his thoughts formed rutted circles, it gave no clear path with which to take. Thus he sat, benumbed. Had it been anyone but Reagan, he thought, I'd know what to do!

Sam rubbed his brow, trying to recall any scrap of evidence that would remove his lingering doubts. He despaired of making a mistake. Perhaps, Camilla had forgotten a guest or two? All at once, a long dormant memory percolated upwards until it burst into his consciousness.

He suddenly recalled overhearing conversation between two guests at a dinner party. One claimed Reagan's father had threatened the owners of Rochester Hotel while the other said he didn't believe the story. And, what was the story? That his son had rented a suite at the Rochester and the old man forced the hotel to kick him out. The mayor had dismissed the account as both men had been well into their cups. It hit him that this was around the time of Camilla's party. How had he forgotten? Surely, this was the proof he needed, the link shackling Reagan to Elizabeth.

All at once, it became clear. He was a father whose daughter was dead. Elizabeth was no less murdered than if Reagan had himself cut her down. And now, deprived of his grandchild, what was there left to live for?

Sam nearly succumbed to a sudden, intense urge to drink. He gripped his knees, beating the craving back through sheer dint of will. He needed to be sober to do what had to be done. It would be soon. If he could never again take pleasure in living, he'd make damn sure Reagan wouldn't be around to enjoy life either.

శ్రాళ

"Let me know if this starts to burn," Amy said as she laid a mustard plaster on the young man's chest. He was among recent arrivals who'd sickened at Camp Chase before reaching the battlefield. "I'll be back to remove it in half an hour."

"Much obliged," Willy said. "Will it make me better?"

"Doctor Alexander says it'll keep your congestion from worsening. We don't want this turning into pneumonia right before Christmas, do we?" Amy pulled a cover over the poultice and then glanced at a watch pinned to her apron. "Try to rest and I'll be back before you know it."

Having finished her immediate duties, Amy turned her attention elsewhere. She pulled one of two wicker baskets from a hall closet where she'd stored them that morning. Filled with different kinds of pines, holly, ivy and mistletoe, she set about decorating walls, doorways and any space soldiers would see. Soon, other nurses lent a hand and the men enjoyed watching their ward transform from drab to a pine-scented wonderland.

Miles watched from the hallway, enjoying his own bit of scenery. Amy had climbed on a chair to hook a wreath on the ward-side of a doorway. With her arms up stretched, she didn't see Miles or his eager gaze as the cloth covering her bosom drew tight, revealing youthful curves. After she had climbed down and with her back to the door, Miles approached, snatching a sprig of mistletoe before stealing away.

chapter 54

"WHAT DO YOU think is wrong?" Camilla asked, her brow knit with affected worry. "This is how I found him when I woke this morning."

Doctor Artemus Turner lit a candle and held it near Leroy's eyes. "How do you feel, Mr. Spelding?"

"Head...hurts...," Leroy rasped, his limbs moving uneasily. "hot..."

"Please unbutton his night shirt." He set aside the candle as Camilla opened the sweat soaked garment. He then situated a stethoscope to Leroy's chest and leaning down, placed his ear on the upturned end. After several moments, he straightened. "I'm not sure what ails him."

He opened his bag and removed an elongated tube. Unscrewing the cap, he tapped out a white powder into a glass and then added water. Swirling until it dissolved, he lifted Leroy's head. "Drink this." Leroy swallowed before coughing weakly. "I know it taste's bad, but it should help." He then turned to

Camilla. "Tell me everything he ate and drank last night." He then listened as Camilla recited his meal as well as his drinks.

"Did you dine alone?" he asked, setting aside the glass.

"No, we had guests. Beau Barrington, Lorelda Hargrove and of course Braegar Calderon who's been visiting these past weeks."

"Did your husband make his own drinks?"

"Everyone had wine from the same bottle. After dinner, I poured the bourbon and sherry."

"Did Leroy consume anything else?"

"Just tea," she said, pointing to a cup and saucer on the side table. "Everyone else ate the same meal. The men drank bourbon and Lorelda and I had sherry."

Artemus lifted the cup and sniffed. He then placed it under the lamp, looking carefully at its interior. "Was Leroy taking Dover's powder?"

"Of course not—I mean—not that I know of."

"Who prepared his tea?"

"I did," Camilla said, pricked with sudden fear. "Is something amiss?"

"I'm not sure. However, I'd very much like to examine the bourbon glasses, if they've not been washed."

"My kitchen help didn't stay due to the storm, so no, they've not been cleaned. I can take you to the parlor," Camilla said, tamping down feelings of panic. She had no idea what the doctor suspicioned, but prayed she hadn't given her husband too strong a dose of sleeping potion.

"No, you stay here. Keep giving him liquids and bathing him with cool water," Artemus said, placing the teacup in his medical bag. "Your maid can show me." He stopped just inside the door. "Did any of your guests spend the night?"

"Lorelda stayed. She's still asleep, though. Beau went home last night. Braegar left early this morning to meet him at Angelo's to discuss ideas for Beau's resort."

"I'll return in a few minutes," he said.

After he left, Camilla paced the floor. She silently prayed the doctor didn't insist on searching the pantry where teas were stored and her vial, hidden. She considered admitting to using the potion with her husband's consent, but soon dismissed that possibility. Assuming Leroy recovered, he'd deny her claim. If anyone suspected foul play, her hope for a favorable divorce would evaporate.

She stopped in her tracks at a sudden thought. What if Braegar feared being linked to Leroy's condition and reneged on their plans? Worse yet, what if Leroy *died*? Would speculation arise that she had somehow been responsible? How then, would it look if she left Cantonsville and moved to Chester? Even she, with all her calculations, couldn't escape the scandal. Camilla cursed herself for not being more careful with the dosage. She could think of no other reason Leroy seemed feverish and weak.

With sudden fervor, she returned to the bed, wetting Leroy's brow. "Rest, my darling," she said sweetly, "and, let me cool you." Moments later, her heart nearly leapt from her chest when she heard from another room, a blood-curdling scream.

Pandemonium erupted as Camilla ran into the hall the same time Tillie bolted from Lorelda's room running straight into Doctor Turner who'd rushed up the stairs.

"She's dead! She's dead!" Tillie said, sobbing. "Miss Hargrove's dead!"

Artemus raced into the room and seconds later ran back out and down the stairs. Tillie collapsed in a heap onto the floor, weeping convulsively.

Abject terror gripped Camilla as she entered Lorelda's room and looked around. The bed appeared to have not been slept in, the covers smooth and folded back. But what struck her most was the bone chilling cold. It hadn't been cold when she entered Lorelda's room last night. *Last night!* Camilla recalled Lorelda's spying in the library as well as her threats. Yet, where was she? Except herself, the room appeared empty.

Feeling a draft from the open balcony door, Camilla stepped onto the snow-filled ledge and looked down. At first, she saw nothing in the morning light but snowdrifts bisecting the brick walkway below.

Upon closer inspection, she saw what appeared to be a hand protruding from a misshapen drift. Moment's later; Doctor Turner skittered to a stop and with both arms, swept snow away, revealing clothing and then, shockingly, Lorelda's body. Brushing snow from her face, he pressed fingers against her neck.

After several moments he looked up, his eyes locking with Camilla's. With a grim look, he shook his head.

And, that was the last thing Camilla remembered.

chapter 55

Sheriff Hadley sat in a chair, pulled close to the day-bed where Camilla had been placed. Covers had been tucked snuggly around her, for despite the newly laid fire and closed balcony door, there was little warmth in the air. She awakened to Doctor Turner waving smelling salts beneath her nose. "Enough!" she said, pushing away his hand. "It's making me gag."

Artemus spoke gently. "Mrs. Spelding, the sheriff's here. He'd like to ask a few questions."

Camilla appeared disoriented as she looked from one to the other. "What?"

Doctor Turner lifted a wrist, feeling her pulse. "You fainted after seeing Miss Hargrove lying in the snow. It seems she's fallen from the balcony. Do you remember?"

"Y-yes!" Camilla's eyes darted around the room. "Where—?"

"She's been taken to my office," he said.

"What happened?"

"That's why I'm here, Mrs. Spelding," Jim said. "We're hoping you'll shed some light on the matter. Do you feel well enough?"

Camilla nodded. "I think so."

Hadley turned businesslike, drawing pencil and paper from his pocket. "Doctor Turner already told me what he's learned. You and your husband had a dinner which included Beauregard Barrington, Braegar Calderon and Miss Hargrove. Is that correct?"

"Yes, it is."

"The doctor told me your recitation of everyone's food and drink. So, I'll only call upon a few specifics," he said, glancing up. "I know this may sound indelicate, but I must ask. Did Miss Hargrove have an inordinate amount of wine with dinner?"

Camilla struggled to sit up, pushing covers to her waist. "She only drank one glass," she said, brushing hair from her face.

"Are you positive?"

"I'm sure of it," she said. "Beau poured it for her."

"And afterward, did she have much sherry?"

She nodded. "Again, one glass."

"I understand Beau departed last night. Do you recall what time?"

Camilla clasped her hands. "It was nine or nine-thirty. We were having refreshments in the parlor. He left about the time Lorelda retired for the evening."

Sheriff Hadley began scribbling. "Tell me, Mrs. Spelding, did you see Lorelda after she retired?"

Camilla appeared to ponder the question, her eyes dropping. "No, I don't believe so. She had a headache and wanted to lie down. Soon after, Beau left and after that, the rest of us went to our rooms."

"Did you hear anything out of the ordinary last night?"

She shook her head. "Nothing but wind. The storm was quite forceful."

"Indeed, it was," Jim said. "And, did any noises wake you this morning?"

"I awoke to my husband asking for water. After lighting the lamp, I could see he'd taken ill. So, I sent Tillie to get Doctor Turner."

"I understand Braegar left this morning for a meeting with Mr. Barrington. Do you know when that was?"

"No. He left before I awakened."

"I see," he said, seeming to digest her words. He didn't speak again until he ceased writing. "I've one last question, Mrs. Spelding. If you didn't hear Braegar arise, and thought him still asleep, why did you earlier tell Doctor Turner he'd already left?"

Camilla opened her mouth, but no sound came forth. She rubbed her brow, knowing she couldn't admit to having entered his bedroom without so much as a knock. "I—I don't know. Maybe in my distress I just assumed he had," she said, looking suddenly anguished and throwing back the covers. "Have we finished? I really must see to my husband." She then looked at Doctor Turner. "Please, could you help me up?"

Artemus held out his hand, assisting her to her feet. "Don't move too quickly until you've become acclimated to standing. We don't want you fainting again."

"I promise," she said. "Will you be returning to check on Leroy?"

"I'll join you as soon as I've answered Sheriff Hadley's questions."

"You won't keep him long, will you sheriff? My husband needs a doctor right now."

"Only a moment longer. Doc assured me your husband's weak, but stable."

"Thank God," she said, looking relieved. "I'd have been devastated had he worsened."

After she left, Artemus glanced at the sheriff. "Do you think it's significant whether or not she knew when Mr. Calderon left?"

"Probably not. But, I've learned if there's even the slightest difference in someone's story, you explore that difference. Mrs. Spelding did seem a little shook up when pressed about it."

"She's entitled," Turner said. "She awoke to an ailing husband and within minutes saw her best friend, dead."

"I suppose you're right. It's enough to scramble anyone's memory."

"Aside from that, I found something you might be interested in since we both want to know what happened last night," he said, moving toward the bed.

"Absolutely." He then stood, placing his pencil behind an ear. "What'd you find?"

Doctor Turner stopped at the bedside table. "I found Miss Hargrove's laudanum," he said picking up the nearly empty flask, "and this." He stooped to retrieve a whiskey bottle hidden beneath the bed. "If Lorelda consumed both last night, she would've been very intoxicated. In that case, she could've easily mistaken the balcony for her bedroom door and plunged to her death. With the storm last night, no one would've heard her scream."

"Are you certain that was her cause of death?"

Artemus sighed as he set both bottles down. "No. I'd first need to examine the body. Also, I'd want to test everything she drank from including these bottles."

The sheriff's brows shot up. "Are you saying she may've been *poisoned?*"

"I'm not saying anything," he said, rubbing his neck. "But, I thought I detected an opiate odor from Leroy's teacup. It made me uneasy because even if he'd ingested poppy seed or wild lettuce tea, he wouldn't be exhibiting all his other symptoms."

"Such as?"

Doctor Turner ticked off his fingers. "Fever, intense thirst, rapid pulse and dilated pupils. Need I go on?"

"What else could it be?"

"I don't know. I never learned of any disease that makes pupils insensible to light. To find out, I'd need to eliminate possibilities of the criminal sort."

"How'll you do that?"

"I'd gone downstairs to examine glasses from the parlor. Thankfully, they haven't yet been cleaned. While doing so, I asked the maid to awaken Miss Hargrove so I could speak to her. Minutes later, Tillie began screaming. I dropped what I was doing and ran upstairs. It's probably coincidental that Leroy took ill the same night that Lorelda had a fatal accident. But still, I'd want to remove any doubt."

"What about the wine glasses? Don't they need to be examined too?"

Doctor Turner nodded. "I'll be visiting the kitchen as well."

"By all means, collect those glasses before they're washed," Hadley said.

"And, let me know if you find anything that points to foul play."

"I will," Artemus said. "I'll ask Doctor Alexander to assist me. In situations like this, two heads are better than one."

Sheriff Hadley laughed. "I think you'd make a formidable team. Unlucky is the man who plots evil of the medical variety."

"Or woman," Doctor Turner said grimly. "Camilla did say she prepared Leroy's tea. That makes her the first person I'd be interested in, if I were you, sheriff."

Jim nodded. "I'm ready to speak with Mr. Calderon now. I had Deputy McCrea fetch him. He should be waiting in the parlor."

chapter 56

"THANK YOU FOR returning so promptly," Sheriff Hadley said as both he and the doctor entered. Braegar, who'd been staring at Camilla's portrait, turned as Jim continued. "Please excuse Doctor Turner; he's become a bit of a sleuthhound for the moment."

"Oh?" Braegar said, his eyes following Artemus as he went to the sideboard. "What seems to be the matter? Besides, the horrible misfortune with Miss Hargrove, that is."

"We aren't at liberty to say. You do understand we're investigating Miss Hargrove's death."

"Of course! Please forgive me," Braegar said, extending his hand. "I don't believe I've had the pleasure of your acquaintance."

Jim shook his hand. "I'm Sheriff Hadley. It's a pleasure to meet you. I'm just sorry it's under these circumstances."

"Me too," Braegar said. "I was fond of Miss Hargrove. I enjoyed her company very much."

Please, have a seat," Jim said. "I've a few questions. It's just a formality, of course." He proceeded once both settled into chairs. "I understand you've been visiting the Speldings for several weeks now. Doctor Turner mentioned your philanthropic work while he tended a prisoner in my jail. Your generosity's commendable."

Braegar waved a hand. "Please, I've been thanked so many times, it's embarrassing. It's been an honor and we'll leave it at that."

"As you wish," Hadley said, pulling paper from a pocket. "Oh, by the by," he said, looking all innocence, "did I hear correctly that you've become involved with the Barrington's due to their recent fire?"

Braegar smiled, seemingly undisturbed. "Indirectly. I read about the fire in the papers. Since we're acquainted and I'm more than able, I offered my help."

"And now, you've become Beau's partner?"

Braegar's eyelids lowered, though his voice remained pleasant. "Sadly, you've been misinformed. It's nothing more than a temporary loan."

Hadley gave him a look of unmistaken meaning. "That seems rather convenient, don't you think? He wouldn't have needed your help if it wasn't for the fire."

"True," he agreed, smiling. "I often find opportunities in unexpected places. It's rather a hobby of mine."

Unable to shake the man's confidence, the sheriff burrowed deeper. "I don't suppose your hobby includes giving fate a little nudge, does it?"

Braegar chuckled, clasping his knee as he propped a leg. "Fate loves the fearless, that's true. I recognized a circumstance and did what anyone in my position would do. Besides, I'm wealthy enough I don't need to cheat."

"But, perhaps, you wouldn't mind a little stratagem?"

"I'm not sure what you're implying," he said, raising a brow. "The paper said a domestic's lamp fell near the woodpile."

"You're right," Hadley said, nodding. "Yet, I'm curious. Wouldn't it have been more fitting if one of Mr. Barrington's associates would've made the loan? I mean, with you being from out of town and all."

"I'm not sure what you mean," he said. "Why would that make a difference?"

"Oh, I don't know, it just seems rather untidy. I'd think he would prefer the known to the lesser known."

"Well, that's where you'd be wrong," Braegar said, tapping fingers on the armrest. "In fact, Beau confided he didn't want money from his friends precisely because they were friends. So you see, I actually fit the bill." Though his tone sharpened, his pleasant visage never wavered. "Is that what we're here to talk about, sheriff?"

"No," Jim said. "Only indulging a bit of curiosity. I'm actually taking everyone's account of last night so I can figure out what happened to Miss Hargrove."

"Yes. Such a tragedy," he said, once again solicitous. "What would you like to know?"

"If you can, I'd like you to describe everyone's food and drink from dinnertime to when everyone retired."

Braegar folded hands in his lap. "Let's see," he said as Jim removed the pencil from his ear, "we enjoyed a fine meal of partridge, boiled potatoes, baked squash and mince pie."

The sheriff began to write. "And, to drink?"

"Wine, of course."

"Do you remember how much Miss Hargrove drank with her meal?"

"I believe she had one glass."

"Did anyone eat or drink anything that wasn't shared by all?"

Braegar rubbed his jaw. "No, everyone had the same fare."

"I understand after dinner drinks were served. Do you recall which beverages?"

"Of course," Braegar said, watching Doctor Turner exit with a tray of glasses. "Camilla poured bourbon for the men and sherry for the ladies."

"Mrs. Spelding poured the drinks?"

"Yes."

"And, how many sherries did Miss Hargrove have?"

"Only one," Braegar said.

"Have you ever witnessed Miss Hargrove consuming more alcohol than normal?"

"Not that I've seen," he said. "If she did it would've been behind closed doors."

Sheriff Hadley tapped his pencil on the paper. "Did you hear anything unusual after you retired for the evening?"

Braegar shifted uncomfortably, uncrossing his legs. "I'm afraid I'm in a difficult situation, sheriff."

Immediately, Jim's gray eyes fastened on the man before him. "What do you mean?"

"Well, I did hear something last night," he said. "But, under normal circumstances it's not something a gentleman would disclose."

"I'm afraid this isn't the time for decorum, Mr. Calderon. If you've information, I insist you say so."

"I hope you understand I didn't consider it sinister at the time. However, in light of what's happened, I can't say that it hasn't any bearing on Miss Hargrove's accident."

"Duly acknowledged. Now, please explain."

Braegar pulled a folded piece of paper from an inner pocket. "I found this slipped under my door last night." He leaned forward and handed it to Sheriff Hadley, who quickly unfolded it. "I've known for some time there's been enmity between Camilla and

Lorelda. However, I mayn't have known the all of it, by what's written."

Jim read out loud. *"I beg you to come speak to me tonight. Camilla's plotting treachery."* He looked up, astounded. "This was signed by Miss Hargrove. Did you speak to her?"

"I waited awhile to make sure everyone had gone to bed. It wouldn't have been decent to be seen entering an unmarried woman's room."

"Go on," Hadley urged. In his mind, the investigation had just shifted.

Braegar rubbed his hands. "When I approached her door, I heard voices. I'm ashamed to say, I listened."

"What did you hear?" Jim asked, the pencil forgotten in his hands.

"It was an argument between Lorelda and Camilla. I only heard snatches of conversation, but I thought Camilla said something about divorcing Leroy." Braegar looked sheepish. "Something of that nature is none of my business, you understand. I decided I could wait until the next day to have a private word with Lorelda. In fact, I'd planned on speaking to her once I returned from my meeting with Beauregard. As you can see," he said, splaying his hands. "I waited too long."

"What else did you hear?" he said, scribbling furiously.

Braegar sat back. "Nothing. I immediately returned to my room, fearful the door would open and

I'd be caught eavesdropping. At the time, it only appeared to be a spat between friends. I never imagined this could've occurred."

"Did you at anytime go into her room, either that night or before?"

"Never."

Jim read his notes before asking, "Have you ever witnessed Miss Hargrove imbibing in hard liquor?"

Braegar appeared surprised. "Not that I recall."

"You said you'd known for some time there was enmity between Mrs. Spelding and Miss Hargrove. Do you know what the conflict was?"

"I'm afraid not. I'd assumed it was nothing more than female squabbling. Something I wouldn't want to be drawn into."

"Had you witnessed any other animosity between them?"

"Now that you mention it, there was one thing. Last night, Lorelda exposed an ugly incident of when Camilla accused the chambermaid of stealing a gown. I'm sure it embarrassed Camilla for I saw her scratch Lorelda with her fingernails." Braegar shook his head. "Again, it seemed so petty; nothing that indicated a dire situation."

The sheriff strove to keep his visage passive, though his mind reeled. If what Mr. Calderon said was true, Camilla had completely lied about her interactions with Lorelda. "Can you think of anything else that might be significant?"

"That's everything I know," Braegar said. "Of course, I pray this is only a horrible accident. I can't imagine Mrs. Spelding being capable of actual wickedness."

"By the way," Jim said. "Mr. Spelding seems to have fallen ill. Had he mentioned not feeling well?"

"Not at all," he said, looking alarmed. "Is he very sick?"

"Doctor Turner's tending him now. I pray it's nothing serious, but in light of what's happened, I must inquire into everything. Can you think of anything that may've contributed to his ailment?"

"Well, nothing that would've made him unwell, but—" Braegar looked uneasy, placing two fingers over his mouth.

"What is it?" Jim pressed. "I insist you tell me."

"I'm sure it's nothing," he said at last. "But, since I'm obligated, I'll tell you. Camilla mentioned having trouble sleeping. She knew of my hobby of botanicals and asked me to prepare a sleeping potion." His eyes rounded. "Surely, she wouldn't have dosed him instead, would she? I promise you, I believed it was only for her insomnia."

"The doctor will have to decide. But, it seems Mr. Spelding's out of danger."

Braegar appeared relieved. "Thank God!" he said, sobering. "Yet, it doesn't seem possible Camilla would've done such a thing. I'm going to assume Leroy contracted an unknown malady."

"We're hoping that's the case," the sheriff said, writing furiously. "I may need to question you further. How long before you go?"

"I'd planned leaving the day after Christmas. But, if necessary, I can delay my departure."

"It's necessary. In the mean time, you may want to find other accommodations. I've a feeling Camilla's not going to be happy you told me all this."

"I'll pack immediately," he said. "I'll stay at the Rochester since Barrington Hotel's closed."

"Thanks. I appreciate your cooperation. I'll let you know if I need another interview."

"Anything to ensure justice is served," Braegar said. "I've no doubt you'll find the answers to this tragedy."

"One last thing," Sheriff Hadley said, rising. "I'm requesting you don't speak about our conversation to anyone until my investigation is over. Do you understand?"

"Perfectly," he said, rising also. "It's the nature of secrecy. Keeps your enemies from knowing what you're up to."

chapter 57

SHERIFF HADLEY WATCHED Braegar's carriage leave before releasing the curtains. He didn't relish his job right now, but there were too many conflicting stories. After questioning Tillie, he had come to the conclusion that Camilla was the one constant in both mysteries. Even though Braegar admitted being outside Lorelda's door, he hadn't made the tea nor had he entered Leroy's bedroom. And despite evidence Lorelda may've become intoxicated and fallen to her death, he couldn't rule out Camilla as a participant until the body had been examined.

Finally, there was Leroy's sudden illness. He needed to know the doctor's findings before confronting a woman who had lost a friend the same day her husband nearly died.

The mantle clock struck half past noon by the time Artemus entered, carrying his medical bag. "Good afternoon," he said. "I'm sorry you had to wait so long."

"Not to worry," Jim said, smiling. He pointed to a table with the remnants of his meal. "I've been supplied with tea and watercress sandwiches. But, tell me, how's your patient doing?"

"Very good," Doctor Turner said. "We've passed the critical stage and Mr. Spelding's now resting comfortably."

"Have you determined what caused his malady?"

"Not entirely, but I've suspicions, which seem to be borne out by Mr. Spelding's recovery once I gave him a dose of alkaline water and then several glasses of lemonade."

"Lemonade?"

"Alkaline water as well as citrus neutralizes certain poisons. I'm withholding judgment however, until I've examined the evidence."

"The glasses, you mean."

"Those and the bottles found upstairs. I placed them in my carriage the moment I collected them."

"When can I expect an answer?"

"I'm going to my office now to examine the glassware and Miss Hargrove's body. I'll ask Doctor Alexander to join me. I'd expect we'll have information by this evening. Would you like to drop by, say around six?"

"I'll be there," Jim said.

❧❧

"Let's get started, shall we?" Amy pulled up a stool and sat before Miles who had already lit a lamp. Her dress pooled in a heap as she sat lower than he, the vibrant flower and plaid pattern contrasting against her porcelain skin. She was curious about the smile playing about his lips, but chose to ignore it as she opened the tin. Taking a small glob of liniment, she applied it to the backside of his hand. With both thumbs, she massaged the scar while applying increasing pressure.

"So," she said conversationally, "what are your plans for Christmas?"

"I haven't thought about it," he said. "I suppose I'll be in my apartment in case the hospital needs me."

"You're not going to visit family?"

"Last night's storm made that impossible. Not that I couldn't travel from Cantonsville, but Orwell's too small to have street cleaners. Not to mention the roads I'd have to travel to reach my parents' place."

"That's too bad," she said, glancing up. "I'd be sad if I couldn't be with my family during the holidays."

"I'm no more entitled than those convalescing. I'm sure they're missing loved ones even more than I."

"I suppose you're right. I'm hoping the decorations will cheer them. Perhaps, even give them a sense of hearth and home." She frowned at his sudden smirk. "What's so funny?"

Miles broke into a full grin. "Oh, nothing."

Flipping over his hand, she began stretching his fingers. "Really, Doctor Alexander! I wouldn't think you'd find my decoration efforts amusing."

"Oh, it's a fine idea. Even the staff thinks the men will enjoy the trimmings."

Amy worked in silence, pondering his unusual behavior. Even though hospital duties kept her from dwelling on her feelings, when in close proximity, she thought of nothing else. Their daily sessions engaged more intimacy than a working relationship allowed. Through them, she had discovered his passion for healing as well as his desire to alleviate human suffering. Her admiration had grown apace with her attraction to his quick and decisive manner while attending patients. Though he lacked Doctor Turner's experience, he possessed a gentle touch, calming even the grievously wounded. She wished she didn't have to be the one to afflict him. Even now, she stole glances at his handsome face, her heart lurching whenever it showed pain from her manipulations.

"Do you need a sip of whiskey?" she asked.

"I can't use that crutch forever," he said, blue eyes piercing her soul. "Please continue."

She nodded, but mentally braced herself. "This is going to hurt," she said, bending his fingers simultaneously. Easing up, she waited a few seconds before reapplying pressure. "I'm sorry," she murmured, noting his furrowed brow, "only one more to go." After extending his fingers one last time, she sighed inwardly. Though necessary, she hated seeing him suffer. Suddenly, Amy had an idea.

"Tell you what! For Christmas, I'll let you skip the rest of your exercises. But, just this once," she warned. "I promised Doctor Turner I wouldn't neglect my duties."

Without waiting for a reply, she tried standing, but Miles' grip prevented her. "What if I wanted a different present? Would you deny me?"

"Of course not," she said. "I'll do whatever task you wish."

"You promise?" he persisted, helping her rise. "You might find it unsavory."

"Yes, I promise," Amy said, nervous at his close proximity. "What is it you'd have me do?"

Miles said nothing but his eyes slowly rose until they rested upon the purloined mistletoe hanging above them. Looking up, Amy's mouth fell open. "*That*, my dear Miss Burnsfield, is what I want for Christmas."

Amy stared, frozen in place. Always before, she had dismissed Miles' bold behavior as the result of using alcohol for pain relief. But this time, he hadn't once imbibed. He was completely sober and asking to kiss her. A hundred thoughts flooded her mind. She knew the impropriety of his request even as it caused her heart to palpitate. Not knowing what to do, she stood immobile until Miles recognized her indecision and took advantage.

Drawing her unresisting form against his chest, he lowered his mouth, slowly brushing his lips against hers. The contact ignited myriad sensations that blossomed into dazzling bliss as his tongue deliberately, gently parted her mouth. She tried pulling back but Miles cradled her head in a hold that prevented retreat. Gradually, she gave in to his demands, melting against him as this alien activity softened her knees.

When he finally ceased, Amy's senses were reeling. "Doctor Alexander," she said, gasping. "This isn't what I thought you meant!"

Miles grinned as he planted another kiss on her lips. "That's quite all right. It's exactly what I had in mind," he said, releasing her. "And, from now on and when we're alone, I insist you call me Miles."

"I most certainly will not!" she said hotly. "Why should I?"

"Because, my dear," he said, opening the door and sweeping it wide, "by this time next year, you and I will be *married*."

chapter 58

"I APPRECIATE YOU assisting me," Artemus said, closing the door after the young doctor entered, "especially after working all day."

"I'm always available," Miles said, removing his coat. He looked at what appeared to be a body lying on an examining table, covered with a cloth. "Is this an autopsy?"

"It's an examination of Lorelda Hargrove, who died under unusual circumstances," Artemus said, sighing. "I was called to the Spelding residence this morning because Leroy had taken ill. While there, the maid discovered Miss Hargrove had fallen from her balcony."

Miles' brows rose in unison. "Miss Hargrove? Why, I met her a few weeks ago!"

"If this is too difficult, I'll understand," Artemus said, laying a hand on his shoulder. "I certainly won't insist."

"No, that's not necessary," he said, rolling up his sleeves. "I've examined bodies of soldiers I'd previously doctored. I just never expected it to happen here."

"It's part of the job no matter where you are," Artemus said. "All patients die eventually."

"Yes, but hopefully from natural causes," Miles said. "Well, doctor, do you prefer I take notes, or do you want the honor?"

Doctor Turner removed the shroud. "You observe. I'll take notes. If we disagree on our findings, I'll make the call. That way, I'll be accountable to the sheriff. This may spill into Christmas. If it does, I want you managing the hospital."

"Including the staff?"

"Of course. Do you have a problem giving orders?"

Miles grinned. "No. As a matter of fact, I've a few ideas in mind."

Artemus opened a diary-like journal, dipping his pen in ink. "As long as you follow regulations, you'll have full authority. An order from you is an order from me."

"And, if anyone refuses?"

"Dismiss them immediately."

"Thank you," he said. "That should take the quarrel out of anyone."

"It better," Doctor Turner said. "I won't have staff refusing my directives."

❦

"I knew you'd come," Caleb said, stretching out both hands. "I knew you'd see me one last time."

Amy enfolded his hands as she sat in a chair kept next to his bed. Throughout the day, she had visited him often; a word here, a touch there, a mop of his fevered brow. With each visit, she prayed for returning color or renewed spark in his expressive eyes. Yet, with sinking heart, she observed only a dreadful gray veil creeping over his face.

She summoned a weak smile. "I'm not leaving yet, Caleb. I promised to stay until Doctor Alexander returns. He needed to assist Doctor Turner for awhile. Is that okay?"

"Yes, m," he said, nodding. "I'd thought to hang on 'til word came from my folk, but I guess it's time I moved on."

Her eyes shone with unshed tears. "Now, don't you be saying such! I sent your letter a few days ago. You'll hear from them, I'm sure."

Caleb's head moved against the pillow. "I fear not. I waited too long. I'd hoped—" he closed his eyes briefly, "—I'd hoped God would answer my prayers to go home—but now—all I want to know is they'll be all right."

Amy bit back the tremble on her lips. Taking clean linen, she gently wiped his forehead before stirring the air with a fan. "Well, Caleb. I'll pray too. Together, I'm sure the Lord will grant your request."

He attempted a smile, but a spasm interrupted his efforts, his eyes becoming wracked with pain. "How long," he said, panting, "must I endure this?"

Just then, Polly stopped at the end of the bed to check his chart. "When's his next dose of medication?" Amy asked. "He's in pain right now."

"He's not allowed to receive anything until nine o'clock," she responded. Ever since she had been upbraided for misreading her own notes, Polly remained vigilant in following instructions to the letter. "I'm afraid he has a few hours to wait."

Amy rose, taking the chart. "Let me see," she said, scanning its contents. Indeed, Doctor Turner's orders indicated pain relief should be administered in six hour intervals. The last dose had been given a mere two hours ago. She looked at Caleb whose strong body, just as the doctor foretold, rebelled against death, fighting every inch of the way. He clenched his hands as another spasm shook him, his eyes turned imploringly toward her. "I'm going to make an exception," she said before abruptly leaving the ward.

Polly followed, not speaking until reaching the hall. "You can't remove medicine from the dispensary or administer it without orders. It's against regulations!"

Amy only walked faster. She knew the ward master on duty held the dispensary keys. She also knew Doctor Alexander kept a second set in his desk. Without ceremony, she entered the small office and retrieved the keys. Polly gasped as Amy then marched to the dispensary, unlatching the door with a quick turn of her wrist.

"You'll lose your job," she said, watching Amy open a bottle of morphine to shake out a few pills. "I—I won't lie for you."

"I'm not asking you to," she said, pushing past Polly. "I'll let Doctor Turner know you forbade me to do this."

Within moments, Amy had returned to Caleb's bedside, assisting him with a drink of water until he swallowed a pill. She then settled back into her chair. "You rest now," she said. "I'll sit here until the medicine takes affect."

He looked at her with brimming eyes. "Please— don't leave—I don't want to be alone when—it happens—"

"Hush," Amy whispered, bending near, touching his hand. "I won't leave you, I promise. We'll do this together."

Caleb nodded and took a deep breath. He closed his eyes. Yet, when she tried lifting her hand, he held tighter. And so Amy kept vigil, allowing her fingers to remain in his. His breath became regular as the morphine took effect and still she sat, silently praying that eternal relief would come before sunrise.

chapter 59

DOCTOR TURNER OPENED the door at the sound of a knock. "Come in, sheriff," he said, stepping aside. "I appreciate your punctuality. It's exactly six o'clock."

Sheriff Hadley crossed the threshold, allowing Artemus to shut the door. "Please, sit near the stove where it's warmer," Turner said, indicating an empty chair. "I've preliminary findings. Unfortunately, that's all I can do until the body thaws completely."

Hadley took a seat. "I understand. Any information is appreciated." He produced a paper and pencil while Doctor Turner retrieved papers from his desk.

"As I said earlier, I asked Doctor Alexander to assist me. Together we came to some conclusions," Artemus said, handing over the top page. "First of all, the condition of the body indicates it fell and wasn't simply placed outside. Miss Hargrove suffered several broken bones along her ribs and back. She also suffered a depressed skull fracture which is consistent with falling from the height of a balcony."

"So, it was the fall that killed her?" he asked, taking notes.

"It would've been the deciding factor," Doctor Turner said.

"What does that mean? Was Miss Hargrove intoxicated after all?"

"It's possible alcohol had a hand in it. However, we found bruising around Miss Hargrove's neck and what could be fingernail marks. But, it's just as likely the fall caused her injuries. It's hard to say."

"If her injuries could've been from the fall, what makes you suspect foul play?"

"The fact her Hyoid bone was crushed is usually indicative of strangulation. Additionally, Miss Hargrove landed face up. It doesn't appear as if she struck anything on the way down, which I looked for when we moved the body. So, I can't explain why the bones in her throat were crushed when she apparently fell onto her back."

"Did you find anything else?"

"Yes. Under a magnifying glass, petechial hemorrhages were observed in Miss Hargrove's eyes. Some could argue that severe intoxication accounts for the blood-shot appearance. But, I can't prove the victim consumed the amount of alcohol required to cause that condition."

"You did find the laudanum and empty whiskey bottle in her room," Hadley said. "Wouldn't that be proof enough?"

"There's a definite odor of alcohol on her clothing," Artemus said. "But, I didn't find any red, spidery veins chronic drinkers have. Besides, from everything I've learned, she doesn't fit the description. You'd need to question her parents about that, if you feel it's pertinent."

Hadley shook his head. "I'm loath to do that. I had to inform her parents their only daughter had died. Poor Alma could scarce take it in and Joseph was devastated, as any father would be. I don't think they could bear questioning right now." The sheriff tapped his lips with his pencil. "Is there a possibility this was the first time she'd drank so much alcohol? Could that explain why she had no signs of being a heavy drinker?"

"That's a possibility. However, that isn't all." Artemus held out a second sheet. "I don't know how this factors in, but both Miles and I thought it meant something."

Jim took the sheet which had four tubular shapes drawn on it. "What's this?"

"We outlined faint marks on Miss Hargrove's left cheek. At first, we could barely see them, but as her skin warmed, they grew more pronounced."

The sheriff held his hand over the drawing. "It looks like a hand print."

"That's what we thought," Doctor Turner affirmed. "As you can see, the markings are small; too small for a man to have made."

Jim let out a low whistle. "Mr. Calderon said he overheard an argument between Lorelda and Camilla. This likely proves he's telling the truth."

"I'll let you make the conclusions, sheriff. But, in my opinion it was a woman's hand that made that mark."

"That reminds me of something," the sheriff said. "Did you find any scratch marks on either of Miss Hargrove's wrists?"

"Why, yes we did," Artemus said. "How'd you know?"

"Mr. Calderon said he witnessed Camilla scratch her. That now makes two things he's been truthful about."

"Things are not looking well for Mrs. Spelding," Doctor Turner said. "She poured the drinks, she prepared the tea and she made two assaults on Miss Hargrove, all in the same night."

"But, could a woman be strong enough to strangle another woman and then throw her off a balcony?"

Artemus sighed as he leaned against the wall. "In a fit of rage, a person becomes several times stronger than normal. So, is it possible? Yes. What keeps me from making that determination is the plausibility Miss Hargrove became intoxicated and fell to her death accidentally."

Hadley noticed Doctor Turner still held a piece of paper. "Is there more?"

"I asked the apothecary to validate my findings on the glasses. One of the bourbon glasses had traces of a reddish-brown powder. Combined with Leroy's symptoms, we both concluded it was most likely Belladonna."

"What's that?"

"It's a medicine that taken in too high a concentration becomes poisonous."

"Could you tell whether the amount was intended to kill?"

"As we doctors love to say 'Sola Dosis Facit Venemum.' Only the dose determines the harm," Artemus supplied. "Which means, it's impossible to tell whether 'twas purposeful or by accident, Leroy survived."

"I see." The sheriff studied his notes, waggling his pencil. "I've established Mrs. Spelding poured the after-dinner drinks. Is it your opinion that's how he got poisoned?"

"Not just that, but his teacup smelled pungent, similar to lettuce opium."

Jim's mouth dropped. "He was poisoned twice? Couldn't he tell his drinks were contaminated?"

"Bourbon's naturally bitter, so he wouldn't notice a difference. Sugar added to tea masks the bitterness of lettuce opium. It's used to treat insomnia. So, it's possible the tea wasn't intended for harm. However, when I asked Mrs. Spelding if Leroy took Dover's powder, which smells similar because it also contains opium, she denied knowledge of it."

"Braegar claims he made a sleeping potion for Camilla, at her request," Sheriff Hadley said. "It now appears it ended up in Leroy's tea."

"That explains the opium. But I can't account for why she withheld that information," Artemus said, handing the sheriff his last paper. "I've written it all down in layman's terms."

"For that, I'm grateful." The sheriff said, smiling. "And what of the bottles found in Lorelda's room? Any indications she'd been poisoned?"

"None. She would've had to drink from Leroy's glass. All the other glasses were free from residue. Of course, I found no glass in Lorelda's room. It's possible it was removed and washed. However, that's unlikely since the other glasses hadn't been cleaned."

"I've one last question. Do you see anything connecting these two incidents?"

"Only that they occurred on the same night in the same house. As to why it happened, I'll leave that up to the law."

Hadley finished his notes before standing. If everything Braegar told him was true, he knew why. Camilla wanted a divorce. If Lorelda threatened to expose her, everything that occurred suddenly made sense. Doubly damning was the fact Camilla had handled the drinks containing poison. He sighed inwardly, recalling Lorelda's written note. *Camilla's plotting treachery*. "Thanks, doctor. It seems this'll be an investigation of at least one attempted murder and a possible actual murder." He folded the papers and tucked them in his pocket. "When...uh...Miss Hargrove—warms up—do you think you'll find anything further?"

"If I do, it'll be soon. Once a frozen body thaws, it decomposes quickly. I'll be up all night checking for evidence. If I find something, you'll be the first to know."

Hadley suddenly felt queasy. "I don't know how you docs do it," he said, sticking his pencil behind his ear. "I never get used to dealing with the dead."

Artemus walked to the door, his face pensive. "Neither do I," he said, opening the portal wide. "Neither do I."

chapter 60

THE HOUR OF midnight had come and gone. Still, Amy hadn't left Caleb's side. When he stirred, she spoke gentle words in his ear. If his brow furrowed in pain, she slipped a pill into his mouth. When his parched mouth begged for water, she moistened his lips. The ward had long grown quiet as others slumbered, yet Amy left her candle burn, illuminating the darkness in case Caleb awoke.

Someone must've summoned Doctor Alexander for though rounds had ended, he returned to the ward, laying his hand upon her shoulder. "Do you need a break?" he asked in a low voice.

Unable to speak, Amy shook her head. If she had, she feared she would've shrieked against the callousness of a God that allowed a man such as Caleb to endure so much pain. Her heart couldn't fathom why wars were necessary when it was the young who suffered and died. And yet, had it not been for the War, she never would've known him or what it meant for a man to surrender his life for the sake of others. And, so she did the only thing left. She kept vigil to alleviate whatever suffering she could.

"He's your favorite, isn't he?" Miles said, drawing a chair from against the wall to sit beside her. When she didn't respond, he placed his hand over hers. "He's my favorite too," he whispered.

Amy dared a look at Miles. "I stole morphine."

"So, I've been told."

"Polly's a nosey tattletale," she said, near whispering. "I wasn't going to hide what I did."

"I know," Miles said. "I understand you stole my keys too."

Amy fished keys from her apron pocket and placed it in his hand. "I suppose this means I'm to be let go," she muttered. "Polly insisted I would."

"How much morphine have you given him?"

She counted the pills still in her pocket. "Two since five o'clock."

Without a word, Miles retrieved Caleb's chart, making a note before returning it to its place.

"What did you do?" she asked.

"Why, I was just checking to make sure you followed my instructions. I distinctly recall ordering Caleb to receive two morphine pills between 5 o'clock and...," he looked at his watch, "...two o'clock the next morning."

Amy's jaw dropped. "I'm—I'm not to be let go? But, I broke hospital regulations. Doctor Turner said he wouldn't allow theft or insubordination."

"Doctor Turner's given me full authority in his absence. He distinctly said an order from me is an order from him."

Amy looked into his face. He looked tired. He had surely been awake far too long. "I'm sorry if I've caused you trouble. I promise it won't happen again."

Miles smiled. "My dear, you've caused me many things, but trouble isn't one of them."

Her eyes involuntarily dropped to his lips as her mind relived their last encounter. Not knowing what to say, she turned to daub Caleb's forehead with linen before cooling him with a fan. "How much longer, do you think?" she asked in a quivery voice.

Miles studied Caleb's face and pale lips. "I'd say a few hours."

Amy nodded, no longer trusting her voice. Soon, Miles rose, leaving her and Caleb alone in darkness kept at bay by the light of a single candle.

જીન્જી

In the space of a day, Camilla's world had crashed around her. Instead of rejoicing in the promise of a new future, she had to work furiously to shore up remnants of her current circumstance. By a happenstance look out the window, she had discovered Braegar deserting her without so much as a by your leave. Fury alternated with fear as she tried making sense of all that had occurred. That Lorelda had obviously flung herself over the balcony to destroy her chances with Braegar had been more disturbing than Leroy's brush with a potion overdose. She could think of no other reason the wench had been found crumpled beneath the snow.

She now busied herself as any dutiful wife should, plumping Leroy's pillow as he sat in a day-bed and bringing him whatever he desired. If Braegar had abandoned her, she needed her husband to believe in her undying devotion. Her last vestige of hope lay with Mayor Hampton. If he openly accused Leroy of debauching Elizabeth, she could still divorce, leaving her reputation intact.

"Are you comfortable?" she asked, smiling sweetly. "Is there anything else you'd like?"

Though pale, Leroy appeared to be regaining strength as a book lay on his lap and remnants of broth on his lips. "I'd very much like to read today's paper, if you don't mind."

"Of course," Camilla said. "I'll get it straight away." She had nearly reached the door when he spoke again. "You sent word to father that I wouldn't be at work today, didn't you?"

With her back to him, Leroy couldn't see impatience flaring in her eyes. "I sent a message after the doctor arrived this morning, dearest."

She departed, gently closing the door before striding down the hall. She threw open the door of Braegar's room and entered, flinging open his wardrobe. Everything was gone. She looked about the room. His bed had been made as a final parting gesture; as if she hadn't shared her body there, she thought bitterly. Suddenly, she noticed a pair of empty shot glasses on a tray atop his nightstand. She could think of no reason Braegar would've needed more than one. All at once, Lorelda's words came crashing back. *It wasn't enough to keep him from coming to me... You're no less a plaything than I...*

The images of them meeting clandestinely, beneath her roof, shook her to the core. She hadn't believed Lorelda's assertions because she couldn't imagine Braegar would consider the spinster worthy of his attentions. How could he, when he had her at his beck and call? All her insecurities came flooding back, confirming her fears.

She stood immobile, trembling. At that moment, pure rage coursed through her body as she cursed Lorelda for ruining her future and then Braegar for abandoning her to her insipid existence. Obviously, the wench had overindulged before falling to her death. It's what she deserved, she thought darkly. She'd never know who Braegar would've chosen for he had fled like a coward.

She paced the length of the room, debating what to do. Never one to take unnecessary chances, she knew she couldn't leave Leroy without securing her future. If Braegar wasn't the man to save her, she would simply find another. Camilla tried to recall anyone who in the past had shown the slightest interest. Only one emerged that she felt she could influence, one that she had always thought would've made a good match had he had more wealth. That man was Beauregard Barrington. He'd have enough riches, she thought shrewdly, if Paradis Pavillon remained his and his alone.

What better way to exact revenge on her lover than to thwart his plans? If she executed perfect strategy, she'd be a heroin in Beau's eyes about the time Sam Hampton accused Leroy of fathering his grandchild. No one could fault her for leaving her husband and whose shoulder to better cry on than her longtime friend? Of course, she'd have to reveal Braegar's plan as if she had innocently—and recently—discovered his treachery.

Camilla strode from the room, feeling a returning sense of control as she tamped her ire to a simmer. First, she would get her husband the damned newspaper. After that, she would send a message to Beau insisting he come on the morrow as she had information in regards to Paradis Pavillon.

chapter 61

THE SOUNDS OF doors opening and closing announced the arrivals of cook and laundress. Amy knew it wouldn't be long before smells of coffee and frying potatoes would wake the sleeping soldiers. Yet, before the aromas could perform their morning ritual, one by one, the men crept near. Apparently, her vigil hadn't gone unnoticed, for soon they formed a circle of faces filled with awe and sorrow. One balanced on a crutch beside another sporting a bandaged eye. Several wore slings or bindings on various limbs amid bare feet and missing appendages. Had they been dressed in their finest uniforms instead of rumpled nightshirts, they couldn't have looked more reverent or honorable.

Though no words were spoken, their eyes betrayed the wonder of Caleb's patience and fortitude in enduring his hard death. It wasn't until their comrade opened his eyes that smiles lit their downcast faces.

"How are you, old boy?" faltered one.

"Most through," whispered Caleb, looking wonderingly at those crowding his bed. "I thank God for that."

"Can I say or do anything for you anywhere's?" asked another.

"Take my things home. Tell them I did my best."

"We will! We will!" choked many in unison.

They grew silent as Caleb turned his eyes toward Amy. "My ring," he said, working the circlet off his finger and holding it out. "Make sure mother gets it. Tell her it brought me through."

"I promise," she said, placing it in her pocket. "I'll let her know how brave you were." Though her heart ached, Amy gave him her best smile. "It's been a pleasure to have known you, Caleb."

"Your hair's so fair," he whispered. "All golden. Like daffodils. Never seen anything so pretty."

"Give him a keepsake," spoke the one with a bandaged eye.

"Yes! Yes!" the motley troupe urged, and soon scissors were pressed into Amy's hand.

Without a care to its placement, she snipped a generous length from her hair and wound its length around Caleb's fingers. He immediately rubbed his cheek with it before holding it beneath his nose. "It smells of lavender," he said, breathing deeply. "Thank you," he said, a tear slipping past his lashes. "Oh, thank you!"

One by one, the men reached down giving a small squeeze or a tender touch, whispering farewells only brothers in arms could give.

"Good bye, soldier."

"You fought the good fight, my boy."

"God speed."

Soon, everyone retreated, allowing a soldier the dignity to privately surrender his final post. Within minutes, Caleb's feeble gasps were the only sounds that broke the silence until finally, blissfully, his soul departed. Only then, when pain no longer wracked his body, did peacefulness settle upon his features.

Amy leaned over and gently kissed his forehead. "This is from your mother," she whispered. "And this," she said, kissing him again, "is from me."

❧❦

Camilla sipped from her second cup of bitter tea. For unknown reasons, she had felt queasy upon arising. By mid-morning, the sensations receded to an occasional twinge and so she dressed as usual. Leroy had recovered sufficiently to spend a few hours at the bank, which was the exact time she had requested Beau's presence.

She needed to look her best to spin her web and so she put on the dress she intended wearing Christmas Day. A stunning white gown with vertical blue stripes encircling three-quarters of the dress with the skirt front completely white except for a double row of blue triangular "points" stretching nearly halfway to her narrow waist. Lastly, she donned a sleeveless bolero jacket the same deep blue as the stripes.

She brushed then twisted her hair into a golden mass atop her head, allowing ringlets to escape pins in a wispy array. After rouging her cheeks and applying kohl to her eyes, Camilla felt as alluring as she looked. She inspected herself in her mirror, turning this way and that. Satisfied, she sprinkled herself with her most expensive perfume. "Mrs. Beauregard Barrington," she said, practicing a small curtsy. "Hello, I'm Mrs. Barrington. Welcome to Paradis Pavillon."

Her musings were interrupted by a timid knock on the door. "What is it?" Camilla said sharply. She knew it too early for Beau to have arrived.

"Begging your pardon," Tillie called from the hall. "But, the sheriff's waiting in the parlor. He's asking to speak to you, ma'am."

A nervous frown creased her brow. *What could he possibly want now?*

"I'll be there when I'm ready," she said. ""Be sure to prepare refreshments."

"Yes ma'am. Right away," Tillie said before hurrying off. It never boded well once her mistress became irritated.

Camilla's usual habit was to make her guests wait. But, today, she descended the stairs the moment she had collected her wits. She needed the sheriff gone before Beau arrived. "Good morning, sheriff," Camilla said with a smile. "It's a pleasure to see you again."

"Good morning, Mrs. Spelding." Sheriff Hadley rose and then waited for her to take a seat before resuming his.

"To what do I owe this pleasure?" she asked, noting his sober demeanor.

"I've a few questions I'd like to ask. I'm afraid there's disturbing information that's come to light. I'm hoping you can clear it up."

"Of course," Camilla said, smoothing in imaginary wrinkle on her gown. "However, I hope it won't take long as I have a previous engagement within the hour."

"I'll not take any more time than necessary," Jim said. "I'll get right down to business." He then pulled out papers from a pocket. Retrieving a pencil from behind his ear, he cleared his throat. "I'd like to review events the night your husband became ill. Is it true that you were the one who poured the after dinner drinks that night?"

"I was," she said, perplexed. "Is that important?"

"And, no one else served drinks?"

"That's correct," Camilla said. "I don't understand, sheriff. What does this have to do with Lorelda's accident? I've already told you what everyone had to drink that night."

"I'll explain shortly," he said, taking notes. "Can you tell me if you've noticed any alcohol missing?"

"Missing? What do you mean?"

"Could you please look to see if any bottles are missing from your cabinet?"

Bewildered by his questions, Camilla rose and went to the sideboard. She opened the door and looked inside. "I know there were five bottles here. But now, there seems to only be four."

"Can you tell which one's missing?" the sheriff asked.

"I don't see the bottle of rye whiskey Leroy drinks on occasion." Camilla immediately thought of the two glasses in Braegar's room. But, since she'd seen no bottle, she kept the information to herself. "How did you know?" she asked.

"One of our theories is that Miss Hargrove may've consumed more alcohol that evening. Doctor Turner found an empty whiskey bottle in her room."

Camilla's brows rose. "Heavens! Is that how she fell? Why, I never would've guessed." She returned to her seat as the maid entered with a tray. She didn't speak again until Tillie departed. "How do you like your tea? We have lemon, honey and sugar."

"Perhaps later," the sheriff said, looking up from his notes. "You don't seem overly upset Miss Hargrove died. Is it possible she could've been a threat to you?"

"A threat?" Camilla poured herself a cup of tea. "I don't know what you mean. We've been friends for years."

"You said that you didn't see Lorelda after she retired for the evening. Are you still certain of that?"

Camilla felt her confidence slip. Had Tillie overheard their argument? "I—I'm fairly certain," she said.
"Why?"

"Because I've reason to believe you did see Miss
Hargrove afterward. In fact, I believe you two may've
quarreled. Is that possible?"

Camilla thought quickly. Even if Tillie overheard their argument, what difference could it make?
Whether Lorelda fell because she drank too much
or threw herself over the balcony, it mattered not. "I
suppose it's possible," she said cautiously. "I'd been so
concerned about Leroy's illness, it slipped my mind."

"What did you argue about?"

"I can't recall. It was nothing important, I'm
sure."

"Would it be important enough to strike her?"

Her teacup rattled against its saucer. "Why
would you think that?"

Sheriff Hadley pulled a piece of paper from his
pocket. After unfolding it, he held it up. "This mark
was found on Miss Hargrove's cheek. Doctor Turner
claims it's a hand-print. A *female* handprint."

The color drained from Camilla's face. She
stared at the paper and then the sheriff. "What are
you saying? You think I had something to do with
Lorelda's accident?"

"That's what I'm trying to find out." He refold-
ed the paper, tucking it away. "Perhaps, a struggle occurred, ending on the balcony."

Camilla's eyes rounded as her cup tilted in her fingers, spilling tea. She immediately grabbed a napkin, daubing wetness from her skirt. "I most certainly *did not*!" she said shrilly. "Why would I want to kill her?"

"I'm wondering if Miss Hargrove may've stumbled upon a bit of information you didn't want revealed. A divorce perhaps? Did she threaten you? Maybe, in the heat of the moment something bad happened."

"If anything, the twit threw herself off the balcony!" Camilla said. "She was jealous! *I* was the one who married well. *I* had friends aplenty. She clung to my skirts, hoping to steal what was *mine!*"

"My question remains. What exactly happened in her room that night?"

Camilla set her cup on the tray. "We had words," she said more calmly than she felt. "She insulted me and I'm embarrassed to say I slapped her. That's all."

The sheriff tapped his pencil impatiently. "Mrs. Spelding, you need to tell me what happened from the time you entered her room to the time you left."

Camilla forced a smile. "Of course," she said, touching her lip. "Well, let's see. I recall going to her room to see if she needed anything. She'd retired early due to a headache. For some reason, Lorelda was upset. She accused me of interfering with her friendship with Mr. Calderon. I assured her I had no reason to do such a thing. You see, I felt sorry for her.

She'd never married and seemed desperate for the attentions of any man. I told her I was happily married and she—*she* was the one who said I should divorce Leroy. It wasn't I who uttered those words."

"Why would Lorelda suggest you get a divorce?" Sheriff Hadley asked.

"I don't know. As I said, she was jealous. I think she realized she couldn't beguile Mr. Calderon, so she began wearing face paint and changed how she acted around my husband." Camilla's eyes hardened at the memory. "At that moment, I'm afraid I lost my senses and slapped her for uttering such rubbish. I immediately felt remorseful, and apologized," she said, resting a hand near her throat. "However, Lorelda was so upset; she demanded I leave. Of course, I did so at once." Her lashes fluttered with precision. "So you see, sheriff, there's no reason for me to have harmed Lorelda. She imagined things. Maybe, in her distress, she decided to end her life." She lifted the tea-stained napkin to her eyes. "I feel so badly. I now wonder if my words may've pushed her to that recourse."

"That's one theory that hasn't been considered," the sheriff said, scribbling. "I'll be sure to mention it to Doctor Turner."

"Mayhap, that explains the missing liquor?" Camilla suggested hopefully. "If I were you, sheriff, I'd weigh that possibility against whatever you think I've done. I mean, really! Do I look like a murderess?"

"That's not for me to decide, Mrs. Spelding. I'm here to gather facts," he said without looking up. "Truthful information should lead us to the right conclusions."

"I'm confidant it will," Camilla said, feeling more at ease. "After all, you found an empty liquor bottle in her room. I'd think it rather obvious what happened."

"Maybe, if that's all we had found," he said. "Can you think of a reason Lorelda would've written this?" He handed her a folded paper.

Camilla hesitated before taking the note. With trembling fingers, she unfolded it, reading swiftly. "I—I don't know," she said, breathing rapidly. "It makes no sense."

"Perhaps it does," he said, retrieving the note. "Perhaps, she discovered what was about to happen and intended to warn Leroy." Jim deliberately let her believe the note had been found in Lorelda's room. He wanted her to divulge what she knew without revealing Braegar was the intended recipient.

"What do you mean?" she asked, dreading being exposed as an adulteress. "I already told you she imagined things. Her words can't be trusted."

"It's not her words I'm talking about, but how one crime could've covered up the other." The sheriff had saved his most damning evidence for last. "Doctor Turner discovered one of the bourbon glasses had poison in it. It explains the symptoms your husband suffered when he became ill. And not only that, Leroy's teacup had traces of a substance that's used for insomnia. Since you're the one who poured alcohol and prepared Leroy's tea, it makes you the only one who could've tainted his drinks."

Camilla couldn't believe her ears. "Poison? That's impossible!"

"Isn't it true you asked Mr. Calderon for something to help you sleep?"

"Yes, but—" her eyes suddenly averted, "—what does that have to do with anything?"

"Why would a substance you asked for be found in your husband's tea? More importantly, if asked, would your husband acknowledge he knowingly drank it?"

Camilla began worrying the napkin in her lap. "No! I mean, maybe I accidentally gave him *my* tea! Yes! That's it. I gave him my sleep potion by mistake!"

Jim's heart quickened, recognizing signs of guilt. "Mrs. Spelding, there was only one teacup in your bedroom. Doctor Turner said you specifically told him you had prepared Leroy's tea."

"I misspoke!" she said, desperation tingeing her voice. "You're confusing me!" She began wringing her hands. "What does this have to do with Lorelda's death?"

The sheriff suspected Camilla was concealing information. If he unnerved her even more, she might spill the truth. "If Lorelda discovered you'd poisoned your husband, you'd need to silence her, wouldn't you? Perhaps you tried convincing her otherwise and things got out of hand. It's best you tell me everything. It'll go easier on you if you do."

Camilla felt unable to breathe. She couldn't absorb this unexpected turn of events. "No! It's not true!" she said, real tears filling her eyes. "How can this be?" She looked at the sheriff, astonished. "I didn't poison my husband! I didn't kill Lorelda!" Her hands curled into fists as she rose in near panic. "It's time that you leave sheriff! This conversation is over!"

Hadley stood, speaking in a clipped voice. "You've not been candid with me, Mrs. Spelding. I'm afraid I'm going to have to detain you on suspicion of murder of Lorelda Hargrove and attempted murder of your husband."

chapter 62

"SACRI BLEU!" BEAU uttered as he viewed Sheriff Hadley escort a weeping Camilla to the jailhouse brougham. After she had been settled inside with Deputy Walsh, Jim shut the door and watched the conveyance leave the Spelding drive.

"What's happened?" he asked, approaching. "Camilla sent a missive saying it imperative to come at this hour. She said she'd discovered something of vital importance about Paradis Pavillon."

Jim's countenance reflected his subdued mood. "Mrs. Spelding is being detained. I'm afraid you won't be able to speak to her right now. Perhaps another day."

"Detained?" Beau's brows shot up. "What's this about?"

"As you know, I'm investigating Miss Hargrove's death—"

"Oui!" he said, interrupting. ""You don't think Camilla had anything to do with it, do you?"

"It's an active investigation. As a matter of fact, I wanted to speak to you as well. Do you have time right now?"

"Of course," Beauregard said, nodding. "Anything to help."

❧

"Beggin' yer pardon, Miss Burnsfield, but I was told to give this to you, straightaway."

Amy took the envelope. "What's this?"

"The ward master said it were forgotten last night," the boy said. "Me'bbe you's to pass it to the right soldier?"

She turned it over and saw *Caleb Callahan* printed neatly above the hospital address. "When did this arrive?" she asked.

"I think, 'twas yesterday," he said, shuffling his feet. "Some mail weren't handed out cuz th' attendant left early."

Caleb's letter!

Amy turned and nearly ran to Doctor Alexander's office. She knocked and then entered immediately. "Excuse me, doctor," she said breathlessly. "I must put this in Caleb's—Caleb's—" suddenly, her face crumpled and she burst into tears as she held out the envelope.

Miles rose to gather her in his arms, holding her against his chest while sobs wracked her body. He took the letter, murmuring softly as Amy clung to him, her face buried against his shoulder in overwhelming grief. Her tears tore at his heart. He knew no words to soften her pain. And so he allowed her to release her sorrow within the protection of his arms. Glaring at curiosity seekers gathering in the hall, he slammed the door shut with a flick of his hand. He didn't move, letting her tears soak his shirt as he rubbed her back consolingly. "I know it hurts," he said finally, brushing hair from her face. "It's all right to cry." When she began to quiet, he pulled a handkerchief from his pocket and placed it in her fingers. "Here, take this."

Amy wiped her eyes and then blew her nose. "I'm so sorry," she said as fresh tears threatened. "I don't know what came over me." She took a step back, fidgeting with the hanky. "Please forgive me."

"Don't apologize. I know the difficulty in holding vigil with the dying."

"It's so unfair!"

"Life isn't fair," he stated simply. "Nor is it easy."

"I don't understand," she said, looking dejected. "Why did Caleb have to die?"

"I don't know. Truly, I don't. We aren't called to question *why*, Amy. We're called to *do*. You did exactly what you were supposed to do. And, that's enough."

Amy took in a deep breath and nodded. "I—I'll try to remember." She then pointed to the letter. "I didn't get that until just now."

"Let's see what we have," Miles said, looking at the missive. "Is it from his family?"

Amy nodded, sniffing. "He—he was waiting for it. I've got to make certain it goes with him; if I'm not too late."

"I'll make sure it's placed in his hands," he said. "In fact, I was preparing his order for burial, so you're not too late."

"Oh, thank you! I'm to send his ring to his mother. With it, I wanted to write Caleb was greatly comforted by having it as well as receiving her letter." She searched his eyes. "Is it wrong to let her think the letter came before he died?"

"If anything, it's a blessing," Miles said, touching her shoulder. "I see no reason to add to her sorrow."

"Okay. That's what I'll do."

"After that, I'm sending you home. I want you alert for the yuletide dinner we're having tomorrow."

Her eyes rounded. "I'd nearly forgotten! I'm supposed to serve wassail cider."

"And, I'm carving turkey. So, we'll both need to be well rested," he said, opening the door.

"Thank you, Doctor Alexander," she said as she turned away. "I'll see you tomorrow."

He caught her wrist. "Call me Miles," he said, grinning. "Anyone who throws themselves into my arms is on a first-name basis with me."

"I didn't—"

He held up his scarred hand. "That'll be all, Miss Burnsfield. I'll see you tomorrow in the pantry, where you'll be free to torture me at will."

chapter 63

"WHAT DO YOU mean?" Leroy sputtered, soon after entering his parlor. "Why would you take *my wife* into custody?"

"Please, Mr. Spelding, won't you have a seat?" Sheriff Hadley said. "I'd first like to ask a few questions, and then I'll be happy to answer all of yours."

While Leroy settled into a chair, Jim took some moments to gather his thoughts. "I'm sorry this seems so sudden," he began. "But, I assure you I've obtained clear evidence, some of which your wife has already admitted to."

"Evidence of what?"

"As you know, Miss Hargrove was found below her balcony. After an examination, Doctor Turner found a bruise on her face resembling a hand print. He says the mark's too small to have come from a man. Wait—" He held up a finger as Leroy began objecting. "Mr. Calderon admitted to hearing Miss Hargrove quarrelling with your wife that night. Mrs.

Spelding has already conceded she argued with and then struck Miss Hargrove."

"*What?*" Leroy's hand thudded against the arm-rest. "Why would they have argued?"

Sheriff Hadley rubbed his mustache. "According to Mrs. Spelding, Miss Hargrove accused your wife of interfering with her friendship with Mr. Calderon."

Leroy stared, recalling Camilla's demand he warn Braegar and her threat she'd do something if he didn't. He hadn't had nerve to follow through, much to Camilla's rage.

Jim noted Leroy's look of cognizance. "Does that sound familiar?"

"Well, yes, in a way," he said slowly. "My wife believed Lorelda desired Braegar's attention. But, I thought it all nonsense. At the very least, it wasn't my business."

"It doesn't look like nonsense now," Jim said, his pencil poised. "What exactly did Mrs. Spelding say about Miss Hargrove?"

"She had asked that I speak with Braegar to—to dissuade any chance of a relationship."

"And, did you?"

"Of course not," Leroy said, throwing up his hands. "It wasn't my place to tell a grown man whose company he could keep. Since both were guests at my table, how could I then demand he avoid her?"

"What did Mrs. Spelding do when you refused?"

"I'm not sure," he said, looking shaken. "She said if I didn't take care of it, she'd do so herself."

The sheriff began scribbling. "During the argument that night, Mr. Calderon overheard one of them mention something about a divorce."

"Who's divorce?"

"I believe it was yours. Am I to understand you've no intentions of divorcing your wife?"

"Of course not!" Leroy said. "Are you saying Camilla wants a divorce?"

"Mrs. Spelding claims Lorelda uttered the words, not she. But, it's unclear who mentioned it."

"How did Braegar overhear *that*?" he asked, rubbing his forehead. "Where was I?"

"You would've been asleep. This occurred after Lorelda retired for the night."

"That still doesn't say how Braegar overheard their conversation."

"He claimed to be outside the door because he'd been called to Lorelda's room with this," Jim said, handing him Lorelda's missive. "I'm sorry, Mr. Spelding, but there's more."

Leroy's hands shook as he read the note. "More?" he squeaked, looking aghast.

"Doctor Turner believes that the night Lorelda died, you became ill due to Belladonna poisoning."

Leroy turned ashen and his mouth dropped.

"Actually, you'd ingested two substances; one in your bourbon and one in your evening tea."

Though Leroy worked his mouth, no sound came out.

"So, I take it you weren't aware your drinks were tainted?" At Leroy's dumbfounded shake of head, Hadley asked crisply, "Is it true, Camilla was the only one who handled your drinks that night?"

৵৶

"Come in," Reagan said at the knock on the door.

"Excuse me, sir, but Sheriff Hadley's here to see you," Aida said upon entering. "He's waiting in the parlor."

"Thanks, tell him I'll be right there," he said, closing his ledger. After straightening his desk, Reagan left his office, soon entering the front parlor. "Hello, Jim," he said, extending his hand. "Are you here as sheriff or friend?"

Hadley laughed. "Neither, officially," he said gripping Reagan's hand. "I thought you needed to know I've not had time to investigate Braegar's chicanery. I've got bigger crimes on my platter."

"I heard about Lorelda Hargrove," Reagan said, going to the sideboard. "Would you like a drink? You look like hell."

"Yes, and I feel as bad as I look," Jim said, taking a seat. "Make mine a double."

Reagan poured two drinks before handing one to the sheriff. He then sat nearby. "So, what brings you here besides my fine whiskey?"

"First and foremost, the whiskey," he said, grinning. "Secondly, my investigation into Lorelda's death is looking less accidental and more homicidal."

"Good Lord!" Reagan's eyebrows shot up. "Don't tell me Braegar killed Lorelda? I thought it had been some horrible accident."

"That's not the direction the evidence is leading," Jim said, sighing. "In fact, it looks like Camilla has her fingers in this pot."

"Are you serious?" he asked. "Why would she do such a thing?"

"It seems your robber baron overheard an argument between the two women the night Lorelda died. A fact, Camilla's admitted. She also admitted striking Lorelda across the face, though she denies killing her."

"But, Lorelda was found outside her balcony. Wouldn't it take a man's strength to push her over?"

"One would think so. However, I've not found evidence of any man in her room. Beauregard left earlier that night and Leroy had been too sick. Braegar is certainly strong enough, but I've no proof to connect him to either crime."

"Either? Was there more than one?"

"Oh, did I forget to mention Leroy had been poisoned? In fact, he nearly died. Both Doctor Turner and the apothecary confirmed he'd ingested two substances that night. Everyone said it was Camilla who poured after-dinner drinks and prepared Leroy's tea; both of which contained narcotics."

Reagan let out a low whistle. "That certainly takes precedence over fraud and arson."

"At least for now. I've sent a message to Mr. Calderon to come to my office for a final interview. And, unless something turns up, it looks like he'll soon be leaving town. I've nothing to implicate him to either crime at the Spelding home."

"I don't understand why Camilla would harm Leroy," Reagan said. "Does it make sense to you?"

"Well, there's more. Braegar received a note from Lorelda mentioning Camilla and treachery in the same sentence. He gave it to me when I first questioned him."

"I wouldn't take his word for it," Reagan said, snorting. "It could've been forged. After all, he's proven he'll do anything to get what he wants."

"I've already thought of that," the sheriff said. "I showed the note to Lorelda's parents and they confirmed her handwriting. It seems everything Braegar's told me has been the truth. He may be a swindler and a thief, but I can't prove him a murderer."

"Do you know what the treachery was about?"

"Braegar says he heard them arguing about Camilla divorcing Leroy. When I questioned Camilla, she claimed it was Lorelda who uttered those words, so it looks like someone said it. Who, I can't be certain."

"It sounds complicated," Reagan said, shaking his head. "I know Camilla's capable of contemptible things, I just wouldn't have imagined this contemptible."

Hadley swallowed the last of his whiskey. "Thanks, for the tipple." He set down his glass before standing. "Until you read about it in the papers, you haven't heard a thing."

"Of course," Reagan said, rising. "I'll see you to the door."

"Please, don't bother," the sheriff said. "I'm used to finding my way out." Of a sudden, he chuckled. "Just be glad you don't have a wife looking to leave her marriage. It's a messy business."

"I'm very glad, indeed," Reagan said, nodding. "I'm a lucky man."

chapter 64

MAYOR HAMPTON AWOKE after having slept for a day and a half. If anything, his sense of purpose had deepened as wisps of having dreamt of Elizabeth clung like cobwebs to his inner mind. He bathed and then shaved several days' growth before dressing in his finest suit. Standing before the mirror, he combed his hair until it lay perfectly. He stared at his face to see if it revealed his intentions. He tried to smile. Shaking his head, he tried again and this time succeeded in lifting his lips into something resembling a grimace. It would have to do, he thought. At least, it would satisfy his purpose.

First, he would visit Elizabeth's grave. After the recent storm, he knew no one else would venture to the cemetery. He wanted to explain to his daughter what had to be done. After that, he'd do it. He would avenge her death and the loss of his grandson. Sam glanced at his shaky hands. He'd have Dudley prepare strong coffee. Food wouldn't sit well anyway.

Walking to his dresser, he opened a small box and removed a derringer. Placing the gun on its half-cock notch, he poured black powder down the barrel then rammed a patched lead ball onto the powder. Next, he placed a percussion cap on the tube before slipping it into his pocket.

❧❦

The sound of jangling sleigh bells could be heard inside Winslow House Hospital. Mallory paused near a window, blowing warm breath on the glass before wiping away melted frost. "Oh, look!" she said. "There's a wagon stopped outside and it's pulled by reindeer!"

Excited chatter accompanied volunteers now crowding around the window until Amy squeezed between them and pulled upward on the sash. Opening the window, cold air rushed inside as they peered at the wagon now being unloaded. "It's not reindeer," one girl complained. "It's only mules, with tree branches tied to their heads!"

"Looks like someone's coming inside," spoke another.

Amy shivered as the wind penetrated her clothing. "All right, ladies, let's get back to work," she said, shutting the window. "The men won't get fed by themselves."

Extra volunteers had been requested in order to carry out the ambitious Christmas Eve celebration. Doctor Turner had readily agreed, even approving funds to purchase games to be distributed among soldiers. Soon cards, checkers and dominos were entertaining those well enough to play. Folding tables had been borrowed from several churches as well as Clancy's dry goods store and set up in each ward. Soldiers confined to their pallets would have a tray brought while the rest dined at tables.

Boxed food had been arriving all morning, and fragrances of ham, turkey, sausage and oysters mingled with aromas of candied yams, boiled vegetables and fresh baked pies. Cook had been busily baking cookies and preparing plum pudding while Amy, with the help of Olivia, made eggnog and wassail.

Doctor Alexander had just finished rounds, prescribing a hearty yuletide meal to most soldiers. The men exuded eager expectation of the coming feast and amid this excitement the front door burst open and a bewhiskered man carrying a large gunnysack over his shoulder walked in. He wore an ancient fur coat beneath a beaver hat that gave little evidence of his identity. Behind him, boys entered and began stacking several crates near the door.

"Hello!" he called, stomping snow from his boots. "I heard there be soldiers here, unable to be with kith and kin for Christmas." He then approached

Amy who was heading toward the kitchen. "Hello, my fine lass. I'm here to deliver gifts."

"Mr. Bruester?" she said, recognizing Amanda's father behind the fake beard. "Is that you?"

"No, lass! I be Saint Nicholas!" he said, winking. "I'm come early for these young men so I won't disturb their sleep, tonight."

Amy smiled. "That's very thoughtful. I'm sure everyone will be surprised."

"Let's get started." He looked around the reception hall. "Where do I go first?"

"Can I take your coat?" she asked, looking dubiously at the garment. It appeared rather shabby for a wealthy businessman. "Or, your hat?"

"No, dearie," he said, before leaning close to whisper, "There was no other costume to be had. It caused quite a stir leaving the house wearing this aged coat." He touched his whiskered face. "And this, I borrowed from the theatre."

"I see," Amy said, smiling again. "Well, Saint Nicholas, I'll show you the wards. It's nearly time for dinner, so we'd better hurry." She then led him to the nearest chamber. Many sat on sides of their beds, awaiting the coming meal. More than a few jaws dropped when George walked in, a gunnysack over his shoulder.

"Hello, soldier," he said, stopping at the first bed and lowering his sack. "I understand you're a bit injured and can't be with your comrades. Here's a little something to pass time until you improve." He pulled out a book and handed it to him. "And, there's socks as well," he said, digging out a pair. "Merry Christmas!"

George made his way around the ward, handing out books, clothing and writing materials which the men received gratefully. When his sack became empty he returned to the foyer and filled it from crates left inside the door. Amy escorted him from room to room, ensuring each soldier received something. By the time he finished, the soldiers were being seated at tables.

"Please distribute any leftover items," George said, indicating the crates. "I'm sure there'll be more wounded to come."

"Thanks for coming," Amy said. "I'll let both doctors know of your kindness."

"Bah! 'Twas nothing. No one can compensate for what these boys have sacrificed," he said, folding up his gunny. "I'll leave you to your task. It looks like dinner's about to be served."

"Merry Christmas," Amy said as she opened the door. "Please come back anytime." After he left, she hurried to the kitchen where Miles stood, holding a knife.

"Oh, there you are," he said, glancing up. "I was told you were escorting around a strange gentlemen." He smiled as he worked his blade clumsily through the turkey. "I trust it's not some swain vying for your affections?"

Amy's cheeks reddened for Olivia stood near-by, ladling eggnog into glasses. "Of course not. It was Mr. Bruester, bringing gifts." She gave him a reproving look. "Besides, my affections are my business, are they not?"

Miles waited until Olivia left with her tray of drinks. "Of course it's my business. We've already settled the matter. We're to be wed next Christmas."

Her retort died, for the knife Miles held, suddenly slipped, slicing several fingers. The utensil clattered to the floor as he quickly pulled away his hand, preventing blood from tainting the meat.

Amy rushed forward, grabbing a towel. Wrapping it around his fingers, she pressed tightly. "This is foolish! You shouldn't be using a knife," she scolded. "I should've known this would've happened. You're hand's better, but it's not strong enough to do this. What were you thinking?"

She looked up, discovering his intent gaze. "What?" she asked fearfully. "Am I hurting you?"

"The pain I'm feeling is a different kind." Amy felt her insides flutter as he put his free hand over hers. Before she could respond, he removed the towel to inspect his injury. "If I'm to be any use, I suppose we should bandage this."

His words snapped her from her stupor. "Come, then," she said, tugging his wrist. "Let's patch you up." Amy led the way to the supply room. Once inside, she opened a bottle of bromine and dribbled liquid over his cuts, letting the towel catch drips. She next cut a length of linen, wrapping it around one finger and tearing the end in two, tied it off. She then did the same to his other cuts. There, you're now fit for duty," she said. "Albeit, without a sharp instrument."

Miles clicked his heels and gave a short bow. "Thank you milady," he said, appraising her handiwork. "I couldn't have done better myself. Let's get back to our duties." Tossing the towel in a pail, he opened the door, finding a flurry of activity.

Volunteers, a plate in each hand, formed a procession that soon filled empty spots before each seated soldier. Once a ward had been served, the chaplain came and gave a prayer of thanksgiving and a request for healing. And then, the eating began. Amy busied herself with a pitcher of wassail, making innumerable trips between floors, deftly skirting cast-aside canes and crutches while Miles found a safer post portioning out various side dishes.

Later, anyone with room left in their stomachs received their choice of many desserts. Volunteers kept a steady procession refilling glasses, removing dishes and fetching needful things while conversation flowed, punctuated with occasional laughter. Long after the meal ended, activity remained high in the kitchen where dishes were being washed and leftovers packed for volunteers to take home.

By the time Amy finished her duties, a northerly wind had caused spidery drifts to congest the walk-way to the stable. The late-afternoon sun, curtained behind gray clouds, cast a mixture of light and shadow along the frozen ground. She buttoned her coat, thinking she would have to keep her skirts lifted or else ruin the hem of her dress. Amy frowned. *How am I to do that while carrying a basket?* Without warning, the back entrance opened and Doctor Alexander walked in amidst a rush of cold air.

"Brrr!" he said, dusting snowflakes from his coat. "It's freezing outside."

"Just what I wanted to hear," Amy said, eying the frosted door panes. "I'm already late. We're dining at my brother's home this evening. I promised my parents I'd be home before five. If not, I'm to take myself to his house."

"How far does he live?" Miles asked as she wound a scarf around her head.

"Further than my house," she said, tugging on gloves. "He built his home on the east side of town, near the new mill."

"What'd you drive here?"

"A gig."

He arched a brow. "Now who's foolish? A gig isn't built for snowdrifts."

"How could I know it'd be so windy?"

"I've a sleigh," Miles said. "I'll be happy to take you there."

"Please, don't bother," she said, picking up her basket. "I'll manage."

Miles looked her up and down. "Those shoes aren't going to keep the snow from getting inside them and you'll likely get stuck somewhere. No, Miss Burnsfield, I think it safer if I take you to your brother's home."

"But, your hand—"

"A source of frustration, yes." He held it up, admiring his bandages. "Yet, serviceable. However, if not for my injury, I'd have never met you." He smiled, his eyes sparkling azure blue as he opened the door and held it wide. "After you."

Amy relented lest her indecision cause cold air to find its way into the wards. She walked onto the back porch, waiting until the door clicked shut. Smiling sweetly, she began descending the steps. "I appreciate the offer Doctor Alexander, but I'm quite capable of handling a one-horse gig."

Before she reached the bottom, Miles had closed the distance between them. In one motion and without further words, he swept her into his arms then strode toward the stable.

Amy gasped at her unladylike position. "What are you doing?" She gripped his shoulder while her free hand clutched the basket. "I assure you, I'll be fine!" Though she'd been caught unawares, then hoisted into his arms, it was her close proximity to his lips that befuddled her most. She dared not look into his eyes for fear he'd read her thoughts. Instead, she stared at his mouth, her face reddening as she was reminded once again of his stolen kiss.

"I'm doing this for your own good," Miles said, kicking open the stable door and walking inside. "There are few travelers this time of day and I'd never forgive myself if anything happened to you."

The cutter sleigh already had a horse harnessed and stationed near the wide doors. With seeming ease, Miles swung her up and through the open aperture, settling her on the seat. He then reached beneath it, pulling out and unfolding a fur robe. "This should keep you warm," he said, spreading it over her lap. He looked sternly into her face. "Don't move," he warned. "I'm taking you to your brother's and that's the end of it."

"What about my horse?" Amy pointed toward the stall. "I can't leave her."

Miles swung open the wide doors and led his horse and sleigh outside. "Every animal here gets fed," he said before shutting the doors and climbing in beside her. "She'll be fine." He picked up the reins, slapping them briskly. As the runners slid thorough the snow, he grinned down at her. "Now, tell me which way to go."

chapter 65

"WOULD YOU LIKE a cup of coffee?" Sheriff Hadley asked, lifting a pot from the potbellied stove. "It's freshly brewed."

"No, thank you," Braegar said, removing his coat and hanging it on a peg. "I had plenty at breakfast."

"Suit yourself," Jim said, pouring himself a cup. He took a sip, studying Braegar's apparel. "Are you leaving town?"

Braegar nodded. "Once I've satisfied your questions, I'm going home. There's no reason to stay. Poor Leroy is inconsolable at this unfortunate turn of events. I'm afraid it's too much for him. I can barely believe it myself."

"Can barely believe what?" Jim walked behind his desk. "Please, have a seat," he said, indicating an empty chair.

Braegar waited until the sheriff sat before settling into his chair. "I can hardly believe what's happened to Miss Hargrove and Leroy. Do you really think Camilla's responsible?"

Hadley didn't answer; instead he busied himself taking papers from his desk. "I'd like you to tell me about any conversations you may've had with Mrs. Spelding concerning Miss Hargrove."

Braegar looked confused. "What do you mean?"

"Did Mrs. Spelding ever mention wanting you to avoid a relationship with Miss Hargrove?"

Braegar rubbed his jaw. "Not outright. However, I got the distinct impression she didn't want Lorelda and I to become too—close—" He looked up. "It wouldn't have been polite to thwart her desires in her own home. I didn't understand it, but felt compelled to defer to her wishes."

"So, you never had a personal relationship with Miss Hargrove?"

"I'm afraid not," he said, folding his hands. "If Camilla said so, she thought wrong."

Sheriff Hadley began taking notes. "Did Miss Hargrove ever mention being fearful of Mrs. Spelding?"

"Not that I recall," he said. "There wouldn't have been much opportunity to speak privately, since we only saw each other with others present."

"And yet, she sent you that note." Jim looked at him intently. "She must've felt she could trust you. Can you tell me why?"

"I'm not sure how to answer that," Braegar said with a tight smile. "I can't pretend to decipher a woman's mind."

The sheriff pursed his lips, realizing he couldn't easily shake the man's confidence. And, even though he had suspicions about Braegar's culpability in either or both crimes, he still lacked proof.

"Have you any idea what the treachery was that Lorelda wrote of in her note?"

"I only know what I overheard. If Camilla wanted a divorce, I must assume that was the treachery Lorelda meant."

"I don't suppose you knew what grounds for divorce Mrs. Spelding would've used?" Hadley's pencil was poised.

Braegar's eyes became impenetrable. "I can assure you, I wasn't Camilla's confidant. You'd have to ask her."

"I have," Jim said, sighing. He tapped his pencil, realizing the evidence kept leading back to Mrs. Spelding. He felt he could make a case with Leroy's poisoning, but Lorelda's death was still murky. Had she fallen in a drunken stupor or had she been pushed?

"The last time we spoke, you said there seemed to be animosity between the two women even before their argument. Has anything come to mind since then to further support that theory?"

Braegar shook his head. "No, nothing." He then tilted his vest watch upward. "Are we about finished? My train leaves this afternoon. I wouldn't want to miss it."

Hadley leaned back. "I've one more question. I noticed during both interviews you started out saying *Miss Hargrove*, but then reverted to *Lorelda*. Are you sure you didn't have a more involved relationship with the deceased?"

Braegar chuckled. "A slip of the tongue, I assure you. I also refer to Mrs. Spelding as Camilla. We've dined together so often, formalities fall by the wayside."

"I see," Jim said, setting aside his notes. He had learned nothing new and no further avenues to pursue. "Speaking of Mrs. Spelding, I understand she's sent you a message asking that you speak to her before you leave."

"Yes," he said, sighing. "I received her message. But, I assumed it wouldn't be allowed since you said I shouldn't talk to her."

Hadley shook his head. "That was only until I'd collected everyone's testimony."

"Are you saying you'd allow her visitors?" he asked, crooking a brow.

"I don't presume anyone's guilt," Jim said, dropping his pencil. "You're free to speak to her." He jerked a thumb over his shoulder. "Mrs. Spelding's in the back room. There's a chair beside her cell."

Braegar looked interested. "If it wouldn't cause any harm, perhaps, I will. That is, if you've finished with me?"

A knock on the door preceded his answer. "Now's seems to be a good time," Jim said, rising.

As Braegar entered the back room, Sheriff Hadley went and opened the door. "Beau! What brings you here?" he asked, stepping aside. "Come in. It's cold out."

"Merci!" Beauregard said, bustling inside, allowing Jim to shut the door. He removed his hat and coat, finding a bare peg. "Forgive me for bothering you, but I can't help wondering what it was Camilla wanted to tell me when she was arrested. I'm hoping to be allowed to speak with her."

"I've not formally arrested Mrs. Spelding. I've taken her into custody. Judge McCleary's visiting his daughter and won't return until after Christmas. Once he does and if charges are filed, I'm sure Mrs. Spelding will make bail."

"Ahh! I see," he said with cheer. "That's good news, is it not?"

"That depends on whether Mr. Spelding offers the funds," he said, lifting the coffee pot. "Would you like something to warm you? It's going to be awhile. Mrs. Spelding has a visitor."

"Oui!" Beau said, rubbing his hands together. "I'm rather chilled."

Both men had just sat with steaming cups when another knock shook the door. "Dash it all!" Jim said, rising. "Who else could be out and about?"

A blast of cold air accompanied Doctor Turner as the sheriff opened the door. "Hello, doc," he said, grinning. "You might as well join the rest of us."

❧❧

"I don't understand," Camilla said, wringing her hands. "How could I be accused of anything?"

Braegar stood still, his face impassive. "I can only repeat what I've been told," he said. "The sheriff claims there's evidence—"

She gripped the bars, her knuckles white. "It *had* to be the sleeping potion!" she said low, her eyes darting toward the door that separated her cell from the office. "I must've given him too much! I don't know how, but the doctor knew something was in the tea. But, that's not all. Supposedly, the doctor found poison in one of the bourbon glasses!"

"So, that's why the sheriff asked who poured drinks that night," Braegar said. "This doesn't look good for you, I'm afraid."

"But, I didn't do it!" she said. "The doctor must be wrong. All I gave him was sleeping potion. Besides, I don't know anything about poisons."

"If he'd been poisoned, I don't see how anyone else could've done it, either."

"I know that!" Camilla said. "The sheriff made that point abundantly clear."

"What did you tell the sheriff?"

"That I must've given Leroy my tea, by accident," Camilla said, tears forming in her eyes. "It made him ill. But, it wasn't on purpose, I swear." She looked at him in sudden hope. "You can tell him! Tell the sheriff it was only for sleep—that it wasn't intended for harm." Tears ran down her cheeks. "Pray, tell him—about—"

"About us?"

"I don't know!" she said, squeezing the bars. "I haven't, but maybe we should. You could assure the sheriff we'd no intentions of hurting Leroy." She offered a tremulous smile. "Would you? Please—it—it's necessary now..."

"I think that would be unwise."

"But why?" Camilla's face reflected dismay. "They think I tried poisoning him!"

"My dear, as an adulteress, everyone would think that's exactly why he'd been poisoned. You'd just be condemning yourself."

"Better adultery than murder!"

"Thankfully, Leroy didn't die," Braegar reminded her. "You'll have a better chance of acquittal if it's not known you gave Leroy sleeping potion in order to hide a tryst."

"Wouldn't it be better if you vouched for me? I'd rather be a scorned woman than end up in prison." She stepped back, smoothing her hair. "We could still be together—once it's over—"

He shook his head. "It's a damn shame this happened Camilla, because either way, your life's ruined. Why drag me down with you?"

She looked at him with imploring eyes. "But, how can I defend myself? I've even been accused of killing Lorelda!"

"Why would the sheriff think that?"

"He somehow knew we'd argued that night. Tillie must've overheard us. I—I slapped her, but, I didn't kill her!" she said, wringing her hands once again. "The mark was still visible." Closing her eyes, she rubbed her temples. "I can't believe this is happening! It's her own fault she's dead!"

He took a step nearer, his voice soft. "What do you know about Lorelda?"

Her eyes flew open. "That she was jealous!" she said, anger mingling with her fear. "The twit must've been drunk and fell to her death. They found a whiskey bottle in her room. But, because of that damning note, they think I killed her!"

"A note? Who was it written to?"

Something in his voice made her stop. At first, Braegar's presence had buoyed her spirits, reassuring her Lorelda must've lied about their clandestine relationship. But now, she realized he didn't seem surprised. In fact, she noticed his look of amusement.

She suddenly recalled the whiskey glasses in his bedroom. Dawning realization of his treachery produced bile in her throat. Her jaw dropped, the impact of his betrayal striking hard. "It was you!" she said, hissing. "She slipped you the note!" She pressed herself against the bars. "Why'd you give it to the sheriff? You could've destroyed it!"

"'Twas my duty."

"Duty? Was it also your duty to screw her?"

"Oh, that," he said with a short laugh. "That happened earlier. It was my way of gaining information. One can learn quite a bit from a wallflower. It was, shall we say, entertaining." He then arched a brow. "Besides, she was so—*grateful*."

"How could you? We were supposed to be together!"

"We were, for a time," he said shrugging. "Why would you expect me to remain any more faithful than you?" He began putting on gloves. "I'm leaving now, my dear. I wish you the best of luck."

"Wait, please!" Camilla begged. "You mustn't leave. Who'll help me, if not you?"

"You're beautiful, and you know how to use it to get what you want," he said looking her up and down. "I'm sure you'll find a good lawyer."

"I'll tell them about us! You'll be sorry, you treasonous bastard!"

"I'd just deny it," he said, shaking his head. "If you force the issue, I'll suddenly recall that you said

Leroy could die for all you cared. How would that look in court?"

Fear flared in her eyes. "I never meant that, and you know it."

"Do you think the sheriff or Leroy would believe that?"

"You wouldn't!"

"I would. And, if forced, I will." He sighed at her stricken expression. "It's over, Camilla. You need to think about yourself. The image you portray will likely determine your fate. My advice is stay with the mantra it was an accident. With your charms, I'm sure you'll pull it off."

Camilla stared, her face pale. "So, you're just going to abandon me?"

"My dear, I can't be associated with an accused murderess. If anyone helps you, it should be your husband."

She held out her palms in supplication. "He hasn't come. He thinks I poisoned him," she said, her voice catching. "I don't know what to do."

"Then I suggest you don't also tell him he's been cuckolded," Braegar said. "You'd lose whatever assistance he might be willing to give." He then gave a short bow. "I bid you adieu, Mrs. Spelding."

chapter 66

SAM HAMPTON STARED at the marker the stone carver made for Elizabeth's grave. If he had known earlier she died because of a lumberman, he never would've commissioned a tree stump. Yet, it was fitting, he thought darkly. As her life was cut short, so too, would her murderer's.

"Why didn't you come to me?" he said out loud. He stood immobile, the cold numbing his cheeks, tortured with thoughts of what he would've done if he had only known. He would've set things aright. There were laws to make a man take care of his responsibilities. However, it probably wouldn't have been necessary. The lumberman would've likely paid far more to keep quiet he had fathered an illegitimate child.

Now, it was too late. Money wouldn't suffice. The only thing left was revenge. "I'm going to fix this," he said, his voice catching. "I promise you won't be forgotten. He'll know exactly what he's done before I send him to hell!"

Sam retraced his steps and climbed into his small sleigh. Leaving the cemetery, he placed a hand into his pocket. Fingering the derringer, the steel felt satisfyingly cold. Soon, Reagan's debt would be paid.

ૐ ❧*

"Good afternoon," Doctor Turner said, stamping snow from his feet. "Or, should I say good evening?"

"Either's fine with me," Jim said, closing the door. "Would you like some coffee?"

"No thanks," he said, noting Beau's presence. "Perhaps, I've come at a bad time?"

Just then, the back door opened and Braegar stepped into the office, smiling broadly. "Why, I'd no idea the jail was a social beehive." He stuck out his hand, to each in turn. "Hello, Beau. Hello, Doctor Turner."

Monsieur Calderon," Beau said, standing. "This is much a tragedy. Have you discovered anything new?"

He shook his head. "Sadly, no. Mrs. Spelding's quite distraught, as you can imagine. Our conversation hasn't shed any new light."

"If you're finished visiting with mademoiselle, I'd like to speak with her," he said.

"Yes, I am." He stepped out of the way as the Frenchman walked past. "Did you have any further questions?" he asked the sheriff. "Otherwise, I'd like to finish packing."

"Go ahead. If I think of anything else, I'll come by the hotel. What time do you leave?"

Braegar reached for his coat and put it on. "Six o'clock." He then nodded to the men. "It's been a pleasure, gentlemen. I'm sorry to end our acquaintance under these circumstances."

After the door closed, Hadley turned to the doctor. "Would you like a seat?"

I'm not sure if I'll be staying that long," he said, pulling paper from a pocket. "I've found an interesting imprint at the base of Miss Hargrove's neck, behind her ear." He then handed it over. "At first, I first missed it due to lividity, which is skin discoloration. However, it became pronounced as the body warmed. I'm not sure what it is, but it looks too intricate to be a button impression. That's the only thing I could think of that'd make such a mark."

Jim looked at the drawing, moving it this way and that. It showed several curved lines between a double set of straight lines on two of four sides. "I can't tell what it is, either," he said, before setting it on his desk. "Does it give any indication to her death?"

"No," Artemus said. "I don't know if it means anything, really."

"What's your final determination? Was Miss Hargrove murdered or did she simply fall due to intoxication?"

"If pressed, I'd have to say the fall caused her death. However, that doesn't rule out activity that happened beforehand. Her injuries just don't reveal whether she fell accidentally or had been pushed."

"So, you're saying there's no proof of foul play?"

"I'm not saying that. But, I can't be certain. Any lawyer could make mincemeat of my findings. With the presence of laudanum and whiskey bottles, I doubt you'd win a conviction against Mrs. Spelding or anyone, for that matter."

Jim rubbed the back of his neck. "I want justice served," he said, sighing. "I'd hoped you'd find clear evidence one way or the other, like you did with the poison."

"I wish I could too," he said. "The markings on her neck are curious, but not conclusive."

Hadley noted tiredness etching the doctor's face. "Aw, hell! You need a drink. Sit down," he ordered. "I'm pouring us something that'll warm us better than this muddy water I brewed." With that, he reached behind his desk and opened the bottom drawer, pulling out a bottle and two small glasses. As Artemus took a seat, Jim poured amber liquid into both glasses. "Here," he said, holding one out. "This'll fix what ails you."

"Thanks," he said as the sheriff also sat. "Just one, though. I'm on duty tonight."

"Sure, I understand," he said tapping his temple. "Those soldiers wouldn't want you getting fogged, jumbling their medicines, now would they?"

Turner savored the bitter taste before swallowing. "No, they wouldn't."

Just then, Beau came bursting out of the back room, skidding to a stop. "Écouter! Monsieur Calderon avait une affaire avec Mademoiselle Hargrove!" he panted, his hands flying as fast as his words. "Vous devez savoir!"

Hadley shook his head. "English, please. I barely understood a word."

Beau nodded, taking a deep breath before uttering, "Shérif! Camilla informed me Monsieur Calderon has admitted to an indélicat romance with Mademoiselle Hargrove!"

Jim sat up in his seat. "What'd you say?"

"Eh bien!" Beau fought the urge to speak French. "Je vous plains!— *Sorry!*" He took another breath, and began again. "Camilla says Braegar has had a romantic interlude with Mademoiselle Hargrove. Not only that, she claims he's a traître in business. He's swindling me out of Paradis Pavillon!"

"And, she just now recalled that?" he asked, perplexed. "Why didn't she say so before?"

Beauregard lifted his shoulders. "She said it was the hotel fire that gave him his opportunity. Not until later, did he divulge that our contract was *sinistre*. Camilla said she planned telling me the day she was arrested."

"Detained," Jim said. "Mrs. Spelding's only been detained." He drummed his fingers thoughtfully. "Seems rather strange we're just now hearing this. Mr. Calderon was adamant there was no relationship between him and Miss Hargrove. I can't help but wonder if Mrs. Spelding's simply trying to throw suspicion elsewhere." He sat back, raising a brow. "Did she offer any proof?"

"Braegar admitted it to her."

"Yet she neglected to tell me?" Hadley scoffed. "I find that highly unlikely."

Beau waved his hands. "You don't *comprendre*. He just now told her!"

"I suppose I'll have to question her about it," he said, sighing. "Tasks keep introducing themselves to me."

Beau didn't respond, his eyes having fallen to the forgotten paper. "Why do you have a drawing of Monsieur Calderon's ring?" he asked, staring.

Sheriff Hadley looked startled. "What?" he said, nearly choking. He thrust the paper into Beau's hands. "Are you sure?"

Beau turned it so the parallel lines were atop and below the curved markings. "Oui. His crest is thus and so," he said, tracing his finger over the lines. "I saw it very clearly when we first met."

"His ring!" Jim stood, looking at Doctor Turner. "Do you know what this means?"

"That if his ring was against her neck, so were his hands!" he responded, standing. "The other bruises *were* from strangulation! Didn't he say he's leaving on the train?"

"He's going first to the Rochester," the sheriff said, reaching for his coat before snatching the paper from Beau's hands. "Doc, I'll need you to verify his ring made that bruise. You're coming with me."

Both men hurried out the door, leaving Beau standing with his mouth agape.

"Didn't anyone hear he's swindling me?" he asked the empty room.

chapter 67

"WHAT A LOVELY tree!" Katherine said, standing by a cloth covered table dominated by a spruce. The deep red coverlet reached to the floor, its fringe skimming the carpet at their feet. "It's breathtaking."

"Thank you," Amanda said, holding Jesse in her arms. "I enjoyed making the trimmings."

The four foot tree, laden with pine cones, ribbons and glass bead garlands was also dotted with sugared fruit and spun glass ornaments. Gaily wrapped presents filled the remaining space on the table with a few large packages resting on the floor. "By this time next year, the boys will be walking," Amanda said. "We won't be able to leave packages where they can reach them."

Katherine laughed. "You could always have a playpen made. You'll find it useful to corral curious little ones."

"I'll be sure to remember that," Amanda said, nodding. "I don't want either of them exploring the hearth when I'm not looking."

"You must have your hands full with two babies," Katherine said. "I give you credit for adopting an orphan."

Amanda looked toward her husband who held a sleeping Gaeran. He seemed deep in conversation with Thomas as they stood near the fireplace. "It was Reagan's idea," she said, smiling. "And, I must admit, I had my doubts. But, I've since come to realize the beauty of giving to others. What started as sacrifice has become a joy."

Moment's later, the door opened and Amy entered on the arm of Doctor Alexander. "Merry Christmas," she said, smiling widely. "I'm sorry I'm late." She looked to her brother who approached, still holding Gaeran. "I hope you don't mind, but I invited Doctor Alexander to dinner. He hasn't any family nearby."

Reagan held out his free hand. "Of course not. Hello doctor. Welcome to our home."

"Call me Miles," he said, shaking Reagan's hand. "I insist."

"Miles, it is." He then glanced toward his sister. "How was dinner at the hospital?"

"A success," she said, "except, Doctor Alexander cut his hand carving the turkey."

"'Twas nothing serious," he said, holding up and wriggling his fingers. "Miss Burnsfield bandaged me in fine manner. I'll be healed in no time."

Amy's cheeks reddened as Miles gaze lingered. "Obviously, Doctor Alexander shouldn't have been using a knife. His hand isn't yet strong enough."

Miles shook his head. "I've repeatedly asked Miss Burnsfield to call me by my given name. I hope you can convince her to, at least while we're outside the hospital."

Reagan looked from Miles to Amy, noting her heightened color. "Hmm," he said, amused at her fluster. "Since it's my home, I guess I get to make the rules." He then gave her a stern look. "Amy, you must allow the good doctor his wishes. I bid you call him Miles. And," he turned back to the doctor, "you're required to call my sister by her given name. Otherwise, it'll sound too formal around our table."

Miles nodded, giving Amy a smile. "Thank you. I've been waiting for permission. And, now that I have it, would you care to sit, *Amy?*"

Before she could respond, a manservant entered the room and approached them. "Excuse me sir, but you've a visitor." He handed Reagan a card. "He's waiting in the study."

Reading the script, his heart lurched. *Sam Hampton!* Reagan's mind raced over possibilities the mayor would ask to see him on Christmas Eve. Did he know? Impossible! Reagan had been in contact with Lars Orphanage and knew of Sam's visit. Mrs. Seymour had assured him the mayor had left with no knowledge of who adopted his grandchild. She had even gone so far as to imply the adoptive parents lived in Indiana. Neither had Reagan heralded his adopting a babe, instead choosing to inform only family and close friends. So, it was likely Sam didn't know about his enlarged family. He hoped it was mere coincidence he had come uninvited, and without obvious reason. With as much aplomb as he could muster, Reagan held out the baby. "Amy, would you please hold Gaeran? I've a visitor."

"Of course," she said, accepting the child. He watched Amy and Miles join the others near the tree where they were soon laughing and conversing together.

Gripping the card, he hurried down the hall, pausing outside the study. He then opened the door and strode inside. "Mayor Hampton," he said with a smile, "to what do I owe this pleasure?"

Sam stood near the fireplace, gazing at a painting of Reagan and Amanda as newlyweds. Since then, they had commissioned a newer oil painting which included a newborn Jesse. As the more recent one now resided in the parlor, this one had been relegated to the study. The mayor had not turned at Reagan's entrance, but continued to stare at the art work. "You've a beautiful wife," he said. "You must be very happy."

Reagan approached, stopping behind Sam. "I am." He waited for the mayor to speak, growing uneasy at his continued silence. After several moments, he tried again. "Is there something I can do for you, sir?"

"I'm glad you've experienced the blessings of having a child," he said. "It's been one of few pleasures I've had in my life." He turned his head, seemingly deep in thought. "Elizabeth was my joy. My reason for living. She—was everything—"

"I'm sorry for your loss," Reagan said. "If there's anything that I can do?" he suddenly felt helpless being witness to the man's pain. What words of comfort could he offer? *I may've unknowingly slept with your daughter and impregnated her? I have your grandchild, but I can't tell you?* He shifted uneasily on his feet. He still didn't know why the mayor had come.

Sam dropped his head, one hand gripping the back of a chair. "I—" he seemed to struggle for words, "—I must know something." He turned toward Reagan, his mien hard as granite. "I must know if you ever loved her."

Reagan stared, sensing a trap. "Of course, I love Amanda," he said, unwilling to believe he'd been discovered. "Why would you think otherwise?"

"I'm not talking about your wife."

Reagan prayed Sam was fishing. He had no intention of admitting something he had never pursued nor wanted. He had no way of knowing how much the mayor suspected. Surely, if Elizabeth had written a second letter, Sam would've come before now.

"Who do you mean?"

"You know damn well, who I mean," he said, growling. "Elizabeth! Did you love my daughter, or did you just defile her for your amusement?" Flinging down the gauntlet, he waited to see if the lumberman picked it up.

So then, he knew something! But, how much? "We never had that kind of relationship," he said, looking straight into Sam's eyes. "On my honor, we didn't."

"Honor?" Sam spat the word. "You've no honor!" He hands curled into fists. "I should've known when Elizabeth had me invite Bertram here, there was something more! You used her to gain lumber contracts. You ate at my table. But that wasn't enough! You defiled her and once she got caught, sent her away. Because of you, she's dead!"

"I'm so very sorry about her death. But I had no hand in it." Reagan hated his partial lie. He certainly had no knowledge of Elizabeth's actions until well afterward. Telling her father he possibly sired his grandchild, no matter the circumstance, would be fruitless.

"You lie!" he said, reaching into his pocket. "I read her diary! It must be you!"

chapter 68

"SHERIFF!" BRAEGAR SAID, clearly surprised. He looked between the two men standing in the hallway. "Is something amiss?"

"Can we come in?" Hadley asked. "We discovered a perplexing bit of evidence and hoped you could clear it up. Before you leave, that is."

Braegar stepped back, opening the door wide. "As long as you don't mind if I keep packing. The train won't wait, you know."

"Of course not. This shouldn't take long," he said, walking in, followed by Doctor Turner. He watched as Braegar strode to the washstand and began placing shaving accoutrements inside a traveling bag. Removing his hat, he hung it on a coat rack near the door. He then braced his feet. "Would you mind letting us inspect your ring?"

Braegar looked at his hand, then the sheriff. "My ring?" he asked, frowning. "Whatever for?"

"You stated earlier you'd never been inside Lorelda's room. Do you still stand by that?"

"I most certainly do," he said, furrowing his brow. "What makes you think otherwise?"

"It may be nothing," Jim said, keeping his voice light. "Do you object to us looking at it?"

Braegar paused before smiling. He began working the ring off his finger. "It's a family heirloom. You must understand my reluctance to part with it."

"I'll handle it with care," Hadley assured, holding out his hand. "May we see it?"

After receiving the jewelry, the sheriff immediately held it up so both he and the doctor could view it. "What do you think, doc? Does it look the same?"

Artemus unfolded the paper he had kept hidden and held it next to the ring, staring intently. He then glanced at the sheriff, grinning. "It matches perfectly! I should've suspected! A ring, if twisted on the hand and pressed against someone's skin, would create a mirror image such as this."

Both men looked at Braegar whose face suddenly darkened. "I don't like the sound of that, gentlemen," he said, hands clenching. "Whatever mischief you're brewing, it won't work."

"I wasn't the one who left a tell-tale mark on Lorelda's body," Jim said. "I'm sorry, Mr. Calderon. You're going to have to come with me. This indicates you were inside Lorelda's room the night she fell from her balcony."

Braegar's eyes grew cold. "I'm getting on that train, sheriff. You'll not stop me with false accusations."

"I'm sure you'll get the best representation," Jim said. "I'm just doing my job. Moreover, I'm sure you'll want to clear your name. No one wants to do business with a man accused of murder."

"You've already arrested the person responsible for Lorelda's death," he said. "I didn't strangle her."

"*Detained*," Hadley said, rolling his eyes. "Mrs. Spelding's only been detained."

He handed the ring to Artemus then drew his gun. "Besides, we never said Miss Hargrove was strangled. Strange, how you knew that," he said. "The guilty often give themselves away." He looked to Artemus, "Would you mind handing him his frock? Mr. Calderon's going to be staying with us a little longer." The sheriff suddenly became all business as he cocked the hammer. "You, sir, are under the arrest for suspicion of murder of Miss Lorelda Hargrove."

"My lawyers will sue you for slander and false arrest!" Braegar said, seething. He snatched his coat from the doctor's hand. "You'll prove nothing!"

"Perhaps, not," Jim said. "But, I've enough evidence to bring charges. Judge McCleary will decide your guilt or innocence."

"Sheriff!" the doctor blurted suddenly, "look what I found!" He thrust out the ring, revealing a hidden compartment beneath the crest. "I felt something and pushed against it. It sprang open and I found a powdery residue inside."

"What is it?" Jim asked. He waited as Artemus wet his finger and daubed the substance before touching his tongue.

"Poison!" he nearly shouted. "It tastes like poison!"

"Well, I'll be damned," the sheriff said, staring wonderingly at Braegar. "You tried killing Leroy too?"

"I never touched his drink! How many times must I tell you? It was Camilla!"

"There's no reason to possess poison except to use it," Hadley said. "At the very least, you're a conspirator with Mrs. Spelding." He shook his head. "I don't know how you did it, but the truth will come out."

"I demand you set bail immediately," Braegar said, stomping toward the door as Artemus stepped out of his way. "This is an outrage!"

Sheriff Hadley donned his hat. "Judge McCleary's out of town. Besides, the court's closed until after Christmas." He glanced at the doctor as he followed his prisoner. "Come with me. I'm going to need a statement."

ॐ✍

Reagan stared at the derringer pointed at him. Beads of sweat popped onto his brow and he lifted his hands defensively. "What are you doing?"

"You took everything from me," Sam said, snarling. "Because of you, my Elizabeth's dead!" He stepped forward as Reagan stepped back. "I lost my grandchild! The only thing left of my daughter. All because of you!"

"You're mistaken," Reagan said, trying to remain calm. "Please put the gun away. You don't want to do this."

"Yes, I do," he said. "I've planned this for a long time. All I needed was to find out who was responsible. *You* were at Camilla's party. *You* were the only married man there. It had to be *you!*"

Reagan backed up until stopped by his desk. He saw the anguish in Sam's eyes and his insides twisted, imagining the pain of losing a child. If he told all, would it alleviate any of Sam's misery? But, at what risk? He groped for another alternative. "Whatever you think, I didn't pursue Elizabeth. I never acted dishonorably, I swear."

"You think I believe you? You had opportunity while staying at the Rochester." He read the shock in Reagan's eyes. "See, I knew it! You bastard! You beguiled Elizabeth with promises and lies. And, when she bore the fruits of your debauchery you abandoned her, forcing her to flee." He cocked the gun, his face suffused with rage. "I'm sending you to hell! After I do and before I hang, I'm going to tell everyone what a despicable beast you are. You'll be dead. But, your family will suffer for the rest of their lives."

Reagan swallowed hard. His worst nightmare had come calling, baring fangs. "I didn't do what you think. You must believe I didn't know anything—about Elizabeth's predicament—until she wrote me." He pointed toward his desk. "I have her letter. Would you like to see it?"

"You're lying," Sam said, snorting. "You likely have a weapon in your desk."

Despite his words, Reagan saw curiosity flicker across Sam's face. "It's there, I assure you. Fetch it yourself. Top drawer on the right." He then stepped aside, hands raised. "Before you shoot me, please read her letter."

A long pause ensued before the mayor moved. When he did, he kept the gun aimed at Reagan while he rifled the drawer, pulling out an envelope. A shiver swept his body as he recognized Elizabeth's handwriting. He looked at Reagan. "She wrote you? Why not to me?"

Reagan pointed with his chin. "Please. Read her letter. Then, you'll understand."

Sam removed the letter and unfolded it, reading swiftly. Within moments, his face had lost all color. The gun began to waiver and tears burst from his eyes. The letter fluttered from his fingers. He let out a keening wail as he sank into the chair, the derringer slipping to the floor. He buried his face into his hands. "Oh, Elizabeth! Elizabeth!" he said, rocking back and forth, "Why didn't you come to me? Why?"

Reagan approached and gently laid a hand on the mayor's shoulder. "I'm so sorry," he said. "Truly, I am." As Sam sobbed, Reagan reached down and snatched up the gun, pocketing and releasing the hammer in one swift motion. He stood still while the mayor's anguish poured out, waiting until the older man withdrew a handkerchief and wiped his face. "I've lost them," he said. "I've lost them forever."

Reagan squatted on his heels, putting a hand on the mayor's arm. "No, not entirely," he said. "You can see your grandchild if you want to."

"No, I can't," Sam said, his voice forlorn. "Someone in Lars adopted him. The orphanage refused to disclose little Sammy's whereabouts." He rubbed his brow. "After reading her letter, I realize they didn't honor Elizabeth's wishes. They adopted him out before you could get there. But, I'm sure you already know this."

Reagan had been watching the mayor's demeanor, weighing his choices. Once Sam had been shown Elizabeth's letter, he no longer seemed to hold Reagan accountable. Her words had exonerated the child's father of a disreputable act. Did he think Reagan the besotted, unnamed man? It didn't appear so, since Elizabeth didn't acknowledge it in her missive.

Could he trust his sudden urge to reveal the child's whereabouts? The man was obviously overwrought. No, *crushed*. He could alleviate some of his pain. Give him back that which he rightfully deserved. Reagan squeezed Sam's arm where his hand still rested. "What if you learned the child's whereabouts? If you were able see him, would you try nullifying his adoption?"

Sam shrugged his shoulders, twisting the cloth in his hands. "I don't see how. My daughter clearly didn't want me to do so. Besides, she's right about the child being stigmatized. I couldn't—wouldn't—do that. It'd ruin his life." He looked up with sorrow. "I must ask your forgiveness. I almost killed the wrong man." He shook his head. "I shouldn't have relied on Mrs. Speldings memory of who attended a party more than a year ago. I beg you to forgive me."

Reagan's heart wrenched. It was he who should be asking forgiveness. His disagreeable behavior had led to him the Rochester in the first place. If not for his actions, none of this would've happened and there'd be no question of Gaeran's parentage. "There's nothing to forgive," he said, standing. "I'm sure I'd have felt the same had I been in your shoes."

"I was wrong," Sam said, wiping away remaining wetness. "What I did is a crime." He sighed, attempting to smile. "Will you have me arrested?"

"Of course not," Reagan said. "But, I will do something for you. Something I should've done before."

Sam looked confused. "What do you mean?"

"You were right. I did contact the Lars Orphanage after receiving Elizabeth's letter. I spoke to Mrs. Seymour."

"Then, you know where Sammy is?" A dawning hope spread across Sam's face. "Do you know who adopted him?" At Reagan's nod he sat upright. "Do you think the family would allow me to see the child?"

"I know they would," Reagan said, compassion filling his voice. "Would you mind waiting here? I have something else to show you."

chapter 69

THE JAILHOUSE DOOR rattled, startling Beauregard who had been pacing the floor for the past hour. His eyes grew wide as a visibly upset Braegar entered, followed by the sheriff and doctor. "Monsieur Calderon," he uttered, much piqued. "I've been informed you a *filou*—swindler!" He clucked his tongue. "Did you déshonneur moi?"

"Now isn't the time," Hadley said, ushering his prisoner toward the back room. "I've more important matters to attend." After they disappeared behind the door, Beau turned to the doctor.

"So! Did monsieur admit his guilt?"

Artemus shook his head. "He denied knowledge of any crime. However," he said, holding an object, "he'll have a hard time explaining this."

Beau peered closely, recognizing the ring. "Ahh, so the drawing matched? Is this good news for Camilla?"

Before he could respond, loud voices could be heard from the back room. Within moments, the door opened and the sheriff came out, slamming the door behind him. "Whew!" he said, grinning. "I've placed them in cells as far apart as possible, but I don't know if they'll stop accusing each other."

"They seem quiet now," Beau offered.

"That's because I told Deputy Welch to stay seated between their cells until one or the other calms down." He took his chair, indicating the men do so as well. "Little do they know the deputy is making note of whatever conversation transpires. It may prove beneficial later on, if there's a trial."

"Doesn't this mean Camilla's innocent?" Beau asked. "Won't she now be free?"

"We still don't know if she's involved with Leroy's poisoning. She won't be absolved until we find exculpatory evidence." After everyone had settled in, Jim reached for paper, handing one to Artemus along with a spare pencil. "Doc, I'd appreciate you writing your findings on Miss Hargrove's autopsy, including the ring impression as well as what substance you believe inside it. And, Beau you're going to tell me moment by moment what everyone did at Leroy's that night in the parlor. Something's missing. We need to discover exactly how Leroy was poisoned."

As Doctor Turner began writing, Jim took a pencil from behind his ear. He looked expectantly at

Beau. "Take your time, and try recalling everyone's movements. Describe what happened, starting with where everyone was sitting or standing."

Beau rubbed his temples with a thumb and middle finger. "Oui! Let me think," he said, closing his eyes. "Camilla stood at the sideboard to pour drinks. We men sat in chairs while Lorelda had the sofa."

"Did Mr. Calderon get up while Mrs. Spelding poured or help pass out drinks?"

"Non. She stood at the cabinet before offering them on a tray."

Hadley looked perplexed. "You mean she didn't hand anyone their drinks individually?"

"Non!" Beau shook his head. "We chose our glasses from the tray."

"Seems hard to believe Mrs. Spelding could've known which glass Leroy would take, doesn't it? I mean, only one drink had been poisoned. What if the wrong person chose it?"

"I know not," he said, shrugging. "It's how she usually served drinks."

"All right, what happened next?"

Beauregard stared into space for several seconds. "I remember now," he said. "I started talking about reopening Barrington Hotel and somehow, conversation turned to Camilla's portrait. That's when Lorelda spilt the beans about Camilla accusing the maid of thievery."

Jim rotated his pencil in the air. "Keep going. That can't be anything. What else?"

"Lorelda soon retired to her room and it wasn't long before I left, as well. After that, I can't say what happened."

Disappointed, Hadley sat back. "That's it? Didn't anyone get up or move around? I can't prove who did the poisoning if that's all I have!" He glanced at the Frenchman. "Are you positive no one approached Leroy?"

Beau tapped his lip earnestly before his face lit. "Oui! I do recall something. Monsieur Calderon arose to look at Camilla's portrait. He stood a few feet from Leroy." He raised his brows. "Does that help?"

"Not unless he leaned over and poured something in Leroy's drink," Jim muttered, tossing his pencil. "It seems we're back to where we started." He clasped hands behind his head. "What do you think, doc? I know you're listening. Is there any other way Leroy could've been poisoned?"

Artemus sighed, having been caught. "I don't rightly know," he said turning Braegar's ring in his hands. After awhile, he put it on his own finger. By discreetly using his thumb, he was able to push the spring, popping open the hidden compartment. "I suppose he might've added it, had no one been looking. But, with all those witnesses, it seems impossible." He laughed suddenly. "I don't suppose he *traded* drinks with Leroy, did he?"

Beau chuckled, shaking his head. "Non! He only set his drink nearby. They did not trade."

All at once, both doctor and sheriff's jaw dropped and stared at each other.

"Qu'est-ce que c'est?" Beau said in a sputter, looking confused. "What is it?"

"That's it!" Jim said, slapping his forehead. "He must've poisoned his *own* drink and then sneakily took Leroy's."

The doctor nodded. "He could've easily poured it into his bourbon. All he'd have to do is swirl it long enough to dissolve the powder."

Hadley grabbed his pencil, scribbling fast. "Now, we're getting somewhere. We've circumstantial evidence it was Braegar who poisoned Leroy. Along with documentation he strangled Miss Hargrove before throwing her off the balcony; I'd say he's been a very busy man." He shook his head. "The only thing I haven't proven is his involvement in the Barrington Hotel fire."

Beau's brows shot up again. "What's this? There's more?"

"Possibly. It depends on where the man enjoyed his smokes."

"Monsieur," he said, perplexed, "I don't understand."

"Let's just say I discovered your friend enjoys the same cigars as the ones we found behind the woodpile."

Beau's eyes rounded. "Sacrebleu! You don't think—"

"Not by anything he said," Jim said, correcting him. "But, by his actions." He began writing again. "I've yet to connect that with his blackmail attempt."

"Now, you say too much!" Beau said, gasping. "What else did that scoundrel do?"

Jim waved a hand, not looking up. "That contract you signed? Reagan tried thwarting it after discovering legal chicanery. However, Braegar outwitted him with even more underhanded tactics."

"Mon Dieu!" Beauregard quickly crossed himself. "I cannot believe my ears! So, that's what Camilla meant about him swindling me. What has Reagan to do with this?"

Hadley glanced at Artemus, whose jaw had fallen slack. "I'm not at liberty to say. However, I can tell you what Braegar said when I questioned him. "Speaking of which," he opened a drawer and pulled out several papers, "sounded vague to my ears, even then." He scanned his hand-written notes before continuing. "When asked how he came to offer you assistance, he said he'd read about the fire in the papers."

"Oui, the story was reported the next morning," Beau said, nodding. "There's nothing *sinistre* in that."

Jim tapped his pencil abstractly. "I found it odd he didn't take umbrage when I inferred darker reasons for his offer of a loan. He simply reminded me a maid had left the lamp near the stove, causing the fire. I couldn't find a chink in his armor, so I assumed it to be a dead end."

"Impossible!" Beau said, looking confused. "The fire warden didn't know how it started until later that morning, after interviewing the staff. That particular information wasn't in the papers."

"Are you certain?" the sheriff asked, suddenly excited. "I'd have to verify that."

"Oui. I kept a copy of the article. You're welcome to it."

The sheriff slapped his thigh. "He must've known who to blame because he'd been outside the hotel that night, looking through a window. Between that and what Mrs. Spelding claims, we may have enough to convict our industrious Mr. Calderon." He chuckled as he began a fresh piece of paper. "You may be right, Beau. Mrs. Spelding will likely be set free."

chapter 70

AMANDA KNEW WHEN Reagan entered the parlor, something was amiss. She immediately excused herself and met him near the door. "What's the matter?" she asked, shifting Jesse to her shoulder. "You look upset."

"I am," he said, taking her hand. "We've a visitor. Sam Hampton."

Amanda drew in a breath, eyes wide. "Oh no," she whispered. "What does he want?"

"He's cobbled together enough innuendo to suspicion me," Reagan replied quietly. "So, I showed him the letter." At her shocked expression, he continued. "Don't worry. He believes Elizabeth professed another to be Gaeran's father, not me." Recognizing Amanda's panic, Reagan decided not to mention the gun in his pocket. "I've calmed him a bit, but he's understandably overwrought."

"What are we going to do?" she asked. "Is all for naught?"

Reagan's gaze went unbidden to where Gaeran lay in Amy's arms then dropped to Jesse. Despite all his efforts, he had failed to protect his family. He stroked his son's hair while the child slumbered. "I think there's only one thing we *can* do." He looked fixedly into his wife's eyes. "We're going to do the decent thing. We're going to introduce Sam to his grandson."

Stunned, Amanda's eyes grew even wider. "What if he wants the child?" she said, struggling to maintain composure. "I—I think that would devastate you—"

Reagan nodded. "It would." He took a deep breath, releasing it slowly. "But, I can no longer live in fear." His heart wrenched with battling emotions. "I may never know if I'm the father, but I know who his grandfather is. If that means we lose him, then so be it. At least, I'm willing to share."

Then, before he could change his mind, Reagan put a smile on his face and walked toward the others. "Amy, I'll take Gaeran," he said, reaching for the child. "I've a secret admirer who wishes to see the newest addition to our family." He gently lifted the babe in his arms and left the room.

Not since he almost lost Amanda two years ago, did Reagan feel so desolate. Then, his foolishness had nearly cost him his wife and unborn son. He recounted those terrifying hours when Derrick had taken Amanda and threatened her life. He had found courage from the resolve of taking back that which was rightfully his. Now, treading the halls, he lost confidence in his claim to Gaeran. Legally, the child was a Burnsfield. Morally, he remained Sam's grandson.

He stopped outside the study door, pressing a tender kiss upon Gaeran's brow. "In my heart, *you are my son*," he whispered as the babe stirred. "No matter where you are, I'll always love you." Then, with a surety he didn't feel, he entered the room, approaching the mayor who sat slumped in the chair.

Sam didn't realize Reagan had returned until he lowered Gaeran into his arms. "Mister Hampton, I'd like you to meet Gaeran Samuel Burnsfield," he said, as the mayor's startled expression turned to shock.

His mouth gaped as he stared, first at Reagan, then the child. "Oh, my God," he stammered, holding him gingerly on his knee. As Gaeran blinked awake, Sam gazed at him in wonder. Suddenly fresh tears threatened. "He has Elizabeth's eyes!" he said, snuffling. "I can't believe it!" He looked at Reagan with bursting gratitude. "Bless you! Bless you for bringing him back!" Then, his expression turned confused. "But, I thought he'd been adopted to a family in Lars? How did you get him?"

"I asked Mrs. Seymour to say that to protect Gaeran and Elizabeth's reputation. I'm sure you can understand why." Reagan held his breath until the mayor nodded.

"I do," he said. "I just can't believe I'm holding him." He watched as the babe rubbed his eyes. "Isn't he beautiful?"

"He certainly is," Reagan said.

By now, Gaeran was totally awake and stared at Sam with inquisitive eyes. "Hello there, little one," the mayor said, his voice soft. "How are you?" he chucked Gaeran's chin, which elicited a smile. "Ahh, there's a happy boy!" The mayor's eyes seemed to devour the child as that one reached up to pluck at a button. "Do you know who I am?" he said, cooing. "I'm your pappy! Yes! And, you're my grandbaby!"

Reagan had stood, his throat constricted with barely contained fear. Would the mayor change his mind now that he had seen his grandson? Would he demand they relinquish the child? A dozen arguments flitted through his mind, but one factor kept pounding them down. Reagan might not be the father. He could lay no claim unless he professed being the rake Sam had thought him to be. Adoption papers would be no protection from the scandal of being taken to court. It occurred to him to damn the devil and admit parentage, regardless of the truth.

But, he knew he wouldn't. He had promised Amanda there would be no scandal. And, though it would rend his heart from his chest, Reagan wouldn't deny Gaeran's birthright. And so he stood silently and prayed Elizabeth's child would never know from him or anyone else, the pain of being betrayed.

❦

"Sheriff!" Deputy Welch came bursting through the back door. "Mrs. Spelding's ill!"

Jim looked at Doctor Turner, who had been about to follow Beauregard out the door. "Can you stay a moment? I'm releasing Mrs. Spelding tonight and I wouldn't want her going home sick."

"Of course," Artemus said, removing his outer coat once again. "Do you have a private area I can use?"

Sheriff Hadley nodded. "Joe, take Mrs. Spelding and the doc to the storage room." He looked apologetic. "It's small, but at least, there'll be no prying eyes."

"If she hasn't a serious malady, do you want me to take her home afterwards?"

"No, I'd better do it," Jim said. "I'll need to explain to Leroy that his wife's no longer suspected of any crime."

Nearly a half hour later, the doctor reentered the jailhouse office. He shook his head at the sheriff's inquisitive look. "Nothing serious, just nausea gravidarum," he said, pursing his lips. "However, time and tide will tell whether my suspicions are confirmed."

At Jim's upraised brows, he continued. "It appears Mrs. Spelding is expecting. According to my calculations, it's fairly early in her pregnancy."

"Oh!" Hadley appeared suddenly uncomfortable. "Had I known, I mayn't have placed her in jail. She never mentioned her condition."

"It appears to be a surprise to her as well," Doctor Turner said, reaching for his coat. "She thought the strain of these past few days had caused her nervous stomach."

"Leroy will be pleased to hear he's about to become a father," Jim said, rising. "Is Mrs. Spelding ready to go home?"

"She's ready to leave, if that's what you mean," he said. "However, she's requested to be taken to her parent's home after stopping at her house to pack some clothes. She seems to be taking the news pretty hard."

Jim put on his hat. "I suppose it's natural to be apprehensive with your first child. My wife was, with ours."

"Dismayed, seems to be a more accurate description," the doctor said, donning his outerwear. "I get the distinct impression she doesn't want anyone to know."

Jim took his coat off a peg. "Women are fickle," he said, shrugging. "Expectant women are impossible. However, she can rest assured I won't say a word."

"Thanks. If you need me, I'll be at Windsor Hospital," Artemus said, opening the door. Otherwise, if I don't see you before, have a Merry Christmas."

"You too," the sheriff said, smiling broadly. "You've been a tremendous help. I'm sure I'll be calling upon you when Mr. Calderon's brought to trial."

chapter 71

LEROY HAD BEEN sitting by the fire when he heard the knock at the door. Having dismissed his help until after the holiday, he rose to answer it himself. "Sheriff?" His brows rose in surprise. "Is anything wrong?"

"Good evening, Mister Spelding. Nothing's wrong. In fact, there's good news to be had."

"Oh?" Leroy's gaze caught a movement past the sheriff and realized with a start that Camilla stood meekly behind him.

Jim acknowledged her presence. "Mrs. Spelding has been released from jail. We've discovered evidence that exonerates her from the death of Miss Hargrove and from poisoning your bourbon."

Leroy's shock was nearly palpable. "But, you said—"

"I know! I know!" Hadley raised his hand. "I'll need to explain. But, could we please come in? Mrs. Spelding wishes to pack a few belongings before going to her parents, tonight."

Leroy stepped back, opening the door wide. As soon as Jim crossed the threshold, Camilla followed, her eyes downcast. "I'll be only a moment," she murmured before hurrying toward the stairs.

Leroy closed the door, looking confused. "You say my wife isn't guilty? What about all that supposed evidence?"

"I'm afraid I was wrong," Hadley said, removing his hat. "Upon further investigation we discovered it was Mister Calderon who committed those heinous acts. As a matter of fact, he's sitting in jail now. We stopped him minutes from boarding the train."

"Braegar? Why in God's name would he have done any of that?"

"I'll leave that up to the plea peddlers," the sheriff said. "However, the evidence is pretty convincing in regards to your poisoning as well as Miss Hargrove's accident. As soon as we discovered the truth, and concluded your wife likely had no part in it, it was no longer necessary to detain her."

Leroy took a long moment contemplating this news. "Tell me sheriff; was Camilla aware of Braegar's intentions?"

"It appears she didn't know about the poison or what happened to Miss Hargrove. However, just today she revealed Braegar tried swindling Beauregard with a fraudulent contract."

"Dear Lord! What *hasn't* that man done?" he said, rifling his hair. "And, if Camilla knew this, why didn't she tell me?"

The sheriff bit his tongue. With Mrs. Speldings knowledge of Braegar's chicanery, it implied a *very* intimate relationship. Coupled with plying Leroy with sleeping potion and her discomposure over her impending motherhood, he suspected a reason. A man would have to be blind not to put the pieces together. In a quandary, only one thought came to mind. "She's been through an emotional wringer," he said at last, splaying his hands. "I'm sure she had her reasons."

"Were you wrong about the spiked tea as well?"

"All Doc Turner could say was the dosage wasn't lethal. It mayn't have had anything to do with anything."

"Except that I didn't know it was added," he said. "That's a worse problem." Leroy rubbed the back of his neck as he stared at the ceiling. "What about the talk of divorce? Did that really happen?"

Jim toyed with the brim of his hat. "I can only go by what Mrs. Spelding said earlier. She claims Lorelda spoke the words, not she. Since Braegar can't be considered a reliable witness, I'm discounting his rendition of the facts."

Leroy turned his gaze to the empty staircase. "I think I need to speak with my wife," he said finally. "You should go home to your family. It's Christmas Eve." He looked at Jim, recognizing uncertainty. "Don't worry; if she still insists on leaving, I'll take her myself." He laid a hand on the lawman's shoulders. "I thank you for bringing her home. Please give my regards to your wife."

Thus dismissed, Sheriff Hadley decided he now had time to question Braegar further. He had a few mysteries that needed solving.

ॐ ॐ

"I must admit, you were very clever." Hadley sat outside Braegar's cell, one leg propped in a figure four as he pulled a pencil from behind his ear. "I've enough information to charge you for murder and attempted murder. We've your ring which left its imprint on Miss Hargrove's neck when you strangled her and found the compartment that held the poison you used to try killing Mister Spelding. Thankfully, he survived. However, if you'd indulge my curiosity, could you at least explain *why* you wanted them dead?"

"Why should I tell you anything? You'll just use it against me."

"Not so! I've reasons that have nothing to do with the law. I'm just curious—"

"Morbid curiosity?" he said, laughing. "My! My! What unscratched itch lurks in your soul?"

"This isn't about me, I assure you. Could you begin with why you poisoned Mister Spelding?"

Braegar snorted as he leaned against the wall, arms crossed. "If I'd intended to kill Leroy, I'd have done it."

"Really?" Hadley appeared surprised. "Then, why make him ill in the first place?"

"To get that woman off my back," he said, his face darkening. "She wanted out of her marriage and expected me to render the means."

"I don't understand—"

"Camilla came to me! She desired a few pleasant romps, which I gladly provided. After awhile, she wanted more. But, she was nothing more than a wife in watercolors. I needed a reason for her staying. Having to care for an ailing husband was my solution."

Hadley compressed his lips, his suspicions of an affair confirmed. "So, you're saying you only poisoned Mister Spelding to make him ill?"

"Murder wasn't the objective," he said, shrugging. "He was a friend who had a conniving wife."

"If you considered him a friend, why'd you—ah—take advantage?"

"I wasn't bound by any vows. Would you've refused such an invitation?"

Hadley coughed before clearing his throat. "Let's stay on the subject. You claim you weren't trying to kill Leroy. What about Miss Hargrove? What happened with her?"

"Why should I tell you? It'll only be worse for me."

"There's already enough evidence to satisfy the judge," Jim said. "I'm asking for her family. They'll want to know why. I'm hoping to give them some answers.

"I'm sure my lawyers wouldn't recommend it."

"Let me correct myself," Jim said, setting down his pencil. "Everything is off the record. None of this will be used against you. You have my word."

Braegar rubbed his jaw, staring at the tips of his custom-made brogans. He seemed to accept Sheriff Hadley's pledge. "It wasn't planned," he said, finally. "At least, not at first."

"Go on," Hadley urged. "What changed?"

"Lorelda slipped me that note, not realizing my involvement with Camilla. It was true I stood outside her room and overheard their argument. After Camilla left, I came, bearing drinks. I thought to convince her to keep quiet about the affair, but she had this foolish notion Leroy must be told."

"She was going to tell him about you and Camilla?"

"Ironic, isn't it? She felt more loyalty toward Leroy than his own wife. If you ask me, he married the wrong woman."

"It doesn't make sense," Jim said. "How'd she even find out?"

"It seems she witnessed a private moment. She overheard me promising Camilla I'd take her with me. I tried telling Lorelda it was a ruse on my part." He laughed bitterly. "She felt betrayed. There was no convincing her."

"Betrayed?" All at once, the sheriff held up his hand. "Never mind. I don't want to know. What happened next?"

"She didn't know I'd already tampered with Leroy's drink. If she then exposed my affair with Camilla, I was afraid he'd believe the poison was meant to kill. In that moment, I chose what I deemed the lesser of two evils."

"You got yourself in a fine fettle," Hadley said, shaking his head. "However, since you knew Leroy wouldn't die, you should've just taken your lumps. You wouldn't now be sitting in jail."

"I had other interests to consider."

"Ah, yes," he said, nodding. "Paradis Pavillon. I'd almost forgotten. With Leroy working at the bank, you'd have lost your contract."

"That contract is binding! Once my lawyers get me acquitted, I'll retain ownership rights."

"That would've been true had Reagan cashed your cheque. But, I have it on good authority, he tore it up."

"What do you mean he tore it up?" Braegar stood upright, eyes blazing. "Doesn't he know he'll be ruined?"

"You'll have to take that up with him. If you gain your freedom, that is."

"I will." Braegar then approached the bars, speaking with assurance. "Your Mister Burnsfield is out of his league. I'll have you know I never lose."

"So far," Jim agreed, nodding. "By the way, do you enjoy smoking cigars?"

"Are you offering one?" he asked, brow rising.

""If I were to ask Mister Spelding if he'd ever made cigars available to you, what would he say?"

"He'd say he wasn't remiss in his hospitality. Why do you ask?"

"I've learned that your host enjoys a specific brand. One that's rather expensive. You offered that same brand of cigar to Reagan."

"So? Are you now accusing me of thievery?" he said, snorting. "I can assure you, Leroy was generous. I didn't steal them."

"It so happens, that's the same brand of cigar we found outside the wood pile behind Barrington Hotel. Whoever started the fire had loitered there, smoking. Since you were the only one who benefited from that mishap, and you had access to that brand, it places you among a possible list of suspects."

"I'll deny having anything to do with that fire," Braegar said. "Your evidence can't prove otherwise."

"No, but your words to me earlier, will."

"I've admitted nothing," he said. "You're trying to trick me."

"You actually gave yourself away when you told me the fire started with the maid's negligence."

"How does that prove anything?"

"That information wasn't in the papers, Mister Calderon. The only way you would've known that, was if you witnessed her leaving a lamp in the kitchen. Perhaps, by spying through the window?"

"That doesn't prove intent," he said.

"There's no other reason a man of your stature would've been hiding behind a woodpile right before the hotel caught fire."

"You've cobbled together an interesting list of theories. But, you'll never trick me into confessing."

"You're not the first person I've hung for murder," Sheriff Hadley said. "I know what kind of evidence I need."

Braegar felt his composure slipping. "I eat people like you with my coffee!" he said, gripping the bars. "You won't be so smug when I'm cleared of all wrongdoing."

"Like I said, I have evidence. Tonight, I only wanted closure for those who need it. And, for that, I thank you."

"You won't thank me when I slip from your fingers. I'm not like everyone else."

"It's double pleasure to deceive the deceiver," Jim said, sighing. "It seems you've been outwitted, Mister Calderon. It's a tragedy what happened, especially to Miss Hargrove. She didn't deserve to die. However, I do appreciate your candid explanation. As promised, I won't use any of this against you. The physical evidence speaks for itself." He stood, tucking his pencil behind his ear. "I bid you goodnight."

"So, you're really going to tell Lorelda's parents what happened?" he taunted. "That makes you as cruel as me, does it not?"

Jim paused. "I'll spare her reputation, of course. I'll let them know their daughter died trying to save Mister Spelding. It'll give them comfort. As for the rest, there's no benefit in exposing the sordid details."

"I may be guilty of gratifying carnal pleasures, but, Hell hath no fury like a woman scorned," Braegar said, folding his arms. "If my lawyers decide it'll help my cause, everything's on the table. And, that goes for Mrs. Spelding as well."

"You're an evil man, Mister Calderon. I don't know how anyone can be so callous." Then, without further words, he left.

chapter 72

"CAMILLA, WOULD YOU please come into the parlor?" Leroy stood inside the doorway, having waited for his wife to descend the stairs.

She bit her lip, looking around the hall. "Where's the sheriff? He was to wait for me."

"I asked him to leave. I'd like to speak with you. Then, if you still want to go, I'll take you myself."

After a moment's hesitation, Camilla set down her bags. She assumed Leroy knew most, if not all, her transgressions. She couldn't imagine he would want to lay eyes on her, let alone speak with her. "If it pleases you," she said, clasping her hands.

"Won't you please come in?" He motioned invitingly. "I've prepared a small repast. I'm sure you're hungry."

Camilla stepped past him and approached the settee. A platter of cheese, sweets and bite-size sandwiches accompanied a teapot sitting next to plates and napkins. She looked at him in wonder. "You prepared this?"

Leroy shook his head at her obvious surprise. "I'm not helpless, madam. Before marriage, I often prepared late night morsels for myself."

She sank onto the sofa, her eyes drawn to the food as Leroy took the adjoining cushion. A sudden pang reminded her she hadn't eaten since yesterday. Her stomach had been unable to tolerate food while in jail. Camilla hesitated, not knowing if he expected her to serve. The choice was taken when he filled a plate and handed it to her.

"Let me pour you some tea," he said, eying her knowingly. "Although, it hasn't any additives, I'm sure it'll be refreshing."

Camilla's hands shook as she accepted cup and saucer. She then took a sip, her lip trembling. "I haven't the words—" she said falteringly, "—to express how sorry I am—"

"Are you, my dear?" He lifted a brow. "I've had quite an awakening these past two days." He leaned back, allowing his arm to rest on the back of the sofa. "You're shenanigans nearly cost me my life. Although I've been told you're not directly responsible for that, or for poor Lorelda's death."

"I didn't know, I swear!" she said, choking. "I'm guilty of many things, but I never wanted anyone to die."

"Speaking of guilt, that's what I'd like to discuss."

Fear showed in Camilla's eyes. "What do you mean?"

"First, you must eat," he said, motioning toward her plate. "My curiosity can wait."

Camilla obediently nibbled on her food until most had been eaten. Then, setting aside her plate, she daubed her mouth with her napkin. "I'm finished," she said at last.

"I've been told by the sheriff, you're no longer under suspicion of any crime," he began, folding his hands over his middle. "For that, I'm grateful. However, I've had two days to do nothing but think. And, I've been disturbed by my conclusions."

"What do you wish to know?" she asked, her voice quivering.

"Before this happened, were you intending to divorce me?"

Though Leroy sat inches from her, Camilla never felt more distant or alone. Being detained for crimes she didn't commit had shaken her to her core. But, could she really say she wasn't responsible? If not for her actions, none of this would've happened. In her mind's eye, she saw the cascading effects of the path she had chosen. She hadn't cared who had fallen in her wake. Now, she realized how many lives had been devastated because of her.

She worried the napkin in her hands. "I—I—"

"You must be frank," he said sternly. "The time for delicate conversation is over. If you owe me anything, *wife*, it's the truth. Do you understand?"

Camilla nodded and though her lip trembled, she responded. "I'll be honest, I promise."

"Good. Now, tell me, were you intending to divorce me?"

Unable to speak, Camilla nodded while gazing at her hands.

Leroy appeared to have braced for the worst, for his mien never wavered. "And, were you planning to replace me with Mister Calderon?"

Again, Camilla nodded.

"Can I assume you and he—?" he left the words unspoken, though his meaning was clear.

"I'm sorry! *I'm sorry!*" she said, tears spilling down her cheeks. "If I could take it back, I would. It was wrong! I was stupid! I—"

Leroy's hand stayed hers and she looked up. "Are you expecting?" he asked thickly.

Camilla looked at her husband with new eyes. Where she once saw weakness, she now viewed steadfastness. For the first time, she recognized real hurt in his eyes, and something else, anger. "It seems so," she whispered.

His hand tightened convulsively on hers. "Is it *his?*"

"I—I don't know," she said dejectedly. "It's possible, but not entirely so."

"So, the child may still be mine?"

Camilla thought for awhile. "It's possible," she said. "I can't be certain."

Leroy sat back, saying nothing. He rubbed his jaw while he looking around the parlor. "It seems we're in a pickle, madam," he said at last. He brought his gaze back to her. "What do you intend to do?"

Camilla lifted her shoulders before dropping them. "I suppose, go to my parents. I don't know what else to do." She wiped her cheeks. "Eventually, I must leave. I can't bear the shame. Nor, should you."

"Are you determined to leave?"

"I've no other choice," she said. "I pray you'll grant an allowance. I know I don't deserve one, but I haven't funds to leave Cantonsville." Camilla sighed, waiting for his dismissal. She wasn't in control anymore. Not over Braegar, who joined forces with her own folly and then deserted her. And, obviously, not over her husband, who surely despised her for her many betrayals. Occupying a jail cell forced her to confront the reality of her treacherous behavior. It wasn't a game. People were hurt. One even died. *It was all her fault!*

"The depth of your deception is breathtaking," he said, drumming fingers on his thigh. "I don't envy you on judgment day. Yet, there's still the child to consider. However small, there's a chance its mine. So, I'll make a proposition." At her shocked expression, he held up a warning finger. "It's completely on my terms, milady. You'll either take it or leave it."

Camilla could barely breathe. She dared not hope for more than a quiet divorce and banishment from society. She had defiled everything sacred. She didn't realize how obvious her remorse, how sincere her sorrow. She looked at him with something akin to dread.

"While you were packing, I had decided to question you about my suspicions. Afterward, I planned writing my lawyers for advice. However, I'm going to temporarily postpone divorcing you until I know whether or not you carry my child. During that time, you'll reside here at my pleasure. Which means you'll do nothing to embarrass or discredit my good name. When we have guests or by ourselves, you'll be pleasant, charming and *kind*. If you cannot or will not abide by my terms, you'll be expelled immediately and without remorse. Since you've proven to be untrustworthy, I've stipulations to protect my interests. You'll memorialize every wrong you have perpetrated on paper and you will sign it. I'll keep it as insurance against the day you betray my generosity. If that occurs, your letter will be enough to grant me an uncontested divorce."

Camilla's mouth dropped. It was the last thing she expected. Suddenly, she burst into tears, nodding vigorously. "I'll do anything you ask," she said between sobs. "I've been a wretched, wretched woman!"

"Considering you've never before apologized, I take this as a first step toward repentance," Leroy said, handing her his hanky. "I'll allow you privacy to write what you must. Leave it on the secretary. I won't read it until you've retired."

"What if you change your mind, once you see it?"

"I doubt anything you confess will be worse than what I've imagined."

Camilla looked at him beseechingly. "If I confess all, I must have your word you won't recant. Or else I won't have the courage to pen the words."

"That bad, is it?"

"I don't deserve your forgiveness," Camilla said, blotting her eyes. "I only ask you allow me atonement. Perhaps, by the time the child comes, you'll find it in your heart to not disgrace me publicly if—if there's to be a divorce."

"I'll honor my word," he said. "If you behave as I demand, you'll not endure public shaming."

"And, if the child is yours?" she asked. "What'll become of me?"

Leroy's voice softened. "Madam, if the child is *ours* I expect I'll have to decide whether or not you'll be in *our* future. No child of mine will grow up outside my protection."

"I accept," Camilla said, taking a deep breath.

"I'll prepare a bath," he said, standing. "I'm sure you're in need of a hot soak and a good night's sleep. You'll stay in our bedroom. I'll take one of the guest rooms."

"I can't ask you—"

"Tut!" His hand rose. "I know it's not been your wont, but you'll do everything I ask, without question or argument. Did I not make myself clear?"

Camilla nodded. "You did. If that's what you wish, I'll happily comply." When Leroy held out his hand, she took it, allowing him to help her rise.

"When you've finished, place your letter in the envelope. I'll retrieve it once you reach your room."

Camilla went to the secretary and sat down; noting writing materials had already been laid out. She looked over her shoulder. Leroy had gone, and so she picked up the pen and began writing. She filled three pages, holding nothing back. Afterward, she read over her words. Recounting her deeds in such bold relief pierced her soul. What senseless, bitter suffering had she caused! Leroy had only wanted to love and protect her. She, on the other hand had abused the privilege of being his wife. Having squandered her position, she had now been reduced to little more than a servant.

It's what I deserve!

Camilla folded the sheets and placed them inside the envelope, leaving it unsealed. With a sigh, she rose and exited the parlor, realizing Leroy had taken her bags from the hall. Going upstairs and into the bath, she found everything as promised. Her fingers flew over the buttons of her now ruined gown and it soon fell to the floor along with her chemise. Then, climbing into the steaming bath, she sank into its depths and holding the washcloth over her face, gave in to deep, wrenching sobs.

chapter 73

LEROY ENTERED THE parlor and approached the secretary. The envelope looked to hold more than one sheet of paper. Sitting down, he stared at it for several moments. He parted the loose flap, yet hesitated removing the missive. His thoughts, unbidden, ruminated over his marriage. How had things gone so awry in the course of a single year? He recalled those first months where Camilla had seemed content. Yes, they argued over household expenses and her allotment for clothes and entertainment. What responsible man didn't curtail costs during these hard times? Her requests had seemed so flimsy. So *female*.

For the most part, he had dismissed them without thought. Upon reflection, he realized he could have easily accommodated many of her requests. He could have compromised. Yet, he chose not to. In his impatience to provide a future, he had prohibited the very things that made life enjoyable, especially for a woman.

Leroy knew he never could've married a beauty like Camilla had he not had wealth. He couldn't lay claim to charm, wit or handsomeness that nature had bestowed on others. He had won her simply because he had been the richest swain available. Despite knowing this, he believed once married, he no longer needed to indulge her wishes. Suddenly, he felt partially to blame.

What hand had he played in Camilla's infidelity? Picking up the envelope, he tapped its edge on the desktop. He had known what kind of woman he married. He willingly accepted her shortcomings because she was beautiful. It had assuaged his ego to troth a comely woman, displaying her much like a huntsman his trophies. Had he not known her family had station but little wealth? She had beauty. He had riches. It was a match well suited. Except, he had reneged by denying her the pleasures she sought through marriage. His contribution weighed less on the scales of iniquity, but it bore weight, nonetheless.

He knew she was now a woman without options. If he chose, he could divorce her, take the child and leave her penniless. She would become a social outcast, living on the largess of aging parents. He held all the proof he needed in his hands. Yet, Camilla's remorse had been sincere. And, even though he had forged his proposal without thought to reconcile, it now weighted in her favor.

Leroy dropped the envelope. Locking fingers behind his head, he stared at the ceiling. He tried imagining life with a babe but bereft a wife. He soon shook his head. If the child was his, Camilla would stay. And, if it wasn't? Would he reject the child along with its mother? He'd have to divulge her adultery, at least to a judge. It could be done quietly. He could bequeath enough funds for Camilla to start anew. He could remarry.

Yet, there remained another option. With this turn of events, he had suddenly achieved all the acquiescence a man could hope to gain from a wayward wife. It was within his power use it to his advantage. Camilla was forever indebted to his good graces. With that power, he would refine whatever decency still dwelt in her heart. Overnight, he could silence her shrewish tongue, tame her disagreeable bent. With little persuasion, he could even regain her bed. But, would he even want to once he knew her deeds; or the depths of her betrayal?

All he had to do was read the contents of her letter.

And then, with the surety of a man who had made his decision, Leroy picked up the envelope. He arose and walked to the fireplace. He tossed it into the flames, watching it curl and then burn completely. Now, he would never know, nor could he ever recount her misdeeds. And Camilla would never know it wasn't locked safely away, to be used as barter for her continued devotion. It would be a lasting pact, born of necessity. In using this maneuver, he made room for forgiveness. And that, he decided, climbing the stairs, was what he would wield to repair his broken marriage.

ॐ∾ॐ

"Merry Christmas, everyone!" Beauregard called as he entered the Burnsfield parlor. Laden with gifts, he set beautifully wrapped boxes atop the already overflowing table. "Merry Christmas! Merry Christmas!"

"Beau! How good of you to come," Amanda said, coming over and kissing his cheek. "Being so late, we thought the weather had prevented you."

"Mieux vaut tard que jamais!" he fairly sang. "Better late than never!" After emptying his arms, he took a seat, accepting a glass of spiced cider. "Ah, mademoiselle, it's a pleasure I've been anticipating all day." He inhaled the warm scent before tasting. "Délicieux!" he said, smacking his lips. "Have I missed overmuch?"

Reagan, who had been standing near the fireplace, drew near. He dropped to his knees where Jesse and Gaeran shared a blanket and began placing wooden blocks before them. "You missed dinner, I'm sorry to say, and both our families as well as Amy's new friend, Doctor Alexander."

Beau lifted a brow inquisitively. "La demoiselle, courted? What say you, mon ami. Is monsieur worthy?"

"He seems rather determined; which means he's a good match to her headstrong ways," he said, laughing. "I've never seen her so disconcerted. She's smitten and doesn't even realize it."

"You know what that means," Beau said, winking. "Courting is the past tense of the word *caught*."

With intimacy only close friends shared, Amanda joined Reagan on the floor where Jesse lay on his tummy. "Here," she said, taking some blocks, "let's spell *J-e-s-s-e*." She laughed as he picked up a wooden block and brought it to his mouth. "Oh sweetie, you're not supposed to chew it."

Reagan arranged blocks in front of Gaeran who sat upright, nearby. "We can't let your brother get away with that. We'll spell your name too." Gaeran picked up a block in each hand as Reagan suddenly leaned over, kissing Amanda on the cheek.

"Reagan!" Amanda blushed, looking apologetically at their friend. "What was that for?"

"For being such a wonderful wife," he replied. "For enduring uncertainties and withstanding troubles. For staying by my side even when I didn't deserve it."

"Agreed!" the Frenchman said, smiling. "Mademoiselle is much to be admired, especially for marrying such a brute as you." Beau's eyes dropped to where Gaeran had set down the blocks after switching them in his hands. "Oh look," he said, pointing. "He spelled *your name*. How coincidental!"

Indeed, the babe had inadvertently set blocks in different places, switching around the first four letters. With the new arrangement, *G-a-e-r-a-n* now became *R-e-a-g-a-n*.

Reagan and Amanda stared at each other, both realizing the truth the same moment. "You don't think—?" she stammered, her hand covering her mouth. "Does this mean—?"

Reagan took the blocks and switched them himself. "I can't believe it," he said. "Why didn't I see this before?"

Alarmed, Beau sat forward. "What is it, ami? Is something wrong?"

Reagan blinked several times as full realization hit him. Elizabeth had given him the answer all along! She had used the letters of his name to name her son. He picked Gaeran up and held him to his chest. "No, nothing's wrong," he said, laughing. He looked at Amanda whose own eyes glowed with love. "Everything is just perfect!"

The End

Thank you for reading *Winds of Betrayal*.

I hope you enjoyed reading it as much as I enjoyed writing the continuation of Reagan and Amanda's story.

If you've not yet read *Threads of Betrayal*, where Reagan and Amanda first meet, I invite you to do so.

Reader reviews are critical to an author's success. I hope you'll consider leaving a review at: Amazon. com
Also available at createspace.com and other major retailers.

In addition to writing, I offer Author Presentations to any group/club interested in having a guest speaker. If you'd like having me as a guest speaker, it would be my pleasure to see if I can accommodate you.

Please contact me at:

www.monicakoldykemiller.com
monicarendell@hotmail.com
Facebook / Monica Young Miller

About the Author

Monica lives on an Indiana farm with her husband, two of her four children, a dog and a pair of barn cats. Before writing her first book, she worked twenty-five years in the medical field of Optometry. During that time, she wrote a human interest story in a medical newsletter and has had poetry published in *Speer Presents.*

When not writing or hauling grain, Monica gives speaking engagements titled Author Presentation/ One Writer's Journey/Lessons in Perseverance. Additionally, she teaches writing and publishing through workshops.

Writing fulfilled a life long dream inspired by her sixth grade teacher, Mrs. Rindfusz who opened up a world of possibilities when she told a shy, eleven year old, "You write the most interesting sentences!"

Made in the USA
Lexington, KY
25 November 2019